PART 1

Truman State University
Kirksville, MO
November 2002

"He's creepy."

"You're jealous."

"I am not. He's creepy and weird."

Linda Kelly smiled as her friend, Karla Sharp, berated the character of the man she was thinking about dating. "How is he creepy and weird?"

"He never looks me in the eyes. He's always staring at my chest."

Linda laughed. "He's a guy. They do that."

"Normal guys glance. This guy stares, Linda." Karla shivered.

Linda Kelly was an athletic woman just under six feet in height. Currently a junior attending school on a woman's basketball scholarship, she started every game. During her sophomore year, she broke the school record for points scored in a season. Her long auburn hair, worn in a tightly braided ponytail for games, flowed over her shoulders on this particular evening. Her hazel eyes sparkled with mischief as she teased her best friend. "Maybe you should show him what you have. Then he wouldn't be curious."

Karla flipped her hand against Linda's arm. "Not in this lifetime." Pausing for a moment, she continued, "I'm serious, why do you like him? Because he's rich and good looking?"

"Maybe."

Everything about Karla Sharp was compact compared to her friend. She stood five inches shorter, her brown hair barely touching her shoulders. Karla possessed more curves than her friend, particularly in her chest. A round face and a slightly upturned nose gave her a natural beauty she enhanced with only a touch of makeup. Like her friend, she was a junior; unlike Linda, she was working toward a degree in biology. The previous summer, her application to the University of Missouri's Veterinary School had been accepted, and she would be attending after her senior year. Her childhood dream of becoming a veterinary was within reach.

The two friends were walking north off campus toward the downtown area of Kirksville, Missouri, their destination a restaurant where they would meet their other roommate for dinner. April Lane worked downtown at a woman's boutique shop and planned to join them after she closed the shop.

"I like him. He's funny."

Karla shook her head. "Funny looking."

"Stop it, he is not."

"Linda, I'm serious, there is something odd about him."

Linda stopped walking and looked at her friend. "You're not kidding, are you?"

"No, I'm not. He scares me." She stopped as well and turned.

Linda stared hard at Karla. "He scares you? How?"

Karla shook her head. "I can't explain. It's his eyes."

Taking a deep breath, Linda sighed. "I haven't had a real date with him yet, but the way he's always looking around does seem a bit odd."

"Odd is not the word. His eyes are evil."

"Oh, Karla, you're exaggerating."

THE COLD TRAIL

J.C. FIELDS

~~~~

Any resemblance to actual people and events is purely coincidental.

This is a work of fiction.

Paperback-Press
an imprint of A & S Publishing
A & S Holmes, Inc.

ISBN-13: 978-1-945669-55-2
~~~~

Dedication

For my cousin, Paulette Sanders Edmondson:
Our time on this earth is short.
Thank you for spending some of yours reading my books.

ACKNOWLEDGMENTS

Writing a novel, to the outside observer, would seem to be a solitary endeavor for an author. But, to quote John Donne, "No man is an island." While placing butt in chair and hands on the keyboard is a one-man operation, the creative phase takes a lot of input from others. Conversations over coffee, the written words of faceless newspaper reporters, talking heads on TV, current event feeds on a smart-phone, the ever-shrinking Time magazine, and, unfortunately, talk radio. All of these uniquely human activities offer ideas for the observant novelists.

Once the creative phase is complete, in jumps the team. Over the course of four novels, this group of individuals has grown. To all, I offer a thank you.

The members of the Springfield Writers' Guild continue to inspire constant improvement in my craft.

Emily Truscott, once again, sliced, diced, and offered advice as my developmental editor. While I do not always agree with her, as a rule, her edits and comments are correct.

Norma Eaton remains my last line of defense providing proofreading, and serving as a beta reader.

Niki Fowler, a graphic artist extraordinaire, continues to create a thematic atmosphere for my book covers.

The newest member of the team is Paul J. McSorley. Paul has become the voice of Sean Kruger with his incredible interpretation of all four novels for Audible.com.

Sharon Kizziah-Holmes, owner of Paperback Press, is stead-fast in her staunch support, and continues to publish my work.

Last, but not least, my wife Connie. She continues to support my writing while reminding me of life and other activities away from the keyboard.

"Am I? Where did you meet him?"

"He watched practice one day."

"Don't you find that a bit strange?"

Shaking her head, Linda did not answer right away. "I really didn't think about it at the time. He was…" She paused. "Cute."

Karla rolled her eyes. "Oh, Linda, you're so naïve."

They started walking again, and the conversation drifted from the man to the upcoming women's basketball season.

***

The conversation was lively, the girls laughing as April told stories about the dress shop. She was a petite woman, large green eyes, light brown hair, a ready smile, and the oldest of the three. She was a senior with plans to graduate in December. Her fiancé was already in St. Louis working as a salesman for a large brewing company after graduating the previous spring. The couple started dating in high school and were preparing to marry in June following her graduation.

As closing time grew near, the only customers left in the café's dining room were the three women. Their waitress, after taking their money, left for the evening. The owner busied himself cleaning and preparing the front end for the next day.

The girls heard a car screech to a halt in front of the restaurant. Within seconds, they saw a tall man with disheveled black hair rush into the dining room. Linda gasped, Karla frowned, and April shook her head.

Linda looked up as the man approached their table, concern etched on her face. "What are you doing here?"

Breathless and wide-eyed, he looked straight at Linda. "Your coach had a car accident…" He paused to steady his breathing. "They've taken her to the hospital and I've been asked to give you a ride."

Blinking rapidly as she assimilated the news, Linda suddenly remembered the words of her father from ten years ago. She blinked again, his words cascaded over her. "*Linda, darling, there is safety in numbers. If you feel threatened, draw your friends around you.*"

If her coach was injured, Linda had to be by her side. She stood and looked at her friends. "I would feel better if you guys go with me?"

Without hesitation, both stood to follow Linda and the tall man with the black hair out of the restaurant.

It was the last time the three women would ever be seen.

CHAPTER 2

Kirksville, MO
Two Days Later

With a latex-gloved hand, FBI Special Agent Sean Kruger flipped through the diary found sitting on the nightstand in Linda Kelly's bedroom. Frowning, he angled the book lengthwise toward the light of a window and studied the pages. So far his examination of the missing women's apartment revealed nothing of value. Except for the diary.

Allen Boone, an investigator for the Missouri State Highway Patrol's Division of Drug and Crime Control stood next to him. Where Kruger was tall, slender, and athletic, Boone was short, at one time, a body-builder. Now a bit overweight, he was a year younger than his friend. Both attended the FBI academy together and graduated in the same class. Boone served only briefly with the Bureau before leaving and joining the Missouri State Highway Patrol. He was dressed in jeans and a Patrol windbreaker. Black hair with streaks of gray just above his ears complimented his round face which was currently tilted to the side.

"What's the matter?"

"Several pages have been sliced from the middle of the book."

"Huh."

Opening the book further, he stared at the barely visible remnants of missing pages. "Looks like three were cut."

Boone produced a plastic zip-top bag from the pocket of his windbreaker. "Let's bag it. Maybe we'll get prints from someone other than the Kelly woman."

As Boone inserted the book into the bag, Kruger looked around the room and observed, "Neither of the other roommates' rooms look disturbed. Someone was in here searching for something. It may point to Linda being the focus of the abduction."

"How can you tell?"

"The pillows."

"What about them?"

"Notice how neat and tidy this room and the bathroom are?"

"Yeah."

"Look at the pillows and the wrinkled bedspread."

"Huh, you're right. Looks like someone sat on it."

"Not a towel is out of place in the bathroom. Everything in this room is orderly, except the bed. Linda Kelly's an athlete with a disciplined mind." Kruger pointed to the bed and pillows again. "My guess is, she wouldn't leave the bed that way. If she did sit on it, she would smooth it out and straighten the pillows, almost without thinking about it. Someone else sat there and leafed through this journal. They found what they were looking for and cut the pages out."

"It's a diary, think it's a guy she might have been dating?"

"Possibly." Kruger continued to stare at the bed.

"One of the local detectives talked to her coach. She didn't believe Linda was seeing anyone."

Looking at Boone, Kruger frowned and remained quiet for a moment. "We won't find the answer here. Let's talk to the coach."

Boone nodded and followed Kruger out of the bedroom.

As they emerged from the apartment, a local police officer handed Boone a note. After reading it, he handed it to

Kruger.

He studied the piece of paper and looked up. "Looks like we need to talk to a restaurant owner."

Boone nodded. "Yeah."

***

"When did this occur, Mr. Drake?" Kruger studied the man.

Glen Drake pursed his lips and rubbed the four-day old whiskers with his left hand, an unlit cigarette in his right. He was the same height as Boone, but skinny. The three men stood in the alley behind the restaurant so Drake could smoke. The man's hands shook as he tried to light the white stick. His face was lined, and his teeth were stained from too many years of smoking. A coughing spell interrupted his first drag, and the man's entire body convulsed as he hacked. Finally, after twenty seconds, he was able to speak. "About five minutes to nine."

Kruger waved the exhaled smoke away. "What happened next?"

"The girls are regulars. They're here every Thursday night and sit at the same table. One of them, I believe her name is April, works at the woman's store across the street. The other two, 'fraid I don't know their names, arrive just before April closes the store and joins them."

"Do they always stay until closing, Mr. Drake?"

Boone stood next to Kruger, his arms folded across his broad chest.

"Yup. April told me their schedules are so hectic, they never see each other except when they have dinner at my café."

"So someone came in just before you closed and spoke to the girls?" asked Kruger.

"That's what I told you earlier."

"Did you get a good look at him?"

Drake shook his head. "I was cleaning the coffee machine

when he came in. By the time I turned around to see who it was, he had his back to me. He had black hair, I did see that."

"Did one of the waitresses see him?"

"I was the only one in the dining room. It was a slow night, and I let the servers go home early. My kitchen staff was in the back cleaning. I went to the storage room for something, I forget why now, and when I came back they were all gone."

Kruger studied Drake as the man spoke. "Have you seen this guy before?"

Drake studied the tip of the burning cigarette. "How the hell should I know, I serve a lot of people in here. Lots of college kids and locals. Since I didn't see his face..." His statement faded into a shrug.

The interview lasted ten more minutes with nothing of importance learned. When Boone and Kruger returned to the Highway Patrol car, Boone sat behind the wheel and turned to Kruger in the passenger's seat. "What do you think?"

"He's not involved."

Boone nodded and started the car. "I don't think so either. Where to now?"

"Let's talk to Linda's coach."

"Why do you think Linda was the subject of the abduction?"

"Several reasons. The Lane woman was engaged, and from what I found in Karla Sharp's room, I don't think it was about her."

"Why?"

"Uh…" Kruger paused and cleared his throat. "Let's just say she wasn't comfortable with men."

"Oh."

"Kelly is a standout on the basketball team. Her stature as the leading point scorer and the media hype surrounding her recruitment by the WNBA give her a media presence the other two women don't have. The exposure could have brought undue attention from a dangerous individual."

"A stalker?"

Kruger nodded. "Let's see what her coach says."

***

"Linda wasn't dating anyone, Agent Kruger. She would have told me."

"Please call me Sean."

"Very well, Sean."

"How can you be sure?"

"Have you ever been on a sports team?"

"Yes, ma'am, I swam in college."

"Then you know. We spend so much time together, we become like family."

Stacy Bell was in her mid-forties, slender and tall enough for her intense blue eyes to be even with Kruger's. Her blond hair was tied back in a ponytail, and she continued to use a tissue to wipe tears.

Kruger nodded. He did understand.

Bell continued, "Linda was a team leader, intelligent and determined to succeed at everything she did."

"Did her dedication keep her from dating?"

"No, she's had a few boyfriends over the past few years. Nothing serious, just college dating. She told me once that getting serious about a man would have to wait. She didn't have time for the distraction."

"So, she did date?"

Bell nodded.

"But, no one at the moment?"

The coach shook her head.

"Any strange men hanging out at your practices or games?"

"No, our practices are closed to the public. Occasionally a student or two will sit and watch if they're already in the building. Games are another thing. I'm normally concentrating on the play, I don't see the crowd."

Kruger understood and nodded.

Bell tilted her head, a puzzled look on her face as she

remembered something. "There was someone about three weeks ago in the bleachers during a practice. I forgot about it until just now."

Kruger raised an eyebrow. "Male or female?"

"Male—he had black hair. Didn't look like a student. Too old."

Boone took out a notepad. "Can you describe what he looked like?"

She shook her head again. "No, I didn't get a good look. I just noticed him. He wasn't there long."

"Why did you remember it now, Stacy?" Kruger's eyes narrowed as he kept his attention on the coach.

"I'm not sure. I thought it unusual, but like I said earlier, if someone is already in the building, they're free to watch. Wish I could remember more."

"Could you check with your other players and see if they can describe the man?"

"Sure. You think it was him?"

"Don't know, but the last person seen with the three women had black hair."

Bell's hand covered her mouth and her eyes grew wide.

***

"Agent Kruger, this is Suzie Green. She may be able to help you."

Kruger smiled as Green entered Bell's office. "Hi, Suzie."

"Hello, sir."

Boone stood in the corner and watched Kruger interact with the young basketball player. Bell sat behind her desk while Green sat in a chair in front of it. Kruger occupied a similar chair next to Green.

"Tell us what you saw, Suzie," Kruger prompted gently.

The young female stared at the coach, who nodded slightly. She returned her attention to Kruger.

"Well, we were walking out of the field house after practice."

She took a tissue from a box on Bell's desk and dabbed at her green eyes.

"Linda was going to help me with a calculus assignment, and we were deciding where to meet." She paused again with the tissue. "There was a tall man waiting about ten yards outside the door. He fell into step next to Linda, and they started talking."

"What did he look like, Suzie?"

"Tall, black hair, dark gray suit which looked expensive, white shirt, no tie. He had his hands in his pockets while we walked."

Kruger glanced at Boone, who nodded and wrote something on a notepad.

"What did his face look like?

"I really didn't get a good look at him. The sun was setting, and he was standing in front of it when I saw him."

"Suzie, this is important," Kruger paused for just a second, "what did they talk about?"

"Something about meeting for coffee."

"Did Linda agree?"

"No, she told him she had plans."

"What else did they talk about?"

"I really don't know, I didn't follow them."

Kruger straightened in his chair. "I thought she turned him down for coffee."

"She did, but she followed him to his car."

"Did you see the car?"

Suzie nodded.

"Can you describe it?"

"I don't know much about cars, except how to drive them."

"That's okay. What did you see?"

"It was dark gray, just like his suit. On the front hood was a three-point star inside a circle."

Boone did a quick sketch on a page of his notebook, tore it out, and handed it to Kruger. He looked at it and showed the drawing to Suzie. "Like this?"

She nodded.

"It was a Mercedes, Suzie."

Kruger heard Bell gasp, and Suzie just stared at him.

After Suzie Green left the office, Kruger turned to Bell and asked, "Do you know if Linda had a cell phone?"

The coach nodded. "All of my players have cell phones. Why?"

"Would you know which carrier?"

She nodded. "Alltel. The university has an agreement with them to provide discounts for students and faculty."

"If she had her phone with her, we might be able to locate it."

"My players are to have their phone with them at all times. Team rules."

Kruger nodded. "It might help us locate her."

***

The search teams consisted of local police officers, county sheriff's officers, two search dogs and their handlers, local residents with knowledge of the area, and Kruger. Now dressed in jeans, hiking boots, polo shirt and FBI windbreaker, he listened to Allen Boone as he gave direction to the searchers.

"The last signal from Kelly's cell phone was received by cell phone towers here twenty-four hours after the abduction." He pointed to a wide circle on the map. "Alltel couldn't pinpoint it any closer, so we have to search this entire area. You guys and ladies know the drill. Let's see if we can find them."

The din of multiple conversations and the whimpering of anxious dogs could be heard as Kruger walked up to Boone.

"What do you think?" Boone asked.

"I'm not optimistic."

"Why?"

"So far, this guy's been careful. We haven't found one witness who can give us a description except he was tall with black hair. He wears suits and drives a gray Mercedes. How many gray Mercedes are in the state?"

"Thousands."

"Exactly. We've got nothing at this point."

"Do you think they're dead?"

"I don't want to think they are, but…"

"I know. I have a daughter. This kind of stuff makes me angry."

Kruger placed his hand on his friend's shoulder. "I have a son. It does me too."

Two hours later, one of the dogs found a spot of interest. Kruger and Boone hurried to the area and found the dog's handler. He was a crusty old gentleman dressed in a brown Carhartt jacket and baggy denim bib overalls. An unlit cigar was in his teeth, and his John Deere hat was tilted back on his head. He stood twenty yards from his dog, a brown and black German shepherd. It stood on point as Kruger and Boone approached.

Kruger walked up to the handler and shook his hand. "What've you got?"

The old man looked at Kruger. "Don't know." He folded his arms over his chest as he nodded toward the dog. "She's found something, I haven't been over there and don't plan to. Seen enough dead bodies. Don't need to see anymore."

Kruger smiled and nodded. "I understand. I'll take it from here. Call the dog back."

The old man whistled a sharp note, and the dog immediately returned to his side. He rubbed the dogs head and knelt down, saying, "Good, girl."

Kruger and Boone carefully walked to the spot the dog indicated. When they arrived, they saw what drew the dog's attention.

Three smashed cell phones.

CHAPTER 3

Jefferson City, MO
Two Months Later

"So they've suspended the search?"

Allen Boone nodded as he poured two cups of coffee in the break room at the DDCC Headquarter Office in Jefferson City.

Kruger sprinkled a half packet of Sweet N Low into the Styrofoam cup and carefully sipped the hot black liquid.

"Why?"

"Manpower and zero results. The girls just disappeared. No bodies, no clues, nothing."

"I was afraid of that. Any fingerprints on the diary?"

Boone shook his head. "Only Linda Kelly's, and yes, three pages were cut out."

"What about the black-haired man? Any other witnesses?"

"Not that we can find."

"Great. So where does this leave the investigation?"

"A cold case."

"I was afraid of that."

After they arrived in Boone's office, he sat behind his desk with Kruger taking a seat in a straight-back chair in front. He reached into his backpack and withdrew a tan envelope. He placed it on Boone's desk.

"What that?"

"Open it."

Boone looked inside the envelope and withdrew a file with numerous pages. After reading the first page, he looked up at Kruger and asked, "Akron, Ohio?"

Kruger nodded. "Caroline Branch, attended the University of Akron on a basketball scholarship." He watched Boone read more of the file.

When he was finished, Boone looked up. "When did you get this?"

"Yesterday. I asked a favor of a research tech at the Bureau. She's very thorough and started looking for similar reports across the country after the girls disappeared."

"This occurred a year ago last fall?"

Nodding again, Kruger pulled two more files out of his backpack. He held them for Boone to see.

"Two more, each a year apart. Kelsey Sorenson in Florida and Jayla Carter in West Virginia. The only difference is that only one woman was abducted in the three other instances."

"Are all the MOs the same?"

"Appears to be. All three women were basketball players and leading scorers on their team. None with Linda Kelly's stats, but they were all well known within their communities."

"Why didn't we know about this?"

"First, they were all a year apart, starting in 1999. Second, they occurred in smaller towns at relatively unknown colleges."

"Akron is not a small town."

"No, but have you ever heard of the University of Akron?"

"No, but I live in Missouri."

"Exactly. Little to no national media attention. They occurred hundreds of miles apart, and local authorities were never able to find credible witnesses. Except in Akron."

Boone said nothing as he waited for Kruger to continue.

Kruger reached for the Akron file laying in front of Boone

and opened it to the last page. "An employee at a McDonalds near the campus was a fan of the women's basketball team. She was manning the drive-through window when she recognized the victim."

"Let me guess. With an older man with black hair."

"Yes, driving a dark gray car with a three-point star inside a circle on the trunk."

"Did she describe the driver?"

"No, he was wearing a University of Akron baseball cap with the bill pulled down."

Boone took a deep breath. "Have any of the bodies been found?"

"No."

"Damn."

"My sentiments exactly," Kruger nodded.

"Is the Bureau going to do anything about it?"

"I plan to bring this to my boss's attention, but with the age and lack of witnesses, that's probably as far as it will go."

Boone continued to stare at the file in front of him. "That's not right for the families, Sean."

"I agree. But without a definitive starting point, it's hard to determine a path forward."

"No, it doesn't, but it's still not right."

***

"Mr. Kelly, my name is Sean Kruger." He held his ID so the man at the door could see. "I'm a special agent with the FBI."

Paul Kelly stared at the man standing at his front door. He blinked a few times, opened the door wider, and asked, "Is this about Linda?"

Kruger nodded, his expression grim.

"Please, come in."

The older man's size surprised Kruger. For someone with a tall, athletic daughter, he was of average height and build. His gray hair was thin and combed straight back. The house was modest, neatly decorated, and smelled of cedar air freshener.

"Is Mrs. Kelly here?"

The older man stiffened and then his shoulders slumped as he answered, "Patti passed away a year before Linda disappeared."

"I'm sorry for your loss, Mr. Kelly."

"What about Linda?"

"I'm afraid I don't have good news."

The man stiffened again. "Why?"

"We still don't have any clues about what happened to your daughter."

"I can tell you what happened, Agent. My daughter was kidnapped and hasn't been found."

Kruger nodded. "There are other incidents, similar in nature to Linda's disappearance."

Kelly was silent as his eyes widened. Finally, he found his voice. "Where?"

"Ohio, Florida and West Virginia."

"Have those women been found?"

Shaking his head, Kruger kept his gaze on Paul Kelly. He could see moisture welling up in the man's eyes. Turning away, he walked toward the kitchen, using the back of his hand to wipe away the tears.

With his back to Kruger, the man said, "My daughter is dead, isn't she, Agent?"

"We can't be sure, Mr. Kelly."

The man turned abruptly and stared at Kruger. "I'm sure, Agent. Why can't anyone acknowledge this fact?"

"Because it's not a fact without a body. At least, that's the viewpoint of the FBI."

"Really. Is it your viewpoint, Agent?"

Kruger shook his head.

"Finally, the truth."

"Reality."

"Yes, the ugly face of reality." The father of Linda Kelly took a deep breath. "What now, Agent?"

"I mainly came here to let you know the truth. The Bureau will keep the cases open, but few, if any, resources will be put against it."

"Kind of what I suspected."

"I wish I could tell you something positive, but I'd be lying."

Kelly nodded. "She was always an adventurous girl. From the moment she could stand on her own, she ran. I don't remember her ever walking, really, it was a struggle to keep up with her. Her mother…" Kelly paused, his voice catching. "Her mother used to laugh and tell her she was going to get a leash. Linda would smile and run faster."

Kruger remained quiet as the grieving father reminisced.

"It was her first day of junior high school. Like her mother, she was tall for a girl. Taller than all of the boys at that age. She was nervous about being teased." He stopped and looked at Kruger. "You know how teenagers can be. Do you have children, Agent Kruger?"

"Yes, an eight-year-old son."

"Keep him close."

Nodding was Kruger's only response.

"I remember telling her that morning, 'Linda, darling, there is safety in numbers. If you feel threatened, draw your friends around you.' Guess she tried to do that, since two of her friends disappeared with her."

There was nothing for Kruger to say. His training and experience prompted him to remain quiet.

"I'm not sure what to do now, Agent. My wife is dead and my only child is gone. I don't even have a body to bury." He looked at Kruger. "What would you do?"

"I don't know, sir. I've never experienced what you are going through."

Kelly nodded and studied the carpet for a few moments before saying, "I can't sell the house and move. What if she is alive and comes home? She wouldn't know where to find me."

Silence fell upon the living room. Kelly turned and looked

out the window leading into the backyard. "Too many memories here. Everywhere I look, something reminds me of Patti or Linda."

The man lapsed into silence. Kruger stood beside him for five minutes before placing his hand on the man's shoulder and saying gently, "I have to leave, Mr. Kelly."

The man nodded, but did not turn around. Kruger showed himself out, leaving Paul Kelly to suffer in his own private hell.

CHAPTER 4

Kansas City, MO

The fall evening was cool but comfortable as Kruger sat on his back porch, listening to the sounds of the city. A siren could be heard in the distance, a dog barked down the street, and the wind rustled leaves in the large oak tree in his backyard. The aroma of charcoal briquettes still emanated from the Weber grill as the fire slowly burned out.

"Steaks were good."

"Thanks, Dad."

Looking up, he saw his father sit down next to him and place two beers on the small table between the two chairs.

The older Kruger looked at his son and observed, "You've been quiet tonight."

After taking a sip of the cold brew, he turned and smiled at his father. "Sorry."

"Brian's asleep, and your mom is in our room, reading."

"Good."

"Want to talk about it?"

"Not much to say. I was just thinking about Paul Kelly and how his world has been shattered over the past twelve months. I'm not sure I could deal with the situation he's experiencing."

"We all make adjustments for whatever life throws at us." The older man took a sip of his beer. "Some do it better than others. You made adjustments when Christine abandoned you and Brian."

"That was different."

"How?"

"Christine hated being married. The only thing she hated more was being a mother. We never discussed having kids while we dated. Guess we should have. After she left, I realized our relationship was more physical than emotional."

"That can happen. It takes a while to truly get to know your spouse. I was lucky when I met your mother. She was someone who wanted to be partners. You'll find someone like that someday."

"I'm not looking."

"We know. That's what I wanted to talk to you about."

Kruger turned to look at his father. "What?"

"Your mother feels our living with you is preventing you from finding someone special to share your life."

"Like I said, I'm not looking."

"Her point," the elder Kruger chuckled. "She's concerned our presence in your house is keeping you from looking."

Shaking his head, the younger Kruger sat his beer down and smiled at his father.

"Dad, right now you and Mom living with Brian and me is the only thing keeping me sane. If I had to disrupt Brian's world by taking him out of school or leaving him with a friend or neighbor every time I had to be out of town, I'd have to quit my job. Like this past week, I was gone for four days. I can concentrate on my job knowing Brian is safe here with the both of you. His life is stable. That's important to me."

"Mary and I love being here, but we don't want to be a burden."

"Trust me, you two are not a burden."

Stan Kruger took another sip of his beer. The father and

son shared many traits, but the main one was a similar body structure. Both were tall, the son over six feet and the father just under. Both were slender, but the elder Kruger lacked some of the son's body mass. Both looked at the world through crystal blue eyes, the older Kruger's assisted by glasses.

"Funny how life works sometimes."

"How, Dad?"

"I'm not sure I ever told you, I didn't retire voluntarily."

The son shook his head. "No, you've never mentioned it."

"The day I turned sixty-five, I was called into the Human Resources department and told when my retirement announcement would be made."

The younger Kruger stared at his father, remaining quiet.

"They told me I had four weeks of vacation banked, which I needed to start the next day. After the vacation, I would officially retire from my position as an IRS auditor. I protested, but was shown a small clause in the Internal Revenue Department employee handbook," he chuckled. "I hated being retired and didn't know what to do with myself. I drove Mary crazy as I tightened every screw on every appliance in the house. Your call, two months later, saved me. Your mother and I feel blessed we were able to help with Brian."

"We're lucky you were in a position to help. I know Brian loves having you two around."

"I probably shouldn't tell you this, but I never cared for Christine. I thought she was too…," the father hesitated, searching for the correct word. "Uh, self-absorbed, for my taste. Those types generally don't stay married long. Did she ever re-marry?"

"Don't know," Kruger shrugged. "I refused to talk to her after she abandoned Brian in the apartment. My lawyer does it for me."

"I still get mad when I think about how she left that little boy by himself."

"It's history, Dad. Brian survived, and I've moved on. He

doesn't even remember it. Which is good."

"Does she ever talk to Brian?"

"Only on Christmas and his birthdays. He writes her letters, but she doesn't write back. I can't tell if it bothers him or not. He's like me, doesn't like to burden others with his troubles."

"Both of you are better off without her."

The younger Kruger stared off into the darkness but did not respond.

The conversation shifted to Brian's soccer games scheduled for the following week. With a planned week of catching up on paperwork and working out of the Kansas City FBI Field Office, Kruger was looking forward to seeing some of the games.

After his father went in for the evening, Kruger sat for a while longer on the back porch. The discussion about having someone in his life stirred emotions he had not felt for a long time. Being a single parent was hard enough; he didn't need the distraction of starting a relationship with a woman. It would be nice once in a while, but where to meet them was the other problem. His distaste for bars and social gatherings did not help.

After turning the lights off on the porch and locking the back door, he noticed how quiet the house was. Taking a deep breath and letting it out slowly, he retreated to his room, got ready for bed, and started reading the files on the missing women again.

***

Wednesday found Kruger working the phone on several closed cases being prepared for trial. A few minutes after completing a four o'clock conference call with a prosecutor in Denver, his cell phone vibrated. Glancing at the caller ID, he frowned. *Unknown* was displayed.

"Kruger," he answered.

"You will never find them."

The voice was electronically modified.

"Who is this?"

"The man with the black hair."

Kruger froze. His mind raced, determining the proper response.

"Which one will I never find?"

"Any of them."

"Aren't you taking a risk calling me? I might be able to trace the call."

He heard a metallic laugh.

"No, you will not be able to trace the call."

"Okay. Why are you telling me this?"

"So you will stop wasting your time."

"Thoughtful of you."

"Yes, I think so."

"May I ask your name?"

"You may ask."

"What is your name?"

More metallic laughter.

"I will tell you this, you will never figure it out. I am smarter than you. Just remember that."

The call ended abruptly. Kruger did not close the line immediately, but picked up his desk phone to call FBI Headquarters in Washington.

***

"What do you mean they can't find a record of the call? I have the number on my phone."

Kruger was pacing on his back deck as he talked on his cell phone. It had taken the FBI technicians two hours to determine the call did not originate with another cell phone.

"I can't explain it, Sean," said Paul Stumpf, a deputy director of the FBI and Kruger's immediate supervisor. "You'd have to talk to the techs. All they told me was the call did not go through Alltel's network."

"Then how did he call me?"

"They think it was done by computer. But since Alltel doesn't have a record of the call, no one knows."

"So, he was right, I wouldn't be able to trace the call."

"Apparently. You reported the voice was mechanical. Do you think it was a pre-recorded call?"

"No, he responded to direct questions. He might have been typing the words, but I don't think so. He laughed several times."

"How'd he get your number?"

"Hell if I know. That's another question I need answered."

"Unless…" Stumpf was quiet.

Kruger waited patiently.

"Who would know you're investigating the abductions?"

"You and the field offices."

"Exactly. Some of your emails probably identified your cell phone number and that we knew about his black hair."

"I don't like the implications of this conversation, Paul."

"I don't either. Let me do a little digging on this end."

"Call me when you know more."

The call ended, and Kruger took a deep breath. As he let it out, a bad feeling rushed over him. With the lack of evidence in each abduction and the sudden appearance of someone who could manipulate the phone system, he feared the case would never be solved.

PART 2

Present Day
Springfield, MO

"Final will be worth twenty-five percent of your class grade."

A moan rose from the students in the room.

"Another twenty-five percent will be determined by your second half paper. Fifty percent of the semester is already in the books. So, those of you with less than stellar results in the first half can re-invigorate your final grade with a second half project. I will be in my office today and tomorrow, after that… See you all on Thursday."

Sounds of chairs scooting, papers rustling, and disgruntled conversations could be heard as the students filed out of the classroom on the third floor of Hill Hall. Psychology professor and retired FBI agent Sean Kruger, PhD, smiled to himself as he placed class notes in his backpack.

"Mean professor."

Startled by the voice, Kruger looked up.

JR Diminski stood in front of his desk, his arms crossed over his chest, a mischievous grin on his face.

"It's Abnormal Psych 251. Fewer than three students, if that, will want the extra project. It's the only undergrad class I have to endure."

"That doesn't sound like you, Sean."

"I'm bored."

"Obviously."

Kruger stood straight, smiled at his friend, and swung the backpack over his shoulder. "What brings you to campus, JR.?"

Diminski shrugged and fell into step behind the dejected professor as he answered, "Thought we were having lunch together."

Kruger stopped and turned to look at his friend.

"Shit, I forgot."

"Do you have time?"

"Always. Let's go off campus. Let me drop off the backpack in my office, and I'll drive."

"Perfect."

Kruger's office was on the third floor, next to the office of the Head of the Psychology Department, a position he would assume at the end of the current academic year. As they approached, both men could see campus police and several uniformed Springfield Police Department officers. As they approached, Dr. Doug Chambers, the retiring head of the department, broke away from the group of officers and approached Kruger.

"Sean, we have a tragedy."

Frowning, Kruger stared at Chambers. "What?"

"One of our graduate students has been abducted. It's Cora Nelson."

Kruger did not reply right away. "When?" he finally asked.

"Her roommate called the office thirty minutes ago. She watched Cora being thrown into an old white Chevy van in front of their apartment."

Taking a deep breath, Kruger calmed himself. He turned to JR to explain, "Cora is a graduate assistant. Very smart, very pretty." He turned back to Chambers and asked, "Did the roommate see the abductor?"

"All she saw was a tall man wearing a hoodie. He had long black hair sticking out from under it. She didn't see his face because his back was to her."

The mention of black hair gave Kruger pause. A distant memory of a similar situation cascaded over him. "Which direction did he drive?"

"She didn't see. She was too busy trying call our office. We called police and campus security."

Kruger looked around and grew angry. "Why are all of these officers standing around here?" he demanded. "They should be at the scene."

Chambers put his hand on Kruger's shoulder. "They have personnel there now."

Ignoring Chambers, Kruger turned to JR. "Do you have your laptop?"

Shaking his head, JR held up a cell phone. "Only this."

"Is it a Wi-Fi hot spot?"

"Of course."

"Can you use my laptop to track her phone?"

"I can do better. I can tell you where the phone is."

Not comprehending, he grabbed JR by the arm and rushed toward the stairs. As they got to the second floor, Kruger asked, "What did you mean back there?"

"Project I've been working on for a client."

"Let's get to the car. Then you can explain."

***

As the Ford Mustang GT screamed out of the faculty parking lot, Kruger turned to JR.

"What did you mean about knowing where the phone is?"

JR was in the passenger seat with Kruger's computer open on his lap.

"If I know a cell phone's number, I can send a signal to make sure the GPS function is on. Even if it's been manually shut off."

"Her phone number is in my contact info. I'm her advisor."

"Good."

Before handing his phone to JR, he pressed an icon. The call was answered on the third ring.

"This is Joseph."

"Do you know any SPD sergeants?"

"Yeah, why?"

"I need to meet one at an address."

"Why?"

"A student's life is in danger."

"Where do you want to meet him?"

Kruger gave him the address.

"I'll call you back."

He offered the cell phone to JR. Glancing briefly at his friend, Kruger asked, "How is this going to help us?"

"I have a trucking company for a client. The owner has a problem with his drivers shutting off the GPS function on their company cell phones. It's against company policy, and he asked me to figure out how to remotely turn it on when they turn it off."

"Sounds like you are turning into the men in black suits you've been avoiding for years," Kruger chuckled.

"Yeah, I've thought of that."

"Hypocrisy?"

"Probably. But the client's fee soothed my guilty conscience."

Before Kruger met JR, he was a computer software analyst for a large privately held software company. The owner of the company decided to bring in new investors to help expand his business. The new investors, through stock manipulation, suddenly owned a majority of the outstanding shares. They proceeded to fire the entire analysis team and outsourced their jobs to India. Within a year, the company was dismantled and sold, reaping millions for the new investors.

After being dismissed, JR hacked the laptop of the new owner and found multiple files outlining illegal activities. He copied the information and tried blackmailing the man, the reason he soon found himself in the company of two men who intended to end his life. JR managed to escape, but in the process, killed one and wounded the other.

Kruger's thoughts went back to their first conversation, when he was still with the FBI and sat down next to JR at a local pub in Springfield. Joseph, who was also sitting at the bar on the other side of JR said, "This is someone you need to talk to. He's fair and will listen."

Joseph stood and left.

"Before you wet your pants," Kruger smiled, "I'm not here to take you back to New York. I know the truth, and I'm here to help you."

The man looked at Kruger calmly. "Don't know what the hell you're talking about, man. I'm just sitting here drinking a beer and watching a baseball game."

Kruger nodded, "Okay. Here's what I know."

He proceeded to tell JR everything he knew while JR stared at the St. Louis Cardinals game on the TV. When Kruger was done, JR continued to stare at the TV. "And what do you plan to do with this knowledge?"

Kruger sipped his beer as he watched the ball game. "Nothing. I need someone like you to help me once in a while. If you want to help me, fine. If you don't, I'll walk out of here, and you'll never hear from me again."

JR turned to him and asked, "How do you know Joseph?"

"Old family friend," Kruger shrugged.

"If I help you, what's in it for me?"

"I'll start the process of clearing your real name."

JR looked at Kruger and smiled. "My name's JR Diminski. Glad to meet you."

They had been friends ever since.

Kruger's thoughts snapped back to the present when JR turned to him. "The phone is two miles west of Ozark on 14, traveling west toward Clever."

"There are numerous turnoffs leading to the James River on that highway."

"Yeah, and the phone just turned south on N."

Kruger's cell phone vibrated. He glanced at his dashboard and saw the call was from Joseph. He pressed the hands-free button on his steering wheel.

"Kruger."

Joseph's voice came over the speaker. "The sergeant's already at the address."

"Tell him we are heading toward Clever on 14. The van turned south on N. I've been down that way. It leads to the James River."

"Got it. I'll alert the Christian County sheriff's department."

"Have them approach with caution."

"Will do."

JR glanced over at his friend and asked, "Can we make it in time?"

Kruger didn't answer. He just pressed harder on the Mustang's accelerator.

***

Twenty minutes later, JR was directing Kruger toward a country lane on the western side of Hidden Valley Golf Links.

"Where the hell does this lead us, JR?"

"Toward the river."

Concentrating on his driving, Kruger asked, "How far?"

"The signal stopped. We're only a few hundred yards away."

Kruger slowed the Mustang as the road deteriorated to a rutted dirt path. The Mustang bottomed out several times as he drove further south.

"When? How far?" His voice sounded strained.

JR glanced at him. Sweat dripped down his forehead, his concentration total. Looking back at the laptop, JR frowned. "Just around this next turn."

Slowing the Mustang, Kruger followed the path. It emerged into a clearing where a dirty white Chevy van sat parked next to the river. Kruger accelerated toward the van and skidded to a halt within fifty feet. He shifted to first, set the parking brake, reached under his seat and extracted a gun, all in one fluid motion. JR recognized it as Kruger's FBI service Glock 19. Before he could say a word, Kruger was out of the car and running toward the van.

CHAPTER 6

Somewhere in Christian County, Missouri

Kruger pressed his back against the side of the van, next to the sliding door. He heard a muffled scream from inside and cringed. Without hesitation, he grabbed the door handle and pulled. As the sliding door flew open, he trained his Glock inside the van. His first impression was of a man kneeling astride a prone figure and removing his shirt.

The man with stringy black hair twisted as he turned toward the now-open door. A knife was in his hand, and he sneered at Kruger. As the man raised the knife, Kruger pulled the trigger on the gun twice. The bullets found their mark, and the man was slammed against the far side of the van. The prone figure scrambled to her knees and crawled as quickly as possible toward Kruger.

***

Kruger sat in the open door of the Mustang. With his hands clasped, he took a deep breath, and studied the grass next to his shoes. Four Christian County sheriff Ford SUVs were now in the open field next to the river. A medivac helicopter from Mercy Hospital was lifting off as he looked up. JR was leaning on the quarter panel of the car and watching over his friend when a larger man with corporal stripes walked up and stood in front of Kruger.

"You want to tell me how you found him?"

Kruger stayed quiet.

JR tilted his head to the side and answered, "I guided him."

The deputy turned his attention to JR and demanded, "Who are you?"

"A concerned citizen."

Corporal Gene Goodman stared at JR. "You being smart, son?"

Kruger could not believe what he was hearing. He shook his head. "I'm ex-FBI, corporal. We knew she was in trouble and were able to help."

"How?"

Looking up at the deputy, Kruger frowned. "Does it really matter? The girl is unharmed and safe."

"And the suspect is en route to a hospital with two bullets in him. I need to know how you found them and why you were involved."

Tired of the exchange, Kruger suddenly stood. The deputy was two inches shorter but outweighed him by fifty pounds. Large law enforcement officers stopped intimidating Kruger early in his law enforcement career. Leaning closer, Kruger stared at the deputy and said in a voice on the verge of a growl, "The girl would have been dead and floating down the river if we hadn't arrived. Do you really want to know the details?"

Goodman narrowed his eyes, but did not divert his gaze or back up. "Eventually. Stand down, agent."

Kruger laughed. "You ex-military?"

Goodman softened his glare and nodded.

"How's the girl?"

"Shaken, but not hurt. Sheriff wants to talk to both of you. Don't leave."

JR just shook his head as the deputy walked away.

Looking over at his friend, Kruger grinned. "That was an unhelpful comment."

"He pissed me off."

"He was doing his job."

"Reminded me of a major I knew in the military."

"Morton?"

JR nodded. "What now?"

"Don't know. Never shot anyone while I wasn't an agent."

JR chuckled. "I have."

Both men started laughing.

Five minutes later, Kruger noticed a man he recognized walking toward them. It was the sheriff of Christian County.

Jessie Summers offered his hand when he stopped in front of Kruger. "Good to see you again, Agent Kruger."

"It's good to see you, too, Sheriff. Although I'm retired from the FBI."

"Yeah, well, once Bureau, always Bureau, right?"

Kruger just smiled.

Kruger met Sheriff Summers two years prior during the hunt for serial killer Randolph Bishop. Bishop murdered a Christian County family of four before Kruger and his team killed the man in a confrontation that left Kruger seriously wounded. It was the last case of his FBI career, and he retired to teach psychology at a large university in Springfield.

Summers, looked at his shoes, cleared his throat. "Uh, we need you to look at something before you leave."

"Okay."

"The guy you shot is well known to my deputies."

Tilting his head to the side, Kruger frowned. "Why?"

"He's been convicted of child pornography and currently a registered sex offender."

Kruger kept his expression neutral.

"I have several deputies at the house he rents," the sheriff continued "Uh…" He looked at the sky. "It's disturbing."

Looking at JR and then back at the sheriff, Kruger nodded. "Let's go."

***

The walls of the dark and dreary bedroom of the small craftsman home were covered in pictures of nude girls. The ages ranged from pre-teen to late twenties. Some of the pictures were old Polaroids, and many were self-printed digital pictures on regular copy paper. Kruger turned to Summers and asked, "How many distinct individuals?"

"I'm told there are at least twenty-four."

"What's his name?"

"Jonathan Luna, goes by the name Jonnie."

"How old is he?"

"We think around forty-five or forty-six."

"You think? You're not sure?"

Summers shrugged, "He has several aliases."

Kruger did the math. "That would make him somewhere around thirty in 2002. Do you know where he was at that time?"

"At this stage, no. I can have someone at the office try and find out."

Kruger just nodded as he looked around the room. "I didn't think you would at this point, but I would like to be notified when you do. It's important."

Summers nodded.

Old news magazines, including Time, Newsweek, and U.S. News and World Report, were stacked in piles throughout the room. A bookcase contained books about true crime and several novels. Truman Capote's In Cold Blood appeared well read. Bending over, Kruger noticed one book in particular that troubled him. Slipping on latex gloves, he retrieved the book from its place in the bookcase.

He looked at the cover and started flipping pages. He stopped on the dedication page. A handwritten note was scrawled in barely legible script. 'This is how it is done.'

JR walked up behind him and looked at the book.

"What's that?"

Kruger was silent.

JR knew his friend well enough not to ask again. After twenty long seconds, Kruger replied. "A book written about a series of abductions I investigated back in late '90s and early 2000s."

"What about them?"

"Four separate incidents. Six women disappeared. Their bodies where never found, and a suspect never identified."

"I vaguely remember hearing about them."

"Apparently, our Mr. Luna likes to study crime." Kruger continued to flip through the pages until he came to a chapter he knew personally. It was the chapter where the author interviewed Kruger about his investigations of the abductions.

"I didn't know you were in a book."

"Not a high point in my FBI career."

"Why?"

"We never found the bodies or the kidnapper."

"Were they all related?"

"We think so. Clues were non-existent. They were all abducted in a public place, never in a place with a security camera and always when the victim was alone. Except the last case, when three women walked out of a café and disappeared. The only connection we could determine was all four abductions targeted college-age female basketball players."

"No clues?"

"None."

"And the bodies were never found?"

Kruger shook his head as he stared at the book.

"Sucks for the families."

"Yeah…"

Extracting himself from his funk, Kruger put the book back into its slot in the bookshelf. Looking around the room, he located Sheriff Summers and walked toward the man.

"Sheriff, I know it's early, but there is a chance, however small, this man may be involved in an unsolved case I investigated seventeen years ago. As soon as possible, I need to talk to him."

Summers tilted his head and glared. "He's in critical condition. It could be days before he's alert enough."

Handing the sheriff a business card with a number scrawled on the back, Kruger stared the man in the eyes. "I was never able to tell a lonely father what happened to his daughter. It's important."

Summers' eyes softened, and he took a deep breath. "Yeah, I've been there. I'll give you a call when he's stable."

Nodding, Kruger started to walk out of the apartment. Summers stopped him with a question. "Agent, what have I got here?"

Kruger turned at the entrance to the house. "Sheriff, you have a predator on your hands. Be prepared to be shocked, saddened, angered, and mad. You will not like what you find in this house of horrors."

Summers stared at Kruger, but did not respond. He turned and started instructing deputies on how to gather the evidence.

JR followed Kruger out the door.

Once they were back in the Mustang and driving toward Springfield, JR turned to Kruger. "What do you think?"

"I don't believe in coincidence, but I have to know for sure he is not the man who abducted those women almost two decades ago."

"How many men like that are out there, Sean?"

"More than I care to think about."

Silence fell between the two friends. Two minutes later, JR glanced at Kruger. "How is this man different from Bishop?"

Taking a deep breath, Kruger exhaled slowly. "Hard to explain. Suffice it to say, they don't feel emotions like you and me. I'm pretty sure this Luna character is not the man I couldn't find in 2002, but he might give me a better understanding of who I'm looking for."

"You going to re-open your investigation of seventeen years ago?"

"Don't know. Maybe..." He was silent for several

moments. “Probably.”

Chapter 7

Springfield, MO

The attic yielded its contents reluctantly. Kruger's FBI notes and files were buried in a corner behind old suitcases from Stephanie's and his days of constant travel. Cardboard bank record boxes, purchased at a local Staples, contained case notes stored for reasons he could not remember. One box on the bottom of a stack in a dark corner contained files and two personal copies of the same book he found on Luna's bookshelf.

One was signed by the author and the other had been given to him by a now-deceased colleague. As soon as he lifted the lid from the box, he hesitated. The contents brought back a rush of emotions. It was an investigation composed of failure, loneliness, loss, and a lack of closure for many families. It also reminded him of a time in his life without Stephanie.

Moving the box to a clear space on the attic floor, he removed the copy of the book given to him by a fellow agent, at one time his mentor. The book contained handwritten notes in the margins that would be read later in the comfort of his home office. For now, the purpose of finding the book was to re-read the last few pages of his interview with the author, pages he had read repeatedly for several years. The title of the book summarized his feelings about the case.

"Lost Lives and Futures."

The author, Christopher Park, contacted Kruger four years after the abduction of Linda Kelly, Karla Sharp, and April Lane. He turned to the page he sought and started reading by the light of a single bare light bulb attached to a stud in the attic.

Park: Agent Kruger, the last abduction occurred four years ago. Since then, nothing. What is the official FBI viewpoint about the investigation?

Kruger: The Bureau maintains an active group of investigators working daily on the case.

Park: You were the lead investigator, correct?

Kruger: Yes.

Park: But you are not involved anymore, is this correct?

Kruger: You are correct. I am no longer involved.

Park: What is your opinion about finding these women after four years?

Kruger closed his eyes and remembered his reaction to this question. Taking a deep breath, he kept reading.

Kruger: I'm not optimistic the women will be found or the investigation closed.

Park: Why?

Kruger: Because after the abduction of Linda, Karla, and April, the kidnappings stopped.

Park: What do you think this means?

Kruger: There are three possibilities. One, the man is dead. Two, he's in prison for something else, or three, he stopped. If he's dead, we will never know the truth. If he's in prison, we might catch a lucky break and learn his identity after he brags about it to a fellow inmate. This hasn't happened, so I don't believe he's in prison.

Park: What about the third possibility?

Kruger: That one bothers me the most. If he quit, he doesn't fit the normal profile of a serial killer. If this is the case, we are dealing with someone who is far more dangerous than we previously thought.

Park: Why?

Kruger smiled at the editorial note made by Park before he wrote the answer to his previous question.

Author's Note: Agent Kruger paused for a considerable amount of time after this question was asked. He stared at me and then turned to look out a window for several minutes. Finally his attention returned and he answered.

Kruger: The vast majority of individuals who we in law enforcement encounter suffer from substance abuse or mental illness. The ones we lose sleep over are the ones who plot out these types of abductions and are never caught. These individuals are usually of high intelligence and can hide their psychosis from those around them. They can be the husband and father next door, even their families are unaware of their particular desires.

Park: Why do you keep referring to this individual as a he?

Kruger: Statistically, they are always male. But, mental illness is an equal opportunity condition. Females can suffer from this type of illness, but generally, as a rule, do not act as sexual predators. They can, but it's rare.

Kruger stopped reading, took his reading glasses off and pinched the bridge of his nose with his fingers. He heard a noise behind him. As he turned, he saw Stephanie's head pop into the attic opening.

Stephanie Harris Kruger was a petite woman seven years younger than her husband. She was strikingly beautiful with naturally curly brown hair she wore touching her shoulders. Her pale blue eyes sparkled in any light, and her smile was infectious. Kruger had fallen in love with her the moment they met.

"You've been up here for hours. Are you okay?"

He smiled and nodded.

"Got involved with a file. I'll be down in a minute."

"Did you forget JR and Mia are coming over for dinner? You're supposed to grill."

"I did not. I just haven't thought about it recently."

"In other words, you forgot." Her tone was playful.

He nodded. "I'll be right down."

Replacing the files back into the box, he scooted it closer

to the opening. Turning off the light bulb, Kruger lugged the box down the folding step ladder and closed the entrance to the attic. The box was set on his home office desk before he joined Stephanie in the kitchen to prepare for their dinner guests.

***

JR Diminski leaned against the handrail of Kruger's back deck and watched his friend clean the iron cooking grates on a large outdoor gas grill.

"When did you learn to cook chicken so good, Sean? Last time we did this, you cooked steaks."

"Stephanie."

Chuckling, JR smiled at his friend. "Care to enlighten me?"

"Stef wants us to eat less beef and more lean protein, like chicken and fish."

"No vegan tendencies, I hope."

Kruger smiled and shook his head. "No, nothing that drastic. I tend to agree with her. We're using more fresh and frozen vegetables and staying away from the canned stuff."

"That I agree with."

The two were quiet for a few moments as Kruger finished cleaning and then lowered the grill's lid. He turned to his friend. "I need your perspective on something."

"Sure, what?"

"I brought down my file notes on the abductions I investigated seventeen years ago."

"Did Luna bother you that much?"

The ex-FBI agent nodded. "Yeah, he did. I need to put a new perspective on them."

"Okay."

"I want to start by looking at what each of the colleges would have in common around the turn of the century."

JR tilted his head slightly. "In what respects?"

Kruger shrugged. "Anything."

"Didn't you do that back when the investigations were fulltime?"

"Yeah, but I didn't have someone like you to bounce stuff off. Other than an older agent I worked with, I was generally by myself on these kidnappings. Budgetary constraints, I was told."

"Okay, so bounce."

"When I reviewed my notes, I found a reference to a phone call I totally forgot about."

"A phone call?"

"Yeah, the voice was electronic."

"Huh." JR was quiet for a few moments. "Lots of ways to make that happen."

"The call was interactive. The caller even laughed at me a couple of times. When I had Washington contact Alltel, they told the Bureau no such call was ever made to my phone."

JR frowned, but remained quiet.

"What do you think?"

"I'm thinking. When did this occur?"

"About two and a half months after the three women were taken. Late 2002."

JR pursed his lips and stared at his friend. "The first keyboard demonstration of a voice synthesizer was in 1939 at the New York World's Fair by Homer Dudley. He used a system invented by Bell Labs in 1930 called a Vocoder. Synthesized speech started getting mainstream in the 1990s. With today's technology, it almost sounds human and can be interactive. But not in 2002."

"Kind of what I thought. What about the lack of a record at Alltel?"

"Not hard to do today, not so much then. You need to look for someone exceptionally skilled with computers."

"We didn't do that."

JR shook his head. "You would have no reason to. Where did the other three abductions occur?"

"1999, Jacksonville University in Florida. 2000, Concord University in Athens, West Virginia. And 2001, University of

Akron in Ohio."

"A year apart?" JR's eyebrows shot up.

"Yes, almost exactly a year apart."

"And no bodies were ever found, correct?"

Kruger shook his head. "No bodies even to this day."

His cell phone vibrated in his pocket. The conversation lagged as he withdrew it and answered the call. JR turned to look out over the back yard as twilight turned to night.

"Kruger."

There was silence as JR listened to the one-way conversation.

"I see… So he was in prison from 1997 to 2005."

More silence.

"That's what I needed to know."

Quiet.

"No, I don't believe I need to interview him. Thanks for the call, Sheriff."

Kruger ended the conversation and placed the phone back into his pocket. JR turned back to look at his friend. "In prison?"

"Yeah. I knew it was too good to be true. Where were we?"

"The call. If we assume the suspect is good with computers, and I believe we have to, he could have been at the schools as a consultant or as a trainer for new software the schools were installing."

"How could we check? That was a long time ago, and admin personnel have probably come and gone over the course of seventeen years."

"Maybe."

"What do you have in mind?"

"Let me think about it tonight."

Mia opened the kitchen door and looked at JR, saying, "We've got to get this little boy to bed, JR. Time to go."

***

The first time Kruger met JR Diminski, he and Mia lived on the third floor of a three-story building in the downtown region of Springfield. His business occupied the second floor, with storage and administrative functions on the first.

When Joseph Sean Diminski was born, the couple sold the building, bought a house across the street from the Krugers and moved the business to a two-story structure on the southwest section of town in a multi-use development a mile from their house.

JR's business had grown from a one-man operation to a nationally known computer security firm employing fifty-one individuals. He let others run the day-to-day operations while he met with clients and did the programing. His sideline business and first love remained the art of hacking.

Kruger stood next to JR as he watched his friend's hands dance over the keyboard while his head swiveled back and forth between three flat screen monitors. "What are you looking for?"

"Personnel records of the four colleges."

"I won't ask how you found them."

"Probably best." JR stopped typing. "Okay," he pointed to four lists on the screens, "these are the individuals at each college with twenty or more years of service. The department where they work is the second column next to their name."

"I didn't realize how many individuals might still be there after so many years."

"Not unusual for a university. Decent pay, good benefits, and the jobs aren't that stressful."

"I would agree."

With his fingers flying over the keyboard one more time, the list changed to only individuals working in the administrative department and the year of their original employment. "You go from forty to fifty individuals to a list of four or five with this filter. Those are the people who could tell you what was going on seventeen to twenty years ago."

Kruger stared at the four lists. It was a start, one he didn't have during the investigation. A new perspective that might help the cold case to heat up again. "Guess I need to talk to Alan Seltzer."

"What's Stephanie going to say?"

"We've discussed it several times over the course of the past year. She wants me to do what I feel I need to do."

"What's that?"

"Go back to the FBI."

JR smiled.

CHAPTER 8

Washington, D.C.
FBI Headquarters

Kruger sat at a conference table in a room adjacent to FBI Director Paul Stumpf's office. Stumpf sat at the head of the table to Kruger's right with a smiling Deputy Director of the FBI directly across from him. Alan Seltzer intertwined his hands and placed them flat on the table. "So, why do you want to come back?"

"Truth, or do you want some PC bullshit?"

"Let's start with the truth, and then we can decide on the BS."

Smiling, Kruger nodded. "There is a developing lead on the missing basketball player's case."

Stumpf's eyes grew wide, and Seltzer stared at Kruger. Stumpf spoke for the first time. "What lead?"

Taking a deep breath, Kruger explained about catching Luna and the conversation with JR. He extracted a sheet of paper with the names of numerous long-term administrative personnel at each university. "I want to interview these individuals. They may help me with a new theory."

"You don't have to re-join the FBI," Stumpf paused for a moment. "We actually have other agents who are trained to do that, Sean." The Director was straight faced as he said it.

Kruger gave Stumpf a half grin. "That's only half of it."

Both Stumpf and Seltzer tried to stifle their amusement. They both failed.

Seltzer covered his mouth with a hand to hide his smile. "Go on."

"It took two years, but I've come to the conclusion I don't like teaching. I was happier as an agent. Plus, I'm slated to be the head of the department at the end of the academic year. You both know I hate politics and most of the duties of the position are political. Plus, I would have to talk to the media on occasion, and we all know how I feel about doing that."

Stumpf chuckled and opened a vanilla folder laying on the table in front of him. He extracted several pages and handed them to Kruger. "Sign these."

After skimming the pages, he returned his attention to Stumpf and asked, "What is this?"

"Acknowledging your leave of absence is over."

"What leave of absence?"

"The leave of absence you've been on for the last two years. You took a sabbatical, don't you remember? You keep your seniority and pay grade."

"Is this the PC bullshit?"

"Yes."

"I appreciate that, Paul."

Seltzer handed Kruger a pen, which he used to sign the documents. After the documents were handed back to Stumpf, a badge and FBI ID appeared in front of Seltzer. Pushing them across the table, he pointed to the ID. "You'll need to get that updated with a new photo before you leave."

Kruger nodded.

Stumpf put the signed papers back in the folder. "Now that you've got this teaching crap out of your system, tell us about your new theory on the missing basketball players?"

Thirty minutes later, after explaining the details of the Luna abduction and his conversations with JR, Kruger folded his hands in front of him and looked at Stumpf. "That's it."

"I think your reasoning is sound. What kinds of resources will you need?"

"Not sure yet. What are Sandy Knoll and Jimmie Gibbs doing now?"

Seltzer answered, "Knoll is in charge of an FBI Rapid Response Team and Gibbs works for him."

"Good, can I have access to them if needed?"

Stumpf nodded.

"If I need anything else, I'll let you know. First step is to interview personnel at the universities."

***

It was the fourth day of his trip to interview administrative personnel at the different colleges. His next interview would be the last for this trip. Afterward he planned to drive home, a four-hour journey.

Emily Douglas was the final individual scheduled. She arrived and sat across from him at the table in a small conference room provided by Truman State University.

She appeared close to fifty, neatly dressed in a gray pantsuit with a light blue blouse under the jacket. Her hair was cut short, but nicely styled, and she wore designer glasses. Now in charge of the accounting department, her promotion had occurred the previous year. After shaking hands, Kruger smiled.

"Thank you for taking time to speak with me, Ms. Douglas."

"Please, just Emily."

"I'm Sean."

She returned the smile.

"Emily, do you remember when the three girls were abducted in 2002?"

"Oh yes, that was such a bad day. I was in records at the time, and we all cried for weeks. Linda Kelly was a student helper there for about a year. She worked when she wasn't in class or at basketball practice. Sweet girl."

This was new information. Kruger made a note.

"Leading up to the abduction, were there any outside contractors working on the computer systems?"

She tilted her head and stared at Kruger for several moments. "Let me think. Yes, yes, I believe there was."

Kruger kept quiet, letting the woman talk.

"A company out of St. Louis was installing a new SIS system, and we had a bunch of individuals installing the program and training us."

"Do you remember the name of the company?"

"No, I'm sorry."

"That's okay. Can you describe any of the individuals from the company?"

"No, only one."

Kruger's eyes widened. "Only one, why?"

She took a deep breath. "Because he was very good at making all of us in records feel we were beneath him." She shivered and shook her head. "I can still see him."

"Describe him?"

"Tall, slender. His face was oval shaped, and he had the darkest brown eyes I'd ever seen."

"What color was his hair?"

"Black."

Kruger straightened. "Who did he work for?"

"The company in St. Louis. He was some kind of supervisor."

"Do you remember his name?"

She paused briefly, "Let me think."

Staying silent, Kruger waited.

"It was Bobby."

"Bobby?"

She nodded. "Yes, his name was Bobby."

"Why do you remember the name?"

"Because he made a pass at me. I was married at the time and told him no. After that, he acted like I wasn't there."

"How?"

"He would talk about me to the other trainers, ignoring

the fact I was sitting right there."

"Huh."

"He said a lot of ugly things. I complained, but was told to ignore him."

Kruger talked to her ten more minutes without learning any additional details. He thanked her and ended the interview.

On the drive back to Springfield, he called JR.

JR answered on the fourth ring. "When are you getting back?"

Looking at the clock on his dashboard, he answered, "Around seven. It's a four-hour drive."

"Learn anything?"

"Not at the first two schools, other than they were all installing Student Information Systems around the time of the kidnappings."

"Any idea of the name of the company?"

"No, no one remembered. I did find out it was in St. Louis. Two witnesses mentioned the company's location. A man in Jacksonville and a woman in Kirksville."

"Okay, I can work with that. What else?"

"One of the ladies I spoke to in Kirksville told me about an individual installing the system who hit on her. His name was Bobby. He was slender with black hair."

"Uh oh."

"Yeah, we need to see if we can find a Bobby who worked for a company with no name, located in St. Louis."

JR chuckled. "I've had less to go on."

"Let's talk tomorrow."

"Deal."

***

"So, you're reinstated?"

Kruger nodded as he unpacked his suitcase.

"Are you sure this is what you want, Sean?"

"Yes, more than the other time I returned."

Stephanie smiled and walked over to hug him. Their embrace lasted several minutes. He kissed the top of her head, the familiar scent of jasmine and vanilla made him smile. "What about you?"

"I will never ask you to quit again. You've been miserable."

He did not respond.

"What about the university?"

"I called on the drive back. I'll be a guest lecturer and student advisor."

"Is that what you want?"

"It was what I enjoyed the most."

"I'm sorry about how I acted two years ago. I was just afraid of losing you."

"It worried me, too. I did work something out with Paul."

"What's that?"

"I'm going to concentrate on unsolved cases."

She raised her head off his chest and looked up. "What does that mean?"

"I don't have to travel unless I need to interview a witness or make an arrest."

She smiled, closed her eyes, and put her head back on his chest.

***

"The name of the company was Infinite Student, LLC. It sold to IBM in 2010." JR pointed toward the left side monitor. "Personnel records were intermingled within the IBM system. No record of a Bobby, or a Robert for that matter, with a background at Infinite Student."

"Are we at a dead end?"

JR shook his head. "I think the guy left before it was bought by IBM."

"What now?"

"I've got one of my snooper routines checking social media for anyone with the name of Robert or Bobby with

Infinite Student in their background."

"Any luck?"

"Not yet."

Kruger straightened from leaning over to look at the screen. "What if he never worked for this Infinite Student, LLC?"

"What do you mean?"

"I was thinking about it last night. What if he worked for another vendor, like say, the hardware company? He might have been there to make sure the hardware and software worked seamlessly together?"

JR blinked several times, but did not respond for about twenty seconds. "Hadn't thought of that." He turned back to his keyboard and started typing again.

Kruger wandered over to the coffee service JR kept next to the conference room and made a cup. He grumbled under his breath about the Keurig system, but remembered he had not bought the drip coffeemaker he was planning on giving JR.

Fifteen minutes later, JR stared at the right screen for at least two minutes. "That," he pointed to the screen, "might be a possibility."

Kruger sipped his coffee and looked at where JR was pointing. "Huh…" He read some more. "What exactly does Haylex Solutions do?"

More typing on the keyboard.

"Network and routing systems. I've never heard of them."

"Really?"

"Really."

"That's interesting."

"It happens. They specialize in academic systems. I don't work with schools, colleges or universities."

"Why?"

JR turned and looked up at Kruger. "They take too long to make decisions. Once they do, their business goes to the lowest bidder. I'm never the lowest bidder."

"Makes sense. Now, what about Haylex Solutions?"

"According to the company website, in 1982, a software engineer named Irving Bush founded the company as a one-man shop. By 1990, the employee count was over one hundred. Infinite Student was his first customer and one of his largest. He died in 1992 after selling the company to a venture capitalist group the previous year. They sold it in 1998 to a group of investors headed by a man named…" JR paused and re-read the name, "Robert Burns. He's listed as the current CEO."

"Uh-oh."

Working the keyboard again, JR paused to read the screen. Shaking his head, he looked up at Kruger. "It's unlikely this is the Bobby or Robert we are looking for."

"Why?"

"Because he was serving as a United States senator from Washington State. Elected in 2000, he retired after two terms in 2012 to become CEO. Plus, he's in his late sixties now. In 2002, he would have been in his fifties."

"That doesn't work, does it?"

JR shook his head.

"Back to Haylex Solutions."

"They were subcontractors for Infinite Student. They installed the networking protocols."

"I don't like the coincidence of the kidnappings starting the year after Haylex Solutions was bought by someone named Robert. If there is a connection, we need to figure it out."

With a slight smile, JR nodded.

CHAPTER 9

Seattle, WA

Robert Burns sipped a glass of Columbia River Merlot from one of the dozen wineries he owned around the state. He studied the skyline of Seattle across Elliot Bay as the approaching darkness transitioned the scene from a forest of tall buildings to a cascade of lights. The floor-to-ceiling windows on each level created the illusion the house was solid glass on the side facing downtown Seattle. He stood in the master bedroom on the top floor of the three level concrete structure and watched the city come to life.

Now late into his seventh decade of life, his presence, wherever it might be, was commanding. His black hair, which he combed straight back, was thinning but still absent of gray strands. Considered the fifth wealthiest individual in Seattle, he rubbed shoulders with the likes of Bill Gates, Jeff Bezos, Paul Allen, and Jerry Baldwin. During the last six years of his two terms in the Senate, he served as chairman on several high-power committees and was outspoken on numerous conservative initiatives.

The tuxedo he wore was well used from attending various campaign rallies and fundraising functions over the past year. The illumination of his beloved city was his favorite time of the day, a sight he rarely missed if at home. Glancing at his watch, he noted it was nearing time to head to the watch party.

Turning to address the individual in the master bathroom, he saw his personal assistant finishing the final touches of her makeup. He smiled. She was beautiful and twenty years his junior. "Allison, when do we need to leave?"

Allison O'Brien's long auburn hair featured streaks of black, which gave the woman an exotic look. She smiled as she stopped applying the finishing touches to her eyes. "Robert, we don't have to leave for thirty minutes."

He nodded and returned to watching the lights of Seattle blink on. Several minutes later he heard Allison ask, "Have you heard any exit polls yet?"

"It is bad luck to listen to exit polls on Election Day."

"No, darling, it's bad luck to see the bride on your wedding day, not to listen to exit polls."

Burns chuckled. Allison was indispensable as his assistant, for which he paid her a substantial salary. She was even more indispensable in his bed, a function which allowed her to share his lifestyle. A lifestyle he had worked forty years to acquire. As tall as Robert, she was slender, athletic, and extremely ambitious. She also knew, if she continued to learn from Robert Burns, she would be the next CEO. The son was not interested in running the family business. She was.

Ten minutes later, she finished in the bathroom and walked over to where he stood. "Beautiful isn't it? The site never ceases to amaze me."

"Me, either. You ready?"

She nodded as he touched a button on a remote control unit sitting on his nightstand. As they walked out of the room a curtain slid silently across the window.

***

By ten p.m. the attendees at the Burns for Senator watch party were drunk with excitement and five hundred bottles of

Washington State wine. Robert S. Burns, Jr. would be the next United States senator from the great state of Washington, beating his opponent by fifteen percentage points in a special election. The previous senator left the position to become the Secretary of Housing and Urban Development.

Robert Senior smiled as he basked in the glow of victory. He had spent close to fifty million dollars on the campaign, the contributions masked through numerous clandestine channels. The amount was immaterial considering the results.

Allison O'Brien walked up next to him, aware that showing affection in public to the senior Burns was strictly against his rules. "Congratulations, Robert. This will be fun."

He nodded. "Yes, it's time Junior understands who is responsible for his election and who will be calling the shots. He also needs to remember who kept his name out of the headlines several years ago."

"Why didn't you run again?"

"I burned a few bridges while I was there. Let's just say Junior will have a fresh start. Besides, his public reputation is clear of any scandals."

"Are you sure?"

"Yes."

"Junior can be a bit… uh, let's say aggressive with the women in his life. Have you ever had someone look into the time he was on the road for Haylex Solutions?"

"There were a few incidents, but they are also behind him and under legal non-disclosure agreements."

"Robert, don't you think it would be wise to double check on Junior?"

Senior shook his head, but did not divert his gaze from his assistant. After several awkward moments, Senior averted his stare. "Should I?"

"Not my decision. But I believe it might be prudent to know if there are other incidents you don't know about."

"Dammit, Allison, you've managed to spoil the mood of the evening."

"Better to know now than have a *Washington Post* reporter explain it to you."

Robert Burns nodded and pulled out his cell phone. He dialed a number and waited for the call to be answered.

***

Joel Moody, ex-police detective and current head of security for Haylex Holdings, Inc., reached for the phone on his night stand and answered on the fourth ring.

"Yes, Mr. Burns."

"How are you tonight, Joel?"

"Fine, sir. I understand congratulations are in order."

"Yes, it was a positive outcome."

"What can I do for you, sir?"

"Uh… This is a sensitive matter, one I do not wish to discuss over the phone. Can you be in my office at eight in the morning?"

"Of course, sir."

"Good."

The call ended, and Moody returned the cell phone to his nightstand. He stared at the digital alarm clock next to the cell phone and sighed. It was approaching eleven in the evening. Burns rarely asked for meetings, which piqued his curiosity. As he lay back down, his wife stirred next to him and mumbled, "What was that all about?"

He smiled and leaned over to kiss her cheek. "Not sure. Burns wants a meeting in the morning."

His response was a gentle snore as his wife settled back into slumber.

Staring at the dark ceiling, his mind raced wondering about the reasons for the meeting. The fifty-year-old detective would never fully get back to sleep.

***

"Would you like coffee, Joel?"

"No, thank you, sir. What did you want to discuss?"

Robert Burns poured a cup of coffee from the service cart his administrative assistant brought in every morning. His office was located on the sixth floor of the Haylex Building in downtown Seattle. He shook a pack of Splenda, tore off an end, and absent-mindedly poured the granules into the steaming liquid. Walking back to his desk, he placed the coffee to his right, intertwined his fingers, and placed them flat on the desk top.

"Joel, I have a delicate issue to discuss. I need your total commitment to secrecy."

"Without being said, sir. Of course."

"Good."

Moody sat ram-rod straight in the chair facing Burns' desk. He remained silent.

"I need to know if my son has any…" He hesitated for a moment. "Uh—embarrassing activity in his past."

Moody blinked twice, but did not answer right away. After several awkward moments, he tilted his head to the left and asked, "Other than the incident in Washington, what kind of embarrassing activities?"

Burns gave his security chief a lopsided smile. "The incident in Washington has been handled legally, and the individual involved is under a strict non-disclosure agreement. She won't be speaking to the press. I'm more interested in any episode with drugs, women, men, illegitimate children, etc."

Moody smiled. "Sir, we did a thorough investigation right after he announced his candidacy, per your request. You know about the affairs at the college campuses. Those women signed agreements and had their tuition paid."

"Were you able to account for all of the trips he took?"

A slight smile came to Joel Moody as he recognized the trap he was being led into. Many a clever defense attorney had tried to trip him up during his years as a Seattle police detective. Few did. "Yes, sir. We covered every trip your son took during his time as a Haylex Solutions consultant. We found nothing nefarious. He had a lot of fun, but nothing illegal."

"Good. Now I need you to look into any personal trips he might have taken."

"Why, sir?"

"Joel, I know my son. Like his father, he has a wild streak. I need to know, before he is sworn in as a senator, if there is anything embarrassing in his past."

Moody nodded.

The meeting lasted another hour before Joel Moody left Robert Burns' office. The task assigned would not be difficult. Joel Moody knew exactly who and what Robert Burns Jr. was. It would be fun watching the loathsome individual fall from his father's grace.

CHAPTER 10

Hannibal, MO

The house appeared old and tired, just like the owner. Since his last visit, seventeen years ago, the trees were larger, the evergreens overgrown and in desperate need of pruning. The house paint was faded from years of sun and neglect. Calling ahead to request a visit, he was informed about the current state of Paul Kelly's health. This news increased his feelings of dread and depression about the questions he needed to ask the still-grieving father.

A round woman in her early fifties answered the door.

"Are you the FBI agent who called?"

"Yes, ma'am. Sean Kruger." He showed her his newly updated ID and badge.

"Please come in. I'm Sara Kelly. My uncle is awake. Hopefully, he will remember you. His dementia is taking more and more of his personality each day."

Kruger paused. "I'm sorry to hear that."

"His short term memory is almost non-existent. Unfortunately, he seems to relive that awful day seventeen years ago over and over. It's so sad. Come with me, I'll show you to his room."

Without saying anything, Kruger just nodded and

followed.

Paul Kelly's appearance had dramatically changed since the last time Kruger interviewed him. The gray hair was gone, replaced by wisps of sparse white hair. He appeared emaciated. Kruger looked at Sara, who was looking at the frail man sitting up in bed.

"The only nutrition his body can digest is Ensure," she said softly.

Returning his gaze to Paul, Kruger walked up to the bed. "Mr. Kelly, do you remember me?"

Paul Kelly's gaze had not strayed from Kruger since he entered the room. His eyes, dulled with cataracts, narrowed, and he nodded slightly.

"You're the FBI agent who was honest with me about Linda."

"Yes, sir."

"I never thanked you."

"There was never a need."

The older man nodded. "Do you have news for me?"

"No, sir. I need to ask you a few questions."

"My memory isn't what it used to be, Agent. I'll do my best."

"Do you remember if Linda ever mentioned the name Bobby to you?"

Kelly stared at Kruger with a blank expression.

"Not that I can recall."

"There's been a new development in the case and I needed to ask."

"I need to give you something, Agent Kruger. There is a box on Linda's bed containing her personal items they returned to me after her disappearance. I want you to have them."

"Why?"

"So you won't forget about her."

"Trust me, Mr. Kelly, I haven't forgotten about your daughter or any of the women who disappeared."

Suddenly a blank expression appeared on Paul Kelly's face.

He frowned and looked up at Kruger.

"You're the FBI Agent who was honest with me about Linda. Aren't you?" he asked.

Recognizing what was happening, Kruger gave the older man a smile. "Yes, sir, I am."

Kruger talked to the man several more minutes and had the same conversation three times. When Paul Kelly turned his face toward a window, Kruger asked Sara Kelly to show him Linda's room. As soon as the door was opened, it was like stepping into a past era. Posters of Kurt Cobain, Sheryl Crow, Stone Temple Pilot, and the 1996 Women's Olympic Basketball team still clung to the walls with yellowed cracked Scotch Tape.

The bed was made with a flower print bedspread adorned with ten pillows and numerous stuffed animals. Cobwebs could be seen in all four corners of the room. A sun-faded curtain still adorned the western window. Stacks of folded clothes lay on the seat of a rocking chair at the foot of the bed. Kruger could see what appeared to be several basketball jerseys within the stacks. The room smelled of dust and stale air.

Kruger looked at Sara. "My uncle has not allowed anyone to touch this room. This is how it appeared when Linda went away to college. We aren't even allowed to clean it."

Nodding, Kruger saw the box sitting on the bed and pointed to it. "Is that the box he mentioned?"

She nodded.

As he opened the top, he saw the reason for his visit. The last time he saw the object was on an apartment night stand seventeen years ago. He remembered flipping through the pages of Linda Kelly's journal, his hands covered with latex gloves. Setting the journal on the bed next to the box, he rummaged through it until he came to a bundle of envelopes held together with a brittle rubber band. He flipped through these and placed them on top of the book.

Further examination of the box revealed nothing else of value to his investigation, until he saw the business card laying upside down at the bottom. He reached into the side pocket of his jacket and extracted a latex glove. He placed it on his right hand and extracted the business card. He looked at it, smiled, and placed it in a small Ziploc bag. This he placed back into his jacket pocket. He turned to Sara. "Is there a picture of Linda I can borrow?"

She frowned and pursed her lips. "Let me think." She turned and surveyed the room. Her eyebrows rose as a small smile came to her face, and she left the room. She was back in less than a minute with a picture in a five-by-seven frame.

"This was her sophomore picture. Truman State handed it out to the media when she set the school scoring record."

Kruger took the picture and saw a tall, athletic woman with auburn hair standing with her hands behind her back and a basketball at her feet. The smile on the woman's face made Kruger sad. He shook the funk off and looked up at Sara. "This is perfect. I will return it with the letters and journal. I assume he will he want them back?"

She shook her head. "Probably not, he's never looked inside the box. It was sealed up until yesterday. When I told him about your call, he asked me to put it on the bed for you. I'm surprised he remembered it."

"I'm not. It's part of a memory his dementia hasn't reached yet. Unfortunately, if he lives long enough, it will."

Smiling, she shook her head again. "As I told you on the phone yesterday, Hospice comes in once a day. The family banded together to help Uncle Paul stay in the house as long as possible. My dad is his youngest brother and has Power of Attorney. He took a reverse mortgage out on the house. It has helped with the expenses, and there should be just enough left for the funeral. It's sad, but he's been able to stay here and wait for Linda."

Kruger gave her a grim smile.

Sara looked at the box. "She isn't going to come back, is she, Agent?"

"No. I'm afraid not."

"Hospice started morphine two days ago. He probably

won't be with us too much longer."

"Probably not."

"My dad told me that his brother died the day he heard about Linda. His body just didn't realize it yet." She sighed. "He was a good man, Agent. Why do bad things happen to good people?"

"I wish I knew, Sara."

***

Linda Kelly's journal was interesting reading. Kruger sat at his home office desk and read it page by page, a task he had performed seventeen years earlier. It revealed a young woman's hopes and dreams about playing in the WNBA someday. From the first page, Kruger could tell if she had lived, she would have fulfilled her dream. A sadness swept over him as he re-read the journal. The final ten pages were the important section of the book. He read them three times before setting it down.

Stephanie appeared at the door of his office. "Did you learn anything?"

He frowned and picked up the book. "Maybe a little. She talks about a handsome man watching basketball practice one day and having coffee with him later. No name, but there are three missing pages after that. If they did have a date, the name and any more detail may have been cut out."

"Maybe one of her teammates would know if they dated."

"I looked at my notes from the case before I read the journal. None believed she did. Her coach told me during an interview Linda's schedule was frantic: practice, school, work, practice, and more practice. She also mentioned Linda didn't like to date during the basketball season. Too many distractions."

Stephanie nodded. "I can understand that."

"From what I've learned about her, Linda was a focused individual. She reminds me a little of you when we first met."

"Are you telling me I'm not focused anymore?" Stephanie

tried to hide her smile, but she failed miserably.

Kruger chuckled. "No, you're just focused in a different direction right now. Linda was on a mission, playing in the WNBA."

She nodded.

"Her dad told me seventeen years ago that Linda was an adventurous individual. In the journal, she mentions the excitement of older men showing interest in her. Apparently, it had happened before."

"Did she and this Bobby have sex?"

"If they did, the reference might be on the missing pages. Otherwise it is not mentioned in the journal."

"Does she describe him?"

Kruger shook his head. "No, it just mentions a handsome man with expensive clothes."

"Do you think his description was cut out?"

"Probably."

"So, in other words, you're right back where you started."

"Pretty much. With one exception."

"What's that?"

"A business-size card with a phone number on it."

Stephanie's eyebrows rose. "Really."

"I've sent the card off for analysis. Getting fingerprints off paper has always been difficult, but the Bureau has some new techniques. We'll just have to see."

"What about the number?"

"JR's working on it."

Stephanie smiled.

***

"What can you tell me about the phone number?"

JR shook his head. "Not much."

"Why?"

"Remember the Bureau couldn't trace the call you received?"

"Yeah."

"I use this type of technology all the time. The phone number was web-based and forwarded any calls to another predesignated number. Pretty sophisticated for 2002."

"So, in other words, he gave her a number that switched her call to a hidden number."

"Yeah, it's a little more complicated, but that's a good explanation."

"So, what do you think?"

"Whoever this guy is, he was ahead of the game with computers."

Kruger pursed his lips. "Like someone who knows network and routing systems."

Nodding, JR was silent for a few moments. "Yeah, like someone familiar with routing systems. What little we have to go on continues to point toward Haylex Solutions, doesn't it?"

"I'm afraid it does."

"Now what?"

"I think it's time I spoke to Robert Burns."

JR smiled. "Before you go, you'll need as much background on the company as possible."

Putting his hand on JR's shoulder, Kruger smiled. "That's your job."

CHAPTER 11

Seattle, WA

Sean Kruger shook the extended hand of Haylex Holdings, Inc. head of security after showing his FBI credentials.

"Thank you for meeting with me, Mr. Moody."

"Call me Joel. I thought you retired after the incident in Fayetteville, Arkansas several years ago."

"Urban legend." Kruger did not feel the need to discuss his personal life.

Moody smiled. "Do you remember Byron Hall from Provo, Utah?"

"I do. A good man, enjoyed working with him. Although the circumstances were a little grim."

Kruger's thoughts flashed back to the murder of eight young homeless women in Provo. Byron Hall was the Chief of Police who had called in the Bureau for help. It was Kruger's first encounter with FBI Agent Franklin Dollar. When the seventh victim was found, Dollar arrested a homeless man and claimed the case was solved. It wasn't. Two days later, with the homeless man in custody, an eighth victim was found. Kruger, with the help of Chief Hall, identified the real killer as one of the detectives investigating the murders.

Kruger continued. "Do you know him?"

"He's a cousin on my mother's side. I see him every year at Christmas. He speaks highly of you."

This gave Kruger pause. Moody knew too much about him. The incident in Fayetteville generated a tremendous amount of media coverage and was understandable. But his involvement in Provo was not generally known. Apparently, Moody made some inquiries after Kruger made the appointment.

Kruger smiled. "How is Chief Hall?"

"Retired."

"Good for him."

They were sitting in Moody's office at a small conference table in the corner. Moody folded his hands in front of him and looked Kruger in the eyes. "What can I do for you, Agent?"

Understanding the niceties of the meeting were concluded, Kruger returned the stare. "I'm re-opening an investigation the Bureau closed twelve years ago."

Moody did not respond.

"Over the course of four years, six college-aged women disappeared. Their bodies have never been found. Four of them held scholarships on the basketball teams of their respective schools."

Moody did not move or make a comment. Kruger recognized it as something an experienced interrogator would do.

Kruger continued. "Recently, new evidence has been discovered about the circumstance of their disappearance."

"What kind of evidence?"

"At the time the women disappeared, each of the schools were installing new student information systems. All were installed by the same company."

Moody's expression did not change as he asked, "Do you know the name of this company?"

"Infinite Student. It was based out of St. Louis at the time."

"At the time?"

"IBM bought it in 2010."

"I see. What does this have to do with Haylex Holdings?" There was a note of irritation in Moody's voice.

"One of your subsidiaries, Haylex Solutions, was a subcontractor for Infinite Student."

Moody returned to being quiet.

"We have a partial description of the suspect in the abductions. He had black hair and was called Bobby."

Moody's expression hardened. "So, because Haylex Solutions was a subcontractor and our CEO is named Robert Burns, you believe he's the kidnapper? Am I following you correctly, Agent Kruger?"

"No." The conversation suddenly went from a friendly chat to confrontational. Kruger smiled to deflate Moody's attitude. "We are trying to cross-reference personnel who worked for Haylex Solutions to see if anybody was at all four schools during the installation of the software. That's all we are doing at this time."

Moody glared at Kruger and took a deep breath. "Legal would require a subpoena to release personnel information."

Reaching inside his suitcoat, he extracted an envelope. "I concur. This will protect the liability of your company. It is specific for only the names of persons who were at the four schools during the dates of the install. I'm in town until tomorrow."

Reaching for the envelope, Moody opened and reviewed the document.

"I will give this to our legal department, after which we can have the records available by late this afternoon. Will that be sufficient, Agent?"

Kruger nodded.

After Kruger left, Moody returned to his desk and called the company's legal department. The lists would be ready in an hour, at which time, a visit with Robert Burns Sr. would be required.

***

Sitting in front of Robert Burns Sr.'s desk, Moody leaned forward and handed the list he received from HR to the CEO of the company.

Burns read the list several times, laid it on his desk and glared at his head of security. "There is no way you are giving this information to the FBI."

"The subpoena was lawfully prepared and submitted."

"I don't care."

"If we refuse to give the information to this agent, there would be consequences."

"What kind of consequences?"

"Lots of FBI agents, accountants and lawyers descending on your company. Bad media coverage, and the declaration of your son as a person of interest in the abductions."

Burns stared at the man sitting in front of him and then back at the list. "What do you suggest?"

"Give him the list, with one name missing."

"Is there a way they can check if it's accurate?"

"I don't see how."

Handing the list back to Moody, Robert Burns nodded. "Give it back to HR. I will call and tell them how to amend the document. Then you can give it to this FBI agent."

Standing, Moody nodded and left the office.

***

At a quarter after four, Sean Kruger was handed the newly modified list of names. It was stamped by a notary public within the HR department and declared official. Kruger scanned the list and looked back at Moody.

"I appreciate your cooperation, Joel."

Moody nodded. "Glad we could help."

Kruger placed the folded document into his inside suitcoat breast pocket, stood, and extended his hand with a business card.

As Moody accepted the card, Kruger smiled. "If you think of anything or have any questions, call the cell phone number on the bottom."

Moody returned the smile and shook Kruger's extended hand.

Back in his rental car in the parking lot of Haylex Holdings, Inc., Kruger retrieved the list from his suitcoat pocket and reviewed it again. Obtaining the names had been too easy. He looked up and stared at the six-story building holding the corporate offices of Haylex Holdings. Something was amiss, and he needed to know what the something was.

Before starting the car, he retrieved his cell phone and sent a two-word text message. His phone rang ten seconds later.

"What did you find out?" JR's voice had a hint of excitement in it.

"I think I was given an incomplete list of names."

"How can you tell?"

"Gut feeling. Getting the list was way too easy."

"Not necessarily an admission of guilt, Sean."

"I know, but I need you to perform a little of your magic on Haylex Holdings."

"Oh, like what?"

"Do I have to spell it out?"

"No. When will you be back?"

"Flight leaves at six in the morning. With the time difference and my layover in Dallas, a little before six in the evening your time."

"I'll have it when you get back."

***

After returning home and helping Stephanie feed and get the kids to bed, Kruger walked across the street a little after eight in the evening. Mia answered the door, gave him a brief hug, and told him where JR was located.

Kruger stood behind JR as he summarized his findings and pointed to the screen of a laptop.

"You were correct in your assessment. There were two lists. The one they gave you and this one." He pointed to a Word document on his screen. "Time stamp is 1:13 p.m. And the time stamp on the document you were given is 2:42. Same list, except one name is missing on the second one."

"I don't like people lying to me, JR. It's a felony."

"I know."

"So Robert Burns was at the school."

"No, not the CEO," JR shook his head. "There's another Robert Burns associated with the company. A son."

Silence was Kruger's response.

"His age in 2002 would be correct for the description you were given. He's forty-six now, looks like his father. Same hair color, tall, slender, and guess what?"

"What?"

"He was just elected to the United States Senate in a special election."

"Shit."

"Yeah, I would agree."

"Can you place the son at all four colleges at the time of the disappearances?"

"Only through this document."

"I'll need more than that."

"I'm aware of that. My next project is to dig into the Haylex Solutions computer. It's separate from the main corporate computer."

"You're hesitating."

JR nodded.

"Why?"

"These guys know what they're doing. I'm going to need to understand their computer security before I start poking around."

"You've hacked the NSA computer more times than we can count. How can this be more difficult?"

He shrugged.

Kruger stared at his friend. "How long?"

"Don't know, day or two."

"Keep me posted."

The next morning Kruger retired to his office and closed the door. He found the stack of business cards he kept bound together with a heavy rubber band. Once the band was off, he thumbed through the stack until he came to the one he needed. He dialed the number and waited for an answer.

***

New York Times reporter Tracy Adkins glanced at her cell phone. The caller ID displayed the name of an individual she had not heard from in several years. Intrigued, she answered on the fourth ring.

"Sean Kruger. Have you been avoiding me?"

"Hello, Tracy. How are you?'

"Curious."

Kruger chuckled.

She continued. "Rumors on the street say you got married and retired."

"You're a reporter, Tracy, you can't rely on rumors. But, yes to the first, no to the second." Once again, he did not feel the need to explain his FBI status.

"Good, you've always been my favorite source within the FBI. What can I do for you?"

Tracy Adkins was an experienced journalist, currently assigned to national politics for the Times. Unmarried, in her mid-thirties with long dark blond hair, Tracy fostered a studious professorial look. She was an attractive woman with dark blue eyes, but in her line of work, she didn't need the person she was interviewing concentrating on her looks. So when working, she kept her hair in a bun and wore unflattering black glasses. Her wardrobe was always conservative, alternating from grays, browns, or blacks, never anything too colorful. She found it kept her interviewees calmer. Plus it contributed to the illusion she perpetuated. The illusion whoever she was interviewing could trust her.

She waited for his answer.

"I need some background."

Laughing was her only response.

"What can you tell me about the new senator from Washington State?"

Kruger frowned when he didn't hear a quick response. "Tracy?"

"Trying to determine why you want to know."

"As you said, curious."

"That's why I like you so well, Kruger. You're as full of shit as I am."

"Ha, ha. What do you know?"

"Is there a story in this?"

"Maybe. But, for now, it's on the QT."

"Will I get the exclusive?"

"If something pans out, yes."

She chuckled. "It just so happens when Robert Burns Sr. suddenly resigned from the Senate in 2012, I did a deep dive for the paper. How much time ya got?"

"As long as you need."

CHAPTER 12

Springfield, MO

"Robert Burns Junior was born with a silver spoon in his mouth, if you don't mind the cliché."

"Kind of what I suspected."

Tracy Adkins chuckled. "You don't know the half of it."

"Enlighten me."

"His father, Robert Burns Sr., is the fifth richest man in Seattle. On the Forbes list of richest men in the world, he's number thirty-nine."

Kruger whistled.

"Yeah, serious money."

"How?"

"Tech and good old fashioned real estate. Starting in 1947, after returning to Seattle from the Second World War, his father bought land for pennies on the dollar, land considered useless. Those properties were all over the state and now some of the most productive vineyards in the world."

"Huh."

"That was just the beginning. He worked for Microsoft for a few years during the early eighties and left after a disagreement with Bill Gates. They are now buddy, buddies."

"Huh."

"Is that all you can say, Kruger?"

"At the moment, yeah."

She chuckled again. "Starting in the mid-90s, Senior started buying up small tech start-up companies and consolidated them into a company called Haylex Solutions."

"Heard of it."

"Good. This was the company he handed over to his son, Bobby Burns."

"He was known as Bobby?"

"In some circles."

"Explain."

She sighed. "Junior was a bit wild. In fact, wild might be too tame. He was crazy. So, Daddy insisted he go by Bobby."

"Why use the word crazy?"

"Do you need details?"

"Yes."

"I'll have to open my computer and refer to my notes."

"Not a problem. I'll wait. So why do you have all these details at the tip of your fingers, Tracy? He was just elected."

"Senior served two terms as a senator. He was a right-wing conservative from a liberal state. I've been curious about Junior. If he's anything like his father, how did he get elected?"

"Money?"

"Exactly. Okay, I'm looking at my notes. What kind of details do you need?"

"Indulge me."

She laughed. "It will cost you."

"Put it on my bill, Tracy."

"Junior was judged to be a genius. His IQ was measured at 151 while still in high school. He graduated early and started Stanford at the age of seventeen. Without Daddy keeping a thumb on him, he got in trouble quickly."

"How so?"

"He was accused of raping a co-ed after a freshman mixer."

"Accused?"

"Charges were dropped after Daddy poured a lot of money into the school and the accuser. Since he was under eighteen, the whole incident was forgotten, and his record expunged. His accuser transferred to another school."

"How did you find out?"

"I don't reveal sources, you know that."

"Sorry, go on."

"Senior hired a security team to keep an eye on him during the rest of his college career. He graduated with honors in three years."

"What was his degree in?"

"Computer science."

"Huh."

"There you go again."

Kruger chuckled.

"After college, Senior decided to keep Junior close to home. He went to work for Haylex Solutions in their research and development department. I've been told his designs revolutionized several of their products, increased market share, and helped the stock price soar."

"Bet Daddy was proud."

"Even more so, because Haylex Solution's stock didn't get killed when the dot.com bubble burst. It remained a solid performer."

"So if he was making all this money, why did Burns run for Congress?"

"Ego. At least that's what I was told. As you can imagine, he has a healthy one."

"Not a crime."

"No, but it can get you in trouble at times."

Kruger hesitated, thinking hard about his next question. "If Senior was busy running for the Senate, what was Junior doing?"

"I'm not sure. Burns made the announcement he would run for the Senate seat in December of 1999. He won the election the following November."

The timing concerned Kruger.

Tracy continued with her narrative. "In 2003, Senior was halfway through his first term and brought Junior to Washington, D.C. to be on his staff. I'm told Junior was more narcissistic than Senior. Half of the staff quit in protest."

"Why 2003, Tracy?"

"I spoke to several of the staff members who left. The senator never explained his reasons, he just did things. I was told Senior was not an easy man to work for. Demanding of his staff's time and energy. Not unusual in Washington, but he broke the norm."

"How long did Junior work there?"

"Until the end of Senior's second term."

"So, why did he not run again?"

"Senior used the old cliché about spending more time with his family. I heard that and wanted to gag. He was widower, his kid was working for him, and he was chairman of several key committees. I suspect he didn't run because he didn't want the public to know about a breach of Senate ethics rules."

"What breach? This is the first I've heard of it."

"I'm not surprised. He struck a deal with Senate leadership. Don't run again, and this little incident will be buried."

"Do you know what he did?"

"Not with any confidence. Rumors, innuendos, and hearsay, were all I could dig up. Nothing concrete."

"What were the rumors?"

"A Senate intern left Washington without giving notification. She claimed the good senator was making unwanted advances. However, she retracted her statement and changed her major in college from government to business."

"Money?"

"I would say so. She's under a non-disclosure agreement and won't discuss the incident."

"It wasn't the son was it?"

"That, my old friend, is a good question. She won't say."

"Do you still have her contact information?"

The reporter paused and was silent for several moments. "Why?"

"It's important, Tracy."

"What if I do?"

"I need to talk to her."

"Again, why?"

Kruger took a deep breath. "If the son is the one involved, it will lend evidence to his being implicated in another more heinous crime."

"You've piqued my interest again, Agent Kruger. What are you working on?"

"Tracy, I can't tell you right now. We have a theory, and that's all it is. A theory."

"I love theories. They generally evolve into great stories."

Kruger sighed. "Give me her contact information. If she talks to me, and if we connect the dots, I'll fill you in."

"Lots of if's in that sentence, mister."

"It's the only thing I can tell you right now, Tracy. Sorry."

"You've always been upfront with me, Kruger. Okay, got something to write with?"

***

"This is the office of Lucile Wilkins, Attorney at Law, may I help you?"

The voice dripped with the accent of Memphis, Tennessee. Kruger smiled. Memphis was only three hundred miles from where he lived, yet seemed like a different country.

"Yes, my name is Sean Kruger. I'm an agent with the FBI. I need to speak to Ms. Wilkins about a case I am investigating."

"What case is that, Agent?"

"I'm sorry, I can only discuss the matter with the counselor."

There was hesitation on the other end, then Kruger heard, "One moment, please."

A long silence followed as he waited.

"This is Lucile Wilkins. What's this about, Agent?"

"Ms. Wilkins, I'm investigating a case that may involve one of your clients. She is not a suspect, but may have been one of the victims."

Wilkins did not immediately respond. Finally, he heard, "I have many clients, Agent, who might that be?

"Heather Grant."

Again the attorney was quiet.

"Ms. Wilkins, there are broader considerations with this case involving a number of missing women. I need to schedule a meeting with you and your client to discuss the matter."

"I will need more details, Agent, before I subject my client to any harassment by the FBI."

"I assure you, I do not wish to harass your client. The case I am investigating is a cold case and involves the disappearance of six young women twelve years ago. None of these women have ever been found, nor have we been able to identify a suspect, until now. Your client may be able to assist our investigation."

"Do you have a subpoena?"

"I was hoping to do this without one."

"Very well. I will have to contact my client. If she agrees to meet with you, it will be at our office. Date and time will be at her discretion. My assistant will call you back with her decision."

"Thank you, Ms. Wilkins, I appreciate any cooperation you can provide."

He sat the cell phone down on his desk after the call. He turned his home office chair to stare out the window behind him. The room was isolated on the west end of their house away from the living area where Kristin and Mikey played. A mature white oak tree dominated the front yard and provided shade for his window during the heat of summer. His desk chair faced away from the window, preventing distractions of the busy neighborhood from gaining his attention.

Picking the cell phone up again, he scrolled through his recent call file and found the number he needed in Hannibal, MO. It was answered on the third ring.

"Hello."

"Yes, this is FBI Agent Sean Kruger. Is Sara Kelly available?"

"This is she, Agent."

"Hi, Sara. How is your uncle?"

There was a long silence which Kruger did not take as good news. Sara finally answered, her voice shaky with emotion, "Uncle Paul passed away early yesterday morning."

"I'm sorry for your loss, Sara."

"He's with his wife and Linda. He's whole again."

Kruger remembered his feelings when his mother passed away, over six years ago. There was sadness, but joy in the knowledge she and his father were together again.

"I apologize for calling at this time, but I needed to know where to return the journal."

"The journal is yours, Agent. My uncle gave it to you."

"I see. I appreciate it. There is a chance it will help lead us to Linda's abductor."

"Let's hope, Agent. Let's hope."

CHAPTER 13

Memphis, TN
Three Days Later

The meeting took place in the office of Heather Grant's attorney, Lucile Wilkins. When Kruger was escorted to the conference room where the two women waited, he found the atmosphere cold and confrontational. After a successful career as a federal prosecutor, Wilkins was in private practice. Her specialty was representing women victims of sexual assaults. Before leaving for the meeting, Kruger's research on the attorney found her to be a skilled and well-known women's rights attorney. Now in her late forties, she was confident and immune to intimidation by law enforcement officers. After introductions, Lucile Wilkins spoke first.

"Agent Kruger, my client is under a non-disclosure agreement which specifically prohibits her from speaking about the incident."

"I understand. In no way do I want her to violate her agreement." He laid Linda Kelly's journal on the conference table so that both women could see it.

The attorney responded with one word: "Good." Heather remained quiet.

Kruger looked at the younger woman. Her eyes were glued to a mug of coffee she held in her hands. Now in her mid-twenties, she was strikingly beautiful. Her long auburn hair looked natural, accented with hazel eyes. He was struck by the similarities of Heather and Linda Kelly. Smiling, he returned his attention to her attorney.

"Ms. Wilkins, I have re-opened an investigation into six missing college students."

The attorney stared at Kruger, but did not respond.

"These women disappeared from college campuses between 1999 and 2002. They have never been found. Six families do not know where their loved ones are or the certainty of their fate. Most realize their daughters and sisters are dead, but they do not have the closure of a funeral."

"How does this involve my client?" Her attitude a bit less combative.

"A good question." He opened the book and took out the picture of Linda. "Notice any similarities?"

Wilkins frowned and Heather gasped. The attorney spoke first. "They are similar in appearance, I will grant you that."

Kruger reached into his inside suitcoat pocket and withdrew an envelope. He extracted three pictures and laid them next to the picture of Linda.

"More than similar, Ms. Wilkins. All four of the missing basketball players resembled your client."

Tears were flowing down Heather's cheeks as she stared wide-eyed at the photographs.

He touched the picture to the left of Linda Kelly's. "Caroline Branch, disappeared in 2001. She played basketball for the University of Akron." Pointing to the next one, "Kelsey Sorenson, Concord University also a basketball player, vanished in 2000." He indicated the fourth picture. "This is Jayla Carter, she was abducted in 1999 while walking to basketball practice at the University of Florida."

The attorney and her client did not speak, they just stared

at the pictures.

Kruger folded his hands on the table and spoke softly. "Heather, did you play basketball in college?"

Heather Grant shook her head as she stared wide eyed at the pictures. "Volleyball."

He nodded and let the answer soak into the attorney. After a few moments, he opened the journal, "I would like to read a passage from the journal of one of these women. Her name was Linda Kelly." Kruger tapped the picture of Linda. "She was a star player at Truman State University in Kirksville, MO. As the top scorer on the team, she had her sights set on playing for the WNBA after graduation."

He paused, but neither Wilkins nor Heather Grant spoke to stop him.

Reaching into his suitcoat pocket, he pulled out half-readers and read the passage.

"I noticed him at practice yesterday, sitting by himself in the bleachers. At first I thought it odd, but today he was back. A fan, was my first guess. After practice I saw him outside the gym waiting for us. Suzie poked me in the ribs and told me he was cute. I agreed with her. His black hair, expensive suit gave him a dashing appearance. He's also charming and polite. A bit old, maybe twenty-nine, but I'm not looking for a long term relationship. I think he's handsome."

Kruger looked up and took off the glasses.

"The next three pages of the journal were cut out. Seventy two hours after Linda Kelly wrote those words, she and two of her friends disappeared, along with the man with black hair. They have never been found."

Still no response from either woman.

He glanced at Heather Grant. She was wide-eyed and studying her coffee mug as she turned it clockwise and then counter-clockwise.

"I interviewed Linda Kelly's father after the incident," Kruger continued. "He was devastated, of course. His wife, Linda's mother, had recently passed away, and now his daughter was gone. He couldn't sell the house, afraid Linda would return home and not be able to find him. So he stayed in a place where everything reminded him of his lost loved ones. It drove him to dementia. He passed away the other day, alone, not knowing what happened to his daughter."

He saw moisture well up in Heather's eyes again.

"From interviews conducted at each of the college campuses, the Bureau has determined the same individual is responsible for the disappearance of all six women. Unfortunately, we do not have a complete description of the suspect. Only that his name was Bobby, and he had black hair. We have circumstantial evidence pointing to an individual who, we believe, created the events leading to Ms. Grant's sudden departure from her position as a U.S. Senate intern. This evidence suggests it was the same individual who abducted these women."

Heather Grant stopped studying her coffee mug. She stared at Kruger, her eyes wide as a tear rolled down her cheek.

Wilkins placed her hand on April's arm. "Agent, you said' circumstantial.' No solid evidence."

"Correct."

"I'm sorry, this is not a compelling reason for her to violate her agreement."

"I'm not asking for her to tell me anything. I realize she is not allowed to speak about it, but she can nod yes or no to questions without violating the agreement."

The attorney blinked several times and leaned over to whisper in Heather's ear. The young lady nodded.

"Very well, Agent. Ask your questions."

"Was Senator Burns ever involved in this incident?"

Heather shook her head.

"Was it Robert Burns Jr.?"

She stared at Kruger, then at her lawyer, who smiled and gave her a slight nod.

Heather Grant also nodded.

"Did Robert Burns Jr. sexually assault you and threaten you if you told anyone?"

Heather took a deep breath, closed her eyes, and nodded.

"Thank you, Heather," Kruger smiled, his eyes sympathetic. "You've given us confirmation we are looking at the right individual. You may have just given six grieving families a ray of hope. This meeting will not be mentioned in my final report. I appreciate your assistance."

As Kruger stood to leave, Heather looked up at him.

"At first, I thought he was charming…"

"They always are."

Wilkins tilted her head. "They?"

Kruger nodded. "Men like Robert Burns Jr. are always charming. The problem is the charm is used to gain the confidence of their prey before they attack them."

"Are you saying the man who attacked April is a psychopath? What are your qualifications for making a statement like that, Agent?" Her tone was again confrontational.

"A PhD in clinical psychology and twenty-five years of putting men like Robert Burns Jr. in federal prison, counselor."

Her stern expression softened and she was quiet for a few moments. She gave Kruger a slight smile. "Then Heather was lucky."

He nodded.

"She's more than lucky she didn't disappear like the rest of these young ladies."

***

The drive back to Springfield gave Kruger time to plan his next steps. He pressed the button on the Mustang's stirring wheel to connect his phone for a hands-free conversation. When asked by the automated female voice who he wished to call, he responded. The call was answered on the third ring.

"Seltzer."

"Alan, it's Sean."

"How'd the interview go?"

"She confirmed it was the son, not the senator."

There was silence on the other end of the call. Finally, after several moments, he heard. "We need to move forward carefully on this, Sean."

"Believe me, I'm aware of that."

"You're investigating a newly elected member of the Senate."

"Again, I'm aware of who I'm investigating."

"Are you sure he's responsible for the six women disappearing."

"I'm sure. But do I have rock solid evidence he did it? No, I don't."

"Proceed with caution. The father still has powerful allies within Congress. We don't want this to blow up in the agency's face."

"Alan, are you more interested in the truth or the agency's image."

"Both."

Kruger didn't answer right away. Taking a deep breath, he counted to ten. "Whatever, Alan. I have no intention of causing embarrassment to the agency."

"I didn't think you did. I'm just saying, get the proof we need to charge this guy for the abductions."

"That's my plan."

"How?"

"I'm working on it."

The call ended with Kruger wondering if his decision to return to the FBI was the correct one.

CHAPTER 14

Seattle, WA

The living room of Haylex Holdings CEO's home occupied two-thirds of the first floor in the three-story structure. The lights of Seattle were clearly visible through the floor to ceiling window on the east side of the room. A fire burned brightly in the see-through fireplace separating the huge gourmet kitchen from the living room. Junior lounged in a leather sofa, his right arm stretched over the top cushion. He brought a crystal tumbler to his lips and sipped the twelve-year-old scotch. Glaring at the man standing in front of him, he sat the glass down on the side table left of the sofa.

"I'm not sure what you're referring to since I'm the one who was elected to Congress. Not you."

Robert Burns Sr. gave his son a grim smile. "True, but without my money you wouldn't have won."

"How do you know?"

"Because the polls were dismal when you first announced. It was only after directing fifty million into your campaign coffers to buy all those negative ads against your opponent that your numbers started to improve. Target specific marketing didn't hurt either."

The younger Burns scoffed. "It's illegal to give that much money to a candidate."

"Only if you do it the legal way. I chose another path."

"Still, I got elected. You didn't."

"A technicality. You'll follow my directions."

"Maybe."

"Bobby, you haven't got a clue what's in store for you. If you want to be taken advantage of, run over, ignored, and basically made a fool, then don't listen to me. The Senate is the major leagues of politics. You'll have to play by their rules, not yours."

"I don't think so."

Senior shook his head. "You may be a genius, but you lack one trait needed on the Senate floor."

"What's that?"

"The ability to make people believe you like them."

"I'm better at it then you think."

"Yes, you are excellent at times, but you lack the ability to keep up the ruse. You have a tendency to ignore individuals you find annoying. You will find ninety percent of your fellow senators annoying. Once that occurs, your effectiveness in the Senate ends. You will not get the plum committee assignments you'll need to help the fine citizens of Washington State."

"I didn't get elected to help them."

"You'd better make sure the news media never finds out. They will eat you alive, my son, and it will be the end of your political career."

"If you know so much about this, why did you quit?"

The older Burns stared at his only son as his face reddened. "Because you couldn't keep your little head in your pants. That's why."

"What are you talking about?"

"Heather Grant. She left town and went straight to an attorney. You're lucky she didn't go straight to the police. Afterwards, to keep it out of the news media, I paid off the intern and made a deal with the Senate leadership. I took the blame and kept your name out of it. Hell, even the majority leader didn't know it was you."

Blinking rapidly, the younger Burns swallowed hard and stared at his father. "Oh, hell, Father, she was after my money. All she wanted to do was trap me into getting her pregnant. It was pathetic. There is no way anyone would have believed I was responsible."

Rolling his eyes and shaking his head, the older Burns took a sip of his scotch. "What would you have done, called a press conference and tell God and everyone you were the one raped? I don't think so."

Robert Junior's face reddened. He stood suddenly and glared at his father. "How dare you make those types of accusations? It was consensual."

It was the senior Burns' time to explode. He got within inches of his son's face and screamed, "Bullshit. She had internal bleeding. You're lucky they came to me first."

"She liked it rough."

Burns glared at his son. Shaking his head, he backed away from the forty-three-year-old man he was finding increasingly difficult to understand. "Go to bed, you're drunk." He turned and walked toward the stairs.

***

Joel Moody looked up from his laptop screen after hearing a tapping on his office door. Surprised to see elder Robert Burns standing there, he stood. Burns spoke first. "Joel, do you have a few minutes?"

Startled at the appearance of the company's CEO at his office door, he motioned to a chair in front of his desk. "Yes, sir, please come in."

Burns shut the door, something Moody never did when he was in his office, feeling it made other associates nervous to have the head of security behind closed doors.

After both men were seated, Burns cleared his throat. "Joel, at one of our last meetings, I asked you to check on

Junior's past."

"Yes, sir."

"Have you made any inquiries?"

Moody felt a trap being set, but nodded anyway.

"Uh, what did you find?"

"Not much."

He saw the CEO relax, slightly.

Moody continued, "However, what I found raised some questions."

"Oh?"

"The FBI agent's inquiry concerned me."

Burns nodded.

"What was Junior doing during the years of 1999 and 2002, while you were campaigning and serving your first two years as a senator?"

The look on Robert Burns' face confirmed Moody's suspicions. His boss did not know.

"He was heading up Haylex Solutions."

"Was it part of his job description to be at installations?"

The older Burns shook his head.

"Hmmm."

"What?"

"Mr. Burns, the only installations he attended during those years were colleges."

The CEO closed his eyes.

"Let me guess, the four colleges where women disappeared."

Moody just nodded.

"I was afraid of that. Are you sure?"

"Confirmed by HR."

"How?" The elder Burns frowned.

"The first list HR prepared for the FBI agent piqued my concern. If Junior was going to a lot of installations during those years, it could be just a coincidence. But he didn't. Those are the only ones he attended."

Robert Burns Sr. stood and paced the small room. He was silent as he placed his right hand under his chin and supported the arm with his left hand. "What else does the FBI know?" he finally asked.

The statement concerned Moody. "All I gave them was the edited list."

"Good."

The room fell into silence again. Moody watched as the older man stared at the carpet as he paced. After what seemed like an hour, but was only a minute, Burns stopped pacing and faced the desk. "If the FBI requests any additional information on Junior's activities during his tenure at Haylex Solutions, please refer them to the company's attorneys."

"Yes, sir."

"I'm very serious about this, Joel. No one in this organization is to speak with the FBI in the future. All inquiries are to be directed to our legal department. No exceptions."

"I understand, sir."

"Good."

Without another comment, Burns turned, walked out of Moody's office, and closed the door behind him.

Joel Moody stared at the closed door, resisting the urge to immediately stand and open it. Taking a deep breath, he retrieved the business card given to him by Sean Kruger from the top drawer of his desk. He committed the number to memory and then placed the card in the shredder he kept under his desk. He would have to find an untraceable landline later after leaving the office for the evening.

***

Kruger glanced at the caller ID and the time on his vibrating cell phone. He frowned. It was past nine in the evening, and the area code was unfamiliar to him. He answered on the fifth ring.

"Kruger."

"Agent Kruger, this is Joel Moody with Haylex Holdings. I apologize for calling so late."

"Not a problem, Mr. Moody. What can I do for you?"

There was silence on the other end for an extended period. Finally, he heard, "I have been informed by our CEO that any additional inquiries about employees of Haylex Solutions or any affiliate of our corporate entity, Haylex Holdings, will need to be made through our corporate attorney's office."

"I see."

"I appreciate your understanding."

"Mr. Moody?"

"Yes."

"Why are you calling me late at night from a number unassociated with Haylex or yourself?"

"You're an intelligent individual, Agent Kruger. I am sure you can infer the reason from the message I was told to relay."

"Very well, Mr. Moody," Kruger chuckled. "Message received."

"Good. Have a nice evening, Agent."

The call ended, and Kruger smiled to himself.

CHAPTER 15

Springfield, MO

"Alan, even though our evidence is circumstantial, the call from Moody last night leads me to believe we're on the right path. Everything we know right now points to the newly elected senator from Washington State as a person of interest in the abductions."

After spending the night thinking about the call from Moody, Kruger waited until the following morning to call Alan Seltzer. Kruger continued, "My guess would be the senator-elect's father is concerned about our inquiry."

"Is he involved someway?"

"Not sure, but he's taken a lot of drastic measures to keep his son out of trouble."

"Sounds like attorneys are involved."

"Probably, but there's something else going on."

"What?"

"I think Moody is hiding something."

"Isn't he their head of security?"

"Yes."

"There you go. He's the company's spokesperson."

"Then why did the call originated from a land line not associated with Haylex? If he wasn't at the office, why not use his personal cell phone?"

"Maybe neither were available."

"In this day and age, Alan? You can't get away from phones."

"Are you reading too much into how the call was made?"

"Maybe. The call originated from a pay phone. Why?"

"Do those still exist?"

"A few still do."

"How do you know about the phone?"

"JR placed an app on my phone a year ago. I know where every call I receive comes from, even if it's spam."

"Got it."

Kruger was silent for a few moments.

"Alan, the only explanation for using a pay phone is he didn't want the company to know he called me."

"Makes sense."

"I want to put Robert Burns Jr. under surveillance."

"Not sure the Seattle Field Office should be involved at this stage, Sean."

"I agree. At this time the local agents don't need to know what we suspect. We need more evidence before we bring them in."

"You can't do it by yourself. Who do you have in mind, or should I ask?"

"I'd like Sandy Knoll involved."

"Call him. I'll send authorization for him to report to you until you have the evidence you need or you determine nothing's there."

"Thanks, Alan."

***

"Great to hear from you, Agent, it's been awhile."

Retired Army Major and now an FBI Rapid Response Team leader, Benedict "Sandy" Knoll held the cell phone tight to his right ear and faced away from the firing range.

"Yes, Sandy, it has." Kruger heard gunfire in the

background on Knoll's end. "Is that weapons fire in the background?"

"Qualification day for several team members."

Knoll was a large man now in his late forties. As a retired Special Forces Major, he still had the physique of a man in his twenties. Bulging bicep muscles stretched the material of his tan t-shirt, which was tucked into desert BDU pants. The pant legs, in turn, were tucked into dessert combat boots laced tight. The man's dark blond hair was worn short, but not as short as his military days. With a face weathered and lined from too many years in the Middle East and an unlit cigar clenched in his teeth, he resembled a Hollywood cliché. He was not.

Kruger spoke a little louder, "Have you heard from Deputy Director Alan Seltzer?"

"Yes, sir. Looking forward to working with you again."

"I have a favor to ask."

"Name it."

"Can you include Jimmy Gibbs?"

"He's already packed and sitting on his duffle bag."

"Thanks, Sandy. See you tomorrow."

When the call ended, Kruger sat back in his office chair and swiveled to look out the window behind his desk. Placing an elbow on the chair's arm rest, he rested his chin on his hand, an index finger covering his mouth. His eyes tracked a squirrel outside munching on an acorn from the large oak tree in the front yard. His thoughts were not about the squirrel, but about how to bring a predator, who had eluded identification for almost two decades, to justice. He needed one more person on his team before he started executing his plan.

***

"Remember when you said you wouldn't work with the FBI unless I was involved two years ago?"

JR Diminski smiled and nodded.

"I'm asking you to team up with me again."

Diminski continued to smile, but remained quiet. They were sitting in a conference room on the second floor of his office building in the southwest part of the city. The walls were glass, which kept the room from feeling claustrophobic, but allowed sound proofing by the use of double paned windows.

"I'm putting the old team together."

Nodding again, JR looked at Kruger. "What about Joseph?"

"He and Mary are in New Zealand."

"Oh." JR fell into silence.

"Are you interested?"

Another nod.

"You'll be designated an independent contractor."

"I will be personally?" JR's body tensed and his forehead crunched together.

Kruger shook his head. "No, your company."

JR visibly relaxed. "Okay, good."

"So, are you interested?"

"Do I have to answer? Of, course I am. I've missed the action."

Kruger smiled. "Thought you would, but I needed to ask."

"So, what's the plan?"

Glancing at his watch, Kruger looked back at JR. "Sandy and his team landed twenty minutes ago. When they get here, I'll bring everyone up to speed."

***

An hour later, Sandy and Jimmie Gibbs entered the conference room. Kruger was pleasantly surprised by the appearance of an additional individual. FBI Agent Ryan Clark smiled as they shook hands.

"When did you join Sandy's group, Ryan?" Kruger asked.

"About a month ago."

At one time, Clark was a detective with the Arlington,

Virginia, Police Department. He and Kruger had worked together several times over the past twenty-five years, most notably investigating the Beltway Sniper in October 2002 and a case four years ago when they chased a group of assassins across the United States. Clark was wounded while protecting then-Congressman Roy Griffin. After his recovery, Kruger lobbied the director to make him an agent. Since then, Clark had made a name for himself within the agency.

"Outstanding." He turned to the big man and shook his hand. "Good decision adding him to the team, Sandy."

"I thought so."

Kruger found Jimmie Gibbs and offered his hand. As they shook, he said, "Glad you could join our little soiree."

Where Knoll was built like a bodybuilder, Gibbs' physique was lean like a swimmer, a sport he excelled at. He currently held several Seal Team records for endurance and distance.

After retiring from Seal Team Six, he allowed his black hair to grow long. He normally wore it in a ponytail extending past his shoulder blades. Being from Southern California, his usual dress was surfer casual: cargo shorts, linen shirt and sandals. Blue eyes rounded out his handsome features and contributed to the tales of his womanizing, a myth he claimed was more urban-legend than reality. Knoll prized Jimmie's pose and level-headedness during missions, especially when events turned sour for the team.

Gibbs grinned, "Wouldn't have missed it, Sean. Glad to hear you're back."

Smiling, Kruger motioned for the group to find seats in JR's conference room. He noticed Clark smiling at JR and shaking his hand. The conversation was not audible from where Kruger stood. He took a seat and waited for all the parties to join him. "Thank you for coming, Sandy."

Knoll nodded.

"Since we all know each other, let's get started."

Sandy Knoll started with a question. "Give us some background and your objectives, Sean?"

"Six women were abducted during the years of 1999 and

2002. Their bodies have never been found, nor has a suspect been identified." He paused for a few seconds. "Until now."

Clark stiffened, Knoll frowned, and Gibbs smiled. JR picked up the narrative.

"Using a variety of…" he paused briefly, "methods, Sean and I have determined a person of interest in these kidnappings is a newly elected senator from the state of Washington."

Knoll's team frowned in unison.

Clark tilted his head. "How?"

JR explained their process.

Knoll nodded, remarking, "Works for me."

Everyone nodded in agreement. Kruger took over. "What we have right now is a lot of circumstantial evidence and a significant amount of conjecture. I received a call from the head of security for Haylex Holdings explaining how any additional requests for company records would have to go through their attorney's office."

Clark nodded. "That would seem to be a prudent step on their part."

"I agree. However, he called from a pay phone."

Gibbs frowned. "Do those even exist anymore?"

JR chuckled. "Yes, a few still do."

"What is significant about calling from a pay phone, Sean?" Knoll was leaning forward with his large arms flat on the table, fingers intertwined, and his brow furrowed.

"Glad you asked. I believe he was making sure no one at Haylex Holdings could check their phone records about him initiating the call. He's a retired cop and, I believe, an intelligent retired cop."

JR placed his elbows on the table and made steeple with his hands. "Checking phone records is simple these days. With cell phones and computer linked phone systems, getting call records is a matter of obtaining a computer readout. If you want to make sure a call doesn't appear on a printout somewhere, a pay phone is your best bet. There are computer protocols available to get around a call being recorded into a database, but you have to know what you're doing. As an ex-cop, even though he works for a high-tech company, my guess would be he doesn't have that skill set."

Nodding, Knoll sat back in his chair. "Why call you in the first place?"

"I believe he was sending a message. In a roundabout way, he even said so."

Gibbs twisted the Styrofoam cup of coffee in his hands clockwise. "He was letting you know you're closer than you think, wasn't he."

"Yes, I believe he was."

"Why do you need us, Sean?" Clark gestured to Knoll and Gibbs.

"We are going to place Robert Burns Jr. under surveillance."

Everyone in the room was quiet.

Knoll grinned. "You could have had the local Seattle field office do that, Sean."

"The Deputy Director doesn't want them involved at the moment, and neither do I. If we find our information about Junior is incorrect, we simply leave and no one will know the senator-elect was suspected. I don't believe that will be the outcome. However, it's better to be careful, just in case."

Ryan Clark asked, "What about this Moody character? Where does he fit in?"

"Since I've had previous contact with him, I'm going to be following him. My plan is to contact him away from his work and home. I'm hoping he will cooperate."

Everyone nodded.

"One more concern." All eyes were on Kruger. "There's a chance the father knows the truth about his son. I believe he's been protecting Junior for years and will prove to be a well-financed foe. In addition, he's spent a lot of money getting Junior elected. It could get dicey when he discovers our investigation is closing in."

Gibbs chuckled. "We can be dicey, too, Sean."

"That, my dear Jimmie, is exactly why I want you guys

working with me."

Chapter 16

The bedroom was dark. The only sound in the room was his wife's gentle breathing next to him. Normally, during sleepless nights, all Joel Moody had to do was listen to her, and he would fall asleep. Not tonight.

With his hands behind his head, he stared at the barely visible ceiling illuminated by a nightlight in their master bathroom. Taking the job with Haylex Holdings was enhancing his financial situation after spending twenty years with the Seattle Police Department. But the conflict he now felt renewed his original doubt about working for the older Robert Burns. He knew the younger Robert Burns was dangerous. But when FBI Agent Kruger started asking questions about the younger Burns' whereabouts from 1999 to 2002, his worst fears were confirmed.

Seventeen years had passed with no hint anyone suspected the son. Now the FBI was asking questions. Moody knew the truth. He also knew secrets about the disappearances no one else knew, including the younger Burns. Those secrets needed to remain hidden. Hidden from both the father and the son. More importantly, hidden from the FBI.

Somewhere around three in the morning, an idea started to form. Ten minutes later, Moody fell into a restless sleep.

***

Kruger watched as Joel Moody backed his car out of the modest Sammamish, Washington, home driveway. The house was tucked away in an area dominated by mature native trees. The neighborhood was quiet, residential, and family friendly, a typical home for a cop. Moody's five-year-old Ford Fusion also told Kruger the head of security for Haylex Holdings was not exploiting his new position with the corporation. A good sign.

This was his second day of following the retired detective, his patterns not yet discernable. If he followed the same route as the previous day, he would stop at a local Starbucks and go inside, forsaking the long line at the drive-thru. If the pattern continued, it was the perfect spot to get the man alone.

The following day, Kruger sat inside the Starbucks when Moody walked in. Their eyes locked, and Moody gave Kruger a half grin. When he received his coffee from the barista, he approached Kruger's table, hesitated briefly, and sat down.

"This isn't a coincident, is it, Agent?"

"No, I wanted to talk to you away from your home and office."

Moody glanced at his watch. "I've got twelve minutes. What's on your mind?"

"Your call last week raised a few questions the FBI needs answered."

Silence was his response.

"Was Robert Burns Jr. at the colleges when the women disappeared?"

Moody did not look at Kruger, but nodded.

"All of them?"

Another nod.

"Can you get me proof?"

"No, not without raising suspicion. But I can point you in the direction you need to go."

Kruger tilted his head. "Why are you helping us, Detective?"

Moody leaned forward over the small bistro table and spoke quietly. "Because Robert Burns Jr. is a dangerous man, Agent. I'm a law enforcement officer first, and he needs to be put away. I'm not in a position to do it, nor do I have the authority anymore to do it myself. Robert Burns Sr. is a powerful man in this town. He's a rich ex-senator and extremely philanthropic toward the arts, which means he's well liked. Within the Seattle power structure, he has a stellar reputation as a man above reproach. In addition to all of this, he's over protective of Junior." He stood, but continued to study Kruger. "My wife is at a ladies church function tonight. I assume by your presence you know where I live. Be at my house at six this evening. Come alone."

After taking a sip of his coffee, Moody turned and walked out of the coffee shop.

***

Jimmie Gibbs sat in a Ford Transit van with the decal of a local cable TV company on the side. He watched as the wife of Joel Moody backed out of her driveway. Her vehicle was a four-year-old Toyota Rav-4. After it drove off, he waited until he heard Clark tell him the woman was merging onto West Interstate 90.

After checking with Kruger, he gathered his tool bag, exited the van, and walked nonchalantly to the back of the Moody home. The back deck was hidden from neighbors by tall cedars and dense pine trees. Extracting a small tool from a leather pouch in his back jean pocket, he was through the door in thirty seconds.

The door opened into the kitchen area, and he stood quietly listening for any sign someone was at home. All he heard was the ice maker filling. When it finished, he stood still for another two minutes. The only sound he could hear was a ticking clock somewhere in the kitchen. Placing the tool bag on the kitchen floor, he extracted a Ziploc bag containing opaque discs with a thin colorless filament attached to each.

He strategically placed one disc in each room of the house, making sure the tiny microphones were positioned to pick up any speech uttered within the rooms. One was placed behind each nightstand in the couple's bedroom.

Gibbs completed his task in less than five minutes and did a quick sound check on each. With this task completed, he picked up his tool bag, relocked the door, and walked out onto the wooden deck. The back lot was relatively flat, with the deck a few inches off the ground. He reached into his tool bag and withdrew a small box the size of a small paperback book. The color of the box blended well with the weathered wood. Kneeling, Jimmie peeled the covers off of four patches on one side of the box and then reached under the deck to attach the object to a support post. With the object now hidden, he stood and walked back to the Ford van.

As he drove out of the neighborhood, he spoke for the first time since entering the house. "Package delivered."

Knoll responded. "Roger."

Turning to Kruger, who was sitting across the table at a local diner three miles from the house, Knoll said, "Okay, now we can listen to your meeting with Moody.'

Kruger nodded and sipped the coffee in the mug he held. "I'm not sure I trust him yet. Let's make sure everyone is close at hand tonight."

"Already planned. Gibbs will be in the trees behind the house. Range of the transmitter is three miles, so he will have no issues listening to your conversation. Clark and I will be parked a few houses down the block. We can be inside in a matter of seconds."

"Good." He sipped his coffee again. "Every action he's taken indicates he wants to help. Why am I not convinced yet, Sandy?"

"It's healthy to be suspicious, Sean. I've survived a lot of shit being suspicious."

Smiling, Kruger nodded.

***

"Would you like coffee, Agent Kruger?"

"No, thanks."

Kruger sat at the breakfast table watching Moody pour himself a cup. Prior to meeting with the ex-detective, Jimmie Gibbs explained to Kruger where the microphones were located and the best chair to occupy. He now sat in a chair across from where Moody would sit. A small glass bistro table located in the breakfast nook separated them. The bug was located under the chair on his right.

As soon as Moody sat down, Kruger asked. "Why did you call me the other night?"

The retired detective sipped his coffee. "Courtesy."

Sitting back in his chair, Kruger crossed his arms over his chest. "Detective, I'm not going to sit here all night and listen to you dance around the subject. Tell me now, or I'm out of here."

"You're on the right track, Agent."

Kruger did not respond, keeping his gaze on the man across the table.

"The list you were given was edited. There was a name removed from the original."

Choosing not to tell Moody he already knew, he uncrossed his arms and leaned forward, placing his arms on the table.

"Uh… that's withholding evidence, Joel."

"I know."

"You're an ex-cop, why would you do that?"

"Technically, I didn't. Robert Burns Sr. ordered the list changed."

"Still, a prosecutor could charge you as an accessory."

Moody nodded. "I did a little more research on you today, Agent. You have a doctorate in psychology and spent twenty-five years tracking down serial killers."

"You're changing the subject."

"Not really. There are a lot of reasons Mr. Burns had the list altered."

Kruger did not respond.

"Over the course of your career with the FBI, I am sure you've dealt with others like Robert Burns Jr."

"What type would that be?"

"An individual who lacks remorse or empathy for what they do to others. Someone who won't take responsibility for their own actions and lie about it."

"Yes, I've dealt with a few."

Sipping his coffee again, Moody put the cup down and stared at Kruger. "When I was an SPD Detective, Agent, I worked vice for a while, then a murder desk for several years. I've had to deal with all types of predators. Most weren't too bright, which made catching them easy. A few were smart, but we eventually caught them." He paused for a moment and stared past Kruger into the dark back yard. "Robert Burns Jr. is a brilliant man. Some of his inventions have made millions for Haylex Holdings. He is also deceitful and impulsive."

"I know about the assault on the Senate intern. I also know it wasn't the father."

"No, it wasn't," Moody shook his head. "The only reason that poor girl is still alive is because I stopped Junior."

Kruger barely kept his surprise from showing. "Oh."

"Yeah, it was my first year as head of security for Senior. The incident occurred just before he would start his campaign for re-election. One of several reasons I was hired. One night before leaving for the evening, I was checking to make sure all the doors in his Senate office were locked. I heard a noise and investigated."

The retired cop closed his eyes. "I'm not going to go into detail, but the girl was tied up, and Junior was on the verge of hurting her. I stopped him and called Senior. Let's put it this way, lots of money exchanged hands and the father took the blame for the son. It ended his Senate career. Junior, to this day, denies the incident even happened. He claims I made it up."

"What does the father say?"

"He never talks about it. I'm not proud of it, Agent, but financially, I was rewarded quite handsomely for keeping my mouth shut about the incident."

Kruger frowned. "How much money did the elder Burns spend to get his son elected?"

Moody shook his head. "I don't know the exact amount, but it's in the millions. Most of it hidden."

"Why is the father so intent on his son being a senator?"

"I don't know, I'm not privy to the palace intrigue. I'm just hired help."

"I need hard evidence Junior was at those colleges at the time of the disappearance. If I can get it, I can issue an arrest warrant for him."

"I would bet the personnel records have been altered by now to make sure Junior's name is gone.

"Can you get me access to the computer system?"

Moody shook his head. "Our IT team is exceptional. They'd spot a breach in a second."

Kruger reached into his pocket and pulled out a flash drive. "Insert this into any computer on the network for ten seconds."

Staring at the object, Moody didn't reach for it at first. "What's on it?"

"Better you don't know. Just make sure it's not a computer you normally have access to."

Moody reached for the drive. "Ten seconds, that's all?"

Kruger nodded.

Chapter 17

Seattle, WA

Arriving early, Joel Moody followed his normal routine of walking the six floors of the Haylex building looking for anything out of the ordinary. But this particular time, he also noted one additional piece of information: whether an office was in current use or vacant. The occupied offices outnumbered the vacant ones by nine to one.

His next stop was personnel, not part of his regular routine, but he made up an excuse for the visit. Gail Johnson was already there handling phone calls from the eastern part of the widespread Haylex empire. When he walked in, she smiled.

"Morning, Joel."

"Hi, Gail. Had your coffee yet?"

The middle-aged woman shook her head. "Phone started ringing the second I got here."

"How do you take it? I'll get you some."

"You're a dear. Just bring one of those pink envelopes, I'll take it from there."

Five minutes later, Joel sat on the edge of an adjacent desk sipping coffee and making small talk to Gail in between phone calls. When the current call ended, she looked up at him and asked, "You want the list of current home office personnel on vacation?"

Moody nodded.

"So, what's up?"

"Checking out a hunch."

"Oh, what kind of hunch?"

Looking over both shoulders to feign he was about to reveal state secrets, he spoke in a voice barely above a whisper.

"Unauthorized long distance phone calls are being made from company phones. I think they're originating from phones on the desk of vacationing employees."

This was a lie, but he doubted Gail would bother to check.

"Oh, my." Her phone rang, and she started another conversation. After a minute, she said, "Please hold for a second." After suspending the call, she returned her attention to Moody. "Give me an hour, and I will have a list for you."

"Thanks, Gail. I'll be back. Don't say anything to anyone, I need to keep this quiet."

"No problem, Joel."

As he returned to his office, the din of a normal morning at Haylex Holdings grew as more employees arrived to start their day.

***

At ten minutes after twelve, Pacific Time, Joel Moody unlocked the door of an office on the fourth floor. Its current occupant, a senior vice president of sales for one of Haylex Holdings' East Coast companies, was on a cruise with her husband. Closing the door, he used a flashlight app on his cell phone to locate the small workstation computer box under the woman's desk. Finding an empty USB slot, he inserted the flash drive given to him by Kruger. He counted to ten, extracted the drive, placed it back in his pocket, and walked out of the office. He was in the office less than thirty seconds. No one saw him enter or leave.

***

"The database with Junior's name is gone. There are no such files within their HR department or any of their archived technical data, Sean."

"You sure?"

"I've checked in all of the HR files for those years, and his name has been redacted from all of them. It's been done expertly. There's no digit evidence it was ever there." JR's voice sounded a bit excited.

"You don't have to be happy about it." Kruger's frustration was reflected in his response.

"That's not it. We're dealing with an IT department with exceptional computer skills. I'll have to be extremely cautious going forward."

"But you got in."

"Yes, the pathway was open, but as soon as I discovered the missing information, I shut it down."

"Why?"

JR took a deep breath. Even though the distance between the two men was over two thousand miles, Kruger could see in his mind's eye his long-time friend's reaction.

"During the short time I was able to stay in their system, I saw evidence of one of the most sophisticated security firewalls I've ever encountered."

"Better than yours?"

"In some ways, yes."

Kruger was surprised by the admission, but let JR continue without interrupting.

"The systems I install for my clients are some of the most secure in the world. Just a fact, not a boast."

"I've heard that."

"This is a private computer network; there are protocols on it I've never seen. To be honest with you, I'm surprised I was able to hack into it as easily as I did the first time. I stumbled upon a flaw, which has since been patched."

"Can you get back in?"

"Maybe, if they didn't detect my intrusion."

Kruger was silent for a while. Finally, he continued, "We're at a standstill here."

"How so?"

"Our suspect is in Washington, D.C., preparing to be the next senator. Sandy and his team are catching a flight this afternoon for D.C., and I'm coming home."

"You're not going to be in the middle of it?"

Silence was his answer. "Okay, what do you need me to do?"

"Not sure at this point. I need better background on both Senior and Junior. Once I have that, I'll understand what we're up against."

"Do you want me to do it?"

"Yes, plus I'm going to get a Bureau analyst to do a work-up. We can compare what they find to what you find. My guess is there will be a difference."

"I'm not following you."

"Something just isn't right. It's hard to explain since I can't put my finger on it."

"Which one do you want me to start on?"

"Senior."

"Got it."

***

Barbara Whitlock had been an analyst for the FBI for as long as Kruger could remember. Having worked with her on numerous cases, he knew her results to be exceptional. She was also discreet. He found her direct number on his cell phone, a number only a select number of agents possessed, and pressed the send icon.

The call was answered on the fourth ring.

"Is this the Sean Kruger who's been ignoring me for over two years?"

"Guilty."

He heard laughter on the other end of the call, then, "I should hang up."

"Please don't."

"Have you divorced that young hussy you married yet? There are broken hearts around here waiting for it to happen."

"No, still married. Happily, I might add."

More laughter. "What can I do for you, Sean?"

"Has the Bureau preformed a work-up on the newly elected senator from Washington State?"

"If they have, I haven't seen it. Why?"

"I need one on him and his father."

"Uh-oh. Should I ask why?"

"I can't tell you right now. Besides, it would prejudice your analysis, you know that Barbara."

"Can't fault a girl for asking, can you? When do you need it?"

"Yesterday."

"Well, guess I'd better get busy, I'm late getting it to you."

They both chuckled, and Kruger ended the call. He stared at the boarding gate for his flight back to Springfield. His concerns about the two men he was investigating was increasing with every piece of information he gathered.

The announcement for his flight interrupted his thoughts.

***

The bedroom was dark, and his hands were behind his head as the prospect of getting to sleep waned. Stephanie put her arm over his chest and snuggled.

"Can't sleep?"

"Hope I didn't wake you?"

"You didn't. Something's bothering you."

He placed his arm around her and brought her closer. "It's been several years since I've had to spend so many nights in a hotel."

"Glad you're home."

"Me, too. It brought back memories I don't care for."

"Such as."

"All those nights we were apart before we got married."

"We were both miserable during those years, weren't we."

"Yes."

"So, what are we going to do about it?"

"I've got to figure out how to balance the traveling and the investigations."

"You will, give it time. Besides, remember our homecomings after being apart for a while?" She slipped her hand under his t-shirt and rubbed his chest.

Smiling, he turned his head toward her as she moved her hand toward his waist. "Yes, I do, they were almost worth the time away from each other. Are you trying to start something?"

"I'm not trying, I am starting something."

He leaned over and kissed her as his hand slid under her night shirt.

***

The next morning was Sunday. Brunch was the first meal of the day and always prepared by the man of the house. As a frustrated chef, he strived to make something tasty and different every Sunday. Most times it was excellent, occasionally it was not. Today's menu was well received by the members of the Kruger household.

While Kristin and her younger brother, Mikey, watched a movie in the adjacent room, Stephanie and Kruger cleaned the kitchen.

"You're quiet this morning." Kruger dried a sauté pan while Stephanie refilled their coffee cups.

"Do you remember Dr. Eunice Maxwell?"

"Yeah, she's the head of the Business College at the university? Isn't she the one who talked your ear off at last year's faculty Christmas get-together?"

Stephanie nodded.

"What about her?"

"She called on Friday."

"Oh."

"Yeah, she wants me to join the faculty as an instructor and start a mentor program matching senior women working toward a business degree with woman business leaders in the community."

"Sounds interesting. Did she give you any details?"

"A few. I told her I would have to discuss it with you before I committed."

Kruger frowned, "Why?"

She punched his arm playfully. "Because we make decisions together, mister. Or did you forget?"

Kruger chuckled. "I didn't forget. Do you want to do it?"

She nodded.

"Well, do it."

"What about the kids?"

"What about them? Give them a peanut butter sandwich and wish them good luck for the day."

Shaking her head, she glanced at her husband. "You're impossible."

He smiled. "Whatever you want to do is fine with me, Stef. It sounds like something you would enjoy."

"I know, it does. But I'm worried about the kids."

"The university has one of the best day-care centers in the city, they'll be fine. Besides, it'll be good for Kristin. She's ready for kindergarten, why not start her there. Besides, being around other kids will help develop both of their social skills."

"Spoken like a psychologist."

"It's the truth."

"I know. I've grown used to being with them all the time."

He smiled and drew her into a hug. "Did you ever think you would put your kids ahead of your own ambitions?"

"No." She shook her head against his chest. "I also never imaged being in love with someone as much as I am with you."

Squeezing her tighter, he kissed the top of her head. "I know. Not sure how I got so lucky meeting you."

Their embrace lasted a few more moments. While he put the sauté pan in the cabinet, she picked up the full coffee mugs and handed one to him. As Kruger watched her, a sense of contentment washed over him, a feeling he was unaccustomed to during the years before they met. Taking a sip, he followed her back into the room where their daughter and son were busy watching a movie about a frozen kingdom.

Before he could sit down next to his daughter, his cell phone vibrated. Sighing, he withdrew it from a jean pocket and glanced at the caller ID. The area code was California and the name under the number read Roy Griffin.

CHAPTER 18

Washington, D.C.

Roy Griffin's office was located on the third floor of the Hart Senate Office Building. Despite his wife's distaste for Washington, she was responsible for the office's décor and appearance, utilizing natural wood, leather, and black steel as the main features of the senator's work space. It was comfortable and inviting to visitors and his fellow senators. More than a few legislative proposals were negotiated on the two leather sofas facing each other in the center of the room.

In his late 40s, Roy stood a bit over six feet tall. He wore his blond hair slightly longer than current fashion and was male model handsome. Even by California standards, he was wealthy. Keenly aware his looks and money were the reason he now occupied a United States Senate seat, he strived to make a difference for the citizens of California. His rise to the Senate was meteoric.

Originally elected by his image-conscious Northern California district as a member of the House of Representatives, he was drafted by his party to unseat the previous second senator from California. The election was not a fair contest. After being caught taking numerous overseas trips, paid for by a huge California defense contractor, the previous senator lost in a landslide to Griffin. Now in his third year as a senator, he was Chairman of the Homeland Security and Government Affairs Committee. With that responsibility, he was privy to information most senators were not.

He stared at the cell phone laying on his desk. A number from his frequent call list was prominently displayed, ready to be called. Taking a deep breath, he let it out slowly and stood. A large floor-to-ceiling window was behind his desk, and he turned to look out at the United States Supreme Court Building. He stood staring out the window with his hands behind his back.

A light tapping on his office door brought him out of his thoughts. He turned to see his Chief of Staff, Sherry Carlson.

"Senator, I'm going to head out. Do you need me for anything else?"

"No, Sherry, thank you for coming in on a Sunday morning."

"Not a problem." She remained standing in his doorway. "Are you alright, Roy?"

One of his rules in the office was first names. Outside the office, more formality was needed, but here in the office, he preferred less pretense. His staff was getting used to it, but slipped at times.

"I'm fine. Just a lot on my mind."

"You sure? I can stay longer if you need me to."

He shook his head and smiled. "Enjoy the rest of the day. It looks beautiful out there. See you tomorrow."

She returned the smile and left.

Griffin returned to his desk, picked up the phone and pressed the send icon.

***

Kruger smiled as he accepted the call. Roy Griffin was a friend, someone he had met almost four years ago during the investigation of a string of assassinations of prominent Jewish businessmen. While not Jewish, Griffin was also a target for assassination. Ryan Clark and he had prevented the congressman and his wife from being shot. Clark took the bullet intended for Griffin.

"Hello, Roy. How are you this morning?"

"Concerned."

Frowning, Kruger's tone turned cautious. "How so?"

"I had a strange call from the Majority Leader yesterday."

"Not sure I know how to help with Washington, D.C., politics."

"Uh…"

"Go on, spit it out."

"Are you investigating a newly elected member of the Senate?"

Kruger hesitated, searching for an appropriate response.

"I'm not sure I understand what you're asking, Roy."

"Me either. He hinted that I needed to call you and put a squelch on your investigation."

"Roy, you're talking obstruction of justice."

"I know. I didn't like his implication and I told him so, but he insisted I call you." He paused for a heartbeat. "Are you investigating a newly elected senator?"

"Just between you and me?"

"Yes."

"It can't go any farther because all we have is speculation and circumstantial evidence."

"I understand. That's the reason for my call. I need to understand why the Majority Leader would risk being charged with obstruction."

"Do you want to what we know?"

"Not sure, maybe. Give me the fifty-thousand-foot view."

"It's a cold case from my earlier days at the Bureau." He gave Griffin a quick summary of the case. After finishing he remarked. "We knew all the incidents are related."

"How?"

"All the victims except two were star women basketball

players, and those two disappeared with a player."

"I kind of remember hearing about this, but it's been a long time ago. The bodies were never found?"

"No."

Griffin was quiet. Kruger let him think. His silence lasted almost two minutes.

"Okay, Sean, I understand why the Majority Leader is trying to intervene."

"Why?"

"Money."

"I'm shocked."

Griffin chuckled, "No, you are not."

"You obviously see a connection I don't. Care to elaborate?"

"I'm sure you know who the father of the new senator in question is?"

"Yes."

"You know how rich he is?"

"I've heard he has a few dollars."

"More than a few. Did you realize how much influence he still has in Washington?"

"I can only guess. But I know he took the fall for something his son did, which ended his career as a senator."

Now it was Griffin's turn to remain quiet. "I'm not following you."

"Officially, Robert Burns Sr. took the blame for inappropriate contact with a young Senate intern in 2012. There was more than inappropriate contact. The son raped her. To keep the incident quiet, he made a deal with then-Senate leadership to bow out of his re-election quest. The intern was paid off, and the whole affair swept under the rug before the news media could catch wind of anything."

"How do you know this, Sean?"

"I can't reveal sources at this time, Roy."

"Oh, boy. What else has the son done?"

"We think he's responsible for the six missing women."

A long stretch of silence from Griffin ensued. Finally,

Kruger heard, "How?"

"I would prefer not to discuss it over the phone. Ryan Clark is on my investigative team, he's in Washington, and he can stop by to brief you. That is, if you want him to."

Griffin took a deep breath and let it out slowly. "Have Ryan stop by."

"I'll call him."

"I never told you why the majority leader is involved."

"No, you didn't."

"Robert Burns Sr. owns factories and businesses all over the United States."

"I'm aware of the size of his company."

"What you probably don't know is the majority leader is from a state whose largest employer is owned by Haylex Holdings."

"You're right, I didn't know that."

"I can only guess what the elder Burns said to make him take a chance on stopping your investigation."

Kruger did not comment immediately. "Which means it won't be the only step he takes."

"I hadn't thought of that."

"Neither did I until you brought it up. I need to mention this to my team." He paused for a few moments. "Do you want Ryan to call you on this number?"

"Please."

***

"That's an interesting development."

"I agree, Sandy." The call to Sandy Knoll was made immediately after ending the conversation with Griffin. "And potentially troublesome for our investigation."

"How so?"

"With Robert Burns Sr.'s political connections and wealth, there is no telling what he will do to try to stop our efforts."

"So far Junior's been a boring individual to follow. He's making the rounds introducing himself to various senators and from what we've heard, receiving a warm welcome."

"People like Burns can be charming when they want to be. Keep an eye on him." He paused for a moment. "I'm more concerned about his nightlife than his meetings with senators."

"Got it. Clark just left to brief Senator Griffin."

"That was fast."

"Yeah, he told Ryan to meet him at his office in the Hart Building."

"Keep me posted."

***

Roy Griffin smiled as he shook the hand of Ryan Clark. "I haven't seen you since you joined the FBI, Agent. Congratulations."

"Thank you, Senator."

"Please call me, Roy."

Clark nodded.

"I never had an opportunity to thank you for protecting my wife and me in San Francisco. Sean tells me you made a complete recovery."

"Except for an ugly scar, yes, I did."

"I... Uh, I'm still embarrassed I didn't believe you and Sean when you tried to warn me about the dangers."

"Glad we were able to keep you safe."

Griffin nodded. "What can you tell me about your investigation so far?"

"Most of the information we have points with a broken line to Robert Burns Jr. We know he was at each of the campuses when the women disappeared. His father owns the company that was installing part of a computer upgrade at each college, and we found information suggesting Junior was at each campus during the installations. Those locations were the only time he assisted. According to a source, he wasn't involved at any others."

"Could be a coincidence."

Clark smiled, "One witness told Sean the man one of the women was seeing was named Bobby. Three witnesses told us the man had black hair."

"Uh-oh."

"Yeah, Robert Burns Jr. went by Bobby up until the time he started working for his father in the Senate. That was 2003, the same year the disappearances stopped."

"I haven't met the man, yet. I'm guessing he has black hair."

"Yes, plus his age is right. He's in his early forties now, which would have made him in his late twenties when the kidnappings occurred. Which is the age witnesses give for the Bobby person."

"Why can't you use this and company information about him being at the campuses and arrest him?"

Shaking his head, Clark pursed his lips. "Wish we could. The information is no longer available in the company computer. It's been deleted."

Griffin knew about JR, but did not say anything. "I see. You're right, lots of information but nothing a good lawyer couldn't shoot holes through."

"Did Sean mention the assault on a Senate intern in 2012?"

Griffin nodded and frowned. "Why wasn't this brought out in the election?"

"Lots of money and a non-disclosure agreement. Not even the Senate leadership, at the time, knew it was the son."

Standing, Griffin turned to stare out his window. "So you're telling me a vicious sexual predator has been elected to the United States Senate, is that correct, Ryan?"

"Sean has a stronger word for it, Roy."

Looking over his shoulder, Griffin responded, "What's that?"

"A psychopath has been elected to the United States Senate."

Griffin chuckled humorlessly. "Some would say it's happened before."

"Yeah, but none this dangerous."

CHAPTER 19

Washington, D.C.

The black Cadillac Escalade pulled into the narrow undercover entrance of the Four Seasons Hotel on Pennsylvania Avenue. It stopped long enough to allow Robert Burns Jr. to exit. After he was inside the lobby, the driver continued on around the u-shaped drive and exited back onto Pennsylvania Avenue.

Burns stopped at the concierge's and made reservations at Bourbon Steak for two at eight. Continuing on to the elevators, he got off on the fourth floor, turned left and proceeded to his room. Dinner would be with a highly recommended individual whom he was planning to hire as his Chief of Staff. Once she was on board, he could leave this dreadful town and return to Seattle.

His day of interviews with Senate leadership left him mentally exhausted. Charming these individuals was easy, but remembering the lies he told them was exhausting. Glancing at his watch, he noted he had time for a shower before heading down for his dinner reservation.

***

"Where is he?"

Jimmie Gibbs sat at the Bourbon Steak bar and nursed his ten-dollar beer. Sandy Knoll's voice was crystal clear in his earpiece, and he answered as he sipped his beer with the small mic attached to the sleeve of his sport coat.

"Sitting at a table, by himself. Looks like he's waiting for someone. He keeps looking at his watch and then around the room."

Knoll chuckled. "He may be waiting a long time."

"Why?"

"Apparently Griffin found out a friend of his was being interviewed for the position of Chief of Staff with Burns tonight. He convinced her not to show up."

"Good. How'd he do that?"

"Don't know."

"Hey, hold on. Burns is taking a call on his cell phone."

As he watched, the newly elected member of the Senate listened, frowned, said something loud, and ended the call. The din of the restaurant kept Gibbs from hearing the response, but everyone around Burn's table turned and stared at the man. As soon as the call ended, he stood and left the restaurant.

"Oops, she must have called." Gibbs was taking another small sip of beer as he spoke. "He stormed out of the restaurant looking extremely pissed."

Gibbs heard laughter through his ear piece. "What floor is he staying on?"

"Fourth."

"Did you get in today?"

"Yeah. We have a room across the hall. I've got six bugs stashed throughout his suite and a camera in the bedroom area. We should be able to hear everything he says."

"I'll be there in ten."

***

"You're the one who recommended her to me."

Burns' cell phone was pressed to his ear. Knoll and Gibbs could only hear one side of the conversation. The video feed from the small camera was displayed on a laptop sitting on a desk in the hotel suite. Words spoken by Burns emitted through the laptop's speaker.

Knoll looked at his team member. "Who's he talking to?"

Gibbs shrugged. "Haven't got a clue. He hasn't mentioned their name yet."

"What happened before I got here?"

"I got to the room several minutes after he returned. By the time everything was up and running, he had his ear on the phone."

Knoll nodded.

They could see Burns pacing the room. He was out of view for a few seconds, then would walk back toward the windows and repeat the process.

"Now what am I going to do, Father?"

More silence.

"Well, now we know who he's talking to," Gibbs whispered.

Nodding again, Knoll remained quiet, staring at the laptop screen.

Burns stopped pacing by the window and stared out, his cell phone pressed firmly to his left ear. "I am calm. But I've just spent the last twelve hours talking to a group of gray-haired, seventy year-old men who are collectively the dumbest humans on the planet. So I am in no mood to listen to your excuses. I need to get someone hired so they can get a staff up and running."

Silence as he listened.

"I am not going to do that, Father."

He continued to study the view out the hotel room window.

"From what I was told today, the staff does everything. The senator just shows up, votes, then talks to the media."

More silence. Burns covered his eyes with one hand as he continued to hold the cell phone to his ear with the other.

His head slowly moving from side to side.

Gibbs leaned in closer to the screen. "Is his body shaking?"

Knoll bent over and studied the laptop. "Can't tell, but it sure looks like it."

"Call Sean."

Taking his cell phone out of his back pocket, Knoll turned his back to Gibbs and pressed the send icon. His call was answered after the first ring.

"Kruger."

"Sean, it's Knoll."

"Uh oh. What's happened?"

"Nothing, yet. Got a question for you."

"Shoot."

"We're watching and listening to a phone call between father and son. Apparently, Junior had a meeting tonight with someone he was trying to hire as his Chief of Staff. He got stood up, and now he's whining about it to his father. You and I both know this type of shit happens, and you go on. Burns is taking it to another level. He's pacing and looks like his body is trembling."

Silence was the only reaction from Kruger.

"Sean?"

"Thinking."

"Sure."

Several minutes passed before Kruger spoke again. "Without actually seeing his reaction or hearing the conversation, I would guess he's struggling to contain his rage."

"Gibbs can send the video to you."

"Send it to JR."

"Got it."

"Sandy?"

"Yeah."

"Don't let this guy out of your sight."

Knoll paused before answering as he stared back at the image of Robert Burns Jr.

"Understood."

***

JR pointed to the forty-inch monitor as he enhanced the image. "Look at his hand before he places it against his eyes."

Kruger leaned over and watched the screen.

"Run it again."

He watched as a noticeably trembling hand rose to cover the pacing man's eyes. As soon as it covered them, Burns stopped pacing. Kruger noticed something else no one had mentioned. Burns slightly raised his right leg and appeared to slam his heel on the ground.

"Stop and rewind five seconds."

JR did.

"Look at that." He pointed toward the leg.

"Hmmm. Kind of childish."

Standing, Kruger hit redial on his cell phone.

Knoll answered immediately. "Yeah."

"What's he doing now, Sandy?"

"Still talking to his father. Mostly listening. He hasn't said much. But he seems to be getting more agitated the more he listens."

"Did he have any drinks?"

Knoll held the phone away from his face. "Jimmie, how much did Burns have to drink?"

"Three low-ball cocktails in about forty-five minutes. Why?"

"Hang on." Knoll spoke into the phone again. "Three on-the-rocks in about three quarters of an hour."

"Has he consumed any additional alcohol since he got back to the hotel room?"

"Yeah, raided the mini-bar twice. Why?"

"So, five cocktails in about, what, hour and a half?"

"I'd say that's right."

"Okay, keep this guy under surveillance tonight. In my experience, alcohol and anger don't mix well with people like

Burns."

"I'll head to the lobby in case he leaves."

"Probably a good idea. Do you have anybody else who can help with surveillance?"

"Yeah, I've called two other guys. They'll be here in the morning."

"Good." Kruger paused for a few moments. "Sandy, I'm probably being overly cautious here, but don't let him out of your sight."

"You've mentioned that several times. What're you worried about?"

"I think he might go hunting tonight."

Knoll did not respond right away. "Uh—boy."

"Yeah. I'll head that way in the morning."

"Not necessary. We've got this covered."

"You sure?"

"If we need you, I'll let you know."

CHAPTER 20

Washington, D.C.

Walking toward the Senate cafeteria, Roy Griffin felt pressure on his right arm. Turning, he saw the Senate Majority Leader looking at him with questioning eyes.

"Roy, can I talk to you?" David Clayton, the senior senator from the state of Illinois and current Senate Majority Leader, held his elbow.

"What about, Dave?"

"I would prefer not to talk here."

Griffin smiled. "Okay, where?"

"My office. I'll have lunch brought in."

Without answering, Griffin followed Clayton. When they were seated in his office, Clayton smiled and clasped his hands together as he sat behind his desk. "Have you spoken to FBI Agent Sean Kruger?" he asked without hesitation.

Griffin tilted his head. He paused for just a moment, determining how to answer, before saying, "No."

"Well, you need to soon."

Smiling, Griffin crossed his arms over his chest. "Now, why would you say something like that, Dave?"

"It's serious."

"Obstruction of justice is serious."

Clayton closed his eyes and took a deep breath. "That was not my intent. Roy, can we be candid?"

Griffin chose not to respond.

"We are facing a philosophical conflict with one of our primary donors."

"Oh? Who's that, David?"

"It's not important. What is important is to keep him happy."

"You didn't answer my question. Who?"

"I am sure you can understand this major contributor to our party is concerned about an unjustified inquisition being conducted by FBI Agent Sean Kruger."

"Oh…"

"Yes, unsubstantiated claims are being directed at a newly elected member of our esteemed body."

Griffin stood. "Senator Clayton, I was a prosecutor and then a businessman before being elected a senator. I find your remarks disconcerting."

"Sorry, not what I was intending." Clayton raised his hands, palms out.

"Then what were your intentions?"

"We have a substantial amount of money, for the party, at stake here, Roy. I'm sure you can understand our concern."

"For the party? Or, for you?"

Clayton frowned, his tone less conciliatory, "The party."

Griffin leaned forward, placing his hands on Clayton's desk, as he snapped, "You're more concerned about money than you are of the possibilities of obstructing a legal and legitimate investigation by the FBI."

Clayton's face reddened, and he abruptly stood, now eye to eye with Griffin. "I do not like your implications, Senator."

"Be careful, Senator Clayton. I am aware of the deal Senate leadership struck with Robert Burns Sr. before his retirement. I'm not sure you want the public to know you and some of your colleague's swept an embarrassing episode under the rug."

The senior senator from Illinois eyes widened as he stared

at Griffin. "How dare you…"

"Spare me your disingenuous indignations, David. I'm not one of your constituents. I know the truth. Senator Burns was not the one who assaulted the intern."

David Clayton did the exact opposite of what Griffin expected. He blinked rapidly for several seconds, tilted his head to the side and narrowed his eyes. "What do you mean, assaulted?" he scoffed. "It was an illicit affair."

"I mean what I said. The intern was assaulted and raped by Senator Burns' son."

"We didn't know about an assault. The Ethics Committee was told it was a consensual affair between the intern and the senator."

Griffin shook his head. "Not according to the evidence Agent Kruger has found."

Clayton sat down and studied the top of his desk, his hands clasped in front of him again. After taking a deep breath, he let it out slowly. "The Ethics Committee was preparing several charges against Senator Burns at that time. When we were told of his supposed indiscretions with the intern, we gave him a choice. Do not seek a third term, or face Senate censure. He chose to retire. He also told us he would continue to contribute funds to the party." He looked up at Griffin. "Please, sit down, Roy."

Returning to his seat in front of Clayton's desk, Griffin remained quiet.

"What do you know that we don't?"

"I tell you this in confidence, Dave. Agreed?"

The senator from Illinois nodded.

"Agent Kruger has two witnesses who will testify, in a court of law, that the current senator-elect, from Washington State, assaulted the intern, both sexually and physically. It was not the ex-senator."

"Why was this not reported to the police?"

Griffin's face hardened. "The father started throwing money at the victim and the witness. I'm told the young lady signed a non-disclosure agreement and the other witness works for the elder Burns as the head of corporate security. But there's more to the story."

Shaking his head, David Clayton closed his eyes. "Oh good grief. Tell me."

"Agent Kruger believes the newly elected senator from the great state of Washington is the man responsible for the disappearance of six women at the turn of the century. Their bodies have never been found."

Clayton's eyes suddenly opened, his head jerked up, and he stared at Griffin. "What?" He pronounced it as a two-syllable word.

Nodding, Griffin crossed his arms over his chest. "Our newest member of the Senate is a suspected sexual predator and murderer."

Raising his hands to his forehead, Clayton leaned forward and pressed the palms of his hands against this eyes, whispering, "Oh, dear god."

The junior senator from California watched the Senate Majority Leader carefully. While he would not necessarily call the man a friend, he trusted him as a colleague and knew he would do what was right for the nation and Senate. He kept his silence, waiting for Clayton to speak. It was several minutes before he did.

Straightening in his chair, the senior senator from Illinois gave Griffin a half smile. "I first met Robert Burns Sr. in 2000, right after he was elected. He was a bit arrogant, but then most of us are, or we wouldn't be senators."

Griffin nodded.

"His arrogance was more profound, to a point I found irritating. At that time I was Conference Chairman and, as you know, responsible for committee assignments. When I meet with him to discuss where he wanted to serve he told me, in no uncertain terms, he wanted to be Chairman of the Commerce, Science, and Transportation Committee. When I told him that wasn't the way it worked, and he would have to serve on a committee with an opening and work his way up to the chairman position, he stood." Clayton paused, and chuckled slightly. "I will always remember his expression and what he told me. 'Mr. Clayton, I have no interest in being just a member of a committee. I will either be the chairman or I won't serve.'"

"I looked at him. I'm sure my expression gave away my feelings, because he smiled slightly. So I stood as well and returned his smile. I said, 'Then I guess you won't serve.' He glared at me and left my office. That was my introduction to Senator Robert Burns. I assigned him to the Indian Affairs Committee and the Joint Committee on the Library. To my knowledge, he never showed up for a single hearing."

"So what did he do as a senator?" Griffin asked.

"Not much. He spent a lot of time in Seattle. He didn't divest his interests in his companies and continued to run them. We didn't see much of him until 2003 when he started working toward his re-election. That was the first time I met Junior. I thought Senior was arrogant, but Junior made his dad look humble."

"How so?"

"Nothing specific, it was his general attitude. He really didn't have a title, but was in charge of his father's staff. The senator already had a Chief of Staff, so they clashed immediately. He was demanding, condescending, lacked empathy for anyone, and made everyone who worked there miserable. Turnover in his staff was the highest in the history of the Senate."

"Why didn't his opponent bring this up in the 2006 election?"

"I don't know," Clayton shrugged. "I was busy with my own re-election."

Griffin and made a note to himself to follow up on this point. "How did your meeting with the younger Burns go today?"

"Not well. He complained about his office assignment and lack of applicants for his staff. I listened, but did not offer any sympathy or help. He was noticeably upset when he left."

"Why was the incident with the intern swept under the

rug?"

"It really wasn't. The only thing we knew was when Burns asked to visit with Senator Manning, who was President Pro Tempore at the time, and myself. He announced his retirement to us. When asked why? He told us about the affair with the intern, and his goal to keep the whole issue out of the news media. We agreed. What Burns didn't know at the time was there was a resolution to censure being prepared to present to the Select Committee on Ethics. When he announced his retirement, the resolution was abandoned."

"Why censure and not expulsion?"

"We didn't have the votes for expulsion. We did for censure."

"In other words, Burns left the Senate with a clean record."

"Yes."

"And no one knew the reason why the intern left suddenly?"

"All we knew was she left for personal reasons."

Griffin stood. "Thank you, David. I appreciate your sharing this with me."

Clayton took a deep breath and let it out slowly. "I'm sure you will be contacted by the President. Burns was a major contributor to his campaign, and they speak regularly."

"I can handle the President."

"Just an FYI."

"I appreciate it."

CHAPTER 21

Springfield, MO

JR stared at the ceiling fan as it slowly turned. Illuminated by light leaking under the closed bathroom door, it was barely visible in the darkness of the room. Mia lay next to him, breathing softly as she slept. Sleep always eluded him when his mind raced with a project or a problem. Tonight, his thoughts were on a problem. Hacking into the Haylex Holding servers was testing his abilities. Abilities, until now, that were superior to any firewall he had ever encountered, even the government's.

The little program Joel Moody ejected into the system was successful, but only allowed access to a small part of the system. Which raised another question: did Moody intentionally select a computer not connected to the core, or was it a lack of knowing? The answer eluded him.

Mia rolled over and put her arms over his chest. "Are you still awake?"

"Yes."

"You haven't had trouble sleeping in a long time. JR, what's on your mind?"

"Haylex Holdings."

"I could have guessed that. Why?"

"I've never encountered a system like it. It seems to know when it's being attacked and takes action on its own."

"AI?"

"Maybe. Although during the brief time I've been in the system, I'm not seeing evidence of AI."

"Do they have any remote sites?"

JR was quiet for a few moments. "Yeah, all over the place. What are you thinking?"

"I would think remote sites have the ability to access to the main server, find one that's vulnerable, and use it for your pathway."

Although she could not see it in the darkness of their bedroom, JR smiled. Ten minutes later, he dozed off while listening to her breathing.

***

"I'll be damned. It worked."

"What worked?" With a freshly poured cup of coffee made by a new Mr. Coffee machine he bought for JR, Kruger sipped the black brew, smiled, and stepped over to JR's cubicle.

"I finally have access to the Haylex servers."

"I thought you already did. What happened to the program Moody inserted?"

JR turned and looked at Kruger. "I've been meaning to talk to you about that. It worked for a short period, long enough to discover the altered files on Junior. But then, poof. The pathway was gone."

Kruger was silent as he sipped his coffee.

"How much do you trust Moody?"

The FBI agent shook his head. "Don't know that I do. Why?"

"A feeling, nothing concrete. The program I gave him should have allowed permanent access. It didn't. Mia thinks they might have an experimental artificial intelligent system monitoring their system. I'm not seeing any evidence of it, but it could be sophisticated. The point is, the program shouldn't have been found, unless he told someone about it."

"So how did you finally get access?"

"The company is huge, Sean. They have subsidiaries in all but three states and twenty foreign countries."

"So?"

"The only states they don't have a presence in are Montana, North Dakota, and Hawaii."

Kruger sipped his coffee.

JR frowned as he watched Kruger drink his coffee. "I hope you're planning to clean the new machine you forced on me."

Kruger chuckled.

"I'm serious. Those things are messy and require a lot of cleaning."

"Don't worry, I'll take care of it. Besides, it makes a better cup of coffee."

"Whatever. I'll keep using the Keurig."

"Back to what you were saying about how big Haylex Holdings is."

"Right, not all their companies are high-tech. They own a lot of food manufacturers, mostly private label packers."

"Really?"

JR nodded. "High sales volume without having to invest in marketing departments."

"Makes sense. What else?"

"A lot of companies in different industries, most I've never heard of."

"So, how did you get in?"

"Bottled water packer in northern Arkansas. It seems their computer system isn't scheduled for an upgrade for another year. It showed me the way into the main server."

Kruger smiled. "So what are you looking for?"

"Emails."

"Really? Why?"

"You'd be surprised what people put in their emails without knowing what they've revealed."

"Have you looked at any yet?"

"No, but I have a little search engine sorting through them."

Sipping his coffee again, Kruger remained quiet.

A full ten minutes passed while he waited for JR's program to sort through the untold tens of thousands of emails. During this period, JR stood and poured a cup of coffee from the Mr. Coffee. He sipped, paused, took another sip, and smiled. "This is better."

"Told you."

"Still not changing."

All Kruger could do was shake his head.

***

Director of the FBI Paul Stumpf was in his late fifties. At one time a dedicated marathon runner, he still maintained a lean body. But after having both knees replaced, he was starting to add a few pounds to his five-eleven frame. His hair was dark brown, perfectly styled, with the first appearance of gray around his temples. Rimless glasses sat on an unremarkable nose in front of arctic blue eyes. During Stumpf's rise within the FBI, he and Kruger worked together a few times in their early careers. Now decades later, he was the director, thanks in part to an investigation Kruger solved four years earlier.

Normally a calm individual and slow to anger, he carefully analyzed situations before commenting or taking actions. This morning, he was anything but calm. Alan Seltzer, Deputy Director of the FBI, stood in front of Stumpf's desk with his hands behind his back and listened to his boss rant, an occurrence Seltzer had never seen during his ten years of working alongside the man. He remained quiet as Stumpf paced and vented.

"I can't believe what I just heard on the phone. I can't believe it."

Seltzer remained silent.

"The President actually ordered me to shut down an ongoing investigation. The President of the United States, for gawd sakes." The pacing stopped and he glanced at Seltzer. "You heard him, didn't you, Alan?"

"Yes, sir. I did."

"What is he thinking? Just what the hell is he thinking? My gawd, we're talking obstruction of justice, pure and simple."

"Yes, sir."

"Kruger has obviously struck a nerve somewhere with his investigation. How can Robert Burns Sr. have enough persuasion to make the President commit an impeachable crime? Can you answer that question, Alan?"

"No, sir. But I can tell you Burns is one of the largest contributors to the President's election campaign."

Stumpf stopped pacing and stared at Seltzer. "How so?"

"Millions."

"How many millions?"

"Unknown. He's donated through a variety of companies his corporation owns and all the money goes to a PAC."

"How far along is Sean in his investigation?"

"He interviewed a Senate intern who acknowledged the son sexually assaulted her. She is under a non-disclosure agreement. Kruger asked her to nod or shake her head to answer his questions."

Stumpf chuckled for the first time since the phone call. "Only Sean would think of that."

"They can place the son at each of the universities at the same time the women vanished. Unfortunately, this information was deleted from the company records after Kruger started his inquiry."

"So, he's making progress."

"Yes."

"Does this remind you of another investigation Kruger made four years ago?"

"Yes, sir."

"Remember what we did then?"

"Yes, sir. We officially took Kruger off the investigation

and unofficially kept him on it. However, this time you and the Bureau are in a difficult position, Paul. Disobeying a direct order from the White House could get you fired."

Stumpf started pacing again and was quiet while he moved.

"Yes, but the aspect of a vicious sexual predator being introduced into the U.S. Senate is more troubling than losing my job."

Seltzer nodded. "This could come back to bite the President as well, Paul."

"Yes, it could. Especially if certain members of the opposite party knew about it."

"You have it on tape, don't you?"

The Director nodded and paced a few more minutes. When he stopped, he looked at Seltzer with a smile. "Okay, let's go to the conference room and get Sean on the phone."

***

Standing on his back deck, Kruger pressed the cell phone to his ear with his shoulder as he listened to Paul Stumpf on the other end.

"I don't want to pull the plug on this investigation if you feel you're making headway, Sean."

Taking a deep breath, Kruger calmed his initial reaction to the phone call.

"Paul, we're dealing with an extremely intelligent individual. He's manipulative and uses his father to divert attention away from himself. We've been able to access some of the company's emails between Senior and Junior. They are… let's say, informative."

"I won't ask how you accessed them."

"Probably best."

"So what's next? I have to get back to the President with something."

"We have to build a case against Junior. He's the guilty one. I don't think Senior's committed any crimes, other than being unethical in his business and political contributions, which I'm not focused on."

"The President was adamant we stop the investigation, unless you had positive proof of Junior's guilt."

"You know we don't have it yet. We might have to actually catch him in the act of assaulting someone to get that kind of proof, and I don't want to put anyone in harm's way."

"Then you have to officially shut down the investigation."

Taking another deep breath, Kruger let it out slowly. "That is not the right move, Paul. You and I both know it."

Stumpf was quiet for a long time. Kruger checked the phone to see if the call had ended. "Paul?"

"You're correct, of course, it's not the right thing to do. Can you get by with your current manpower?"

"Yes."

"Then I will tell the President we are not putting any additional assets into the investigation."

Kruger chuckled, "Sounds like something I would come up with."

"I learned from the best."

"Thanks, Paul."

"Don't thank me yet. Just make sure Burns doesn't suspect he's being followed."

"When we have enough evidence, we'll arrest him."

"Get to the truth, once you have it, I can deal with the fall out. For now, stop this psychopath, Sean."

"That's the plan."

Chapter 22

Washington, D.C.

Robert Burns Jr. stared out the window of the Uber driver's Honda Accord. His destination was a trendy nightclub in Georgetown suggested by the hotel concierge.

The phone call from the candidate for his open Chief of Staff position created emotions not experienced in several years. She had been blunt about her reasons. After further research into his character and history, there was no way she would work for him. She even told him his reputation in Washington would make it difficult for him to hire any competent staff, no matter how high the salary. She wished him well and ended the call.

This was his father's fault. His father had talked him into running for the Senate, and it was his father who greased the wheels of the election with millions of dollars for him to do something he simply did not want to do.

Old feelings exorcised from his psyche years ago flooded back. The old desires and needs bubbling up from the heat of his rage. When the Uber driver parked the car in front of the nightclub, Burns exited immediately without a word, his bill already settled with a credit card on file with Uber.

The din of the club assaulted his senses the minute he

walked in. A smile came to his lips as he pushed his way through the crowd toward the bar. He was on the hunt, and it felt good. Several minutes later, he stood surveying the room, sipping on an incredibly expensive single malt scotch on the rocks. As he took in the crowd, he saw two intoxicated women sitting at a table, their arms animated as they tried to communicate with each other over the music.

Without hesitation, he walked over and sat down.

Two minutes later, both women stood and walked away from the table. Burns shrugged slightly and sipped his drink as he surveyed the area for his next conquest.

As he scanned the room, a tall slender woman stepped up to the table. Turning his attention to her, his eyes widened and he felt his heart race. Her hair was blond, cut in a pixie style exposing darker hair above her ears. The face was heart shaped, with a petite turned up nose, full lips and green eyes sparkling in the flashing lights of the nightclub. A form-fitting dress exposed cleavage and ended twelve inches above the knees of her muscular legs. Burns' breathing rate increased. She bent over, exposing more of her breasts.

She spoke next to his ear. "Did your friends leave?"

He nodded and yelled so he could be heard over the thumping bass line of the music. "They're in a relationship. No males allowed."

She grinned and offered her hand. "I'm Linda."

Shaking the offered hand he replied. "I'm Bob. Want a drink?"

Sitting down next to him, she nodded.

***

Jimmie Gibbs slipped into the nightclub followed by Ryan Clark. Gibbs went left, Clark went right. Sandy Knoll waited in the car, a small radio receiver in each ear. His left ear would be communications from Gibbs and his right ear from Clark. He winced at the sound of the club in his ear, as it bordered on deafening.

Gibbs was first to respond. "Got him, he's sitting at a table talking to a pair of women."

Clark was next. "I see him."

Knoll let the two agents assess the room before asking, "What's he doing?"

"Just talking." Gibbs spoke in a deep voice trying to overcome the background noise.

There was no communications from the inside team for a minute. He heard Clark. "Wait one."

Knoll did not respond.

"They just stood and left."

Smiling, Knoll nodded. "Good."

"Hold the thought. Looks like they're being replaced by a tall blonde. Damn, son, she is beautiful."

"Hold your comments, Jimmie, we're working."

"Doesn't matter, she's gorgeous." Using his cell phone, he took several pictures of the two, making sure he had a good photo of the woman.

Clark and Gibbs were quiet as they watched the woman bend over and talk into Burns' ear. After shaking hands, she sat down and the target of their observation ordered drinks from a passing waitress.

Clark was the first to speak. "They're leaning toward each other. The girl is smiling and laughing. Burns is animated, talking her head off."

"Careful, Ryan, he might be plotting to take it off." Gibbs smiled to himself after the comment. His concentration was on Burns' lips, trying to read what he was saying.

Burns and the woman suddenly stood and headed for the front exit.

"They're moving, Sandy, headed your way." Clark started toward the exit when he saw something over Jimmie's shoulder across the room. Before he could say anything, a man, similar in size to Knoll, approached Gibbs from behind.

"Jimmie, watch out…" Clark's warning was useless as the large man started to clamp a massive hand on Gibbs' shoulder. Instead of moving to follow Burns and the woman, he pushed his way toward his teammate.

***

Sensing something moving behind him, Gibbs reacted faster than the man who attempted to grab him. The hand barely touched his right shoulder before Gibbs' left hand seized it and he spun around. The brute probably outweighed him by a hundred pounds, but skill and training overcame the disadvantage. Before the big man knew what had happened, Gibbs leveraged him around and pinned the larger man's arm behind him.

He growled in his ear. "FBI, dickhead. You're interfering with a federal investigation."

The large man, surprised at the turn of events, shook his head. "You're bothering our customers. You have to leave."

Gibbs raised the arm further toward the man's neck and heard an audible gasp.

Clark appeared with his FBI credentials and shoved them into the large man's face. "What the hell are you doing assaulting a federal agent?"

The big man grimaced as he felt the tendons of his left arm stretched to the point of snapping. "Ouch… I'm security here, let me go, I'll explain."

As the crowd dispersed around the confrontation, Sandy Knoll emerged from the throng of people, his FBI credentials attached to a lanyard around his neck. He stood in front of the security man, crossed his arms over his massive chest, and leaned forward inches from the other man's nose.

"Why did you attack a federal agent?" he demanded.

Knoll was actually larger than the man Gibbs still held immobilized.

"Let me go, and I'll explain."

Looking at Gibbs, Knoll nodded. The security man's arm was released, and Gibbs stepped back several paces. By now the music was silent, and an odd quiet permeated the nightclub. The security guard rubbed his newly freed left arm.

"We have a two-drink minimum." He twisted around and motioned with his head toward Gibbs. "He wasn't drinking."

Knoll closed his eyes and brought a hand to cover his mouth. After a few seconds, he lowered it and touched his ID. "You have got to be kidding me."

The other man shook his head. "Sign's on the door."

Knoll turned to Clark. "See if you can spot Burns. They may be long gone by now."

Clark nodded and headed toward the door.

Returning his attention to the security guard, Knoll asked, "Does this establishment have an agreement with any working girls?"

The bouncer shook his head.

Gibbs leaned close to the man and warned, "Careful. Don't add lying to a federal agent to the assault charge."

The security guard jerked his head back and stiffened. "I didn't assault you."

"So you say. You put your hand on me without my permission. Not good in a judge's eye."

The man blinked rapidly several times and continued to stare at Gibbs.

Knoll asked again. "Hey, does this establishment have an agreement with any working girls? Answer me."

Returning his attention to Knoll, the man nodded.

"Do you have their names and addresses?"

"Nothing in writing. Just a verbal agreement."

"Shit. What's her name?"

"Linda Smith's all we know."

Knoll frowned and turned to Gibbs. "We have to find Burns and the woman. She may be in real danger."

"Got it."

He started toward the exit, but before he left, he heard the security guard ask, "How'd you do that?"

"Do what?"

"Twist me around so fast."

Gibbs smiled and leaned closer. "Boy Scouts."

***

When Knoll and Gibbs returned to the agency Tahoe, Clark was already there, his hand pressing a cell phone to his ear. When they approached, he held up his index finger. "Yeah, Sean, we lost him. Can JR track Burns' cell phone?"

Silence as he listened to the response. "Yeah, tell him to hurry. The lady with him may be in trouble."

Again, silence returned to this side of the call.

Knoll broke the quiet to ask, "Can he track it?"

Clark nodded. "He's having the phone pinged right now. If it's on, we can get a direction."

"Good."

There was a sixty-second silence. The only sound was the renewed muffled sound of music coming from the club.

"Got it," Clark jotted something down on the back of one of his business calls. "Yeah, we're headed that way. Ask JR to see if he can pinpoint it further. I'll call you back in a few."

Ending the call, he handed Knoll the card. "We need to head south on 495. JR's trying to pinpoint it. All he can do right now is tell us the phone is in Camp Springs."

"Got it, let's go."

***

The Motel 6 hallway smelled of cigarette smoke, stale beer, and Pine-Sol. Linda handed Robert Burns the keycard with a smile.

"I like to keep this little get-away ready for all kinds of occasions," she said. "It isn't fancy, but it is quiet. Is that okay with you?"

As Burns opened the door, he smiled and turned back to her. "Fine with me."

Standing aside, she walked into the room as he followed. After locking the door, he noticed she had already taken her shoes off and was unzipping her dress. It fell to the floor, revealing a skimpy bra and a thong.

Burns felt a stirring in his groin as he watched her. Still with her back to him, she undid the bra and turned. Holding the cups against her, she smiled. "Like what you see so far?"

He nodded, but remained where he stood.

She threw the bra aside, revealing her breasts. "Come closer so we can get acquainted and have a little fun."

Stepping closer, he stood in front of her while she unbuckled his pants. When she reached inside, the blindness took over. He slapped her so hard, she fell back onto the bed. Before she could scream, he clamped his hand over her mouth.

"Oh yeah, I'm going to have fun."

CHAPTER 23

Camp Springs, MD

The agency Tahoe screamed south on 495, its recessed emergency lights flashing and siren blaring. Knoll concentrated on driving while Clark stayed on the phone with JR. "Okay, JR. we're heading south on 495, approaching Suitland Parkway."

JR's voice was calm. "Ryan, you need to exit 495 and get on Allentown Road."

Clark turned toward Knoll, "Sandy, have you seen an exit for Allentown Road?"

"Yeah, two miles ahead."

"Take it."

Knoll nodded. Clark returned to the phone. "What else, JR?"

"Once you're on Allentown Road, the phone is south of Auth Road."

Clark frowned and turned to Gibbs in the back seat to ask, "Does Auth Road sound familiar to you?"

"Yeah, Joint Base Andrews is close. Why?"

Returning to the phone, Clark asked, "Is this phone close to Andrews?"

"Hold on." The call was silent for several minutes. "Yeah,

a bit north, southwest of Auth Road."

Gibbs leaned forward and put his arms on the back of the two bucket seat in the front. "There's a Motel 6 just past Auth Road if I remember correctly."

"I know where it is," Knoll nodded. "Do you think?"

"Nothing else fits the location."

"Then that's where we'll start."

***

Gibbs leaned over the check-in desk, his cell phone held so the night clerk could see the picture.

"She here tonight?"

The clerk was tall, somewhere in his mid-twenties, skinny with gelled hair swept back on top and shaved on the sides. His pock-marked face showed the signs of untreated acne. He shrugged.

"Dude," Gibbs palmed his FBI creds so the clerk could see them. "She's in serious danger. Is she here?"

Another shrug.

"If something happens to her, you'll be considered an accomplice."

The clerk's eyes grew wide, and he answered quickly, "Room 145, close to the back entrance."

"I'll need a passkey," Gibbs demanded.

The young man stared at Gibbs for several moments, then searched a file box and handed him a plastic card.

"Thanks, dude."

The three men approached the room with their guns gripped in both hands and pointed at the floor. Cigarette smoke permeated the hall as they spread out in front of the door to room 145, Clark to the left and Gibbs slightly to the right of the door. Glancing at each of his partners, Gibbs poised to knock, while Knoll stood behind him and nodded.

Knoll used his hand to count down front three fingers to one. When he made a fist, Gibbs knocked and spoke in a heavy Spanish accent, "Room service."

No response from the room.

He knocked again. "You called room service."

Still no response.

Gibbs inserted the card into the lock and glanced at Knoll and Clark. They both nodded. He heard the click, saw the green light, and Clark pushed the door open.

The room was pitch black. Light from the hallway illuminated a bare leg draped over the side of the bed. With his gun extended before him, Gibbs was first in yelling, "FBI". Knoll was right behind and flipped the light switch next to the hotel door. Training kicked in as Gibbs swept the open bathroom and the small living area, his Glock extended in front of him. He yelled, "Clear," and rushed to the body on the bed.

The woman was nude, her face swollen and disfigured from repeated blows. His hand felt the carotid artery of her neck and felt a faint pulse. "She's alive, call 911."

Clark backed out of the room and punched the emergency code into his cell phone. Knoll found a blanket and covered the unconscious woman. He glanced at Gibbs, who was using his paramedic skills to make sure she was stable.

Knoll stood off to the side watching his teammate work.

"How long?" he asked.

"Don't know, she's in shock. We'll be lucky if she makes it until the paramedics get here."

"I'll call Sean. He'll want to know."

Gibbs nodded.

***

"I can be there early morning. I'll call Alan. They need to start looking for Burns."

"Have them go to the Four Seasons. He's got a room there."

"Will do."

Knoll ended the call and stepped out into the hall. He noticed two men enter the hotel from the back entrance and stop when they saw Clark and him in the hallway. The one on the left had a folded black plastic object tucked under his arm. Both men stared, hesitated, and quickly walked back out the door. Knoll sprinted after them and emerged just as they jumped into the side of a Ford Transit van and speed away, its license plate obscured.

Watching as the van disappeared around the side of the building, Knoll raised his cell phone up and hit re-send.

"Kruger."

"Funny thing just happened."

"Yeah."

"Two guys entered the back entrance of the hotel. One had a body bag folded under his arm. Apparently, we weren't supposed to find her this fast."

"Really?"

"Yeah."

"Okay, I just got off the phone with Alan. They have a Swat Team headed toward the Four Seasons. If he's there…"

"He's guilty, Sean. We have him."

"Keep me updated on the girl."

"Will do."

***

Gibbs called Knoll from the hospital two hours later.

"She didn't make it, Sandy."

Knoll took a deep breath. "They've got Burns in custody and stashed away in a military brig on Andrews. He's screaming about false arrest. I'll tell them to change the charges from assault to murder."

"We have evidence."

"Oh?"

"Semen. They'll have to do a DNA analysis to be sure, but the blood type matches Burns."

Knoll smiled.

***

The next morning at two minutes after eleven, Robert Burns Jr., was shown into an interrogation room in the Joint Andrews Base brig. Sean Kruger sat at the table looking over a file folder in front of him. Once Burns' shackles were secured to metal rings in the floor the MPs left.

Burn's looked at Kruger, who ignored him. "I want a lawyer."

Kruger continued to look through the file and remained quiet.

Burns spoke louder, "I want a lawyer."

"I heard you."

"Well?"

Looking up, Kruger smiled. "No."

"I beg your pardon, it's my right."

"Yes, it is your right, but I wonder what happened to Linda Smith's rights."

"Who?"

"Linda Smith."

"Who is that?"

"The woman we found last night with your semen in her."

"Consensual sex. I didn't even know her name."

"She died after your consensual sex, Bobby."

Burns stared at Kruger, his eyes widening slightly when the nickname was used. "When I left, she was fine. Smoking a cigarette, if I remember."

Kruger smiled. "She didn't smoke, and there were no cigarettes in the room."

"Nevertheless, she was alive when I left."

"I'm sure she was." Kruger pointed to Burns' right hand. "Nasty bruise on your hand. Hit something?"

"I'm done talking to you. I want my lawyer."

Kruger stood. "I'm sure you will have one shortly."

He turned and tapped on the door. It opened immediately. Before he left the room he turned to look at Burns. "You might want to know the Senate is having an emergency meeting on your status as a future senator. Doesn't look good for you."

Before Burns could respond, Kruger walked out.

As Kruger exited the facility where Burns was being held, Sandy Knoll and Jimmie Gibbs met him. Knoll spoke first.

"Well?"

"As we suspected, he denied knowing her, but when I told him his sperm was found on the body, he changed his story to consensual sex. He has a rather nasty bruise on his right hand. Did they get pictures of that?"

Gibbs nodded. "I made sure they did last night."

"Good, you two come with me, we have an appointment with the director at one. Seems we stirred up a hornet's nest."

***

Director Paul Stumpf chuckled as he read a memo in the file in front of him. He sat at the head of a long conference table in the room next to his office. Sean Kruger, Sandy Knoll, Jimmie Gibbs, and Ryan Clark sat on his left. Deputy Director Alan Seltzer and Senator Roy Griffin sat to his right. He looked up at Kruger.

"You've been re-instated for less than a month and have successfully pissed off the President of the United States, a variety of senators, the governor of the state of Washington, and the thirty-ninth richest man in the world."

Kruger gave the director a half grin and shrugged. "It's a gift."

"I'm proud of you, Sean."

"I'm just getting started. Burns will be transferred to the Morningside Police Department holding cell at four this afternoon."

Alan Seltzer handed Kruger a printout from a file, saying, "The lab rushed this one, but preliminary DNA analysis of the semen found on the victim's body belongs to Robert Burns Jr. They'll do a thorough and complete test later, but so far, it's him."

"Good, we can hold him on that for a while. When's his

initial appearance?"

Knoll spoke next. "Tomorrow morning at ten. Apparently, his father's attorney in Seattle appointed a temporary lawyer here until they hire one. That guy showed up an hour after we left."

Jimmie Gibbs tapped his finger on the conference table, but did not speak. Seltzer looked at him and prompted, "What's wrong, Gibbs?"

"Make sure the lab tests the bruises on her face. I'll bet they find skin cells from Burns' hand. He beat her severely."

Seltzer nodded. "They've already taken samples. We should know before his appearance tomorrow."

Taking a deep breath, Kruger let it out slowly. "We need him held without bail. No matter how large the judge makes it, Burns Sr. will post the bond."

"Bureau lawyers are already working on it, Sean," Stumpf said. "I'm told the U.S. Attorney for the District of Columbia will make the case for no bail."

"Good," Kruger smiled. "I'm glad this is being taken seriously."

"Very much so. I've seen her in action, she'll make sure he's held without bail."

Stumpf turned to Senator Griffin to ask, "Senator, what is the status within the Senate concerning our detainee?"

"Not much we can do at the moment. He hasn't been sworn in. But, assuming he demands to be sworn in, we already have more than two-thirds of the membership ready to vote for expulsion."

"The question now is how far Daddy Burns will go to protect Junior?" The question came from Sandy Knoll.

Stumpf cocked his head to the side. "Why do you say that?"

"We know Senior took the blame for Junior's assault on the Senate intern, right?"

Everyone nodded.

"We know the bodies of the women kidnapped around the turn of the century were never found."

Kruger frowned. "What are you thinking, Sandy?"

"Last night, after we found Smith, a couple of thugs walked into the hotel carrying what looked like a folded body bag. When they saw Clark and me, they scurried out of the hotel and sped away in a white Ford van."

Still frowning, Kruger nodded slightly. "Junior walks away from the Smith woman…"

Gibbs interrupted, "Her last name was Ramos."

Everyone looked at Gibbs, who was reading the screen on his cell phone.

"Just got the ID back," he continued. "Linda Ramos. She lived in Clinton, Maryland, and was only twenty-two."

The room was quiet. Kruger cleared his throat and asked, "Junior walked away from Ramos without trying to cover it up. Why?"

Seltzer spoke next. "What are you suggesting, Sean?"

"I'm not suggesting, I'm speculating. We have one incident where Senior stepped in and protected Junior. We have to guess, but the men Sandy saw last night were probably hired to clean up."

Clark took up the narrative. "There's the reason all the women kidnapped from the colleges were never found. Someone was hired to clean up the mess?"

Kruger nodded. "It may also be why no one has ever claimed responsibility. One person killed them, but unknown individuals, different in each case, disposed of the bodies.

CHAPTER 24

Seattle, WA

Joel Moody stared at his cell phone screen.

The Haylex building was quiet. The only associates present were dealing with issues in the eastern part of the country. It was a little after seven in the morning in Seattle, three hours behind Washington, D.C. The leading stories on all the news feeds he monitored were about the newly elected senator from Washington State being charged with murder. Moody had not heard from Robert Burns Sr. yet, but expected the inevitable to occur at any moment.

At exactly seven-twenty-one, Senior stormed into his office. "What the hell is going on in Washington, D.C., Joel?"

"You know as much as I do, Mr. Burns."

"Have you made inquiries?"

Moody took a deep breath. "With all due respect, Mr. Burns, my job is security for Haylex Holdings. I am not Junior's babysitter."

The senior Burns' face grew crimson, but he did not say anything immediately. Finally after a few moments, he said, "Since Robert Burns Jr. is a part of this company, his security is your concern, Mr. Moody."

"CNN reports he's been charged with kidnapping, rape,

and murder. He finally got caught, Mr. Burns. After all these years, he got caught."

"Has his attorney been notified?"

Moody shook his head.

"Why not?"

"I will attend to it immediately, Mr. Burns."

Moody was already tired of the accusations and blame. Knowing Robert Burns Jr.'s true personality and keeping quiet about it was a burden he was tired of carrying.

The thirty-ninth richest man in the world leaned forward, putting his palms flat on the front of Moody's desk to support himself. He bowed his head and closed his eyes. "Mr. Moody, in times of crisis, we all must do our part for the good of the company. Your focus for the foreseeable future is to travel to Washington, D.C., and make sure my son does not go to prison." He raised his head and looked Moody straight in the eyes. "Is that understood?"

Moody stared back at the man, suddenly questioning his loyalty to this family. But a surge of greed and ambition made him slowly nod.

***

Kruger finished reviewing the Bureau's evidence against Robert Burns, Jr., concerning the murder of Linda Ramos. He closed the file and slid it across the table to the U.S. Attorney for the District of Columbia.

Carol Welch was in her mid-forties, dark-haired, and petite. Her blue eyes were glued to the folder as she picked it up. After earning her JD degree at Yale she joined the U.S. Attorney's office and gained a reputation as a buttoned-up, hard-nosed, and no-nonsense prosecutor. Now she occupied the top spot for the district. Her gaze went to Kruger.

"I was told you have additional concerns about the suspect, Agent."

"Yes, ma'am."

"Care to share?"

"We can prove one other woman was sexually assaulted by the suspect."

Her eyes widened, but she remained quiet.

Kruger summarized the assault on Heather Grant. When he was done, he sat back and waited for a response.

"Why was he not prosecuted for it, Agent?"

"Money."

She smiled and tilted her head. "Go on."

After informing Welch about the intervention of the father, the non-disclosure agreement, and reviewing his meeting with Heather Grant and her attorney, Kruger once again grew quiet, waiting for a response.

"I see. Did she violate her agreement and talk to you about this, Agent Kruger?"

"No ma'am, her agreement is emphatic about not speaking to anyone about the incident. There is nothing in the agreement about non-verbal responses."

Welch almost grinned, caught herself, and nodded.

Kruger continued. "She confirmed the attack was made by our suspect, not the father."

"Okay. That's two sexual assaults. Why do you think he's a flight risk?"

"There's more."

She took a deep breath and closed her eyes. "Okay, tell me."

Kruger summarized his renewed investigation of the missing college basketball players and laid out his new theory for the prosecutor.

Carol Welch sat back in her chair and blinked several times. "You have my attention. Anything else?"

"One of the agents who found Ms. Ramos reported seeing two men on the night she was attacked carrying a body bag toward her room. We suspect they were there to dispose of the body."

Now Welch's eyes were wide as she stared at Kruger. "Agent, are you suggesting what I think you're suggesting?"

Kruger nodded. "Our suspect has been at this for a long

time. We need to put this guy away forever before another woman is attacked. If he's released, I guarantee he will disappear."

"Can you prove anything about the six missing women?"

Shaking his head Kruger hesitated for a second, "Not yet."

She made strong eye contact with him. Pressing her lips together, she stood. "Find the proof, Sean. I'll make sure he's not released on bail."

"Thank you, Carol."

***

The United flight from Seattle's International Airport landed at Washington, D.C.'s Dulles International a few minutes after seven a.m., Eastern Time. Haylex Holdings allowed associates at the director level and above to fly first class. Moody was Director of Security, so his seat in the second row of the plane allowed him to be one of the first passengers to depart. With his body on Pacific Time and having slept fitfully during the overnight flight, he needed caffeine before his ten a.m. appointment at the D.C. law firm of Rothenberg and Sandifer.

Another perk of working for Haylex Holdings at the director level allowed him to hire a limousine versus having to use Uber or, God forbid, a taxi. After checking into the Grand-Hyatt and a stop at a Starbucks, Moody arrived fifteen minutes early for his appointment at the law firm.

Immediately escorted to a large conference room, he was offered coffee, which he accepted and was told one of the partners would be with him shortly.

At exactly ten a.m., a tall gentleman with professionally styled silver hair walked into the conference room and offered his hand. "Kyle Sandifer, Mr. Moody."

Moody shook the man's hand, noting the Brooks Brother dark gray suit, white on white shirt with a maroon striped tie. Three inches taller than Moody, Sandifer's grip was firm. He appeared to be in his early sixties, dark tan, with few wrinkles and a clean shave.

"Thank you for meeting with me, Mr. Sandifer."

"Call me Kyle."

Two additional individuals entered the room without saying a word and sat down across from Moody. Sandifer nodded in their directions, not introducing them but saying, "These are two of our associates who will be taking notes during our meeting. Now, what can we do for Haylex Holdings?"

Clearing his throat, Moody stalled for a few seconds by taking a sip of his coffee. "As you may have heard, our CEO's son has been falsely accused of a heinous crime."

Sandifer nodded.

"Your firm was recommended by our attorneys in Seattle for your aggressive defense of high profile individuals accused of an unsubstantiated crime."

Again, a nod.

"Haylex Holdings would like to hire your firm for the defense of Robert Burns Jr."

A slight smile came to Sandifer's lips. Moody realized the man was seeing dollar signs dancing in front of his face.

"A wise decision to hire our firm, Mr. Moody."

Moody did not invite Sandifer to call him Joel. Years of dealing with defense attorneys gave him a slight distaste for lawyers.

"Who in your firm will be handling the defense of Mr. Burns?"

"Considering the importance, I will personally oversee the defense strategy, but one of our partners will do the day-to-day due-diligence."

Moody smiled, knowing full well this statement meant the firm would be double billing for Sandifer's time and the attorney actually doing the work.

"Very well. Do you have a contract for representation ready?"

Sandifer nodded as one of the functionaries handed him a file folder. Extracting several pages from the folder, he handed them to Moody, who skimmed the document for the rate. Not that he cared, but was curious. He half grinned when he saw the fee the Washington, D.C., firm would bill Haylex Holdings: $1,000 per hour. Insane.

"I believe you will find this agreement spells out our responsibly for the defense of Robert Burns Jr. I'm told you possess Power of Attorney for the father in these matters. Is that correct?"

"Yes."

"Very well, if the agreement looks in order…" Sandifer handed Moody a pen, then sat back and waited.

Continuing to skim the document, Moody noted, in subtle legalese, the firm included an exit clause should they decide the case was unwinnable. Interesting. Wouldn't want to ruin a perfect winning streak.

With a flourish, Moody signed the document and handed it back to Sandifer.

"Excellent, we will get started immediately."

CHAPTER 25

Washington, DC

"I'll be here for a few more days."

Stephanie Kruger smiled, even though her husband could not see it. "That's fine. My sister will be here tomorrow. If you were here, you'd be bored listening to us."

"I would not."

Kruger secretly was glad to be gone. He liked his wife's sister, but when the two got together, mind-numbing boredom was his normal reaction.

"Sean, you are a horrible liar."

"I am not. I love it when your sister visits."

She laughed and was quiet for a few moments. "I'm worried about you."

"I'm in court or the Hoover Building. Not much can happen at either."

"Just be careful."

"I will."

They talked about other matters for the next thirty minutes before ending the call.

His next call was to Carol Welch for an update on the first appearance. She answered on the fourth ring.

"U.S. Attorney Welch."

"What happened today, Carol?"

"I was wondering when you would call. He was denied bail."

"Good. Did he have an attorney?"

"The attorney explained to the court he was temporary until the family could hire a local firm in Washington. He looked relieved he didn't have to defend him. Burns said nothing, only listened. One of our Assistant U.S. Attorneys handled the hearing and spoke to Burn's temp lawyer later."

"What'd he say?"

"Apparently, a gentleman by the name of Joel Moody is already here or will be sometime today. He has an appointment with the firm Rothenberg and Sandifer."

"Who are they?"

"High profile criminal defense attorneys. Their specialty is white collar crimes, but they've defended a few sexual predators over the years. They're very good and very expensive."

"Daddy can afford it."

"So I've heard."

"I've met Joel Moody. He's an ex-Seattle cop and now the Director of Security for Haylex Holdings. The father hired him for security during his Senate days."

"Oh?"

"I'm a little surprised about him being the representative. He doesn't like Junior."

"How do you know that?"

"Oh, let's just say he knows who Junior really is."

"Is he the witness who saved the intern?"

"Yeah."

"Oh, boy. What's going on, Sean?"

"I'm not sure. One thing bugs me about this case."

"What's that?"

"The ten-year gap between the missing women and the assault on the intern. It's extremely inconsistent."

"Maybe there are others you don't know about."

Kruger tilted his head in thought. "Possibly…"

"Back to Joel Moody."

"At one time, I considered him an inside source at Haylex Holdings. But, so far, he hasn't given us anything."

"Will he testify about the intern?"

He could hear Welch tapping a pencil or something on her desk. "Good question. Not sure."

"Very well. I'm late for an appointment and have to run. I'll give you a call when we know the arraignment schedule."

"Thanks."

The call ended, Kruger sat at the small desk in his hotel room. He pursed his lips and drummed his fingers on the faux wood surface. He dialed a number only he and one other person knew. JR Diminski answered the call on the third ring.

"How's our nation's capital?"

"It hasn't changed. I still hate being here."

"What's going on with Burns?"

"Denied bail and still locked up."

"That's good."

"I've got a question. When Moody supplied you with a path into the Haylex server, you told me it only worked temporarily, is that correct?"

"Yes."

"Huh."

"What are you thinking, Sean?"

"Moody may not be the inside source we thought he was."

"There's always that."

"He's here in Washington representing the father and hiring lawyers. From what I was told, he hired one of the best."

"Not surprising considering who his father is."

"I think I need to have a chat with him and figure out whose side he's on."

"Be careful."

"You sound just like Stephanie."

***

After calling Joel Moody and his call going straight to voicemail, Kruger left the hotel and drove to the Hoover building. With his credentials on a lanyard hanging around his neck, he went directly to the cubicle of Barbara Whitlock. She was on the phone, so he leaned against the frame of her cubicle wall.

"Yes, Agent, that is correct, I couldn't find any additional charges against the man." She paused. "You're welcome." After ending the call, she turned toward Kruger, crossed her arms over her chest, and smiled. "Couldn't stay away, could you? I didn't think you liked Washington."

"I don't, but I like you."

Barbara Whitlock was in her mid-to-late forties. She wore her dark hair long past her shoulders, and Kruger noticed a few gray strands intermixed with the dark brown ones. With an oval face and intense green eyes, she was an attractive woman. He noticed a picture on one of the cubicle shelves of her and her husband, Bob, dressed formally. They stood with a younger couple between them, one in a tuxedo, and the other in a wedding gown.

He pointed toward the picture. "When did your daughter get married?"

"Last summer. Bob and I really like him. He's an up-and-coming agent with the FBI."

Kruger nodded. "How's Bob?"

"Made Battalion Chief a year ago. I don't have to worry about him as much now."

"Glad to hear."

She cocked her head to the side and gave him a mischievous grin, her arms still folded comfortably across her chest. "What brings you to my little slice of paradise?"

"I need information."

"You always do."

He smiled. "This one could be a little tricky."

"You say that every time."

"You've heard the new senator from Washington State was arrested, right?"

"Only a hermit wouldn't know. It's the only thing everyone in this building is talking about. What about him?"

"I don't think this is his first time."

Her smile disappeared and she uncrossed her arms. "Coming from you, that's serious."

Nodding, Kruger continued, "I have reason to believe he may be a serial killer."

Whitlock just stared at him, waiting for him to finish his thoughts.

Looking at her again, his expression was grave, "I need to know if there are any missing person reports from the year 2003 to the present in the D.C. area and in the northwestern states of the U.S."

Her eyes widened. "I can guarantee there will be. Any additional criteria?"

"Women, eighteen to twenty-six, probably engaged in prostitution, and never found. Time frame will be between October and December of each year. And especially women who are tall, slender, with auburn hair."

"That is getting specific. Why the narrow time frame?"

"Just a hunch. Most serial killers have a pattern they follow."

She took a deep breath and let it out slowly. "That specific of a search could take a while."

"No problem. I just need it…" he paused, smiled, and glanced at his watch, "…before you go home."

Barbara Whitlock gave him her best you've-got-to-be-kidding-me look and crossed her arms again. "Really?"

"No, but I need it in the next day or so."

"That, my dear Sean Kruger, I can do. How long are you in D.C.?"

"At least until Friday."

"It's Wednesday. Check with me late tomorrow."

He smiled. "Thanks, Barbara."

As he walked away from Whitlock's desk, his cell phone vibrated. He glanced at the caller ID and accepted the call.

"Kruger."

"I see I missed a call from you, Agent Kruger."

"Well, Detective, I heard you were in town and thought I would invite you to dinner."

There was silence on the call.

"Not sure being seen with the investigator of Mr. Burns' son would be appropriate for either of us, Agent."

"You're probably correct. But I did want to thank you for pretending to help us at our last meeting."

There was another long silence. "Not sure what you're talking about."

"Sure you do. Who'd you tell about a possible computer hack?"

After another long pause, Kruger heard, "I'm staying at the Grand-Hyatt. There's a Starbucks next to the hotel. How soon can you be here?"

***

Kruger arrived twenty minutes before his appointment with Moody. He sat in the back of the coffee shop sipping on a plain black coffee, something he did not feel Starbucks did well. The purpose of arriving early was to observe patrons in the shop and determine whether someone was paying too much attention to him. Jimmie Gibbs and Sandy Knoll sat at a table in the front of the shop, having arrived ten minutes prior, and totally ignored Kruger.

Moody walked in five minutes before the agreed to time and frowned when he saw Kruger already there. After getting a coffee from one of the baristas, he sat down across from Kruger. "You got here fast."

"Traffic was light."

Nodding slightly, Moody took a sip of coffee. He looked at Kruger and asked, "Why would you think I told someone about the program I inserted?"

"The pathway allowed us access for less than an hour before it was shut down."

Moody studied his cup of coffee before he said anything.

"Huh." He took a sip. "Our IT department is good. Sorry."

Smiling slightly, the response confirmed Kruger's suspicions. "So, why are you here, Joel?"

"I was appointed by Mr. Burns to make sure his son doesn't go to prison."

Kruger nodded. "Or?"

"I'll no longer be employed by Haylex Holdings."

"Ahhh..." Taking a sip of his now cold coffee, Kruger glared at Moody and said dryly, "Thought you didn't like Junior."

"I don't. But I like being employed."

"That's good to know, Joel."

Kruger sat his coffee down, stood, and walked out of the Starbucks.

Gibbs and Knoll did not leave. Both remained in their chairs, Gibbs watching Moody's reflection in the front window. After several minutes, Moody stood and walked toward the exit.

Knoll spoke in a whisper, his right hand holding a coffee cup to his lips and obscuring his face. "Guy on your right, middle of the room, next to the wall."

"Got him."

"Tracked Kruger when he left, doing the same to Moody. Now he's getting ready to leave."

"Got a plan?"

"I'll follow Moody. You keep an eye on this guy."

"Sounds fun."

CHAPTER 26

Washington, DC

"He's three cars behind you. Do you see him?"

"Yeah, white Ford Fusion."

Kruger was on his cell phone with Gibbs. Despite his history of detesting FBI pool cars and renting Mustangs when in D.C., he was glad to be driving an agency vehicle tonight. It was an aging Dodge Charger with over a hundred thousand miles, but it gave him access to a radio.

"That's the one," Gibbs replied. "He's been with you since you left the Grand-Hyatt."

"He was in the Starbucks, middle of the room against the wall, right?"

"That's him." Gibbs was four cars behind the Fusion in a Chevy Equinox, his cell phone funneled through the vehicle's hands-free option. "What do you want to do?"

"Let's have a conversation with him."

"Love to. How?"

"I'll call in reinforcements; they're a mile behind us. Stay on the call."

"Got it."

Traffic on Suitland Parkway, at this time of day, was close to gridlock. The slow flow of cars and trucks suited Kruger's plan. Minutes ticked by, and traffic crawled forward. Ten minutes later, he noticed a black Chevy Suburban in his rearview mirror approaching the white Fusion on its right. Jimmie Gibbs' Equinox was also inching forward, positioning itself directly behind the target car.

He keyed the mic on the agency car, putting him in touch with the agents in the Suburban, "I'm going to slow down and let the car behind me pass. When it does, I'll stop, and we execute the plan."

"Roger, will follow your lead."

Slowing the Charger down allowed several of the cars between him and the Fusion to pass. Finally, the Toyota Camry behind him blasted its horn, found an opening in the right lane, and sped around on his right. As he passed, the Camry driver flipped Kruger the bird and sped on. The Fusion was now positioned directly behind Kruger, with the Suburban on its right, the Equinox hugging its bumper, and a guardrail on the left.

Kruger slammed on the brakes.

When the Charger skidded to a halt, the trapped Ford Fusion stopped just before colliding with the rear bumper of the Dodge. At the same time, the Suburban turned on its hidden emergency lights, stopping inches from the right side of the Ford. With Gibbs stopped against the rear bumper of the Ford, the driver had nowhere to go. He had just enough room to open the driver side door, which he kept closed for the moment.

Kruger drew his Glock, opened the door, and took a Weaver stance, his weapon pointed at the stopped Ford.

Gibbs exited the Equinox and stood behind the open SUV door, his Sig Sauer drawn and pointed at the driver's side of the Fusion. An agent in the black Suburban stood behind the engine compartment, his service weapon drawn and pointed at the car.

"FBI," Kruger yelled. "Out of the car now. Hands above your head."

The driver glared at Kruger, then shifted his attention to

the agent standing behind the Suburban's engine compartment. Finally, after looking back at Gibbs, he returned his focus to Kruger.

Cars jammed up on the freeway as drivers craned their necks to see what was going on. Keeping his Glock aimed at the Ford, Kruger moved so the Dodge's driver side door was between him and the man in the Fusion.

Kruger repeated his instructions to the driver.

Finally, the door slowly opened, and a hand emerged above it.

"Both hands where I can see them," Kruger yelled again.

Kruger heard Gibbs yell above the din of traffic moving in the opposite direction on Suitland Parkway.

"GUN!"

All three FBI agents opened fire on the man, who suddenly stood up above the roof line of the Ford Fusion, his hands holding a Springfield Armory XD pointed at Kruger. Shots rang out as his fingers pulled the trigger as fast as possible.

***

"You were lucky, Sean."

Kruger sat in a cubicle on the second floor of the Hoover Building, working on his report. Alan Seltzer stood in the entrance, leaning against the edge of the cubicle wall.

Not turning his attention away from his laptop, Kruger stopped typing.

"Is he alive?"

"Barely."

Kruger nodded.

"We found three bullets in the door you were standing behind."

"Don't tell Stephanie. She thinks I'm just doing paperwork and sitting in a court room."

"No problem. It was a righteous shooting. No need to worry."

"I'm not worried, it was righteous. What concerns me is the guy had no escape and still tried. Why?"

Seltzer crossed his arms over his chest. "He had something in his car," he answered slowly.

Kruger leaned back in the desk chair. He tilted his head slightly, "What?"

"A small Samsung tablet. The only information on it was a file with your picture and bio."

Silence was the response from the seated FBI agent.

Seltzer continued, "The ID on him was false, but fingerprints identified him as Yaakov Romanovich, born June 1, 1988, in Kiev, Ukraine. Parents, Stefan and Mariya, immigrated to the U.S. six months after the December 1991 fall of the Soviet Union. The family was granted citizenship in 2001. Yaakov joined the Army after high school and earned a dishonorable discharge after spending a couple of years in the brig for assault. The family never left New York City. The mother died in 2007 and the father in 2010. Our shooter has been picked up numerous times for assault and racketeering charges, but never convicted."

With no comment from Kruger, Seltzer stood straight and entered the cubicle, lowering his voice. "He fell off law enforcement radar for several years, then in 2012, an extortion charge landed him in a New York City jail. Charges were dropped when several witnesses recanted their stories."

Kruger gave Seltzer a half grin. "Gee, imagine that."

"NYPD believes he belongs to a Brooklyn-based Russian gang known for racketeering, murder-for-hire, smuggling, and human trafficking. They haven't had any contact with him since 2012 when he dropped out of sight."

"How'd you find all this out so fast?"

"Ryan Clark."

Kruger grinned. "I told you he'd be good."

Seltzer nodded. "Clark spent some time in New York with our organized crime group before transferring to Rapid Response. When he heard the name, he called a buddy with the NYPD, and they filled him in. Before we knew all of this, an inquiry was sent to Interpol to see if they had anything on him. Apparently he's well known to them as well."

"Oh?"

"Yeah, do you remember a Ukrainian cop named Brutka?"

"Sergey Brutka, yeah, met him in Paris. What about him?"

"He's with Interpol now. He wants a few moments with Romanovich, so he's catching a flight to Dulles. Should be here late tonight."

"Interesting. Why?"

"He's following up on an investigation."

"What kind?"

"Human trafficking."

"Huh." Kruger was quiet for several moments. "So how did Romanovich know I'd be at the Starbucks?"

"More to the point, who hired him?"

"Maybe Sergey can help find out."

"Is Moody under surveillance?"

"Sandy Knoll has that under control. He's being watched 24/7."

Seltzer nodded.

Kruger stared out of the cubicle past Seltzer. "Who's pulling the strings, Alan?"

"Good question."

"My bet's on Junior."

"Do you think he's the one paying to have the bodies disappear?"

Kruger nodded and stood. "Yeah, I do. I need to know what Junior's been up to since 2003, and I know just who to ask."

***

The meeting took place in Carol Welch's office, with Sean Kruger, Alan Seltzer, FBI lawyer Lorene Norton and Ryan Clark present. Carol finished reading the summary in front of her, took her glasses off, and looked at the others sitting at her conference table. "This is all very compelling, but I need admissible evidence or a judge is going to grant bail. All we have, for sure, is his DNA on the victim. He admits they had consensual sex, but claims she was alive when he left."

"Which is true, she was," Lorene said as she reviewed her notes. "But lab analysis found trace samples of the skin from his right hand in her facial wounds. He beat her."

"Coroner's report states she died of internal bleeding and head trauma," Kruger said.

"I understand, but Sandifer will concede all of this. His function right now is to get the suspect out on bail. Without being able to connect Burns with the Senate intern and the women on the college campuses, the judge will be compelled to grant bail."

Clark spoke next. "What about the attack on Sean?"

"Immaterial. At this point we don't have a direct connection between Burns and the Russian."

"What if we can get it?"

"Will it be admissible in court?"

Shaking his head, Clark frowned. "Not at this time, but we're working on it."

"Look, this is as frustrating to me as it is to you four. I can stall another day on the bail hearing. Get me the evidence, and I'll keep this clown in jail."

"We'll get it, Carol," Kruger's voice did not convey confidence.

CHAPTER 27

Washington, D.C.

"I appreciate you jumping on this so fast, Barbara."

"No problem, Sean." She handed him a half-inch thick eight-by-eleven envelope. "What you requested is there. I looked at all the data again and where we can place Burns. There are only a few cases that match the criteria you gave me."

"Really?"

She pointed at the envelope. "Between the years 2004 and 2014, I found seven cases with the same circumstances as the college students. Women last seen with a tall man with black hair and never heard from again."

"Huh." Kruger pursed his lips and studied the metal clasp holding the envelope flap closed.

"Those cases didn't receive the same media attention as the missing basketball players."

Kruger looked up. "I'm not going to like the reason, am I?"

"Probably not, I didn't. The women were on the fringe of society, drugs, prostitution, homelessness, plus numerous other reasons."

Opening the envelope, he glanced at the summary sheet

Barbara had prepared and asked, "Why these particular cases?"

"Once you read them, I think you'll understand why."

He turned his attention to her. "Give me the highlights."

"October 25, 2004, Rena Renfro, 23, Baltimore, disappeared from a bar in the downtown area. Last seen by her roommate talking to a tall slender man with black hair. They left together, and she's never been seen again."

Kruger stared at the summary page following Whitlock's narrative.

"November 1, 2005, Ruby Torres, 19, Richmond, a street walker, last seen getting into a Honda Accord driven by a man with black hair. Witnesses could not see his face. Her body has never been found."

Another nod from Kruger as he flipped pages.

"November 22, 2006, Carol Valenti, 17, run-away from Pittsburg staying at a halfway house in Baltimore. Several days before her disappearance, she told a friend she met a man who wanted to help her get her life together. A journal she kept mentioned a tall attractive man named Bobby who befriended her at the café where she worked part-time. Her parents have never heard from her and a body has never been found.

"October 1, 2009, Fredericka Casteel, 25, Newark, NJ, another street walker. Same scenario as the Torres woman, last seen getting into a car with a dark haired man. She's never been found."

Looking up again from the pages he was studying, "What about 2007 and 2008?"

Her head shook, "Nothing I can collaborate like the others."

He nodded and went back to following her narrative.

"December 13, 2010, Bellingham, WA. Keena Tamayo, 21, a waitress at an all-night diner was seen flirting with a tall slender man with black hair. He would arrive an hour before her shift ended. On the third night, they left together. She and the black-haired man never returned to the diner. She is still listed as missing."

Silence was Kruger's response.

"October 31, 2011, Carin Trudeau, 20, originally from Ontario, disappeared after her shift at a fast food restaurant in Spokane. Employees remember her talking to a tall man with black hair."

Kruger nodded, not looking up. "Where was Junior during those years?"

She smiled slightly. "Seattle. His father was spending more and more time at home during the last three years of his term. Senate records show he did not cast a single vote during the second halves of 2010 and 2011."

"Huh."

"Nothing in 2012, but that was the year the intern was assaulted, correct?"

"Yes."

"Okay, last one. November 15, 2013, Portland. Joselyn Medeiros, 18, street walker, same story as the two other ones about getting into the car of a man with black hair. Nothing since then I can collaborate."

Kruger returned the pages to the envelope. "I'll give these to Carol Welch and see what she can do with it. Anything else?"

Barbara nodded.

Tilting his head slightly, Kruger kept his attention on the analyst, "What?"

"I included documentation in the file about Robert Burns Jr.'s location during those timelines."

"And?"

"When his father was in Washington, so was he. When his father was in Seattle during the second half of 2010 and 2011 and after his term ended, so was the son."

"We knew that, but you're saying you have documentation?"

She nodded. "Dates, times and eyewitness accounts."

"What kind of eyewitnesses?"

"Newspaper and magazine articles with pictures.

Remember, his father was extremely rich and a senator through 2012. Seattle media coverage was plentiful and at times harsh when he wasn't in Washington. Then, starting in 2013, your suspect was considered one of the movers and shakers of Seattle society. Highly visible and voted most eligible bachelor in 2014 and 2015. It's all in the file."

Kruger smiled.

"Thanks, Barbara."

***

Carol Welch also smiled after reading Barbara Whitlock's research. "This is good, Sean. It sets up a pattern that, while not conclusive, allows us to at least offer probable cause to deny bail."

"Yeah, but once we get to court, it won't hold water."

"No, but we can delay, delay, delay, until you can get the evidence we need."

"How do we prove flight risk?"

She sighed. "We can't prove it, but we can suggest the possibility in several ways. Let's say you find a passport in another name, or if he has a residence in another country. We know he has the funds to travel, so a combination of these points and any others we can find would be a starting point for our argument."

Kruger nodded, almost absentmindedly, his thoughts miles away.

Welch was beginning to appreciate and like this FBI agent's thoughtfulness and measured manner. "What are you thinking?"

Blinking several times, he looked at her. "I have one other resource researching our Mr. Burns. I need to follow up with them."

Placing her elbows on the table and clasping her hands together, she rested her chin on them. "He was denied bail at his initial appearance because he didn't have a full time lawyer in place. Sandifer is pushing to move the arraignment up, and the earliest opportunity on the court docket is next Friday. Can you put together what we need before then?"

Standing, Kruger slung his backpack over his shoulder. He half grinned at the attorney, "I've got a good team. We'll have something for you."

As he walked out of the building, he pressed the call icon on his phone and waited. The call was answered on the third ring.

"I was just about to call you."

"What've you found?"

"Are you in a place where you can be on a computer?"

"No, just walking out of meeting with the Carol Welch. Why?"

"I need to show you something."

"I'll call you from the hotel."

"I'll be here."

***

"Notice the gentleman on the far right?" JR asked.

Kruger was staring at a picture on his laptop screen. "Yeah."

"Look familiar?"

"Looks like Burns."

"It is. Facial recognition software confirmed it's him."

"Where did you find the picture?"

"I used the Russian search engine Yandex. It's more popular in Russia than Google."

"Okay, but you didn't answer my question."

"I'm getting there."

Kruger didn't say anything.

"The picture was taken at a 2015 meeting of Russian high-tech companies announcing a joint venture in research to develop the next generation of artificial intelligence."

Again, Kruger did not comment.

"The text under the picture is in Russian. It identifies the individuals in the picture, all of whom represent Russian companies involved with the venture."

"Let me guess, it doesn't identify him as Robert Burns."

"Nope, it doesn't."

"What's he calling himself?"

"He's identified in the pictures as Mark Hoehmann."

"Huh."

"There's more."

"Okay."

"The article indicates he's a network engineer with a Haylex Holdings company called Genise Solutions, which just happens to be Haylex Solutions' European equivalent."

"So he does have a fake passport."

"Actually, the passport is real. The name on the passport is fake."

"How's that possible?"

"It's easy."

Kruger chuckled. "You love to torture me, don't you?"

"One of my personality flaws. I can't help it."

"What country?"

"Austria. It has loose citizenship requirements, as long as you have a lot of money and open a business there."

"But the passport is under a different name."

"Correct."

Pausing, Kruger blinked several times. "That's the key. He is a flight risk. With an Austrian passport under another name, he could disappear."

"One problem, Sean."

"What's that?"

"Where's the passport?"

Kruger didn't say anything for several moments. "When the Seattle field office searched his home, there was no mention of finding one, nor did our agents here in D.C. find one in his hotel room."

"It's either in a safe deposit box somewhere, or it's hidden in his house in Seattle," JR guessed.

"I would agree. Guess someone needs to search his house."

"Got anyone in mind?"

"Yes, I do. He loves that kind of stuff."

***

"What am I looking for, Sean?"

"He has an Austrian passport under the name Mark Hoehmann. We need the passport to show opportunity to flee."

Jimmie Gibbs' room was several doors down from Kruger's. He was packing his carry-on bag as they discussed his pending trip to Seattle.

"The Seattle field office didn't find other passports during their initial search of the house. But, in all fairness, they weren't searching for them."

Gibbs nodded. "You think he's hidden it somewhere?"

"Yes, I do. With the kind of money the family has, no telling what's hidden in his house."

Nodding, Gibbs stopped packing and looked at Kruger. "Who knows I'm going to Seattle?"

"Sandy and myself."

"Good, the fewer people who know the better. Gives me freedom and tactical options."

"Kind of what I was thinking."

Gibbs gave Kruger a grin. "Any restrictions on rules of engagement?"

"None, use your imagination." Kruger placed his hand on Gibbs' shoulder. "Jimmie, we know of at least seven women, six of whom have never been found. One of them is dead and we can assume the other six are as well. There is a possibility of seven others. We know of one who survived, but her life has been scarred forever. That's a total of fifteen. We have no idea of how many others. Find the passport, Jimmie. Find it and anything else you can to help us put this guy away. We have to stop him. Now might be our only chance."

***

Sergey Brutka shook Kruger's hand as he displayed a toothy grin.

"Agent Sean Kruger," he pronounced it KRUGAR with a hard G and R. "It has been, what, ten years?"

"At least, Sergey. It's nice to see you again. I understand you're with Interpol now."

"Yes, yes. They finally recognized my talents."

Kruger chuckled.

Brutka was tall for a Ukrainian, and the two men stood at eye level with each other. A massive callused hand engulfed Kruger's as they shook. The Interpol detective wore Levi Jeans, a beige cable knit turtleneck sweater and an oversized corduroy sport coat. With disheveled dark brown hair and an untrimmed drooping mustache, he was a throwback to fashion of the early 1980s. As he spoke, his bushy eyebrows danced with delight. "This is my first time in America."

"Really, but then I've never been to Ukraine."

"You would love it, Agent Kruger. It is beautiful country."

"I'm sure it is, Sergey."

Alan Seltzer and Ryan Clark watched as the other two men in the room greeted each other. Seltzer pointed toward a small round conference table occupying one corner of his office. "Agent Brutka, why don't we all sit down and you can tell us about your interest in Yaakov Romanovich."

Brutka nodded. After everyone was seated, Brutka slipped an envelope out of his sport coat inside pocket. He extracted a small stack of color pictures and placed them side by side on the table top. The pictures appeared to be either passport or driver's license photos. There were ten. All were of young women in their late teens or early twenties.

Kruger stared at the photos. Each of the women featured similar characteristics, blond hair, blue eyes, and haunting blank stares. He looked up at Brutka. "They're all missing, aren't they?"

Brutka nodded, but remained quiet.

Clark spoke for the first time. "How many of them have never been found?"

"None have been found."

Pursing his lips, Kruger picked up one of the pictures and studied it. "Over what time frame?"

"The first in late 2012. The young woman in the picture you hold disappeared in early 2017. They are from various countries in the Baltic Sea area, Sweden, Finland, Latvia, Norway, and Denmark. All were last seen in the company of a man matching the description of Yaakov Romanovich."

Kruger put the picture back on the table. "NYPD lost track of him in 2012. Was he overseas?"

"Yes. He is what you call person of interest."

Picking up one of the pictures, Clark looked at Brutka. "What were their occupations?"

Giving Clark a grim smile, Brutka leaned back in his chair and swept his hand over the pictures. "Prostitutes. Unsuccessful students, women on the edge of society. None were married, and all were barely surviving."

Clark put the picture back on the table. "Women who wouldn't be missed."

"Correct."

Seltzer looked over his glasses at the Interpol detective and asked, "Do you think Romanovich will tell you where they are?"

Brutka shook his head. "No, I doubt he knows. He is more of, what you call in America, a gopher. He doesn't think, he only does what he is told. I want the name of the man who told him."

Kruger turned to Seltzer. "What is Romanovich's condition?"

"Last I checked, stable."

Standing, Kruger looked at his watch. It was late. He turned his attention to Brutka. "Meet me at the hospital in the morning, we'll arrange a meeting."

CHAPTER 28

Washington, D.C./Seattle

The six a.m. flight out of Washington's Dulles International Airport made one stop in Detroit on its way to Seattle. Jimmie Gibbs bought a cup of coffee at a Dunkin Donuts kiosk across from the gate where his flight to Seattle would board. Because of the time difference in crossing the continental Unites States from east to west, even with the in-flight and layover time, he would arrive late morning in Seattle. Plenty of time to scope out his objective.

He sipped his coffee as he studied the faces of the passengers waiting for their flight to Seattle, looking for anyone who might be paying too much attention to his presence. He saw none. His eyes settled on a woman in her mid-to-late twenties, blond hair, with the physique of a swimmer.

The memories of his sister flooded back, causing him to close his eyes. He saw her as she was the day she disappeared. Two years his junior, she would have turned fourteen in a week. Long blond hair, blue eyes, tall, slender, athletic, and a better swimmer than he. Every swim coach she worked with said the same thing: she was destined for the Olympics. She would win gold someday.

He rubbed the back of his hand against his cheek, wiping away the stray trickle of water seeping from his eye. He blinked several times to clear the funk. As a former Seal and now an FBI agent, Gibbs kept his personal life private. Few individuals knew about his sister. There were a few high school buddies with whom he still maintained contact who knew, but no one else. Her disappearance, and later the discovery of her body, had literally killed his parents. His family was never the same.

He remembered his mother's faraway stare during the trial and his father's unrelenting depression after the suspect was found guilty, but only sentenced to twenty-five years. Both parents never stopped grieving.

Two years after the trial, his mother was diagnosed with advanced breast cancer and died several months later. His father withdrew from society and committed suicide six months after Jimmie joined the military. All of these events drove him to set swimming and endurance records during his Seal training days, records that still stood within the Seal brotherhood. He silently dedicated those records to his lost sister.

When his flight was called, he stood and walked toward the gate. He didn't know what he was going to find, but he was determined to make sure Robert Burns Jr. was never again allowed the opportunity to kidnap someone's daughter, sister, girlfriend, or wife. He would not allow the man to destroy another family.

***

Located in Clyde Hill, Washington, east of Seattle across Lake Washington, the house was high-end, but not estate level. During his initial reconnaissance of Robert Burns Jr.'s residence and surrounding neighborhood, Gibbs drove past the house twice. Making mental notes of landscaping and neighboring homes, he determined the best approach for his next visit. Driving away from the neighborhood, he made a cell phone call. Kruger answered on the second ring.

"Kruger."

"It's Gibbs. Just drove by the house."

"What do think?"

"It's doable. Do you have the details from the Seattle field office's search?"

"Yes, they didn't find any evidence of a hidden safe or hidey-hole."

"How thorough do you think they were, Sean?"

"Not sure, I'm not familiar with any of the agents out there."

"It's a big house. If there is a hidden safe, it might take some time to find. Possibly a few trips."

"Too risky. If you don't find anything on your first trip, we'll re-think our strategy."

"Do we know if he rents a safe deposit box anywhere?"

"If he does, it's under a different name. That's why I believe he has it hidden in the house somewhere."

"Can JR find out if the house is monitored by a security company?"

"I'll have him call you."

"Thanks."

An hour later, Gibbs received a call on his cell phone showing the number as Unknown. He smiled and answered.

"Jimmie, good idea about checking for security," JR told him.

"What'd you find?"

"House is monitored both electronically and physically by a company based in Tacoma."

"I don't suppose you found the security password for the house?"

"Yes, their computers aren't that secure. I've got it arranged so their system will not recognize the alarm being off from six p.m. tonight until six a.m. in the morning. Is that enough time?"

"Should be. What about this physical monitoring?"

"Scheduled for four in the afternoon and ten at night. Nothing else."

"I'll keep that in mind. What's the code?"

JR chuckled. "Real original, his birthday backwards." He recited the code.

"Anything else?"

"No, I'll monitor the company tonight for you. If I see somebody getting suspicious about the house, I'll call you."

"Thanks, JR."

"All part of the service."

Gibbs smiled and ended the call. He glanced at the time on his cell phone. He had time to check into his hotel, catch a few hours' sleep and be back in the neighborhood at midnight.

***

The dense landscaping surrounding Robert Burns Jr.'s house hid Jimmie Gibbs' approach to the rear entrance. A large deck surrounded by older cedar and fir trees was invisible to prying neighbors. Dressed in black military utility pants, a black long-sleeved t-shirt accented with a black tactical vest, black socks and Reeboks, black latex gloves, black watch cap, and his face smeared with military face paint, he was invisible in the darkness.

He gained entry to the house with the aid of a specially designed tool. A small Bluetooth earbud was snug in his right ear and connected to his cellphone in a pocket of his vest. The only weapons he carried were a Walther PPK .380 ACP pistol and a Gerber auto folding combat knife.

Inside, he paused next to the door and listened. The only sound was the ticking of a massive grandfather clock somewhere in the house. With night vision goggles in place, he quickly walked to the security system panel and punched in the code JR had given him that afternoon.

The house was dark, no night lights or automatically timed lamps were in this part of the house. From plans provided by

Kruger, he knew the house was bi-level. Located on the first level was a gourmet kitchen, a formal dining area, breakfast nook, living area, a master bedroom, a master bath, and a half bath near the front entrance. A three-car garage was located next to the kitchen, separated by a mudroom and laundry. Four bedrooms were upstairs, two on each side of the hall with Jack-and-Jill bathrooms between them.

After gaining his bearings on his position in the house, he headed toward the master bedroom to start his search. Time dragged as he checked the floor and walls of the walk-in-closet next to the master bedroom. Nothing. Following the same procedure, he checked all four upstairs bedrooms with the same result. Nothing.

He glanced at his black diver's watch and noted the time was three a.m. Three hours, and nothing for his labor. His next stop was the laundry room. Nothing there, either, nor did he find anything in the garage.

With only half an hour before his self-imposed exit time of five a.m., he stood in the middle of the kitchen and surveyed the room. On a hunch, he pulled the refrigerator away from the wall.

There it was.

A recessed wall safe with a number pad for entrance.

Reaching into one of the pockets on his utility pants, he extracted a small aerosol can and sprayed the keys. The residue left by the spray glowed brighter on certain keys. The numbers touched most often standing out with the night vision goggles. He noticed a similarity to the numbers of the security system and tried the same code. The door popped open.

Flipping his goggles up, he used a small mag light to peer into the dark interior of the safe. Passports, paper currency, handguns, and a bound book could be seen. Reaching for the passports, he flipped through them. Without hesitation, he retrieved his cell phone and hit a speed dial.

Kruger answered on the second ring.

"Did you find anything?"

"Four passports, all different names. There's cash, lots of it. Wait a second, I need to look at something."

Replacing the passports, he extracted the book and flipped through the pages.

"Ah, shit, he's got pictures, Sean."

Silence was his answer. Finally, he heard, "Where did you find them?"

"Hidden safe behind the refrigerator."

"Next question, how did you get it open?"

"Code is the same as his security system, the six digits of his birthday backwards."

"Close it up, and I'll send the field office back in with the excuse we know there is a safe in the kitchen somewhere."

"Got it."

"Jimmie?"

"Yeah."

"Well done."

***

Kruger ended the call with Gibbs and took a deep breath. An excuse was now needed to send the FBI back into the house to find the safe. He paced within the confines of his hotel room. Glancing at his watch, he noted the time in Springfield was a few minutes before seven. He dialed JR's number. The call was answered on the second ring.

"Did Jimmie find something?"

"Yeah, he did."

"Good or bad?"

"What we needed. I need something else from you."

"Name it."

"How hard would it be to find out if the safe Jimmie found came with the house or was installed later?"

All he heard was silence for almost a minute.

"Not sure. I can start with public records on when the house was built and by who. If it came with the house, it would be on the blueprints. If we get nothing there, I can go back into the security company's computer and see if they installed it."

"How long will that take?"

"Couple of hours."

"Do it."

CHAPTER 29

, D.C.
George Washington University Hospital

Having been recently moved from intensive care to a room designed for easy observation, Yaakov Romanovich was still connected to monitors and IVs. Brutka and Kruger stood in the hall looking through the windows at the sleeping patient. A uniformed guard sat in a chair in front of the room's entrance. Brutka stood with his hands behind his back as he studied the man in the bed.

"I wonder what his dreams are like."

Kruger smiled, "Probably nothing like yours or mine."

"Ahh... Probably not." Brutka did not divert his eyes. "When did the doctor say I could speak to him?"

"Anytime. He's been conscious for twenty-four hours. He's stable."

"Then I believe it is time to have a friendly chat."

Both men showed identification to the guard, who wrote their names in a notebook. As they walked in, Romanovich opened an eye and saw Brutka. He stiffened and closed his eye again. Kruger stood off to the side as the Ukrainian stood by the right side of the bed.

Brutka spoke in his native language, with Kruger catching

Romanovich's name at the end of the statement.

The patient shook his head.

Brutka turned to Kruger. "I asked him if he was Yaakov Romanovich. He shakes his head like we are stupid. As I suspected, he is not smart."

Turning his attention back to the patient, Brutka spoke in their native language again for a long time and then waited.

The man lying on the bed shook his head and said two words Kruger didn't understand.

Brutka chuckled and turned to Kruger to explain, "He is definitely not too bright. I explained why I was here and what information I needed. He is not being cooperative and thinks we should go away."

Kruger crossed his arms over his chest and leaned against the wall. He knew from their time together in Paris ten years ago that Brutka was a highly competent interrogator.

The conversation between the two Ukrainians continued for several more minutes as Brutka's voice grew stern. The wounded man commented less and shook his head rapidly after each question. Finally the Interpol detective pursed his lips and leaned closer to Romanovich's ear. Kruger could not hear the conversation, but the patient's eyes grew wide and the heart rate monitor showed a drastic increase in his pulse.

Brutka straightened and crossed his arms. He glared at the prone man.

Finally, Romanovich closed his eyes and spoke two words. "Dmitri Orlov."

Brutka smiled and motioned for Kruger to follow him out. When they were out of hearing range of the police officer guarding the door, he turned to Kruger. "Dmitri Orlov, have you ever heard of him?"

Kruger shook his head. "Should I?"

"No, I do not believe you would have an opportunity to know this man. He is well connected in Russia. Out of my reach, but maybe not yours."

"Explain."

Brutka did.

CHAPTER 30

Hoover Building
Twenty-Four Hours Later

Carol Welch walked into the conference room followed by two assistants. She nodded at the three FBI officials already in the room, Director Paul Stumpf, Deputy Director Alan Seltzer and Sean Kruger.

A white evidence box sat in the middle of the table.

As she sat, she looked at Sean Kruger. "Okay, what was the urgent summons all about?"

"Look in the box." Kruger stood and pushed the box closer to the District Attorney.

She removed the lid and glanced inside. Smiling, she lifted out four passports and flipped through each one. "My, my, I was hoping for one."

"Four, to be exact. The Austrian one is actually legit, the name isn't, but the passport is. The rest are as fake as the names."

She glanced back in the box and frowned.

"The book, what's in it?"

Director Paul Stumpf cleared his throat. "Robert Burns Jr.'s key to a prison cell."

She hesitated to touch it. Kruger smiled. "It's been

fingerprinted and all we found were his. You can look, but beware, the images are not pleasant."

She did not touch the book. "How many?"

Kruger's face was grim. "All six of the college women, others we knew about, many we didn't. There's a total of thirty. He's been at this a while."

"Are they identified in any way?"

Kruger nodded. "Dates and names. He was at least meticulous in his recordkeeping. This is a grim characterization, but the pictures appear to be trophies."

"How was the evidence recovered?"

"Lawful search of his property. First search revealed nothing, then a careful review of the home's blueprints revealed a built-in safe installed by the contractor when the house was remodeled ten years ago." His expression remained neutral. "With this information, the Seattle Field Office secured a second search warrant. Everything was by the book, Carol."

"Good." She hesitated for a second. "Does it give locations of the bodies?"

Seltzer gave Welch a frown, "For the first ten, yes. After that, no."

"When did he stop revealing the location?"

"1998. We are assuming this is the year he started paying others to hide the evidence."

Stumpf spoke next. "I've sent teams of FBI agents and forensic technicians to the locations identified. We will keep you informed on what they find."

She stood. "Gentlemen, I believe we've got him by the balls."

Kruger smiled.

Hesitating before she walked out of the meeting, she turned again to Kruger to ask, "Did the Interpol detective learn anything?"

Nodding, Kruger did not say anything.

Seltzer answered. "Uh… we're looking into it. As soon as we know more, we'll update you."

She frowned and then nodded.

***

"I've got a late afternoon flight out of Dulles, should be landing a little after nine." Kruger held the cell phone to his ear with his shoulder as he placed his computer in his backpack.

"Good. I've missed you." Stephanie's voice was cheery, and her tone made his homesickness worse.

"I've missed you too, Stef. Has your sister left?"

"This morning, lucky you."

"Not fair."

Stephanie Kruger laughed. "Kristin keeps asking when Daddy's coming home."

The words were like a punch in the stomach. He took a breath, "Tell her she can stay up until I get home."

"She'll be grumpy tomorrow."

"I'll take her to the park. That'll cheer her up."

They talked for several more minutes as he cleaned out the work space used during his stay in Washington. As he ended the call, Sandy Knoll walked up.

Kruger looked up at the big man. "I don't like the look on your face, Sandy."

"Got a problem."

"What?"

"Joel Moody checked out of his hotel suddenly this morning. The hotel told us he had a reservation for another five days. We followed him to the airport."

"Seattle?"

Knoll nodded. "What do you want to do?"

"Call the Seattle office and have someone there. They're embarrassed they missed the wall safe. They seem to be keen on helping now."

"Got it. One other thing."

"Yeah…" Kruger's tone was cautious.

"Jimmie stuck around a few days to watch Junior's house."

"And?"

"There's been someone there 24/7 since the news broke

about the evidence found in the wall safe. Gibbs indicated they aren't your usual rent-a-cops, they look like pros."

"Huh." He paused momentarily. "Jimmie would know."

"Yeah, he would."

"What's your gut telling you, Sandy?"

"We missed something."

"Mine's telling me the same thing. Let's keep Jimmie in Seattle a little while longer."

"He won't care. He likes the West Coast."

***

The first class seat on the United Airline flight to Seattle was next to the window. Joel Moody stared out at the passing clouds below the plane, his elbow on the armrest with his hand pressed against his chin. The sudden command by Robert Burns Sr. to return to Seattle unnerved him. The man's normal tone was always matter-of-fact with a touch of superiority, but on the call demanding his return to Seattle, Burns was on the verge of hysterics.

His only experience with this side of Burns was during the events surrounding the Senate intern. Moody feared with Junior now accused of being a serial killer, the ex-senator would become unhinged. He checked his watch. The flight time was seven hours, which meant he still had six before touchdown and his meeting with his boss. A passing stewardess stopped and leaned over.

"What can I get you, sir?"

"Scotch and ice, please."

***

Robert Burns Sr. paced as Allison O'Brien watched. It was approaching seven p.m., and the phone call from Joel Moody was the reason for the pacing. He would arrive within the next fifteen minutes.

"Robert, there is nothing you can do about Bobby. You've

always known he was a bit odd. We just didn't know the extent of it."

Burns stopped pacing and glared at his companion. "Moody should have told me about the safe behind the refrigerator. He's the one who approved the plans. He should have known Bobby would hide…" he paused for a second, "things in it."

"Did you know he had four passports?"

"No, I didn't," the elder Burns shook his head. "I knew about the dual citizenship in Austria, but thought he held it in his real name."

O'Brien stood and walked over to the man she had chosen to live with. With her hands on her hips, she stared at him, her brow furrowed and eyes narrow. "Be careful of what you say to the press, or anyone for that matter, about your knowledge of Bobby's indiscretions. It could come back on you."

She watched as his face grew crimson, and he set his lips tight together. His body tensed, his breathing rate increased, and he glared at her. Twenty seconds went by, their eyes locked together. She did not move, nor did he. Finally, he relaxed and took a calming deep breath. "You are, as always, correct, my dear. I'm not sure I can save him this time."

She placed a hand on his chest. "Robert, Bobby was lost a long time ago. You just didn't acknowledge it. There is no saving him. You need to divorce yourself and the company from him before he takes you and Haylex Holdings down, too."

Burns stared at her for a long time, his anger fading as the cold reality of the situation emerged. With his face returning to its normal mask of indifference, he nodded. "Yes, Allison, you are correct. In the morning, you will need to direct our corporate attorneys to remove Bobby's name from the company structure. We will need to issue a press release disavowing any knowledge of his actions and strongly condemning them."

"Very well. Should I make the statement from you?"

He shook his head, "No, make it from the Board of Directors."

She suddenly realized that Robert Burns Sr. was not done trying to protect his son.

***

Joel Moody was met by Allison O'Brien at the door. She smiled, "Come in, Joel. Robert is in his study. He's expecting you."

Moody nodded. This was not his first trip to the concrete monolith known as the Burns House. With as much dignity as he could muster, he walked toward the hall leading to the enormous room holding a library and a massive oak desk. He knocked on the closed door and heard, "Come in, Joel."

When he stepped in, Robert Burns stood and offered his hand. Closing the door, Moody moved quickly to shake his boss' hand and then returned to a parade rest, hands behind him.

"Can I get you a drink, Joel?"

"No thank you, sir."

The elder Burns returned to his chair behind his desk. "I'm sure you are wondering why I summoned you back from D.C. so fast."

"Yes, sir. The thought crossed my mind several times."

"With the new revelations about Bobby's past, the company has decided to cut all ties with him. How did you set up payment for the defense attorney fees?"

"Through Bobby's trust fund, per your instructions."

"Excellent."

Moody relaxed slightly. The conversation was going in a different direction, one he had not anticipated.

"Was bail arranged?"

"No, the hearing will be tomorrow. But from what I was told by his attorney late last night, it will probably be denied."

"I see."

The conversation stalled as Moody recognized a sudden

change in the demeanor of the elder Burns.

"Were you aware of the hidden wall safe?"

"I vaguely remember discussing it with the contractor and didn't find it all that unusual."

"Vaguely remember. I would think something that unusual would create a memorable moment."

Without knowing what direction the discussion was headed, Moody shrugged. "Like I said, I didn't find it strange and dismissed it."

Burns suddenly stood, placed his palms flat on the desk and leaned forward, his face crimson.

"You knew of Bobby's indiscretions and you didn't think it odd to have a wall safe installed behind a refrigerator?"

Moody frowned and stared back. "No, I didn't."

Bowing his head and sighing, the elder Burns shook his head. "Then I overestimated your abilities, Mr. Moody."

The final scotch and ice consumed an hour before touchdown kicked in. Moody crossed his arms over his chest and glared at his boss. "With all due respect, Mr. Burns, I was not hired to watch over and protect your son from himself. I was hired for corporate security. If my services are no longer needed, I will take my leave and bid you a good night."

Standing straight, Robert Burns returned the gesture and crossed his arms over his chest. "Your services…," a slight smile came to his lips, "…are still needed, Mr. Moody. More so than ever."

"Do you need me to return to Washington, D.C.?"

"No, communicate with the attorneys from here. Bobby is now on his own."

CHAPTER 31

D.C. Central Detention Facility
Washington, DC.

Jolene Sanders was three years out of Georgetown Law School and in her second year with Rothenburg & Sandifer. Twenty-nine years old, tall, slender with black hair worn short, she was a no-nonsense attorney with an attitude to match. Defending sexual predators was not one of the reasons she became an attorney. Robert Burns Jr. was, in her mind, the worst kind because he hid behind his wealth and used it to proclaim his innocence.

She waited in an interview room reserved for attorneys and their clients for Burns' arrival. Today was almost her last day with Rothenburg & Sandifer. Having learned she was assigned to the Burns case, she requested a meeting with Kyle Sandifer. The purpose of the meeting was to inform him she wished to be removed from the case, or she would tender her resignation.

"Yes, we assigned you to the Robert Burns Jr., defense, Ms. Sanders."

Jolene stared at the senior partner of the firm and tilted her head. "You are aware of my contract with this law firm, aren't you, Mr. Sandifer?"

"I am mindful of your stated desires, Ms. Sanders, but you are the best criminal defense attorney currently associated with our firm. We have plans for you. Plus this case will go a long way toward your becoming a partner."

This revelation gave her pause. She had only been with the firm for two years. Making partner normally took ten and sometimes longer. With the glut of attorneys in the Washington, D.C. area, it was not unusual for a ten-year associate to be terminated and another slid into their slot.

"How?" she asked.

"As you may be aware, Mr. Rothenburg is planning to retire in six months. I will be taking his position as managing partner, and another senior partner will take my place. This will leave a hole in our partnership ranks." He paused and gave her one of his signature jury persuading smiles. "Please don't take offense to this next comment, but we need to add some diversity to our partnership structure."

Jolene's left eyebrow rose, and she remained quiet.

"Ms. Sanders, your skills as defense attorney are what is important to us. I could care less about the fact you are a female whose parents emigrated from Jamaica. Lobbying still comprises the bulk of our revenue, but we see building our criminal defense team as a growth opportunity. You would be in charge of this endeavor."

"I'm not sure what to say, Mr. Sandifer."

"No need to say anything at the moment. I understand your repugnance about defending this individual. If his father wasn't the thirty-ninth richest individual in the world, I would have turned it down. The son is offensive to me as well. But defending him will generate a seven figure income for the firm. Possibly eight figure with appeals."

"Really?"

"Yes, as much as we would like to remember our naïveté from law school about doing the greater good, the reality is we are a business. A business that must generate revenue. Robert Burns Jr. is a cash cow we cannot let slip through our fingers."

She smiled and shook Sandifer's hand.

So here she was, her first meeting with Burns.

When he was led into the room, his shackles were attached to the rings in the floor and table, severely limiting his range of movement. The two jailers looked at her, she nodded, and they left the room, closing the door behind them.

"Who the hell are you?" Burns' demeanor was immediately defensive.

"I am your attorney, Jolene Sanders."

"I don't give a fuck what your name is. You are not my attorney. You're too young, a girl, and you're black."

She smiled and clasped her hands in front of her. "And you, sir, are accused of being a serial killer."

"Lies. I've been set up."

"Really, by who?"

"Joel Moody. He put that stuff in the safe, not me."

"Oh, is he the one who killed Linda Ramos."

"Who?"

"Linda Ramos, the woman at the Motel 6 with your sperm on her."

"I didn't kill her. The sex was consensual. Moody followed me in and killed her. She was alive when I left room."

Sanders frowned. "This isn't going to work if you lie to me, Mr. Burns."

"I don't want it to work, I want another attorney."

"Can't have one. I'm the best in D.C., and your best bet to beat death row."

Burns stared at her. "Death row? What do you mean?"

"With all of the evidence found in the safe and the murder of Ms. Ramos, the U.S. District Attorney is calling for the death penalty."

"Like I told you before, the stuff found in the safe was planted."

"What about the four fake passports? Were those planted also, Bobby?"

His face grew crimson as he stared at the attorney. "My name is Robert."

She opened a file and took out four photographs. "We received this in a discovery package from the U.S. Attorney's office this morning. Each picture is of a passport found in your wall safe. Your picture is in all four. However, your name is not."

Burns said nothing.

"Unfortunately, Bobby, the existence of these passports allow the prosecution an argument that you're a flight risk."

Still no response came from Burns.

Replacing the pictures back in the file, Jolene removed another photograph.

"Recognize this?"

Burns stared at the picture, but continued to be silent.

"Did you know the FBI has ten teams searching the locations identified in this book? What are they going to find, Bobby?"

"I don't know. I've never seen it before."

She took a deep breath and let it out slowly.

"Really. This was found in your hidden safe along with the passports."

"The passports are mine, but I've never seen the book."

"Your fingerprints are on it."

"Not possible. I've never touched it."

"The book identifies where some of your victims are buried. Are they going to find bodies, Bobby?"

"How many times do I have say this, counselor, I don't know anything about the book. And I certainly don't know about any bodies."

Jolene Sanders sighed and started replacing everything back in her briefcase. "I will have to get back to you on this, Mr. Burns. Your lack of cooperation is disappointing."

"I'm not lying about the book. Look at it, it's the same type of three ring binder we use at the office. I could have touched it there and then someone put all that crap in it, but it's not mine."

"If you want me to use that as a defense, it will be complicated. The passports you admit to, correct?"

He nodded.

"But you deny knowing about the book."

"I've never seen it before."

"Very well, I will be in touch, Mr. Burns."

***

Most of the associates were gone for the evening, which made the building oddly quiet. Not the normal buzz of the hectic schedules maintained by attorneys at Rothenburg & Sandifer. Kyle Sandifer sat in his office chair, his back to the office door, a tumbler containing a few ice cubes and three fingers of Johnny Walker Black in his hand. He stared at the night sky of D.C., his thoughts miles away. He heard a knock from behind and swiveled around to see who was there.

Joseph Rothenburg leaned against the door frame. "Did she buy it?"

"Yes, I believe she did."

Rothenburg walked into the office and went straight to the mahogany cellaret on the far wall of Sandifer's office. He found a tumbler, grabbed a few cubes from an ice bucket, and poured three fingers of Maker's Mark bourbon. Once the drink was complete, he sat in a wing chair in front of Sandifer's desk, crossed his legs, and smiled. "Good."

"She's an ambitious young attorney, Joseph, and she's good."

"She'll eventually make partner somewhere. Just not with us."

Sandifer nodded. "Have you heard from the investment firm?"

"That's what I wanted to talk to you about."

"I'm listening."

"Landing the Burns case could not have happened at a better time. How much are you projecting our billings to be?"

"Minimum eleven to twelve million this year alone. It will be Ms. Sander's only case. "

"Huh, that much?"

Nodding again, Sandifer took a sip of his scotch.

"We're effectively billing $2,000 an hour with the agreement signed by the client's representative. As the senior attorney on the case, I'm billing the same amount as Ms. Sanders. This case could go on for years, with appeals and delays."

"Better than I projected. It will help the firm's valuation when we close the sale."

"When?"

"Six months."

"Have you informed the other senior partners?"

"Townsley knows and so does Murphey. Both are on board. They're tired of D.C. and ready to retire somewhere warm with a slower pace."

"As am I." Sandifer was quiet, studying the sweat beads forming on the outside of his tumbler. "This case will make her reputation in this town, Joseph."

Rothenburg nodded thoughtfully. "Yes, if she plays her cards right, the new owners will make her an offer."

"I hope so, she's a better attorney than I ever was. She'll be mad we didn't tell her."

"We're not telling any of the associates or the junior partners."

"Still…"

"It has to be that way, Kyle. Terms of the sale."

"Yes, I know."

"On to more important matters. Have you talked to Robert Burns Sr.?"

"No, only his representative, Joel Moody."

"I spoke to several individuals with knowledge of the case today."

"Oh…" Sandifer took a sip of scotch. "At the Hoover building?"

Rothenburg nodded. "Were you aware they had agents at ten locations where bodies are supposedly buried?"

"That information was not in our discovery packet."

"If they find bodies, it will be hard to keep him off death

row."

"Yes, but it will increase the number of appeals to be filed."

Rothenburg chuckled, drained his glass, and stood. "Kyle, the longer the appeal cycle, the more potential revenue we can project for valuation. Six months will go by in a flash, then you and I can get the hell out of here."

CHAPTER 32

Springfield, MO

Kristin ran to her daddy as he walked into the kitchen from the garage. Kruger scooped her up and wrapped his arms around her, being careful not to squeeze too hard. She squealed with delight as he twirled her around.

"Where were you, Da-dee?"

"I had to catch a bad man, Kristin."

"Did you catch him?"

"Yes, Kristin, we caught him."

"Good." She hugged her father's neck and then put her head on his shoulder.

Stephanie stood off to the side, smiling. "She's been checking the garage every five minutes to see if you were home."

Kruger started to say something, but his throat constricted. Blinking rapidly, he leaned his head against his daughter's and closed his eyes.

"I'm home now."

Kristin was asleep before he could get halfway through her favorite story. He placed the book on her nightstand, straightened the blankets on her bed, and closed the door, leaving it slightly ajar. Before he and Stephanie went to bed, he would open it all the way.

As he unpacked his travel bag, Stephane sat on the bed and watched him. "Well?"

He looked up. "Well, what?"

"You didn't tell me what happened."

"Of the ten sites, eight produced bodies. Plans are to expand the search area at the other two sites."

"Then you have him."

Taking a deep breath, he nodded. "Yeah, we have him. Maybe."

"What do you mean, maybe?"

"Money, lawyers, more money, you name it. This guy's father worries me."

"Why's that, Sean?"

Looking at his wife, he gave her a grim smile. "I'm not able to put my finger on it yet, but something about finding the book makes me nervous."

"Uh-oh."

"Yeah."

"Why?"

"I don't know, that's the problem. To me it just felt too…" He paused and furrowed his forehead, "convenient. The guy goes to all the trouble to hide the bodies, yet he leaves this book in a wall safe with evidence he did it. I don't know. Maybe I'm giving him too much credit."

She stood and walked over to where he stood. "Sean, think about it for a few moments."

"I have been."

"No, think about it from his side. Why would he keep pictures?"

"Trophies. A reminder of what he feels he's accomplished. It's a way of reliving the moment. But…"

"Go on."

"There is something about this one that bugs me. I just can't figure out what that something is."

"Let's get ready for bed; you look tired. Bet you haven't slept well, have you?"

"Not really."

"Maybe you can think clearer in the morning."

***

The digital clock on his nightstand read 4:12, two minutes later than the last time he glanced at it. Sleep had come easy the night before, but now, six hours later, it was elusive. His conversation with Stephanie as he unpacked played in his mind over and over. There was something there, yet just beyond his grasp. Stephanie lay asleep next to him, her gentle, rhythmic breathing a sound he missed when away from her. Normally the sound acted like a sedative, helping him get him back to sleep. It wasn't working this morning.

As quietly as possible, he got out of bed and walked down the hall to his office. Before turning on his desk lamp, he closed the door. When he arrived home the night before, he placed his backpack on his desk chair and left it for the next day. Removing his computer and placing the bag on the floor next to the desk, he opened his laptop. While it booted up, he stared at the screen as it showed the progress of activation. When ready, he opened a file and started to read.

Leaning back in the chair, his left elbow was on the armrest, the hand supporting his chin. His index finger moved slowly across his lips as he moved the mouse with his right hand. The file was his official report written after his investigation of the abduction and disappearance of the female college students. Even though he had read it dozens of times, each time through the report sparked new questions. On his second reading, he stopped and tilted his head to the side. A question he had not considered before stared him in the face. He read the passage again and took a deep breath. Glancing at the clock in the lower right corner of his computer, he reached for his desk phone.

***

Teri Monroe, PhD, MD, and longtime friend of Sean Kruger, was now the Director of the FBI Forensic Science Division. She answered on the fourth ring.

"Monroe."

"Teri, it's Sean Kruger."

While he couldn't see it, Teri smiled. "Sean Kruger, I haven't spoken to you in—how long?"

"It has been awhile, Teri." He heard a noise in the background he couldn't place. "I hope I didn't wake you."

"Nonsense, I was just about to step into the shower." The noise stopped. "I thought you retired?"

"Urban legend."

She chuckled. "So, what do I owe this early morning phone call to?"

"The Robert Burns case."

"How are you involved?"

"I'm leading the investigation."

"I heard that, but thought it was a rumor."

"No, it's me."

"What can I do for you?"

"Has your team identified any of the bodies found?"

"As of last night, no."

"Anything you can tell me?"

"Without the report in front of me, not much. Except the ones found were all female. Small females."

Kruger frowned. "Kids?"

"No, mature skeletal structures. While the DNA analysis will take a while to confirm our assumptions, skeletal and skull structure suggest the bodies are of Asian descent."

"Huh."

"Do you want me to call you after I clean up and can get to my computer?"

"That would be great, Teri."

An hour later, Kruger listened as Monroe briefed him on what the forensic teams found.

"Instructions on where the bodies were buried led us to eight at present count. All were located in the northwestern states of Montana, Idaho, and Oregon."

Kruger used Google Maps to zero in on the area. "How far from Seattle?"

"Good question. None were more than four hundred miles away."

"A hard one-day round trip, but doable."

"That was our conclusion as well."

"So your team believes these women are Asian?"

"They do."

Taking a deep breath, Kruger let it out slowly. "If they were part of a human trafficking network and illegal, you won't be able to ID them."

"Trust me, that thought has occurred to us."

"I take it nothing personal was found with the bodies."

"No, not even clothes."

"Really?"

"We know Burns is an intelligent individual, but it's almost like a cop buried them. He knew not to leave anything that would help with identification."

Kruger could almost hear the pieces of the puzzle fall into place as they coalesced into a picture he previously did not see.

"Teri, would you call me if you find the other two bodies? I want to physically see the site."

"You got it, Sean. I'm supposed to get an update mid-morning. I'll call you."

"Thanks, Teri."

***

The call came at 11:13 Central Time. Kruger was at his desk and answered on the second ring. "Kruger."

"Sean, it's Teri. They found another one."

"Where?"

"Mount Hood National Forest, about fifty miles east of Portland."

"I'll call the travel desk and get a flight."

"No need. I just spoke to the director. An agency plane will pick you up in two hours. They can have you in Portland by late afternoon."

Smiling, Kruger appreciated the offer. "That sounds real good, Teri. I'll have to thank Paul later."

The call ended and he sat back in his chair. His go bag was always ready, so packing wasn't an issue. He made another call.

"Gibbs."

"Jimmie, it's Sean. How fast can you get to the Portland airport?"

"About three hours, why?"

"I need you to pick me up. We have a crime scene to examine."

"Text me your arrival time. I'll be there."

***

Kruger and Gibbs stood outside the yellow tape, putting covers over their hiking boots and slipping latex gloves on their hands. The terrain was rugged and the tree canopy thick. Bright halogen lamps illuminated the scene, allowing them to examine the site even though it was approaching 9 p.m.

Kruger looked at the site supervisor, a young forensic technician from San Francisco.

"How deep was the body?"

Raetia Tom was in her early thirties with black hair worn bundled tight under her FBI cap. Her brown eyes were almond shape, similar to JR Diminski's wife, Mia. Her demeanor was professional, but when she looked at Gibbs, it softened.

"About six inches of dirt, with twenty plus years of decomposing leaves increasing the depth slightly and helping hide the body."

Gibbs looked at her, an expression of surprise on his face. "You think she's been there twenty years?"

She nodded. "Probably twenty-one, she's the last one

identified in the Burns' notebook. Plus, there isn't any soft tissue remaining. Once we get her to the lab, we'll know for sure."

Nodding, Kruger looked toward the open grave site.

"May I look?"

"Come on."

Kruger walked cautiously toward the excavation site and stopped several feet away. The skeleton was curled into a fetal position, allowing the grave to be small.

"How did you find her?"

"Ground penetrating radar. The information we were given about the body was at least one hundred meters off."

Gibbs knelt down to take a closer look. He stayed in the position for a solid ten minutes while Kruger walked to the other side of the grave. He too knelt next to the skeleton. Gibbs pointed to a spot on the skull.

"Raetia, is that what I think it is?"

"Yes, blunt force indentation of the pterion. The blow probably ruptured the middle meningeal artery, causing an epidural hematoma. But since there is no soft tissue remaining, it will be hard to determine exactly if that was the cause of death or a posthumous injury."

Kruger remained quiet as he examined the burial site. In the bright illumination of the halogen lamp, he saw something clutched within the skeletal hand under the body. He pulled a small mag light out of his jacket pocket and trained the beam on the hand.

"I have something here, Raetia."

She moved next to Kruger and bent down. "Looks like a small pendant."

"Yeah, could you have your team get that for us?"

She nodded.

Thirty minutes later, Kruger sat in Gibbs' rental car, looking at the small pendant in a plastic evidence bag. There was an inscription on one side that was hard to make out. Holding the object at a slight angle allowed him to see it better.

Gibbs sat next to him, his hands on the steering wheel. "Can you make it out?"

"No, looks like logograms."

"Let me see."

Kruger handed the bag to Gibbs, who studied the pendant at various angle toward the light of the car interior.

"Yep, it's Chinese."

"Can you read it?"

Gibbs smiled at Kruger.

"It's a name."

CHAPTER 33

Portland, OR

With his shoulder pressing the cell phone against his ear, he studied the pendant, still in its official evidence bag. While he and Gibbs checked into a hotel and got a fitful night of sleep, the pendant had been examined and fingerprinted by the Portland FBI Field Office. They were in luck. A partial print was pulled from the pendant. Whose print it was remained a mystery, but Kruger was optimistic it was the victim's.

"JR, Peng My-lai is the name on the pendant. Her age was probably early to mid-twenties when she died in 1997."

"Kind of a needle in a haystack search, Sean."

"I understand, but if I have the Bureau do it, I'll still be waiting for an answer a year from now. You can do it faster."

"Okay, I'll start with missing person reports and newspaper reports from the upper northwest area. I'll include Oregon up through British Columbia. What kind of a timeline do you want?"

"Try 1990 to 1997. Not sure how many you will get, but it might give us a starting point."

"Got it. I'll call you when I have something."

Kruger turned to Gibbs, who was standing at the cubicle

entrance.

"What's next?" Gibbs asked.

"I think we need to pay Mr. Joel Moody a visit."

Gibbs smiled. "You thinking the same thing I'm thinking?"

Nodding, Kruger gave Gibbs a crooked smile. "Maybe. Something's not kosher about him."

"I think he's a lying sack of shit."

Kruger grinned.

***

The phone call came when they were twenty miles south of Olympia. Kruger answered on the second ring.

"Kruger."

"You were correct to assume the name was important."

Recognizing JR's voice, Kruger smiled. "Tell me."

"The name on the pendant was the woman's daughter. Peng My-lai is a twenty-seven-year-old high school teacher in Yakima. Her mother disappeared when she was seven."

Kruger was silent. "How did you find her?"

Gibbs shot a quick glance at the senior FBI agent and then returned his attention to the road.

"Most daily newspapers have gone digital over the past two decades, and their archives are also digital. I used one of my snooper programs. It got a hit in the archives of the *Tacoma News Tribune* about the disappearance."

Feeling a jolt of excitement, Kruger extracted a notebook from the backpack on the floor board in front of him. Pressing the phone to his ear, he said, "Give me the details."

"She teaches mathematics at West Valley High School, 9762 Zier Road in Yakima. Her Facebook profile indicates she's single and lives in an apartment complex on 72nd Avenue."

"Boyfriend or roommates?"

"Not according to her Facebook profile."

Kruger glanced at his watch and asked, "It's 10 a.m. here.

How far are we from Yakima?"

There was a brief pause and then JR returned, "About three hours."

"I'll have the Seattle field office contact the school and ask what would be a good time to talk to her today."

"I'll keep searching for information on the mother."

"Sounds good. Thanks, JR."

***

Having the Seattle field office secure an appointment with Peng My-lai reduced the tension of two FBI agents appearing at the school. They were offered use of the principal's office after arriving. Kruger also requested a school counselor or close friend of the woman's to be in attendance, mainly due to the nature of their discussion.

Thirty minutes after school was dismissed for the day, Peng My-lai opened the door to the principal's office and walked in. She was a petite woman, five feet tall, with black hair flowing midway to her back. Her brown eyes surveyed Kruger and Gibbs with a reserve bordering on suspicion. She was followed by an older woman in her mid-forties.

Kruger started the conversation. "Ms. Chang?"

The woman nodded.

"My name is Sean Kruger and this is Jimmie Gibbs. We're both Special Agents with the FBI."

This revelation startled the woman standing next to Peng My-lai.

After studying Kruger for a few moments, she nodded and asked, "Is this about my mother?"

Kruger nodded.

"She's dead, isn't she?"

Nodding again, Kruger gestured for her to sit down at a small conference table in the corner of the office.

After everyone was seated, Kruger tilted his head slightly and asked gently, "Did you believe she was alive, Ms. Chang?"

The woman shook her head, visibly relaxed, and clasped her hands in front of her.

"No, I've always known she was dead, but when you don't have a body to bury, there's always a chance. Where was she?"

The older woman placed her hand on Peng's shoulder, preparing for the news.

Gibbs answered. "Ms. Chang, she was found in a shallow grave fifty miles east of Portland. She had a pendant grasped in her hand with your name on it."

"I gave that to her for Christmas. She disappeared the next fall. How long was she there, Agent?"

"At least twenty one years."

Peng nodded. "I'm not surprised."

Kruger frowned. "Why is that, Ms. Chang?"

"My mother had an adventurous streak in her, Agent Kruger. She took a lot of chances she should not have taken."

"Why?"

"I don't know, I was young at the time. I remember a lot of strange men came around. I also remember policemen coming by on occasion."

"Where did you live at the time?"

"Seattle."

Both Gibbs and Kruger stiffened. Gibbs spoke first. "You said policemen came around, why?"

"I never knew for sure, but my aunt always thought there were drugs involved. I don't believe it was. Now that I am older I believe it was something else."

Kruger spoke in a soft voice, "Sex?"

She took a deep breath, let it out slowly, and nodded. "I can remember many times a man would visit, and my mother would put me to bed. A few hours later, I would hear him leave our apartment."

Silence filled the room as her gaze concentrated on the ceiling. Tears welled up in her eyes. "After Mom disappeared, I lived with my aunt and her husband."

Gibbs started to say something, but Kruger smiled at him

and slightly shook his head.

"I've had to live with the fact I never knew who my father was and that my mother disappeared when I was seven. Do you know how embarrassing that is for a child?"

In a gentle voice, Kruger replied, "No, I don't."

"Well, I was determined not to follow in her footsteps. I worked my way through college and now I have a good career. I'm sorry if I don't cry about her. It's been a long time, and she chose her own path."

"I can appreciate that, Ms. Chang. What we are trying to determine is who might have abducted her."

"One of her guests, I suppose."

"Possibly, however, we believe she may have been the victim of a serial killer now in custody. We are trying to piece together who she might have had contact with on the day she disappeared."

Peng stared at Kruger for several moments, not speaking. Finally she said, "How many victims?"

"We've found nine victims so far. There are more, we just haven't found them."

Her eyes grew wide, and she grabbed the hand of her friend. She sat quietly for a while. Kruger did not say anything.

Finally she relaxed and sighed. "I remember the day she disappeared, a policeman visited."

"Was he in uniform?" Gibbs asked, leaning forward.

She shook her head, "No, coat and tie."

"Can you remember what he looked like?"

"No, but I do remember he had black hair."

***

Neither man spoke during the first thirty minutes of the drive to Seattle. Gibbs broke the silence. "What color of hair does Moody have?"

"Not sure, he shaves his head."

"Exactly. He might have black hair."

"He might," Kruger nodded. "His eyebrows are dark. We need more information about his tenure with the Seattle Police Department. Did he leave on his own, or was he asked to leave?"

"Don't know. But I know someone who might be able to tell us."

Looking over at the younger man, Kruger smiled. "Who?"

"A guy I served with in the Navy is an officer with the SPD."

"Call him."

***

"It's good to see you again, Eric." Jimmie Gibbs shook the hand of a tall man wearing the navy blue uniform of the Seattle Police Department.

"Good to see you too, Jimmie. So you're with the FBI?"

"Rapid Response Team." Gibbs nodded. "This is Special Agent Sean Kruger."

Kruger shook the man's hand, but stayed quiet as the two old friends talked and he studied the police officer. Eric Chavez was several inches taller than Gibbs. Where Gibbs was wiry, Chavez was muscled like a body builder. With short brown hair, green eyes and a handsome face, he projected the image of a police department recruiting poster.

Having met the FBI agents in the parking lot of their hotel, the officer was leaning against the front driver side fender of his Ford Police Interceptor SUV.

"Moody left before I joined the SPD. After you called, I asked around. Not too many guys would say much. I don't think anybody cried about his departure, at least that's what I surmised."

Gibbs frowned. "Anybody give you a reason?"

Shaking his head, Chavez didn't answer right away. "Let put it this way, no one was surprised the FBI was interested in him."

Kruger frowned and stiffened. "Did anyone explain?"

"The only guy who made a comment said, and I quote, 'Maybe the pervert finally got caught,' but that's all he would say."

Kruger crossed his arms and frowned. Gibbs gave his friend a grin. "Think any of those guys would talk to us?"

"Doubtful," Chavez shook his head. "From the reception I got by just asking, Moody is persona-non-grata around the department. The less said the better."

They spoke to Chavez several more minutes before he drove off. Gibbs turned to Kruger. "What do you think?"

"We need to have that chat with Moody. He lied to me."

"Where?"

"I know where he'll be first thing in the morning. How do you like your coffee?"

CHAPTER 34

Seattle, WA

Kruger sat at the same table in the same Starbucks where he met Moody several weeks earlier. Jimmie Gibbs occupied a table within eavesdropping distance. When Moody saw Kruger, he hesitated, and looked back out the entrance. He returned his attention to the FBI agent and walked closer to the table.

"What do you want, Agent?"

"You lied to me, Joel. I don't like people lying to me, especially ex-cops."

His expression, neutral and uninterested, did not change. "Not sure what you're talking about. I've never lied to you, Agent Kruger."

"You didn't tell me about the wall safe."

"Why would I tell you about the wall safe? I barely remembered it and certainly didn't know what was in it."

"Sit down."

"Can't, I'll be late. Besides this conversation is over." He started to walk toward the barista station.

"The book gives the location for ten bodies. We've found nine of the ten."

Moody stopped, but did not look at Kruger. Gibbs moved

over a table.

"We will need to use DNA to identify eight of them, and once we do, those families will have a little closure."

Turning to look at Kruger, Moody's nostrils flared.

"I will repeat myself, Agent Kruger. I didn't know about the book."

"SIT DOWN."

Moody sat across from Kruger. Gibbs moved to the adjacent table and positioned himself behind Moody, who turned to look at the newcomer.

Kruger nodded in Gibbs' direction, "Joel Moody, meet Special Agent Jimmie Gibbs. Jimmie is a retired Navy Seal."

Gibbs just stared as Moody turned back to Kruger. "Where's this going, Agent?"

"Not sure if you picked up on what I said early, but we identified one of the bodies. One that disappeared in 1997."

Moody remained quiet.

Holding the pendant up, still in a plastic evidence bag, Kruger showed it to Moody. "Do you recognize this, Detective?"

Frowning, Moody snorted, "No, should I?"

"The pendant has the victim's daughter's name engraved on it. It was grasped in the dead woman's hand. We found the daughter who identified the pendant as her mother's."

"Who is she?"

Shaking his head, Kruger smiled.

"Nice try."

Gibbs leaned over and whispered, "The daughter told us the last person she saw her mother with was a policeman who didn't wear a uniform."

Moody twisted in his chair to glare at Gibbs.

Kruger picked up the questioning. "What color is your hair, Detective?"

Whirling back around, the ex-cop stood suddenly. "Any further discussion will need to involve the company attorney, Agent. Good day."

Moody walked quickly toward the exit and left.

Gibbs smiled. "He forgot his coffee."

"Yeah, I noticed."

"Bet he never comes back to this Starbucks again."

Kruger chuckled.

"Probably not."

***

Two hours later, Joel Moody sat in front of Robert Burns Sr.'s desk and summarized the encounter with the two FBI agents. He conveniently forgot to tell his boss this was the second meeting at the coffee shop.

When the narrative was completed, Burns stood and started pacing.

"I didn't know about the book either, Joel. Did you talk to Bobby about it?"

Shaking his head, Moody did not verbally respond.

Burns stared at his security chief. "Why not?"

"You recalled me to Seattle, Mr. Burns. I didn't have the chance."

"And you're saying you didn't know about the book either."

"No, sir."

Burns was quiet, and the pacing resumed. Moody sat and watched the man move from one side of the room to the other and repeat the process.

The silence was broken when he stopped next to his desk. "This will complicate Bobby's defense. Is there a way of claiming the book was planted by someone else?"

"I don't see how. I called his attorney's office, and they told me the only fingerprints on the book were Bobby's."

"Damn."

The pacing resumed. Finally, after another two minutes, Burns stopped again and stared at Moody. "I believe you had better figure out a way to explain the book in the safe."

"Mr. Burns," Moody stood, "I will not make a false statement to a member of the FBI or in a court of law. Yes, I work for you, but that does not mean I will perjure myself during the course of my employment."

Burns glared at Moody for several seconds. Then his facial features softened.

"No, I don't suppose you would, Joel. Forget I mentioned it."

Returning to his desk, he sat down and opened his laptop. He ignored Moody.

Sensing the meeting was over, Joel Moody knew he was walking out of Robert Burns' office for the last time.

***

"How soon can you be in Seattle, Sandy?" Sean Kruger held the phone to his ear as Jimmie Gibbs drove.

Sandy Knoll replied, "How fast do you need me?"

"Jimmie and I are going to put Joel Moody's place under surveillance. As soon as you can."

"I'll call you when I know about my flight."

"Good. Thanks, Sandy."

Gibbs glanced at the senior agent and asked, "What's the plan?"

"Time to enlist the help of our fellow agents here in Seattle."

Four hours later, the owners of a house directly across the street from Joel Moody's home agreed to allow the FBI to set up an observation post in their bonus room above the garage. No reason was given, but the owners did not mind because they didn't like Joel Moody in the first place.

In conversation with the husband, Erik Perkins, Kruger learned Moody's neighbors felt he and his wife lived above their means.

"Why do you think that?" Kruger asked.

"He's a cop, right?"

"Yes."

"They're always bragging about the cruises they take." Perkins shook his head. "It drives Nancy nuts. I make good money and we're lucky if we can go out to dinner in Seattle. Those two," he pointed across the street, "are always leaving for week-long cruises."

"Huh." Kruger paused for a moment. "If you guys don't speak to each other, how do you know?"

"They always ask the Allisons to check on their house. They won't ask us. Harry Allison is one of my golfing buddies. He tells me all about it."

When Kruger relayed the conversation to Jimmy Gibbs, he chuckled. "More reasons to not live in the suburbs, Sean. Too much drama."

"We don't have that issue where Stef and I live."

"You're lucky."

Kruger took the first twelve-hour shift, and Gibbs would take the second. Knoll would arrive late the following day.

When an agent from the Seattle field office arrived, Kruger was pleasantly pleased. He had met the man two years ago in Las Vegas during the search for the serial killer Randolph Bishop. Kruger shook his hand and smiled.

"When did you get transferred to the Seattle office, Tim?"

"A little over a month ago."

"It's good to see you again. I didn't realize I knew anyone in the local office."

"Glad to be here, sir. I'm looking forward to working with you again."

Tim Gonzales was three years out of the FBI Academy. He stood right at the minimum agency height requirement, but made up for it with his strength. Broad shouldered with a thin waist, he could bench press three hundred pounds without straining. Born in Fort Worth, Texas, his proud parents were new citizens of the United States, having taken their oath the day after Tim's graduation. Clean shaven, with short, coal-black hair, his face was tanned and male model handsome. He spoke English like a Texan and Spanish like a native of Mexico City, one of the reasons he was in a rotation of working field offices in the western United States.

The two FBI agents were in the bonus room. Gonzales

was looking through binoculars when he asked, "What are we looking for, Agent Kruger?"

"Call me Sean, Tim."

"Yes, sir."

Kruger shook his head and grinned. He liked the young agent. His enthusiasm was contagious.

"I'm not really sure what we're looking for. Something unusual, strange visitors, late night comings and goings. Our Mr. Moody has a dual personality. He says he will help us, but when you push him…"

Gonzales nodded. "He doesn't give details."

"Exactly. Plus he lied to me."

Not taking his eyes away from the binocular, the younger FBI agent asked, "How?"

"He knew about a hidden safe in a suspect's house, yet didn't tell us about it."

Kruger stood behind Gonzales, staring at the house of Joel Moody. Turning, Gonzales frowned.

"How is that lying to you, Agent Kruger?"

"Tim…"

"Sorry, Sean. How do you know he did it intentionally?"

"Good question. The issue with the safe was part of a series of lies. We prepared a subpoena requesting names of Haylex Solutions employees working at four college campuses from 1999 through 2002. Moody gave me an inaccurate list and didn't tell me. To me, that is inexcusable and a lie."

"Whose name wasn't there?"

"Robert Burns Jr."

Gonzales smiled. "The guy you arrested in Washington, D.C.?"

"One and the same."

"So you think Moody is running interference for the father?"

"I don't think it, I know it. Now, how we prove it is the next question."

"Interrogate Robert Burns Sr."

Kruger smiled and placed a hand on the young FBI agent's shoulder. "Tim, someday you'll understand that there are two types of individuals you can interview. Those who have no choice, and those who have the money to have a choice. The Burns family has the money."

"Doesn't seem right."

"It isn't, but at this point in time, it's reality."

"So now what?"

"We wait."

Jimmie Gibbs showed up early for his shift and was talking to Kruger when Gonzales put the binoculars down and got behind the high-end digital camera with a telephoto lens. "Got something." He started the camera's video feature.

Walking to the window, Kruger peered out and asked, "What's going on?"

"Car just pulled into the driveway. Looks like Moody's."

"Ford Fusion?"

"Yes."

"Yeah, that's Moody." Kruger glanced at his watch. Ten after 10. "Kind of late to be getting home." He returned his attention to the house.

Gibbs sat in a chair away from the window. "Anything happen before this?"

Kruger shook his head. "Note the time, Jimmie. I got a call from two agents watching the Haylex building. They reported he left a little after seven, but traffic kept them from following him too far. We need to know where he was."

Twenty minutes later, a black SUV pulled into the driveway. Gibbs was behind the binoculars now. He reached down and started the camera again, saying "Uh oh."

Kruger looked up from checking emails on his phone. "What?"

"Black SUV, looks like a Denali, just pulled into the driveway."

"What's it doing?"

"Nothing at the moment, just sitting in the driveway." Gibbs was silent for a few moments. "Shit, two dark clad individuals just ran out of the house got into the SUV. They both carried something big. Now the truck is backing out."

Kruger was on his feet before Gibbs finished talking and headed toward the stairs. Gibbs and Gonzales were right behind him.

As he exited the house, he withdrew his Glock from his belt holster and started running toward the Moody house. Gibbs, younger and faster, caught up.

"What're you thinking?"

"Two possibilities. One, someone was in the house when he got home. Second, that was Moody and his wife."

"I was thinking number one."

As they reached the front door, both men noticed it was slightly ajar. Kruger put his back against the wall on the left of the entrance, and Gibbs withdrew his weapon. The elder FBI agent pointed at Gonzales and whispered, "Secure the camera, and call for back up."

The younger agent nodded and ran back toward the observation house.

Kruger, using the tip of his gun, pushed the door open a little wider.

"FBI, Joel. I need you to come to the front door."

Silence.

"Joel, this is Sean Kruger. Come to the front door."

More silence.

Looking at Gibbs, he whispered, "Probable cause?"

"Looks like it to me." He raised his Sig Sauer. "I'll take lead."

"Go."

PART 3 – THE FUGITIVE

Seattle, WA

Gibbs entered the house first. With his Sig Sauer held with both hands extended in front, he turned to the right. Kruger entered the house behind Gibbs, his Glock in both hands stretched in front of his eyes as he turned to his left. Both men were silent as they moved into a wide vestibule. Each moved methodically as they swept the house for threats.

The next room was a formal sitting room. Kruger noted an ornate wood coffee table positioned in front of an uncomfortable looking coach with several upholstered accent chairs adjacent to it. A grandfather clock stood against the wall behind the couch with multiple strategically positioned oil paintings on the wall next to it. Everything in the room screamed big-box-store-home-décor. As they finished clearing the room, their eyes met as they approached a large opening leading to the remaining area of the house.

Pausing briefly, they nodded at each other, remaining quiet.

Kruger noticed at this point the house was eerily quiet. The only sound emanating from the kitchen was the ticking of an oversized wall clock.

Gibbs kept his Sig Sauer in front of him, but used his left

hand to count down to three. As he replaced his hand on the gun, they moved through the opening. Once again, Gibbs to the right, Kruger to the left.

The room was an open area consisting of a gourmet kitchen, breakfast nook and a well-equipped family room. Repeating the process used in the formal sitting room, the two men methodically swept the room for threats. They continued this process until all rooms of the house were searched.

When the house was clear, they both holstered the guns and returned to the couple's bedroom.

The room was ransacked. Doors and drawers were open on a large armoire with clothes and undergarments scattered on the floor. Kruger stepped carefully around the mess and entered the master bedroom closet. The same scene met his gaze. Empty clothes hangers were on the floor, and an empty space under the remaining hanging clothes suggested it was where suitcases had once resided.

One object in particular caught his attention. An open floor safe. He walked up to it and peered inside. The safe was empty.

"Jimmie, I've got an empty floor safe in here."

Gibbs appeared at the door of the closet. "Just checked, both cars are in the garage."

Kruger nodded. "I believe we have possibility number two. They've made a hasty escape."

"Why?"

"Good question. We need to look at the video Tim shot."

An hour later, Gonzales, Gibbs, and Kruger reviewed the video from the camera on Kruger's laptop. They were in the formal living room of Moody's home with the computer on the coffee table, while the rest of the house buzzed with activity as FBI agents and forensic technicians methodically searched each room.

Kruger crossed his arms. "Fast forward to the shot of the SUV."

When the video reached the part where the SUV

appeared, Gibbs leaned close to the screen.

"I can barely make out the license plate." He retrieved his cell phone from his jeans pocket, stood, and walked outside the house.

"Tim, when did Moody's wife get home?"

"I started watching the house at three. The camera wasn't set up yet when her car pulled into the driveway and parked inside the garage. We never really saw her."

Without comment, Kruger continued to watch the video.

Gibbs returned to the room. "License plate belongs to an executive limo service."

Kruger "Where's it going?"

"When I called, they wouldn't tell me. Asked if I was really with the FBI and had a warrant."

"Great. Okay, let's do this by the book."

Turning to Gonzales again, Kruger asked, "Tim, call your office and put out a BOLO for Joel Moody and the SUV. Have them send someone to the limo service with a warrant. We need to know where that car is taking them."

"Sure, for what reason?"

"A person of interest in the 1997 murder of Peng My-lai's mother, Peng Xi-lan."

***

"What can I do for you today, Agent Kruger?"

Gilbert Tucker, known by his fellow officers as Gil, ran the Seattle Police Department's detective department. His gray hair was cut military short. Hazel eyes stared at Kruger and Gibbs with a wariness produced by twenty years as a police officer and a general distrust of the FBI.

Standing in the lobby of the Seattle Police Headquarters in downtown Seattle, Kruger smiled.

"I appreciate you taking the time to see us this late, Detective Tucker. Is there somewhere more private we can talk?"

Tucker looked at Kruger and then at Jimmie Gibbs.

Returning his attention to Kruger he asked, "Is this about Joel Moody?"

"Yes."

"Follow me."

They were led to a small conference room next to the Chief of Police's office.

"Our chief's gone for the day; she won't be needing the room. Have a seat."

Kruger suppressed a smile as he recognized the attempt by Tucker to control the meeting. Neither he nor Gibbs sat.

"This won't take long, Detective."

"Okay, what do you need to know?"

"How well did you know Joel Moody?"

"How well did anybody know Joel Moody would be a better question. The answer is not well. He was an average detective on a good day, a lazy detective on most. He wasn't well liked in the department. When he left to work for Robert Burns, there was a collective sigh of relief heard throughout the department."

Kruger tilted his head and crossed his arms over his chest. "Why?"

"Have you ever worked with someone you didn't trust?"

"Yes."

"Then you know why. No one trusted him. Not good for a police officer."

"No, it isn't. Why was he not trusted?"

Tucker leaned against the corner of the conference table and, like Kruger, crossed his arms over his chest.

"Moody worked vice while he was with the department."

"Just vice, nothing else?"

"Yep, just vice."

"He told me he worked a murder desk during his last few years as a cop."

"If he did, it wasn't for the Seattle Police Department."

"Huh. Sorry, go on."

"We could never prove anything, but the feeling was he was being paid under the table by someone. He bought a new house, started taking trips, spending more money than a police officer makes."

"How did he explain it?"

"Claimed his wife had a new job that paid well."

"Did she?"

"Internal Affairs checked it out, nothing ever came of it, so…" Tucker shrugged.

Nodding, Kruger relaxed a little and pulled out a chair. Gibbs continued to stand. Kruger asked, "If he was such a poor detective, how did he land a job working for one of the richest men in the world?"

Tucker chuckled. "As I mentioned, Moody worked vice. We think he had some dirt on Burns' son. At least that was the scuttlebutt at the time. With all the recent events, apparently it was true."

"Did Moody ever arrest Junior?"

"No record of it. Conjecture within the ranks was he caught the son doing something, and instead of arresting him, called the senior Burns."

"When do you think this happened?"

"Not too long after he joined the vice squad."

Gibbs had kept silent until now. "What do you think happened, Detective?"

Smiling, Tucker shook his head. "Agent, I try not to speculate, but I can add two and two together. After Moody started vice, he requested to work alone. We generally don't approve those types of requests, but everyone refused to be his partner. So I conceded to his wishes. He bought the house a year later. Internal Affairs could never pin anything on him."

"What was his arrest rate like?" Kruger was standing again.

"Horrible. Oh, he'd bust a small time gambling ring once in a while, bring in a couple of hookers, or nab a group of teenagers for smoking dope, but never anything major. To be honest with you, if he hadn't left to work for Burns, he would have been busted back to patrol."

"That bad?"

"Yeah."

Leaning against the table and on a prearranged signal from Kruger, Gibbs asked. "Do you have any problems with Russian Mafia here in Seattle?"

Tucker stared at the younger FBI agent for a long time. Finally he nodded his head, "Yes."

Kruger stiffened. "How so?"

"Drugs, sex trafficking, extortion, all the usual stuff."

"Could Moody have gotten sucked into their control?"

"We never looked at it from that standpoint, but I guess anything is possible. Why do you ask?"

Hesitating while internally debating how much to say, Kruger answered, "Right now we don't have any solid evidence, but we believe Robert Burns Jr. has a connection to them."

Tucker frowned. "What makes you think so?"

Gibbs responded, "They tried to kill Agent Kruger in Washington while he was investigating Junior. That much we can prove. We also have evidence Moody spoke to someone associated with the Russians while he was in Washington."

"Shit."

"A fair assessment."

Tucker blinked several times and relaxed his shoulders. "What do you need from us?" he asked.

"We'd like to review all of his arrest reports. There might be something there."

"I can do that."

"One last question." Kruger tilted his head to the side.

"Sure."

"What color was Moody's hair before he started shaving his head?"

"Black."

***

Tucker led them to a couple of empty cubicles with keyboards and computer monitors. After he showed them how to access the arrest records, he left them alone. Gibbs turned to Kruger and asked, "What are we looking for, Sean?"

"Not sure, but somewhere in these records there might be a hint to what happened while Moody was a vice cop. It could be subtle or it could be glaring, but we won't know until we see it."

Gibbs looked at his watch.

"Knoll caught a late flight into Seattle. His plane lands in three hours. You want me to meet him at the airport?"

Kruger nodded. "Yeah, I'll stay here and start the search."

After Gibbs left, Kruger pulled out his cell phone and called a number. It was answered on the fourth ring.

"I've been expecting a call from you. What's up?"

"JR, there's a pattern starting to emerge. How hard would it be for you to hack into the Seattle PD computer?"

"Can you get access to a terminal?"

"Yeah, I'm staring at one right now."

"Cool, I'll walk you through what I need. Ready?"

"Yeah."

Once the information was given to JR, Kruger ended the call and started looking at Moody's reports for the last ten years of his career with the SPD. The work was tedious, but a pattern emerged. Moody was a lazy detective. He started to question why the Seattle Police Department allowed him to keep working, but then he remembered how long it took the FBI to discipline their own underperforming agents.

An hour passed before his cell phone chirped. "What'd you find?"

"Kind of what you thought. Seattle has a huge problem with the Russians. They just haven't figured it out yet."

"Did you find anything tying Moody to them?"

"Yeah. Are you looking at Moody's files?"

"Yes."

"I'm going to give you a case number. Go to the file and read it. Call me back when you're done."

When Kruger read the file, he smiled and sent it to a

printer. Just as he picked up the report from the machine, his cell phone vibrated. Looking at the ID he accepted the call from Gonzales.

"What've you got, Tim?"

"Sean, the car service got the call for the pick-up at seven p.m. from Moody. Apparently, he called from his car. They dropped them off at the Marriott near the airport. I just heard from the agents who were sent there. No one by the name of Moody ever checked in."

"Did they show a picture?"

"Yeah, they had a copy of his police ID photo. No one at the front desk recognized him."

"Did they talk to everyone in the night crew?"

"Yes, everyone."

"Did they check the security tapes?"

"Uh, I don't think so."

From past experience, Kruger knew how to find out what the Moodys did after being dropped off.

"Okay, thanks, Tim, I appreciate the rapid response from your team."

"Your welcome."

Kruger ended the call and took a deep breath. Moody was going through a lot of trouble to disappear. Without hesitation, he called JR back.

"Now what?"

"I know it's late there, but I bet you weren't in bed yet."

"Not yet, why?"

"I need the Seattle airport Marriott's security cameras hacked."

"Again, why?"

"Remember the stunt you pulled in New Jersey by having a taxi drop you off in front of a hotel and then walking away?"

There was silence, then a hesitant, "Yeah."

"Moody must have read your playbook; he just pulled the same stunt. Limo service dropped him and his wife off at the Marriott, and they never checked in."

"I'll call you back."

Chapter 36

Seattle, WA

Kruger handed the printed file to Gil Tucker, who flipped through the pages. He stopped on the fifth page and read the highlighted section. Frowning, he started again on page one and read with more scrutiny. When he was done, he closed the file and handed it back to Kruger. "It explains a lot."

Nodding, Kruger remained quiet.

"How did you find it?"

"They're your department's files. Why didn't someone internally find it?"

"I don't have a good answer."

Smiling, Kruger nodded. "It happens. Reports get skimmed over and forgotten. Sometimes they don't even get read."

Tucker stared at the file in Kruger's hand and sighed. "It explains why Moody kind of withdrew. He felt threatened."

"Particularly if no one within the department cared. I would guess, no one read through the report far enough to see the notation of the threat."

"I can't defend the department. Just because we don't like a guy…"

"Isn't a reason to ignore him, right?"

"No, it isn't. This report indicates Moody was being intimidated by members of a Russian gang in the late '90s after he discovered they were importing Asian women to work in the sex trade on the West Coast."

Kruger nodded. "Since no one in the department questioned him about it or followed up with him, he figured no one cared."

Tucker's color faded several shades as he stared at the report. "This makes me sick to my stomach."

"I'm sure it does. But it also explains why he stopped caring. I didn't find any mention of Robert Burns Jr. anywhere. There's a connection between Moody and Junior we don't know about. That connection, whatever it might be, paints a pretty ugly picture."

"Not sure I'm following you."

"There is a crossing somewhere we haven't found. Moody is threatened by Russians if he exposes their sex trade activities here in the Northwest. A few years later, Moody is hired by Robert Burns Sr. as his Director of Security. Why?"

"Don't know."

"Neither do we, but it's part of the picture."

"Okay."

Gibbs was leaning against a wall with his arms folded across his chest. "Gil, you mentioned earlier rumors were floating around your department about Moody and Junior. What caused the rumors?"

Tucker blinked several times. "Trying to remember." He studied the floor for several moments and then looked up. "The dates are fuzzy, but it was a couple of years after Senior was elected to the Senate. The son was a celebrity of sorts in the local media. I remember he was on the cover of a local magazine, *This is Seattle*, at least every other month. At least it seemed like it. Then all of a sudden, he's in Washington working for his dad. That's when the rumors started."

Kruger frowned. "Why then?"

"Not sure. But it was also around the time Moody stopped

undercover work."

"You never mentioned he was allowed to go undercover."

Nodding several times, Tucker half grinned. "Got him out of the station for long periods of time. Everyone was happier when he wasn't here."

Gibbs tilted his head and asked, "When was this, Gil?"

"I remember 9/11 happened during this period, so, that would be, what, 2001?"

Kruger frowned.

Standing straight, Gibbs asked. "1999 to 2002?"

Tucker nodded thoughtfully. "Yeah, that sounds about right."

Kruger stared at Tucker without comment.

"Why are those dates so important?"

"Robert Burns Jr. is a person of interest in a series of abductions during that period. We think, and this is speculation, Moody was protecting the son with the blessing and financial backing of the father."

Tucker stared wide-eyed at Kruger. "Shit."

"What?" Kruger and Gibbs spoke in unison.

"When did these abductions take place?"

"Late fall of each year."

Tucker's face grew pale. "That's the time of year Moody always went undercover."

"Gil, I'm going to call the FBI in. We need to get a federal warrant for Moody's cell phone records, his bank records and credit card bills. Jimmie Gibbs will assist with getting a federal judge to sign the warrant. Do you want your department to be involved?"

Tucker nodded.

***

Early the next day, after only three hours of sleep, Kruger ducked under the yellow crime scene tape and entered Joel Moody's office at the Haylex corporate office. Seattle detectives, local forensic personnel, and several FBI agents

Kruger didn't know were busy gathering files and evidence for closer scrutiny at the local crime lab.

Sandy Knoll stood in a corner, his massive arms crossed over his chest as he supervised the process. He nodded to Kruger as he approached.

"Heard anything from JR?"

"Not yet," Kruger answered. "Anything of importance here?"

Knoll chuckled. "Yeah, corporate attorneys keep threatening us. Claiming this is corporate property and not subject to seizure."

Smiling, Kruger nodded. "Standard procedure. Seen anything of Burns?"

"No."

"They've got this under control." He pulled a folded sheet of paper from the inside pocket of his blazer. "I need you and one of the computer techs to accompany me. A federal judge just signed this search warrant for Moody and the younger Burns' work records. When the three of us show up at their HR department, attorneys are going to be coming out of the woodwork. My guess is we'll meet Burns then."

Knoll grinned, "Wish Charlie Craft was here."

"I spoke to him before I arrived. He recommended Krista Tam; is she here?"

Pointing toward a twenty-something woman sitting at Moody's desk, "That's her."

Krista Tam was in her late twenties, tall, with a round face, almond-shaped eyes, black hair pulled back into a ponytail, and black rim glasses sitting on a petite nose allowing brown eyes to focus on her work. She was dressed professionally in a light gray pantsuit and an open collar silk blouse.

Knoll walked over to her. "Krista, could you come with me?"

She looked up at the big man. A slight grin appeared. "Sure."

Standing, she followed Knoll and Kruger out of Moody's office.

***

The receptionist in Haylex Holdings HR department stared at the search warrant with wide eyes and no comment. Refusing to touch the document, she finally picked up the phone on her desk and touched three numbers on the keypad.

"Ms. Potter, uh… We, uh… Could you come to my desk, please?"

She was silent for several moments, listening to the person on the other end of the call. "There are three FBI agents with a search warrant standing in front of my desk," she whispered into the phone.

More silence as she listened and stared at the warrant still in Kruger's hand. "Thank you."

She replaced the receiver, looked up at Kruger, then Knoll and back to Kruger. "Ms. Potter will be out shortly."

Kruger smiled. "Thank you."

The clicking of heels on marble tiles could be heard as the Director of HR walked toward the reception area of her department. The pace was hurried, not panicked, but rapid.

Sheryl Potter was a mature woman, Kruger guessed in her late fifties, with a stern demeanor and attitude. She was immaculately dressed in a navy pantsuit with a light blue sweater underneath. A pearl necklace accented the ensemble. Her shoulder-length white hair bounced as she strode into the lobby. Her hazel eyes glanced from Knoll, to Krista Tam, and finally settled on Kruger.

"What's this about a search warrant?" she asked immediately.

"My name is Sean Kruger, we are special agents with the FBI. This is a federal search warrant, duly signed by a judge, for the Haylex Holdings personnel records of Joel D. Moody and Robert Burns Jr." He handed her search warrant.

With a slight hesitation, she accepted the paper. "I'm going to have to contact our attorneys before I let you into our records."

Shaking his head, Kruger gave her a frown. "Doesn't work that way."

"Well, I can't just let you waltz in here and start tearing up the place and looking through everyone's personnel records."

"We're not interested in anybody else's records. Only Moody and the younger Burns."

She tried to hand the search warrant back to Kruger, who made no effort to accept it.

"I will not let you at our records until our attorneys are present."

Kruger turned to Knoll, "Agent Knoll, please place Ms. Potter under arrest for impeding a rightfully served federal search warrant."

As Sandy walked toward the woman, her eyes widened, the color drained from her face, and she put her palms up in the air toward Knoll. "You can't…"

"Yes, we can. Now do you want to cooperate, or does Agent Knoll lead you off the premises in cuffs?" Kruger's jaws clinched and his brow furrowed.

She lowered her hands, stared at the search warrant, and then slowly nodded her head. "Very well, follow me." She turned toward the receptionist. "Linda, please call Mr. Burns' office and let them know what is going on."

Ten minutes later, a tall man in his late sixties walked purposely into the officer where Krista Tam was working on a Haylex Holding computer terminal. His face was red, his breathing labored, and his nostrils flared.

"What the hell is the meaning of this intrusion?" he demanded.

Kruger, who had been waiting for his opportunity to confront Robert Burns Sr., smiled slightly. He walked toward the man with his credentials held in his right hand.

"FBI."

When the man reached for them, Kruger withdrew his arm and placed his ID back in his inside suitcoat pocket. He stepped forward, "Special Agent Sean Kruger. We have a search warrant duly signed by a federal judge for the personnel records of Joel Moody and your son, Robert Burns Jr. Do not interfere."

"Do you know who I am, Agent?"

"Yes, I know who you are. But quite frankly, I don't care. Federal law applies to everyone."

Burns' breathing rate became more erratic as his jaw tightened. Through clinched teeth he said, "I am the CEO of this company and a former Senator. I demand you stop this illegal search immediately."

Kruger smiled slightly and leaned closer to Burns. "Not going to happen. Now please leave this office."

"I will have your badge, Agent, so help me."

"Others have tried. I still have it."

Both men stood and glared at each other, Kruger standing straight, his arms now crossed over his chest, as he observed the elder Burns. Finally, the older man's breathing slowed and became more normal, his face softened.

"May I speak to you privately, Agent?"

Kruger tilted his head slightly. "Why?"

"I want to understand the reason for the search warrant."

"It's simple. We need company records concerning Mr. Moody and your son's whereabouts while traveling on corporate business."

"Why my son?"

"He's a person of interest in a federal investigation."

"Just because he's been wrongfully accused of a crime does not give you the right to violate his rights."

"Your son is a person of interest in a series of abductions seventeen years ago."

Burns stared at Kruger, the realization of his worst fears about his son's future suddenly materializing. In a less confrontation tone, Burns asked. "Once again, Agent, may we speak in private?"

Kruger turned to Knoll and Tam and asked, "Sandy, could you two give us a few minutes?"

Knoll nodded and motioned Krista to follow.

While they walked out, Kruger reached into his pocket and touched an icon on his phone. He then redirected his attention to Burns. "Is this private enough for you?"

The older man crossed his arms over his chest. "How much?"

"How much what?"

"How much money to make you forget this investigation?"

Smiling slightly, Kruger shook his head. "I'm not following you, Mr. Burns."

"Do I have to spell it out for you, Agent? I'm one of the richest men in the world, and I will spend whatever it takes to defend my son. You can do yourself a favor and be the recipient of some of my money instead of it going to a bunch of lawyers."

Kruger smiled at Burns, knowing he now had an ace up his sleeve. An attempt by Robert Burns Sr. to bribe an agent with the FBI. He reached into his pocket again and turned off the recording app.

"I'll think about it. In the meantime, I have an investigation to conduct."

Chapter 37

Seattle, WA /Springfield, MO

"I'm at the airport waiting for my flight. Did you find anything on the Marriott's security cameras?" Sean Kruger held the cell phone tight to his ear with his shoulder as he walked toward his departure gate at the Seattle-Tacoma International Airport.

"Yeah. Moody and his wife watched the SUV drive off and then walk toward the parking lot. Exact same thing I did in New Jersey. It was a ruse."

"Did you see where they went?"

"SUV in the far corner of the hotel parking lot. He knew where the security cameras were because there isn't a clear picture of the car or the license plate."

"Can you make out the model?"

"I'm not sure, either a KIA or a Hyundai."

"What color?"

"Dark, either black, dark red, or dark blue. Parking lot lights and distance make it hard to distinguish."

"Can you enhance the picture to make sure?"

"I can, but it will take a little time."

"Fine, one more thing."

"Yeah."

"Gibbs is going to send you a file on Moody. I need you to do a deep dive on him."

"What are you looking for?"

"I don't want to put any preconceived solutions in your head."

"What if I don't find anything?"

"If you don't, hey, you tried. But there's something there, JR."

"Okay, if you say so. How far back do you want me to go?"

"1997."

"Okay. Challenging, but doable."

"That's the JR I've grown to love."

"Ha ha."

"I'll be in town by tonight."

"Let's talk tomorrow."

Kruger ended the call just as he entered the departure gate. He took a deep breath, his current absence from home weighing heavy on his mind. After checking the departure time at the gate, he dialed Stephanie's cell phone. It was answered on the third ring.

"Hi, is your flight on time?"

"Hi back. So far. Sorry for staying a couple of days longer than I thought."

There was silence on the call. Finally, he heard. "Did you make any progress?"

"I think so. JR is helping now."

"Good."

"How are the kids?"

"They're fine. Kristin keeps asking when Daddy will be home and Mikey's always smiling."

He closed his eyes and took a deep breath. The emptiness of being away from his family over the past week suddenly engulfed him. Taking another deep breath, he settled his feelings. "I'll be home tonight by six, if the flight out of Dallas is on time."

"Good. I have some news, if you're interested?"

Another pang of guilt swept over him. With a cheerier voice than he felt, he answered, "Of course I'm interested."

She chuckled. "It'll have to wait until you get home. We'll get the kids to bed and then I'll tell you."

"Not fair."

Another chuckle. "Tough, see you tonight."

The call ended and his mood darkened even farther.

***

Kruger straightened the blankets on the sleepy little girl's bed. After kissing his daughter goodnight, he walked out of her bedroom and left her bedroom door slightly ajar. When he walked into their bedroom, Stephanie was already in bed with the covers pulled up.

"So what was the big news you wanted to tell me?"

She smiled, but did not respond.

"Are you finally going to tell me?"

"Get ready for bed. You're tired."

"I'm still on Pacific Time. My body thinks it's seven."

"Go on, it's late, get cleaned up and come to bed. I'll tell you then."

Five minutes later, he slipped into bed and snuggled against her, feeling bare skin. "So what's the big news?"

"I love you."

"I know that."

"No, you're feeling guilty about being out of town for a few days and afraid your family is slipping away from you. I heard it in your voice when you called. Trust me, we are not."

"Are you naked?"

"Yes."

"Why?"

"Because I want you to quit worrying about being away from us and do what you do best. Then, after you quit worrying, I want you to make love to me."

He pulled off his t-shirt and embraced her.

***

As they lay next to each other, the warmth of their intimacy comforted Kruger. Stephanie lay with her head on his chest, and his right arm was draped over her shoulder. The silence and the joy of being together more important than talking. He took a deep breath.

After a few minutes, he decided to ask, "So what was the good news?"

"Remember I told you they wanted me to teach part-time and mentor senior women?"

"Yeah."

"The head of the department changed her mind."

"I'm sorry, I thought you were excited about it. Why is that good news?"

"There's more."

"Oh…"

"She offered me a full-time position as an instructor."

He smiled and squeezed her tighter. "That's wonderful. When do you start?"

"Next semester. They also want me to start working on my doctorate."

"Even better. Where?"

"Here."

"Business?"

She shook her head, but did not answer.

"Finance?"

"No."

"Then what?"

"You'll laugh."

"I promise, I won't."

"It's a new program they've been thinking about for several years and want me to be their first doctorate candidate."

"IN WHAT?"

"Gender Studies. Mainly about women balancing work and personal life."

"Really?"

She nodded.

"I think it's wonderful. How did this come about?"

"She likes the fact I rose to a senior VP position and then walked away to raise a family. The fact I have a master's degree didn't hurt. I'll still get to mentor senior women business majors."

"Good. You said yes, didn't you?"

She shook her head again.

"Why not?"

"Remember we make decisions as a couple now. Or did you forget?"

"No." His thoughts went back to his reluctance to rejoin the agency until she told him it was his only choice.

"I wanted to be intimate with you before we discussed it."

"Bribe?"

She poked a finger in his rib. "Of course not." She paused briefly. "Well, maybe."

"Is this what you want?"

"Yes, more than I thought I would. It's exciting. Plus, I won't have to travel or be away from you and the kids."

"Tell her tomorrow you accept."

She raised her head and they kissed.

"I will."

***

After dropping Kristin and Mikey at their new day-care facility, Kruger parked his Mustang in front of JR Diminski's office building in a visitor's parking slot. When he walked in Jodie Roberson, vice president and general manager, was talking to the receptionist and made a bee-line toward him. After a quick I-haven't-seen-you-in-a-long-time hug, she smiled.

"I understand you're back with the FBI?"

"Yes. How've you been, Jodie?"

"Busy. Trying to keep JR grounded is exhausting work."

"I can only imagine. Is he here?"

She pointed toward the ceiling. "Second floor, his normal cubicle. I got here at seven and he was already engrossed in something. No telling how long he's been here."

Kruger smiled. "I gave him a homework assignment last night."

"Good, it'll keep him from interfering with our normal routine."

Chuckling, he walked toward the stairs leading to the second floor. Kruger remained amazed at how JR's small regional one-man company had grown into a fifty-one employee national enterprise.

As he approached JR's cubicle next to the glassed-in conference room, he saw his friend's head swiveling as he surveyed three flat-screen monitors in front of him. Stopping at the table behind JR, Kruger looked at the Mr. Coffee machine. It looked well used, but he did not see any coffee for it.

Without turning, JR said, "Everyone is using it, but think it's someone else's duty to buy coffee. If you want a cup, you'll have to use the Keurig."

Shrugging, he picked a coffee pod, placed it in the Keurig and pushed the flashing blue button. So far, JR had not diverted his attention from the monitors. When the coffee was done, JR turned to look at him. "Make me one, too."

Kruger placed his untouched cup in front of JR and waited for a few moments. "Your welcome."

"What?"

"I said, you're welcome."

"Uh, okay. Uh, thanks, I guess."

Chuckling, Kruger returned to the machine to fill another mug with coffee. While the water was forced through the pod, he leaned against the table and asked, "Find anything?"

"Yeah, finish making your coffee and pull up a chair."

When Kruger sat down, JR broke his concentration on the screens and looked over at his friend. "What were you expecting to find about Moody?"

Looking at the steaming coffee, Kruger took a sip of coffee, grimaced, and returned his attention to JR. "Moody is dirty. Beyond that, I really didn't know what to expect."

"He's more than dirty. Moody has over ten million dollars in an account in the Cayman Islands."

"Interesting. Did you determine the source of the funds?"

"A bank in Switzerland."

"And?"

JR smiled. "There are multiple accounts transferring funds to him. One is an account owned by a European subsidiary of Haylex Holdings. The rest are controlled by a corporation tied to a Russian oligarch named Dmitri Orlov. Currently he runs the bank while maintaining a relationship with the FSB."

Kruger frowned, stared out over the cube farm, and sat back in his chair, his coffee forgotten.

JR glanced at his friend. The silence was unusual. "What's the matter?"

Shaking his head, Kruger didn't answer right away. Finally he returned his attention to JR. "Nothing. Go on.

"Remember, this is not my first time tracing international money transfers. A normal search, like the Bureau conducts, wouldn't find the connections."

"Tell me about this Orlov person. What's his story?"

"He travels to the U.S. East Coast on a regular basis. I found a couple of pictures of him and Putin vacationing at a resort near the Black Sea. They appear to be buddies. What little information I can find indicates they may have served together in the KGB."

"Huh."

"Orlov's bank has a branch in New York City and Washington, D.C."

Kruger did not smile, but tilted his head to the side. "Really?"

JR nodded and glanced at his friend as he asked, "Ever hear of a guy called Yakov Romanovich?"

Hearing the name, Kruger raised his eyebrows. "Maybe. What'd you find?"

"Works for Orlov in New York City. So you've heard of him?"

Nodding, Kruger studied the cooling liquid in his coffee mug. "Let's just say he's currently a guest of the FBI in Washington, D.C."

Sitting back in his chair, JR crossed his arms over his chest. "Why?"

"He tried to kill me in Washington, D.C. Gibbs put three bullets in him before he could put one in me."

"Really?"

"Yes."

"Glad he missed."

"Me too."

Kruger sipped the now cold coffee. "So, just exactly what is the connection between these two?"

"Romanovich was an enforcer for the Russian mob in New York City. Disappeared around 2012, and I can't find any references to where he was."

Sipping his coffee again, Kruger was quiet. Finally after a long moment of silence he said, "He was in Ukraine."

JR's head turned and he frowned. "How would you know that?"

"Long story."

Sitting back in his chair, JR folded his arms over his chest. "Why am I doing all of this when you already know about it?"

"You're helping to put pieces of the puzzle together. That's why."

"Well, here's another piece. Did you know the New York group is offering a bonus to anyone who can silence you?"

"Say what?"

JR nodded. "Twenty-five thousand dollars."

"Shit."

"I would agree."

"Where the hell did you find all of this?"

"Dark Web chat room for the Russian gang in New York City."

"You're scary."

"I've been told that."

"How did you find it?"

JR smiled, but did not answer the question.

"So these guys discuss openly what they are doing?"

"Yes, remember, I said Dark Web. The chat room was password protected, but not well protected."

"So is there any reference to Moody?"

"No. But someone else you're interested in was. I found a reference to a cleanup job in a Motel 6 near Joint Base Andrews."

Kruger stared at his old friend.

Letting his FBI friend think, JR's fingers played on the keyboard as he displayed a string of email messages. He pointed to it. "This is the conversation I was talking about."

Looking at where JR pointed, Kruger saw the name Burns. "Senior or junior?"

"This segment of the communication doesn't specify which, but if I had to guess, I would say senior."

"Why?"

"Once the chat room was found with the reference to Burns, I did a search for the name. It is in several conversations over the past seven years. In one string, it mentions a friendly source within the Senate."

"When?"

"A conversation occurring in the fall of 2011."

"Between who?"

"Orlov and someone else within the hierarchy of the New York City Russian organization. Apparently, that individual is now deceased."

"I'm going to chase rabbits for a minute."

"Go on."

Kruger stood and started pacing. "What if there is a connection between Burns and this Russian mafia that dates back to his run for the Senate. This could be the time his son starts going after higher profile victims, and they disappear without a trace."

"Okay."

"If the references you found about the incident in Cave Springs, Maryland, are correct, the Russians are the ones cleaning up after Junior."

"Makes sense."

Kruger stopped pacing and gave JR a slight smile. "Why? Why would that make sense?"

"The women disappeared without a trace. That's hard to do consistently."

"Exactly. I'm speculating here, but what we know would suggest either Burns reached out to the Russians to help protect his son, or the Russians found out about the son and got to the father before he was elected to the Senate."

"I prefer the latter."

"So do I. It makes more sense."

"How did they find out about the son?"

"Moody," Kruger smiled. "That's why he's pulled this disappearing act. He either thinks we know about his connection with the Russians or he's trying to hide from them."

JR tilted his head and stared back at the FBI agent. "That could explain a lot, Sean."

"I know."

Both men were quiet for several moments.

"Let me do some more digging." JR paused for a moment and pursed his lips. "This Orlov character intrigues me. I'm wondering who else he's connected to."

"I think you have an excellent idea." Kruger hesitated, not wanting to break the string of JR's thoughts. Finally he decided to ask, "Did you determine anything about Moody and the parked SUV?"

JR nodded.

"I went back about twelve hours and started looking at the same camera. Moody parked it there around eight. He walks back to the hotel and grabs a cab."

"That would explain the three-hour difference between leaving his office and getting home."

"Yes. The SUV is a black Kia. It had a temp license plate on it."

"How many black Kias are in Washington State?"

"Don't know, but I'll bet it's a bunch."

"Yeah. If he's put a real license plate on it, it'll be like trying to find a needle in a haystack."

"I would agree."

CHAPTER 38

Washington, DC

Carol Welch stared at United States District Court Judge Todd Lewis, her disbelief growing with each word the man spoke.

A fragile-looking man, his black robe hung two sizes too large and gave the impression of a small child pretending to be judge. His receding hairline exposed a massive amount of forehead on an equine face. The dark brown hair on each side, which he combed straight back, puffed out above his protruding ears. Green eyes glared at her over half-readers positioned halfway down an oversized hawk nose. The voice was grating and slightly high pitched.

"Ms. Welch, your argument concerning the defendant's flight risk doesn't hold water. I grant you, having four illegal passports is of great concern. However, the FBI has confiscated them, and they are no longer available to Mr. Burns. Also, the lack of prior offenses and his status as the senator-elect from the state of Washington lead me to grant bail in the sum of ten million dollars."

"With all due respect, Your Honor, the wealth of the Burns' family makes this sum a paltry amount."

"This court does not recognize nor does it care about the

wealth of the family, Ms. Welch. Bail is still ten million dollars."

He turned to the defense lawyer, Jolene Sanders, to say, "Ms. Sanders, inform your client he is not to leave the Washington, D.C., area under any circumstance. He will be required to wear an ankle monitor. If he tries to remove the bracelet and leave the area, bail will be revoked. Is that clear?"

"Yes, Your Honor."

"I understand he was staying in a hotel prior to his arrest. Is that correct, Ms. Sanders?"

"Yes, Your Honor."

The judged nodded and wrote a note on something in front of him no one could see.

"Then inform him that until he can establish a permanent residence the court recognizes as legitimate, he will remain in custody, even if bail is arranged."

"Your Honor, how is he to accomplish this if he is in custody?"

"Not the court's concern, Ms. Sanders." He displayed a grim smile. "As Ms. Welch has pointed out, his resources are extensive. He'll figure it out."

No one spoke as his attention went from Sanders back to Welch. "Any other questions?"

Carol Welch stood and started to say something.

The judge held up his hand, palm toward her. "If you're going to protest my decision, Ms. Welch, don't."

His tone was defiant and his stare intense.

She kept her intended comment to herself.

"Very well, court dismissed."

The judge continued his intense glare at the district attorney as he stood and walked out of the court room. In stunned silence, Carol Welch stared wide-eyed at the empty space the judge just vacated. She sat back and did not move.

Jolene Sanders glanced over at her, a slight smile on her lips, as she gathered her files and placed them in her briefcase. She had won round one. Round two would not be as easy.

***

Two hours later, Carol Welch returned to her office, shut the door and called Sean Kruger. He answered on the third ring.

"How did the bail hearing go?"

"Not well. Bail was set at ten million and within an hour, the one million was deposited. He will be released as soon as he can establish a permanent residence in D.C., and the ankle monitor is calibrated."

Kruger was silent for several moments. "Disappointing. You realize he will disappear, don't you."

"I mentioned the small bail amount to the judge. He didn't care."

"Who was the judge?"

"Todd Lewis."

"Isn't he a recent appointee by the current president?"

"Yes. It was the first time I've been in front of him. He has small man syndrome."

"The president tried earlier to shut down the investigation, Carol."

"I heard."

Silence returned to the conversation. Finally, Kruger said, "Carol, Robert Burns Jr. is a clever individual when it comes to electronics and computers. He'll figure out a way to defeat the bracelet. Once we know the address, I can get a 24/7 surveillance in place. Do you know where that will be?"

"Not yet. The law firm representing him owns several furnished condos around town. My guess is they'll lease one to him."

"They own condos?"

"Yes, they use them to house out-of-town expert witnesses and partners from their offices in Chicago and Dallas. Cheaper than hotels and a great tax write-off."

"Huh."

"I have to go, just thought I would update you."

"Thanks, Carol."

The call ended and Kruger laid his cell phone back on his desk. Taking a deep breath he let it out slowly. He knew full well having 24/7 surveillance on Burns for the period of time until his trial would be cost prohibitive for the Bureau. A feeling of futility washed over him as he made the call to arrange for surveillance.

***

"What do you mean, I won't be released until I have a permanent residence? How the hell am I supposed to do that? I'm stuck in here."

Robert Burns Jr. stared hard at Jolene Sanders, his face growing crimson, his arms flat on the table between them, and his hands clinched so tight his knuckles were white.

"Do you know anyone you can live with here in D.C. until your trial?"

Burns was silent for a few moments, then shook his head.

The young attorney smiled and opened a file laying on the table in front of her. She withdrew several documents and turned them so they faced her client.

"The firm is offering you a six-month lease, with the option of extension, for one of our furnished condos. It's extremely nice and located in the Georgetown area."

She leaned back in her chair, crossed her arms over her chest and watched her client. He scanned each page of the document and lay it back down on the table. Looking up he stared at his attorney.

"The monthly rent is a little high don't you think?"

She shrugged. "Not for D.C."

He looked back at her. "Where are my things from the hotel?"

"In the possession of the firm. I had someone retrieve them and settle your bill. I can have them taken to the condo after you sign the lease agreement."

"How long before we go to trial?"

Again she shrugged. "Couple of months, maybe a year, depends."

"Depends on what?"

"What evidence the FBI has and how cooperative you are as a client."

His eyes narrowed as he glared at her. "What's that supposed to mean?"

"Exactly how it sounds. We need to know the truth so we can provide the best defense."

"The FBI doesn't have proof of anything."

She leaned forward with a grave expression, her hands clasped in front of here. "Mr. Burns, Linda Ramos…"

"Who?"

"Linda Ramos, the dead women the FBI found with your DNA on her."

"She was alive when I left."

"Yes, we know. But she died of her injuries."

"She was alive last I saw her."

"Your denials are getting old. Did you know they found your skin cells in the cuts on her face?"

Burns stared at her, but remained silent.

"I didn't think you did," Sanders continued. "This is what I'm talking about, Mr. Burns. If you aren't going to tell us the truth, we won't be able to properly defend you. Did you beat her?"

Burns nodded.

"Good. Now we're getting somewhere. How much did you have to drink that night?"

"I don't know. Couple of drinks at the hotel bar, a few at the night club, then a few back in my hotel room. Why?"

"After your arrest, your blood alcohol level was just under .200. They estimated it might have been as high as .230 at one time. It's the beginning of a defense. We go from first-degree murder to manslaughter, plea bargain, and work on getting your sentence reduced to probation with counseling."

"I didn't kill her."

She closed her eyes and shook her head. "Please don't

insult my intelligence, Mr. Burns. No one was in the room after you left until the FBI discovered her."

He did not respond.

"Did you have any involvement with a Senate intern in early 2012?"

He shook his head.

She sighed.

"In our discovery packet from the DA, there is mention of evidence you did. If this is true, it sets up a pattern that could contradict our defense strategy for the death of the Ramos woman. So you're telling me the FBI won't be able to prove your involvement with the intern, correct?"

"That's correct."

"I hope not. If they do, any hope of a manslaughter charge is out the window."

"I don't want to plead guilty to manslaughter. I'm innocent."

"Save it for the jury, Mr. Burns. I'm your attorney, not your priest."

Burns' eyes narrowed, and he stared at the young lawyer but remained quiet.

"Do you want to sleep somewhere besides jail tonight?"

Without comment, Burns nodded.

She handed him a pen. He scribbled his name where she pointed. Afterward, she placed the signed documents back into the file folder and slipped it back into her shoulder bag briefcase.

"I'll have you out of here in time for dinner."

She stood, and Burns looked up and asked, "Does the condo come with a cleaning service?"

"No."

"Who's gonna to clean it?"

"You, I would guess."

"I don't clean."

"Learn."

He closed his eyes and took a deep breath. The rage starting to build again. After several calming deep breaths, he opened his eyes.

"I'll pay for a maid and a cook?" he suggested.

"I'm sure we can find a company willing to provide those services. They will be male, however."

"You think I killed that whore in the hotel, don't you?"

"Mr. Burns, it is immaterial what I think or believe. I'm your attorney."

With those words she walked out of the interrogation room toward the building's exit. Yes, she did believe he killed the woman in the hotel. And after this session with him, probably more.

***

From his third-floor window, Robert Burns Jr. looked northeast and watched the lights of D.C. illuminate the skyline. The Capitol Building was a prominent element of the scene. The condo was decorated in an industrial minimalist format using whites and blacks for contrast. He hated the design, but didn't really care. He had no intentions of living here any longer than necessary.

As he sipped on a single malt scotch, he stared out the window, contemplating his predicament. The ankle bracelet was irritating and distracting, but bearable for the moment. His thoughts centered on various ways to defeat the small device. He had a few options.

The bigger problem was how to get out of the country. Access to funds was not the issue. Obtaining the proper paperwork was. Communicating with the individuals he needed to contact was the most pressing issue at the moment. The FBI had possession of his cell phone, and calling on the landline in the condo would be foolish. He needed a cell phone no one knew about.

As his eyes tracked a passenger plane approaching from the north and preparing to land at Reagan National Airport, he smiled to himself as an idea formulated. Once he obtained a cell phone in the morning and a few electronic odds and ends, he would start working on getting out of his current situation.

CHAPTER 39

Springfield, MO

For the first time in several weeks, Kruger was not at the airport on a Monday morning preparing to fly somewhere. Dropping Kristin off at her new kindergarten class enhanced his feeling of normalcy.

With two small children, the Kruger household was always boisterous. Now, with Kristin in school and Stephanie and Mikey at the university to introduce him to his new daycare facility, the house was unusually quiet. He sat at his home office desk and listened. With a slight smile, he plugged a cord into a slot on his laptop and turned on speakers he kept on his credenza. Opening the Pandora icon on his desktop, the sounds of a well-used station started immediately. The first stanzas of Richard Elliot's *Ricochet* emanated from the speakers, one of his favorites. The energetic saxophone of the jazz musician's composition always put him in a good mood.

Half way through the piece, his cell phone vibrated. Looking at the ID, he turned the volume down and accepted the call.

"Kruger."

"Busy?"

"Not yet. What's up, JR."

"Think you need to get over here."

"Oh?"

"Yeah, just linked Junior with the abductions in Kirksville."

"I'll be right there."

***

Kruger leaned forward in the chair as he sat next to his friend. JR pointed to a screen on the left hand side of the cubicle desk. "Department of Licensing, Olympia, Washington, has a record of a dark gray Mercedes SL500 being registered to a Robert Burns Jr. in 1997. License was renewed regularly until January 2003 when it was reported stolen."

"Huh."

"Odometer readings on the registration indicate the car was driven more than 25,000 miles per year."

"Not unusual."

"No, but here's the clincher." He pointed to the middle monitor in the series of three. "Traffic ticket for speeding, November 2002, Kirksville, MO."

"I'll be damned. Junior received a speeding ticket in the afternoon on the day the women disappeared."

"Yup."

"How'd you find all of this, JR?"

"Don't ask."

Kruger smiled slightly. "So if I made the request I could get a copy of the ticket?"

JR nodded and smiled. "You now have verification he was in Kirksville, at the time of the kidnapping, outside of company records. Which, by the way, have been expunged from the company server."

"Do you have any verification he was in the other locations the previous years?"

His response was a smile. JR's fingers danced over the keyboard as images started appearing on the screen. "What do you think?"

As he read the documents contained in the PDF files, his heart rate quickened. On the screen were forms in various formats, but all were records for temporary parking permits issued for a gray 1997 Mercedes SL500 with a Washington State license plate. The locations were University of Florida in 1999, Concord University in 2000, and the University of Akron, 2001, all signed by Robert Burns Jr.

"Did you find a permit at Kirksville?"

"No, just the speeding ticket."

"That's enough." Kruger sat back in his chair and stared out over the cubicle farm. There were numerous employees milling about and ignoring the two individuals seated at the cubicle next to the conference room. Kruger did not see them as his mind raced. "I need to use your conference room. Want to listen?"

"Wouldn't miss it."

After both men made cups of coffee, they sat in the soundproof conference room at a long table. Kruger placed the parking permit and the speeding ticket printouts in front of him for easy reference. He heard Carol Welch's cell phone ring. The call was answered on the fourth ring.

"Can I call you back, Sean? I'm in a meeting."

"We have proof Burns was at each of the colleges when the six women were abducted."

Silence was his answer. "I'll call you back in two minutes."

The call ended, and Kruger smiled. "That got her attention."

Exactly one minute and fifty-seven seconds later Kruger's phone received her call.

"Okay, what proof?"

"We have registration records of a gray 1997 Mercedes SL500 being registered to a Robert Burns Jr., from 1997 till 2003. The car was reported stolen in 2003. We also have records of temporary parking permits being issued for the same 1997 Mercedes at each of the schools during the same timeframe when the basketball players were abducted. The only school we don't have a record for is Kirksville."

"That's not good."

"There's more. We have a copy of a speeding ticket issued to a Robert Burns Jr. on the same day the three women disappeared in Kirksville. Better than a temporary parking permit."

Silence was once again heard on the phone call. Kruger waited.

"Okay, Sean, will the Grant woman testify against Junior?"

"Can't answer that at the moment. I'd have to talk to her attorney."

"Do it. Then we can raise the possibility that the murder of the Ramos woman wasn't his first. We can ask for bail to be revoked."

"Kind of what I was hoping. I'll call Heather Grant's attorney."

***

"Agent, it was one thing for my client to nod or shake her head in response to your questions, but I will not allow her to go through the trauma of testifying in front of a judge, jury and the accused."

Lucile Wilkins' voice was non-threatening, but firm. Kruger took a deep breath.

"I understand, Ms. Wilkins. I do not wish to put her in a position to be traumatized. We now have solid, compelling evidence Burns was at each college when the six co-eds disappeared. With Ms. Grant's testimony, we can establish a pattern of prior behavior. It will be enough to revoke bail and, hopefully, keep him out of society for the rest of his life."

"I will have to discuss it with her. But I'm inclined to advise her against it."

"When you are talking to her, keep in mind she will be helping to save potential future victims."

Wilkins was quiet for a while, then asked, "How

compelling is your evidence about the colleges?"

"Without going into details, we have documents placing him in each locale at the same time as the abductions."

"Very well. I will discuss it with her. We will let you know her decision as soon as I speak to her."

"Thank you, Ms. Wilkins."

The call ended, and Kruger sighed.

"Well, what'd she say?" JR took a sip of coffee after asking the question.

"She'll have to discuss it with Heather."

"And?"

"I'd say there is a fifty percent chance she will."

"Which means a fifty percent chance she won't."

Kruger smiled. "I'll take the positive road, thank you."

"Okay, now what?"

"I think it is time the FBI sent agents to the colleges with subpoenas for the information you found."

"Make sure you word it so it's a generic search."

He stood and looked at the computer hacker.

"This isn't the first time we've done this, JR. I know how to word it."

"I know, I was just… well, you know."

Kruger chuckled, stood, walked around the table and as he was getting ready to leave, placed his hand on JR's shoulder. "Yes, JR, I know. You did a good job on this, we'll get him."

When Kruger was back in his home office, the house was still quiet. This time he did not turn on music; he just concentrated on next steps. Taking a legal pad out of a drawer, he started making a list of what needed to be accomplished.

After the list was complete, he called Ryan Clark. The call was answered on the third ring.

"Clark."

"Ryan, it's Kruger."

"What's up?"

"How's the surveillance going?"

"Boring. He's only left the condo twice. Both times to

have dinner and stop at a liquor store, and then a CVS."

"Does he know he's being watched?"

"Probably, we haven't been real subtle about it."

"Good. I have good news."

"Oh? I could use some. Tell me."

"We finally have evidence he was at the colleges at the time of the abductions." Kruger gave him a summary of their findings and outlined what Clark needed to do.

"When do you want me to get the warrant?"

"As soon as we have the evidence secured by a legal search."

Clark chuckled, "Who found it first? JR?"

"Yeah, JR."

"Glad he's on our side."

"Me too."

CHAPTER 40

Washington, DC
Two days later

The warrant for the arrest of Robert Burns Jr. was signed by a judge at nine a.m., and the caravan of three FBI vehicles, two sedans and a Suburban, screeched to a halt in front of the building containing Robert Burns Jr.'s condo at 9:32 a.m.

Ryan Clark stepped out of the lead vehicle, looked around while he buttoned his suit coat, and waited for the agents in the Suburban to exit. He had four agents from the local SWAT team in full gear ready for the arrest. Two other agents, both of whom Clark had worked with in the past, joined him as they reviewed their plan.

"We will execute like we discussed," he began, then pointed toward the SWAT team. "You four will make first contact. The rest of us will follow with the warrant. Let's get this done. Ready?"

Everyone nodded, and they headed toward the front of the building.

The initial knock on the door went without a response. The second attempt received the same. No answer. Clark took out his cell phone and walked down the hallway. His call was answered immediately.

"When was the last time anyone physically saw Burns?'"

One of the agents on the day team watching Burns' condo answered. "Last night, he took a walk, we had a team following him."

"Where's the ankle monitor."

"In the condo. I'm looking at the signal right now."

"Shit."

"What's wrong?"

"He's not answering the door."

"Probable cause?"

"Yeah, medical emergency."

Clark heard a chuckle. "Go for it, we concur."

With a smile, he returned to the group of agents waiting outside Burns' door. "There could be a medical emergency. Force entry if he doesn't answer this time."

The lead SWAT agent, known to Clark simply as Mark, knocked again.

"FBI, Mr. Burns, we need you to come to the door. Repeat, we need you to come to the door."

Again, no response. Clark nodded at the agent. "I believe we have a medical emergency, please open the door, Mark."

The SWAT leader pointed to a team member with a one-man battering ram slung on his shoulder.

"Your turn."

This agent, whom Clark had only met earlier in the morning and could not remember his name, nodded and unslung the ram. Two agents drew their weapons and stood to the side of the door, one positioned on each side.

The agent with the ram positioned himself in front of the door and looked at Mark. When the agents by the door nodded, Mark raised his hand and used it to silently count down from three.

The force of the forty-pound steel tube filled with synthetic concrete shattered the door jam. The door slammed against a wall inside. The two agents on the side of the door were in first, weapons in front sweeping the room for hostile opponents. There were none.

Clark followed the SWAT members into the room, and while they swept the rest of the residence, he holstered his gun and stared at a dining room chair sitting in the middle of the living area. On the chair was Burns' ankle monitor attached to a small Samsung tablet. Burns was nowhere in the apartment.

Retrieving his cell phone, he dialed Kruger's cell phone. It was answered on the first ring.

"Is he in custody?"

"He's gone. Ankle monitor is here, but he isn't."

"Damn."

"What now, Sean?"

"Put a BOLO out on him. How long do you think he's been gone?"

"Surveillance team reported he went for a walk last night. It was the last time they saw him."

"He could be anywhere by now. I'll call Seltzer."

"We'll secure the place and wait to hear from you."

***

Carol Welch was furious. District Judge Todd Lewis refused to take her call, she was forced to leave a message for him. After slamming the phone handset back into its cradle, she looked up at FBI Agent Ryan Clark and took a deep breath. "So what is the Bureau doing to find him?"

"We have the U.S. Marshall Service involved, and all local law enforcement agencies on the East Coast have been notified of his escape."

"You realize he is probably miles away."

"Yes, Sean thinks he had help from his Russian contacts."

She frowned and stared at Clark. "Why?"

Clark shook his head, "He didn't say, but he seemed pretty sure of himself."

"Find out."

The FBI agent nodded as he left her office.

***

"When did the Russian chat room go silent?"

"Early this morning. There was a flurry of messages and now nothing."

"Do they mention Burns?"

JR shook his head. "No, but there is mention of a package to be picked up in Georgetown."

"When was that message?"

"About eleven p.m."

"When did the messages stop?"

JR looked at his monitor and then back up at Kruger. "Last one was at ten minutes after one a.m., then nothing."

"What did it say?"

"*Ich habs.*"

"That's German. It means 'got it.'"

"Why German?"

"Remember, Burns had an Austrian passport."

"Oh yeah, forgot. Think they picked him up?"

"I don't think it, I know it. I just can't prove it."

***

Robert Burns Jr. opened his eyes, groggy from whatever was in the shot he'd received after climbing into the black Chrysler 300 behind his condo. His hands were immobile behind him and both legs were taped to the legs of the chair where he sat. His neck was stiff from supporting his head while unconscious.

Blinking several times, he saw a large man reading a newspaper in a chair next to a door. The room he occupied was sparsely furnished and smelled of gasoline and tires. Newspapers covered windows that started half way up the wall and extended to the ceiling. Only two walls had windows; the two remaining were solid cinderblock.

The man reading the paper looked up at him, stood, and

stepped out of the room. He returned a few minutes later followed by another man, this one not as large.

"Well, Mr. Burns, I see you are awake." The voice had a distinct European accent. He was of average height, big boned, with a bulbous nose, dark wavy hair, bushy eyebrows, and cheeks scarred by untreated ache.

Burns stared at the man. "Where am I?"

"A long way from where you were. You are violating terms of your bail."

"Again, where am I?"

"New York City. An old warehouse close to Hudson River."

Burns glared at the man, but did not respond.

"You don't seem surprised. Which is good, since you contacted us to help you leave Washington."

"Why am I tied up?"

"Because we wanted to make sure you understand why you were brought here and why you are no longer important to us."

Burns' head snapped back, and his eyes grew wide. "What do you mean, no longer important?"

"You are idiot, Bobby," the man emphasized the second syllable of his name.

"I don't understand. My dad has an agreement with you."

"The correct tense of the word is 'had.' Had an agreement with us. You were supposed to be a senator, but you could not keep dick in pants."

Sweat popped out on Burns' forehead. The conversation was starting to concern him.

"You're sweating, Bobby. Why? Nervous? Good. You should be."

"What do you want? Money? I've got lots of money. How much?"

The man shook his head and smiled. "Money, I have. Influence in Congress, I don't. You were supposed to give me influence."

"Who said so?"

"Your father. He told me you would do anything he told you to do. Just like when he was a senator. He did what we told him."

Robert Burns Jr. stared at the man in front of him as his stomach knotted and bile reached the back of his mouth.

"No, we are done wasting money on the Burns family. We will deliver a message to your father. In fact you will help with the message."

The man pulled a .22 caliber pistol with a long tube on the barrel from underneath his sport coat. He pointed the weapon at the center of Burns' forehead. "Goodbye, Bobby."

The pistol spat with a muffled sound, and the head of Robert Burns Jr., snapped back and then slumped forward. Blood trickled from the small hole in the center of his forehead.

The dark-haired man returned the pistol to his sport coat pocket and looked at the man sitting next to the door. He was still reading the newspaper and paying little attention to the execution of Robert Burns Jr.

"Clean up the mess and make sure his head is sealed in an airtight bag before you FedEx it to the father."

The larger man stood, nodded, and folded his paper before placing it on the seat of the chair.

CHAPTER 41

Seattle, WA
Two Days Later

Sean Kruger opened the back door of the agency pool car and threw his overnight bag onto the back seat. After slipping into the front passenger side of the car, he turned to the driver.

"Thanks for picking me up, Jimmie."

"No problem."

Gibbs pulled the car away from the passenger pick-up lane curb and accelerated toward the airport exit.

"Did you see it?"

Gibbs nodded.

"Who called?"

"Burns' secretary. She was, uh…" He paused for a second. "Beyond hysterical."

"What about the father?"

"He's the one who opened the package. It was addressed to Senior and had 'Your Eyes Only' stamped all over it."

"Where's Burns now?"

"Local field office has him in protective custody. His attorney encouraged him to take the offer. He's shaken up and wants to speak to you and only you."

Kruger frowned. "Why?"

"Don't know. He won't talk to Sandy or me."

"Where is the package?"

"Lab."

"Other than not having a body attached, were there any wounds?"

"Twenty-two caliber hole in the center of his forehead."

Nodding, Kruger turned and stared out the front window. "Damn, we may never find the women now."

"Maybe Senior knows."

Tilting his head slightly, he turned to Gibbs and mused, "You think…"

An hour later, Kruger walked into a starkly furnished room containing an eight-foot table and six folding metal chairs. The walls were bare and painted a shade of cream bordering on dirty. It smelled of human sweat and cigarettes. There were no windows. Robert Burns Sr. was pacing in an open area near the far wall. When he looked up, he frowned.

"Why did it take you so long to get here? I've been stuck in this horrible place for over twenty-four hours."

Kruger didn't answer. He just stood next to the table and placed a file folder in front of a chair.

"Are you going to answer me?"

"Why did you want to talk to me, Mr. Burns?"

Taken aback by the FBI agent's refusal to answer his question, Burns snorted. "I would think it obvious. The death of my son."

Sitting in a chair on the other side of the table, Kruger opened the file. "Why do you think your son was executed and his head sent to you in a FedEx box?"

"Isn't it your job to answer questions like that, Agent?"

Looking up from the file, Kruger kept a neutral expression. "Perhaps. But I think you know why. It will be my job to find the individual who did it. Now sit down."

Burns narrowed his eyes and put his palms flat on the table across from Kruger. "How dare you speak to me that way. I'll have your badge."

Shaking his head and sighing, Kruger took out his cell phone and pressed an icon.

The voice of Robert Burns Sr. was heard trying to bribe the FBI agent.

Burns' eyes grew wide. "You recorded a private conversation without my permission."

"Put a sock in it, Burns, and sit down."

"That's a violation of my rights."

Narrowing his eyes, Kruger glared at the elder Burns. "Do you know what the penalty for attempting to bribe a federal agent is, Mr. Burns?"

"How dare you imply I was bribing you…"

"SHUT UP AND SIT DOWN."

Burns' eyes were now like saucers, but his expression softened, and he sat.

"I'm used to being in control of the situation, Agent. At the moment I'm not. I apologize."

Kruger clasped his hands together and tilted his head to the left. "Good, now we can talk."

Nodding his head, Burns placed his hands in front of him and studied the top of the table. Kruger stared at the man. In that moment, he realized Burns had never faced a situation he could not control. It was a new and uncomfortable experience for him.

In a less confrontational tone, Kruger asked, "Mr. Burns, why would someone execute your son?"

"Sins of the father, Agent. Sins of the father."

"Care to elaborate?"

"Should I have my lawyer present?"

"Your choice, but you are not currently charged with anything. Has anyone read you your Miranda rights?"

Burns shook his head.

"Then there is no need for your attorney, unless you would feel more comfortable with one present. I'm trying to establish why someone would execute your son, that's all."

Folding his hands together in front of him and turning his gaze toward the ceiling, Burns took a deep breath and let it out slowly.

"Bobby was always a problem. I don't know if it was the fact I was never at home or that his mother died when he was three. I couldn't keep a nanny for any length of time to care for him because he was always in trouble."

"How so?"

"Acting up in class, not paying attention. Normal behavior for a bright bored young boy."

"I understand he had a high IQ?"

Nodding, Burns continued, "He was gifted with an IQ of 151. That's in the top one percent, Agent. Once they found this out, he was moved into classes more challenging. His behavior changed a little, but he didn't understand how to socialize with people. He found them…" He sighed. "Not sure how to say this correctly."

"It's just the two of us here." Kruger had failed to tell Burns the conversion was being recorded.

"He thought of most people as inferior."

"Including women?"

A grim smile appeared briefly. "Especially women. That was why I had a hard time keeping a nanny."

Kruger nodded.

"He started Stanford on his seventeenth birthday. Things were fine. He enjoyed the challenging classes, finally dealing with people he felt were his equal." He paused. "During his first semester, he was invited to a fraternity party. He drank too much and assaulted a young woman."

"What happened?"

"As you know, Agent Kruger, I am extremely wealthy."

Kruger nodded. "So I've been told."

"I made my first of multiple mistakes with him. I paid his way out of trouble."

"As a father, we're allowed mistakes raising our kids."

"Do you have a son, Agent Kruger?"

"Yes." As was his habit, he never elaborated about his family.

"Then you understand how we want to protect them."

"Yes, I understand."

Burns studied the ceiling tiles again. Kruger thought he saw moisture in the corner of his left eye. After blinking rapidly, Burns returned to watching his clasped hands.

"As I told you, it was my first of many mistakes with Bobby. The young lady transferred to another school where I made sure her tuition was prepaid and a trust fund set up. I understand she's a doctor now.

"Anyway, I hired an ex-Army sergeant who was starting a security company. He was charged with keeping Bobby out of trouble. That lasted for a while, until Bobby graduated early and came to work for me at one of my technology companies. He was barely twenty-one and designing revolutionary computer equipment. The company's stock soared, and he became rich in his own right.

"I thought his trouble with women was in his past. I was wrong."

"What happened?"

"Joel Moody happened."

"Excuse me?"

Burns nodded. "Joel Moody was a Seattle vice cop. He caught Bobby with a hooker who was barely alive. He recognized who he was dealing with and brought him to me, instead of arresting him."

"So that was the connection?"

"Yes, that was the connection. I then made my next horrible mistake. I paid Moody to watch over my son and keep him out of trouble. This was when I decided I needed to become a senator. Another mistake in hindsight."

Kruger frowned. "So Joel Moody was keeping tabs on your son while you ran for the Senate. When was that, Mr. Burns?"

"I started in 1998, won the election in 2000, sworn-in during a ceremony on January 3, 2001, and started serving the citizens of Washington for the next twelve years."

"Where was Bobby during this time?"

"I am sure you know by now what he was doing."

"I have some suspicions. Why don't you confirm them?"

"He was running Haylex Solutions and helping to install student accounting software at various colleges."

"Yes, I was aware of that."

"Are you aware that Joel Moody traveled with him?"

Kruger felt a jolt of energy with the confirmation, but kept his expression neutral. "No."

"He did. You also probably know that Bobby's tastes changed at this time don't you."

A quick nod was Kruger's only response.

"Joel Moody had made connections with some rather unsavory Russians in Seattle. He was taking money from them to look the other way while they smuggled in young girls in from China, Thailand, and Vietnam. Moody is a greedy man, Agent Kruger. He didn't act like it, but he is."

"When you said Bobby's tastes changed, what are you referring to?"

"Don't play naïve with me, Agent. You know perfectly well what I mean."

"I'm a little slow sometimes."

"Bobby started hurting the women he was with. Moody cleaned it up."

"By hurting, what do you mean?"

"Rape. Beating. Erotic asphyxiation. Worse. You name it, Bobby was doing it."

"What was Moody's role in this?"

"He got them to the hospital and paid them to keep quiet."

Kruger leaned back in his folding chair and stared at the older man, finally understanding.

"Mr. Burns, how much money did Moody receive to pay off the women?"

"Anywhere from five hundred thousand to a million each, depending on the circumstance."

"Why did you do that, Mr. Burns?"

"Bobby's contributions to the company were generating profits one hundred times that amount, Agent."

"So Bobby hurt them, Moody took care of them, and you paid them off. Does that summarize it, Mr. Burns?"

The elder Burns nodded. "I'm not proud of it, but it kept the company profitable."

Kruger took a deep breath and pushed his anger deep within himself. He stood and paced for a few moments. Burns continued to study his hands as Kruger paced. Finally he returned to his chair and sat down.

"Mr. Burns, the women Bobby attacked have never been found. They were not taken to a hospital, nor were they reunited with their families. They simply vanished without a trace. Moody used part of the money to hire men to dispose of the bodies and then pocketed the rest."

Kruger stood again and walked toward the door. He paused to say, "Think about that for a few minutes while I consult with my team."

Burns stared at the door after the FBI agent left. The revelation about the victims of Robert Burns Jr. and his part in those events caused him to bend over and violently start retching.

***

Kruger walked straight to the men's room and bent over one of the sinks. While he was splashing cold water on his face, Sandy Knoll walked in. He leaned against the wall and watched his friend settle down.

"Do you believe him?"

Nodding, Kruger stared at his own image in the mirror. He barely recognized the face gazing back at him. The hair was grayer and the dark circles under his eyes more pronounced.

"Yeah, I do. All the pieces fit. It helps explain the ten million dollars JR found in an account owned by Moody. Plus, Junior's insisting the Ramos woman was alive when he left. It makes sense now. He never tried to kill any of them. He just hurt them and walked away."

He turned to look at Knoll. "Did Moody kill them and the Russians dispose of the bodies? Or did Moody just turn them over to the Russians?"

"That's a good question. Wish I had an answer." He paused for a moment as he judged the current state of mind of his friend. "There's been a development in Moody's disappearance."

"About damn time. What?"

"Moody's wife was detained by TSA as she went through security at Denver International. She had a ticket to Grand Cayman. Denver field office has her in custody."

"Any sign of him?"

Knoll shook his head.

"Is she talking?"

"No, says she'll only talk to you."

Kruger shook his head. "What is it with these people? Can't they talk to anyone else?"

Smiling, Knoll chuckled. "It's because you're so likable."

"Funny, Sandy, very funny. Let's get to the airport."

CHAPTER 42

Denver, CO
Denver County Sheriff's Department Building

Kruger studied the passport he held in his hands.

"Betty Norman. Huh. It looks real."

FBI Special Agent Marcie Kincaid from the Denver field office stood next to him while he examined the passport. Stocky and several inches shorter than Kruger, her medium-length brown hair was tied in a ponytail. Kincaid was a twelve-year veteran of the Bureau. Kruger had met her two years prior during the hunt for serial killer Randolph Bishop. She stood silently with her hands behind her back as she waited for Kruger to finish with the document.

She pointed to the various entry stamps and observed, "Best one I've ever seen."

Nodding his head, he closed the booklet. "Any sign of the husband?"

Kincaid shook her head.

Looking through the one-way glass, he watched the woman fidget as she sat in one of the interrogation room chairs.

"She looks nervous. Did she make a statement?"

"No."

"Has she asked for a lawyer?"

"Not yet. She makes eye contact, says she'll only talk to you, and then looks away."

"Wonder what that's all about? I've never met her."

Sandy Knoll walked up behind Kruger and announced, "Just finished looking through her luggage."

Turning to look at the big man, Kruger asked, "Anything unusual?"

Smiling, Knoll nodded. "Three bundles of hundred dollar bills and her real passport." He handed the passport to Kruger.

Taking it, Kruger returned his gaze to the woman in the room. "Thirty thousand, huh. Wonder what that was for."

Knoll also looked at the woman. "An extended stay overseas, maybe?"

Kruger placed both passports into his inside breast sport coat pocket. "Marcie, would you accompany me?" he asked.

She nodded, and they walked toward the interrogation room door.

Beverly Moody looked up as Kruger and Kincaid entered the room. Her eye narrowed as she stared at him. "Are you Sean Kruger?"

Kincaid stood by the door as Kruger scooted out the chair across from the wife of Joel Moody. She was of average height, unnaturally skinny, and wore her straight brown hair short. Her green eyes looked weary. The wrinkles on her forehead and next to her eyes screamed stress.

Sitting across from her, he removed the passports from his sport coat. Placing them on the table, he answered her question.

"Yes, I'm Agent Sean Kruger, Ms. Moody."

"Finally. Why am I being detained?"

Smiling, he tapped the fake passport. "Violation of US Code 1543, use of a forged or false passport."

She blinked several times.

"It's a felony with a prison term of ten to twenty-five

years, depending on your purpose for it. Was the thirty thousand dollars for a drug purchase, Ms. Moody?"

Remaining quiet, she continued to stare at Kruger and blink rapidly.

"Do you wish to have a lawyer?"

She shook her head as she lowered her gaze and studied the tabletop. "No, I'm tired of the charade."

"What charade?"

"The lie I've been living for the past twenty years."

"Want to tell me about it?"

"Are you going to arrest me?"

"Not yet. If you lie to me, I will. But for now, no. I want the truth about Joel Moody."

"Where do I start?"

He smiled. "The beginning is always a good place."

"Can I have a cup of coffee?"

Kruger nodded.

Twenty minutes later, after she was escorted to the restroom and given a fresh cup of coffee, she sat still while grasping the Styrofoam cup with both hands. Kruger placed a digital recorder on the table and pressed the record button.

Kruger spoke first. "Statement of Beverly Moody, Denver County Sheriff's Department, Denver, Colorado." He stated the date and looked at her. "For the record, will you state your real name?"

"My real name is Gayle Patterson. I've been living under the name Beverly Moody for the past twenty years."

"Why?"

"Originally to avoid being arrested for drug smuggling, then because I liked the lifestyle Joel provided."

"So you weren't married?"

"I'm not sure. When we got married, he didn't let me use my real name. I guess we aren't really married, are we?"

Kruger only shook his head.

"Joel had a crush on me. Why, I don't know. He told me he was a plainclothes cop for the Seattle PD when he caught me the first time. I had sex with him, and he let me go, minus the drugs, of course."

"Of course."

"Second time he caught me was a few weeks later, with even more drugs."

"Why were you in possession of drugs?"

"I wasn't a user. I was a mule, getting paid a lot of money to pick up drugs smuggled in through the Port of Seattle. Joel knew about it and was always watching me. I didn't know it at the time, but he was. He waited until I had a really big shipment of heroin in my possession before he busted me again."

"What happened?"

"He offered a deal. Pretend to be his wife, with all the fringe benefits and get out of smuggling. Or—go to prison for a long time."

"So you took the deal?"

She nodded. "For the first twelve years it was good. He gave me a new ID, a new Social Security number, and a nice house. He was a gentle man, never abused me or hit me. I wasn't used to that. Most of the guys I knew liked to use me as a punching bag. I really thought he loved me. So I stayed."

"So what happened?"

"Robert Burns Sr."

Kruger tilted his head to the side. "Excuse me?"

She wrapped her arms around her and curled her legs under her. Moisture leaked from her eyes. "Joel changed after he went to work for Burns."

"How?"

She shrugged. "I doh-know, he just did."

"What do you want me to call you? Beverly or Gayle?"

She shook her head and hugged herself tighter. Tears were now streaming down her face. "I don't care, Beverly is fine. I haven't been called Gayle since high school."

Kruger eyes narrowed, and he gave her an understanding nod. "Beverly, what do you think Joel was doing for Robert Burns Sr?"

She didn't answer for a long time, her eyes locked on the

top of the table between them. "I was never told, but I can guess."

"Indulge me."

"I think he was cleaning up the messes created by that bastard son."

In a voice barely above a whisper, Kruger leaned forward and asked. "Why do you say that?"

The fury flared immediately. She snapped her head up and she glared at Kruger. "Because Joel never touched me sexually after he started working for the father."

Sitting back in his chair, Kruger looked at Kincaid and then back to the sobbing woman.

"I'm sorry, Beverley."

She did not respond.

***

Todd Norman watched as a female TSA agent escorted the woman formally known as Beverly Moody away from the security line. When the two disappeared through a door next to the security line, the man formerly known as Joel Moody turned from his observation spot and headed toward the airport terminal exit for the parking lot shuttle.

Using her as bait was not his first preference, but he had to know if the FBI was after him. They were.

Fifteen minutes later, he was back at the Kia SUV purchased in Seattle three days ago. During his walk to the SUV from the shuttle stop in long-term parking, he passed a similar Kia with a Colorado license plate five rows from his vehicle. After the other newly dropped off travelers were in their vehicles and driving away, he returned to the other Kia. After checking the visible security cameras, he ducked down behind the vehicle and removed the back plate with a Swiss Army knife. Returning to his Kia, he drove to the exit gate and paid the minimum parking fee. After driving south on E-470, he exited and headed east on I-70.

In Goodland, Kansas, he found a locally owned fleabag

hotel, paid cash for one night, and retired to the room. Backing the Kia into the parking slot in front of his room, he removed the temporary license tag and replaced it with the plate stolen at the Denver airport. Once this was done, he locked the room's door and collapsed on the bed.

Exhausted from three days of steady driving and constantly looking in the rearview mirror, he surveyed the shabbiness of the hotel accommodations. Updates and maintenance were non-existent components of the room. It smelled of Lysol and cigarette smoke. Weariness overcame his repulsion as he laid his head on the dirty pillow. The next thing he knew, it was mid-morning the next day. In the daylight, the room was even more depressing than the night before.

Swinging his legs over the side and sitting on the side of the squeaky bed, he sat and buried his head in his hands. His escape plan was in total ruin.

***

Knoll, Kruger, and Marcie Kincaid were back at the Denver County Sheriff's department at nine a.m. the next day. Beverly Moody was led to the interrogation room. She looked disheveled and fatigued.

When she saw Kruger, her first words were almost hysterical. "I thought I wasn't under arrest?"

Kruger smiled. "You aren't."

"Then get me out of this hell-hole NOW."

"We have you under protective custody, Beverly."

Moody turned her attention to the female FBI agent. "I don't need protective custody. I want out."

"Beverly…" Kruger's voice was calm and soothing. "Why did you and Joel make such a hasty exit from Seattle in the middle of the night?"

"He told me it was time to go."

"At ten o'clock at night?"

"He didn't tell me why. He just said it was time to go."

"But surely you had suspicions."

"Are you going to get me out of here?"

"Maybe… Depends."

"Depends on what?"

"How cooperative you are."

"I've tried to answer all of your questions. How much more cooperative can I be?"

Kruger smiled, glanced at Kincaid, then back at Moody. Kincaid asked, "Beverly, what was the thirty thousand dollars for?"

Shaking her head, Beverly stared at the tabletop. After a long silence she sighed. "Joel had the same amount. We were taking separate flights to Miami and we would fly on to Grand Cayman together. The plan was if we got separated, we would both find our way there and meet later. The cash was for emergencies."

Nodding, Kincaid handed Kruger the file folder she held. He placed it on the table in front of Beverly. He pulled out a few sheets of paper and looked up at her.

"Know what this is?"

She shook her head.

"Seattle police file on Gayle Patterson." He withdrew half-reader glasses from this suit jacket front pocket and placed them on his nose. "Seems you lied to us yesterday about your background, Beverly."

She stared wide-eyed at Kruger.

He read from the top sheet: "Three counts of possession with intent to sell, four counts of solicitation, one count of aggravated assault, and the grand finale, human trafficking. Care to comment?"

"I didn't lie to you. I just didn't tell you everything."

Kruger chuckled and nodded.

"How much do you know about Joel Moody's connections to the sex trade in Seattle?"

"He protected the Russians who were bringing the girls in."

"How?"

She chewed on her lower lip and stared at the ceiling. "You get me a deal and I'll tell you everything I know."

"We haven't charged you with anything yet, Beverly."

"Then let me out of here."

Kruger sat back in his chair and folded his arms over his chest. He did not respond.

"You can't hold me more than forty-eight hours without charging me, Agent."

He nodded.

"Charge me, get me a public defender, and then make the deal. I know more than you think I do."

***

While Marcie Kincaid attended to the details of getting Beverly Moody assigned to a public defender, Kruger and Knoll met in a conference room.

Kruger spoke first. "What do you think?"

"If she can shed light on the real relationship of Joel Moody and the Burnses, I'd say do it."

"Senior's given us his side of the story, which I'm beginning to doubt. Junior is dead, and Moody's in the wind." Kruger studied his shoes for a few moment. "I agree, I'll call Carol Welch. Maybe she can expedite a deal with the district attorney out here."

CHAPTER 43

Goodland, KS

Moody paid cash for another night at the Sunrise Inn and spent the day determining what his next steps should be. A trip to the local Walmart provided a no-contract cell phone with a thousand minutes of pre-paid time and an HP Chromebook computer. At a pawn shop, he bought a Kahr CT9 pistol and several boxes of 9mm hollow point ammunition.

After his shopping trip, he settled into a booth at a local diner with free Wi-Fi and started planning his trip. By three in the afternoon he had a route, using secondary roads and less traveled highways, back to Seattle.

Funds were not an issue. Besides the original thirty thousand dollars in his suitcase, there was another fifty thousand in tens and fives in the Kia's spare tire well. Cash would be all he used on his trek to Seattle. Plus, he figured no one would expect him to return.

The route would take three days traveling mostly at night. But once he arrived in Seattle, Robert Burns Sr. would understand the word payback.

***

Kruger turned over the details and administrative duties of working out a plea bargain for Beverly Moody to the Denver Field Office and Federal District Court of Colorado. He caught the first direct flight from Denver to Springfield. He would return when it was time to take her statement about Robert Burns Sr. Knoll had a brother who lived in Denver, so he stayed and would keep Kruger up-to-date on the progress.

The ten a.m. flight got him to Springfield a little before one p.m. local time. The house was quiet when he walked in from the garage. Stephanie was at the University, Mikey at the day-care facility and Kristin at kindergarten. As soon as he unpacked his go-bag, took a shower, and called Stephanie to let her know he was home, he headed over to JR's office.

JR was at his cubicle working on a project for a client when Kruger walked up to the coffee service behind JR. He had brought a bag of ground coffee for the Mr. Coffee unit. After starting a pot, he leaned against the table and waited for JR to acknowledge his presence.

"I told you the Mr. Coffee pot would be a pain in the ass."

Kruger shrugged. "I'm perfectly fine with making my own coffee."

Turning around so he could look at this friend, JR asked, "So what is going on with Moody?"

"He's in the wind, and his wife is cutting a deal with Carol Welch to tell all she knows."

Nodding, JR turned back to his computer and minimalized the screens he was working on. He opened a file with what appeared to be a surveillance camera image. The image was of Joel Moody.

"Yesterday morning, our Mr. Moody identified himself as Todd Norman and bought a Kahr CT9 at a pawn shop called Bobs Gun's and More in Goodland, Kansas. Background check was clean and the sale went right through. He paid cash."

Kruger stood with his mouth open as he stared at the

screen. Finally after a few moments, he took a deep breath. "I was supposed to be notified if something like this happened."

"You will be, but the wheels of the FBI bureaucracy turn slowly."

"How'd you find it?"

JR smiled. "You probably don't want to know."

"Probably right. Anything else on him?"

"Not that I can find right now. If he had thirty thousand dollars, like his wife, he's probably using cash to prevent a money trail. He is an ex-cop."

"Yeah, he is. So now he has a gun." He poured a cup of coffee while he pondered the news.

JR asked, "Can he get out of the country on an airplane? Or do you have TSA on the lookout for him?"

"We do. I believe that's why he sent his wife through security first. He sacrificed her to see if anyone was after them."

"Nice guy."

"To answer your question, he could, but it would be risky." He took a sip of the hot beverage, smiled, and continued. "They weren't really married."

JR frowned.

"Long story. Let's just say she's pissed and wants to testify against him."

"So what's he going to do? You're the psychologist."

"Psychologist, yes. Mind reader, no. There's a difference."

JR chuckled. "I been around you a few times when I thought you could read minds."

Kruger stopped raising his coffee half-way to his lips. He lowered the cup and set it on the table next to the Mr. Coffee. His eyes stared at a point only he could see.

"Uh oh, I've seen that look before. What?"

"I was remembering my two conversations with Moody. The so-called help he was going to give us by introducing your little program in the Haylex system."

"I've thought about that. Didn't he say he used the computer of a VP of sales while they were on vacation?"

"Yeah."

"From what I learned during the short time I was in their system, they have it separated into three silos. Sales, Affiliates, and Others. There is zero communication between the silos, so if you access the sales system, you don't have access to the other two and vice versa."

"How does Senior find out what he needs in sales?"

"That's the beauty of their system, Sean. Senior had access to all the silos."

"So if Moody had placed the flash drive into an admin computer, we would have had the access we needed."

"Correct, but we didn't know that at the time."

"Did he?"

"As their head of security, I would think so."

"That, JR, was Moody's first lie. He was pretending to help us. Probably trying to determine how much we knew. The second was telling us he didn't know why Senior was so intent on protecting Junior. He was right in the middle of it, and he told me he was just hired help. Hell, he was the man keeping Junior out of trouble."

"Sean, what do the Russians and sex trafficking have to do with all this?"

Kruger shook his head and once again stared off at distant point. He stayed like that for several moments. "Ah, shit," he finally murmured.

"What?"

"This may be way off base, but the only information we've been given is about importing women from Asia."

"Yeah."

"What if it goes the other way? What if there is also a network of American women being smuggled to other countries?"

"How would we check?"

"Not sure we could, but I need to know how many missing person reports are never resolved. The Bureau will have that info."

***

"Barbara Whitlock."

"Barbara, it's Sean Kruger."

"You keep calling and people are going to start talking. Is this social or business?"

"Business."

"You always spoil our conversations with work. What can I do for you?"

"Remember the missing person search for the D.C. and Northwest US a few days ago?"

"Yes."

"I need the same search for the entire country."

"You're kidding me?"

"Nope."

"What are my criteria?"

"Same as the last search, but don't limit it to known prostitutes. Include any women declared missing and never found."

"Sean, sometimes they come back, and no one tells us."

"I'm aware of that, but I still need you to do the research."

"For you, no problem. I'll email you the results."

"Thanks, Barbara."

He walked out of JR's conference room and stared at the back of his friend's head.

"What do you think she'll find?" JR turned around.

"I may have cast too big of a net."

"I looked up some statistics while you were talking to her."

"Okay, tell me."

"First, about 900,000 people are reported missing in the U.S. each year. Of those, only 50,000 are over the age of eighteen. So that means most of the missing are kids, which you are not interested in."

"No, at least not yet."

"Fair enough. Half of the missing adults are white, thirty percent are African Americans, and twenty percent are

Hispanic. The number of women outnumber the men by just a fraction over fifty percent. These statistics vary year by year, Sean. So each year, you could have over thirty thousand or more missing women."

"How many are found?"

"That statistic's hard to determine."

"So what are you telling me, JR?"

"You have a huge number of individuals to investigate."

"Who speaks for them? Who's their advocate?"

JR didn't answer.

"That's what I thought. No one."

***

Kruger spent the rest of the day working the phone between Knoll in Denver, Carol Welch in Washington, and Jimmie Gibbs in Seattle. By the time Stephanie returned home, he had completed what he felt needed to be accomplished from his remote locale. The rest of the evening was spent with the kids and talking to Stephanie.

As he was turning out the light on his side of the bed, Stephanie leaned up on one elbow. "Are you getting adjusted to being with the FBI again?"

Laying down, he was quiet for a few moments. "I slipped back in so easily it was almost like I never left."

"Kind of what I thought would happen. It's who you are, Sean. Don't fool yourself again and think you can do anything else and still be happy."

"There's still one thing that bothers me."

"What's that?"

"Being away from you and the children."

"Good. Don't stop letting it bother you." She leaned over and kissed him.

"I miss those when I'm gone, too," he said with a smile.

"Don't stop missing them either, mister."

They both chuckled and settled in for the night.

Kruger was barely asleep when his cell phone chirped.

Without hesitating, he grabbed it from his night stand and glanced at the ID. Not recognizing the number, he accepted the call.

"Kruger."

"Is this FBI Agent Sean Kruger?"

It was a woman's voice, the cell phone connection weak leaving the voice thin.

He responded with a tentative, "Yes, who's this."

"Tanya Brown. I'm the night dispatcher for the Gallatin County, Montana, Sheriff's Department. I'm looking at a BOLO from the FBI for a Black 2016 Kia Sportage. It gives us this number to call if we spot it."

"Yes, Ms. Brown. Where was it spotted?"

"West of Bozeman on I-90. One of our deputies stopped it because it had a stolen license plate on it."

Kruger frowned. "A stolen license plate?"

"Yes, a similar make and model Kia had the rear plate stolen at the Denver International Airport. Owner of the car didn't know when it was stolen, but when he returned yesterday and putting his luggage in the back, he noticed it missing. Since it was from a black Kia, our deputy stopped the vehicle to check."

"What happened?"

"When the deputy walked up to the driver's window and asked him to step out, he did. Next thing the deputy knew, he was on the ground, and his front tires were flat on his patrol car. No sign of the Kia."

"The suspect is an ex-cop."

"Kind of explains it."

"How is the deputy?"

"More embarrassed than hurt. It could have been worse."

"Much worse. When did this occur?"

"About a two hours ago."

"What direction was the Kia heading when it was stopped?"

"West."

Kruger paused and imagined a map of the western United

States. "Ms. Brown, how far is Bozeman from Seattle?"

"Oh, probably over six hundred miles, through the Flatheads."

"Beg your pardon?"

"The Flathead Range, part of the Northern Rocky Mountains."

"Oh. How long to drive to Seattle, seven or eight hours?"

"More like ten."

"He's headed back to Seattle. Thank you, Ms. Brown."

"What do you want me to do about the BOLO?"

"You've done exactly what we needed."

Kruger ended the call and immediately called Jimmie Gibbs.

He answered on the second ring. "Yeah."

"Moody's been spotted in Montana, heading your way. Where's Burns?

"Went home. Lawyers convinced him the danger was over."

"Shit."

"Want me to head over there?"

"No, I want you to pick me up at the airport. If I can swing a ride on an agency plane, I can be there before Moody makes the drive."

"Call me when you know."

Kruger ended the call and sat on the edge of the bed. Stephanie chuckled. "Let me guess, you're leaving?"

He closed his eyes and took a deep breath. Not wishing to make any excuses, he let his breath out slowly. "I hope for the last time on this case."

"Sean, don't worry. We'll be here. Take care of business."

He turned and smiled.

CHAPTER 44

Seattle, WA

At 4:23 a.m., Joel Moody parked the black Kia several blocks from the glass and concrete monolith known as the home of Robert Burns Sr. The original temp tag was now displayed and the stolen plate discarded. The street was quiet, the lights of the Seattle reflecting off the bay water to his right and the imposing home ahead on his left. Gaining entry would be easy. He was the individual responsible for having the security system installed and knew the correct codes to gain entry. Knowing Burns the way he did, he doubted the old man would think to have the codes changed. That was a job for someone else.

As he approached the wrought-iron fence, he looked up at the glass front and saw Seattle's skyline reflected. The cost to buy the bay side property, tear down the existing structure, and then build this concreate monstrosity was more money than some developing country's yearly GNP. It was also a slap in the face to the historical nature of the surrounding landscape. Moody shook his head as he tapped out the entry code on the eye-level keypad attached to a concreate support column. The lock clicked, the iron-gate opened, and he walked through.

At this hour of morning, Robert Burns and his live-in companion would be asleep in the third-floor master bedroom. He gained access to the interior through a rear door using the same access code. This door led to a laundry mud-room combination. The entire house was illuminated at night by built-in night-lights imbedded in the baseboards. Between the laundry room and the back stairs was an oversized gourmet kitchen. Due to the house being constructed of steel and concrete, there was little concern about the stairs squeaking as he ascended the steps.

At the third floor landing, he heard snoring. One was louder than the other, which meant Burns and Allison O'Brien were present.

Withdrawing the Kahr 9mm from the holster at the small of his back, he entered the bedroom.

***

Jimmie Gibbs drove the agency Tahoe toward the home of Robert Burns Sr. He noticed something and glanced back at an SUV on the side of the street.

"Sean, there's a black Kia Sportage back there with a temp tag. Do you think?"

Kruger glanced at his watch, 5:01 a.m. "Yeah, he beat us. Call for back-up."

After making the call, Gibbs parked the big SUV in front of the wrought-iron gate and looked over at his fellow FBI agent.

"Now what?"

"We wait. Let's see if we can start the day without somebody getting killed."

***

Allison O'Brien was naked and clutched the sheet tight to

her neck to keep from exposing herself. Robert Burns stared at his ex-head of security as he sat with his back against the headboard. Joel Moody sat in a bedroom chair moved to the foot of the bed, his 9mm pistol trained on Burns.

"Strange turn of events, don't you agree, Robert?"

"What do you want, Joel?"

"My life back."

Burns snorted. "You made your own choices. I had nothing to do with them."

Moody shook his head. "Typical rich guy. Never taking responsibility for anything."

"Joel, what is this going to accomplish? Nothing. We'll call my attorneys and get this misunderstanding cleared up."

"You don't get it, do you, Robert? There is no misunderstanding. Your son was a sexual deviate who liked to hurt women. Sometimes they died. Most of the time they didn't, and our Russian friends took care of the mess. What happened to those girls, Robert? Do you know?"

Burns shook his head.

"No, I didn't think you would. Too busy throwing money around protecting your scumbag son."

"I did what a father—"

"SHUT UP."

Burns glared at Moody.

"What exactly did you do to the Russians that pissed them off so bad they sent Bobby's head to you in a FedEx box?"

"I don't know."

"Sure you do. Did you break a promise? Were they still mad about you resigning as a senator? What could you have possibly done to make them do such a thing?"

He saw a tear leak out the side of Burns' eye.

"Son of a bitch, you do have emotions," he marveled. "I didn't think you had the capacity to feel for anyone but yourself."

"You don't know me very well."

The cell phone on the nightstand next to Burns started vibrating.

Moody smiled. "Answer it, Robert. That will be the FBI. I'm sure they know I planned to visit you."

Burns picked up the phone and accepted the call. "Hello."

He was silent as he listened. "Yes, this is Robert Burns." More silence. "Yes, he is sitting in front of me with a gun pointed in my direction." Burns stared at Moody while he listened. He took the phone away from his ear and offered it to Moody. "They want to speak to you."

"Toss it to the foot of the bed."

Burns complied and tossed the phone. It landed in front of Moody at the foot of the bed. He picked it up. "Yeah."

"Joel, this is Sean Kruger."

"I suppose you're going to try and talk me out of ending the life of this sorry excuse for a human being sitting in front of me. Aren't you?"

"That's one of the things I'd like to accomplish. But first I want to know if there is anything you need at the moment."

"Spare me the hostage-negotiation 101. I took the course."

Kruger frowned. Negotiating with someone who knew the drill would be challenging. He took a different track. "Is Allison O'Brien there?"

"Yes."

"Have you hurt her, Joel?"

"Not yet."

"Joel, exactly what are your plans?"

"Haven't got that far yet. I needed to have a chat with Robert."

"Have you?"

"We just got started when you interrupted."

"Let Allison go, Joel. Your interest is Robert, not her."

"Not going to happen, Agent. This conversation is going nowhere, I'm ending it."

He took the phone from his ear and placed it on his right thigh, the end-call icon untouched.

***

Kruger looked at the phone screen, the call was still active. He muted his microphone and turned to Gibbs. "He didn't end the call, he wants us to listen. Call JR, he can record calls on my phone."

He returned to listening.

***

"Now where were we, Robert?"

"This is madness, Joel, they know where you are. They'll storm in here and arrest you."

"Not necessarily. You see, they know I have two hostages being held at gunpoint. Because of that, they will not endanger your life until I give up, or they believe they have no other choice."

"You don't know that."

"Yes, I do, Robert. You see I completed hostage-negotiating training. There are strict guidelines on how to handle hostage situations. So, for now, we have a few hours to discuss why the Russians sent Bobby's head to you in a box."

"I don't know."

Moody pointed the gun at Allison. "Do not underestimate my resolve on this matter, Robert. Allison is nice to look at, but that won't stop me from killing her."

"You won't do it, Joel."

Glaring at Burns, Moody took the cell phone in his left hand, stood, and walked over to the side of the bed where Allison was sitting. She looked at him with wide eyes. Pointing the gun at her head, he tilted his head slightly. "Want to find out?"

She gasped and looked at Burns. "Tell him, Robert. Tell him." Her voice was on the verge of panic.

Burns looked at her and then Moody. "Very well, sit down, Joel. There is no need to harm Allison."

***

Gibbs ended the call to JR and turned back to Kruger, who was still listening to the events playing out on the third floor of the Burns house.

"JR has the recording going. What's happening?"

"Moody just threatened to kill Allison unless Burns tells him about the Russians."

"Is that why he didn't end the call?"

Kruger nodded.

As they spoke, additional police and FBI agents in tactical gear arrived at the scene. Gibbs left Kruger's side to start coordinating the next phase of the operation.

***

"From the beginning, Robert. Don't leave out any details."

"You of all people know how it started. You brought my son's indiscretions to my attention."

"Robert, don't call them indiscretions. He was a sexual predator who liked to beat up hookers."

"Regardless of what you wish to call them, you brought his activities to my attention. The individuals responsible for bringing those types of women into the country didn't like the fact he was harming their assets."

Moody laughed out loud. After shaking his head, he tilted his head. "You're as sick as your son, Burns. You just called human beings assets."

"To the individuals responsible for their presence in Seattle, they were assets. If you're going to interrupt me every time I say something, this situation is never going to end."

"Go on."

"Needless to say, they were watching you and found out Bobby was my son. This was the event leading to my introduction to Dmitri Orlov." Burns took a deep breath and let it out slowly. "He had a problem and determined I was the perfect individual to solve his problem."

"What was his problem, Robert?"

"He needed help getting a few banking regulations relaxed in the U.S. to help his banks do more business. When I asked how I could possibly help, he told me I needed to become a U.S. Senator."

"Just like that? Become a senator and save your son."

"Yes. I funded my own campaign and discovered I enjoyed politics. Once I was in congress, Orlov explained what regulations needed to be relaxed. As it turned out, there were several like-minded senators who co-sponsored the legislation and helped me convince the President. The regulations were relaxed and in some instances, repealed."

"What happened then, Robert?"

"The Great Recession was a direct result of relaxing the banking regulation Orlov wanted changed. When I learned what I had helped create, my enthusiasm for the Senate waned. I lost interest and started spending more time in Seattle."

"So my catching Bobby raping the intern was your excuse to get out of the Senate."

"Yes, it was a perfect out."

"That was the part I didn't understand, why you agreed so quickly to not seek re-election."

"That was the reason."

"So Orlov explained to you why that was a bad decision and you had to do something to make amends. Get Bobby elected."

"Yes."

"Who paid for his election?"

"It was mostly laundered Russian money."

"Why were they so adamant about having someone they could control in the Senate?"

"Orlov told me the Great Recession was an unanticipated consequence of relaxing the regulations. They decided if they had enough senators in their pocket, they could over time destabilize our government."

Moody stared at Burns, his mouth gapping. "You're kidding, right?"

"No, that was their plan."

"So they killed Bobby to send you a message."

"Yes."

"Did you get the message?"

"Yes."

"What was it?"

"Finance the campaigns of their hand-picked candidates."

"By hand-picked, you mean candidates they've compromised?"

"Yes. They will make sure those candidates will support changing laws to help destabilize our government."

"And you're going to do it."

"No, I've caused enough damage. I haven't told Orlov yet, but once I tell him, I'll be dead within a month."

Moody smiled and brought the cell phone back to his ear. "Did you get all that, Agent Kruger?"

Kruger unmuted his phone. "Yes, it's all been recorded. Now, put the gun away and we'll get everybody out of this alive."

Moody placed the phone back on the bed near Burns' feet. He smiled at Burns and shook his head.

"You get off easy, motherfucker."

Without hesitation, Moody placed the barrel of the Kahr 9mm under his chin and pulled the trigger.

CHAPTER 45

Springfield, MO
Two Weeks Later

JR Diminski sat in the soundproof conference room on the second floor of his office building. Kruger sat across from him, staring at the Polycom VoIP Conference Phone. On the other end of the call was Director of the FBI Paul Stumpf, Assistant Director of the FBI Alan Seltzer and Attorney General Brian McAlister at the Hoover Building, with Washington District Attorney Carol Welch in her office.

"What's our next step?" asked Director Stumpf.

"I want to know what happened to all the women who've disappeared at the hands of the younger Burns."

"So do we, Sean. Do you have any ideas?"

"Since his arrest, the father has been cooperating with our Seattle field office. He confirmed Moody was the conduit for alerting Orlov about the son's activities. I think the Russian knows what happened to them."

McAlister spoke next. "Getting Orlov to talk could be a problem, Agent Kruger?"

"Does he have diplomatic immunity?"

"No, he has a visa."

Kruger paused and thought for a few moments, then suggested, "Revoke his visa and issue an arrest-on-sight warrant."

Seltzer said, "That's an interesting idea."

"It could work. After the arrest warrant is issued, I want him to know I'm the one responsible."

"Why?" Stumpf's voice held a note of concern.

"Because I want a meeting."

"Are you sure?"

"Yes, I'm sure."

"Why?"

"I want to know what happened to the college students."

The meeting lasted another ten minutes as details for the arrest warrant were worked out.

After the conference call ended, Kruger looked at JR. "Would you be able to find a cell phone number for Orlov?"

JR looked up from the laptop in front of him and nodded. "Been working on it since you mentioned having a meeting."

"Any luck?"

"Yes, apparently he has the number on his business card."

Kruger smiled slightly. "You're kidding."

"No, he portrays himself as an international banker, therefore he freely gives the number out."

"That's not the number I want to use. He has to have another less public phone."

"He does. I just found it."

"How?"

JR smiled. "Trade secret."

Kruger chuckled.

***

Kruger was back at JR's office the next day. During the twenty four hours since the phone call, the State Department notified Orlov via email about the revoking of his visa. At the same time the email was being sent, the Department of Justice issued a warrant for his arrest. Now it was time to have a quick chat with the man.

Sitting at the conference table, he waited for JR to set up the call. "Will he be able to trace this call back to you?"

JR shook his head. "If they try, it will appear to be coming from a coffee house in Abuja, Nigeria."

Kruger chuckled and just shook his head. "Amazing."

"Not really." A minute later, he looked up from the laptop. "Ready?"

Kruger nodded.

"Here we go." He touched the enter key and both men looked at the Polycom unit. After a few moments, a voice said, "Da."

"Dmitri Orlov?"

"*Kto eto*?"

Kruger looked at JR, who turned the laptop around. A translation program displayed the meaning: *Who is this*?

Kruger nodded. "This is FBI Special Agent Sean Kruger, Mr. Orlov."

The Polycom box was silent. JR shook his head and whispered, "Call's still connected. He's thinking, trying to figure it out."

"I've heard of you Agent Kruger. You have been a busy FBI agent recently and the one responsible for a sudden change in my status in the United States."

"Yes, I am. I wanted to give you a courtesy call about your situation."

"Interesting. How did you get this number?"

"Phone book."

There was a small chuckle from the Russian. "Apparently, I forgot to tell them it was unlisted."

"Mistakes happen."

"Yes. Now, what did you want to tell me about my visa?"

"I understand you received an email explaining why it was revoked."

"A clerical error, I am sure."

"No, it's not a clerical error. Were you aware of an arrest-on-sight warrant issued by the Department of Justice?"

The Russian was silent again. Finally, he returned to the conversation. "You are just full of good news today. Why would your Department of Justice issue an arrest warrant? I am just a businessman."

"They don't think so."

"Ah… What do you think, Agent Kruger?"

"My opinion doesn't matter. The opinion of the DOJ does."

"How do I change the DOJ's opinion?"

"They believe a meeting between you and me would go a long way in settling this misunderstanding."

"A meeting."

"Yes, a meeting."

"Where? In the United States? I would be arrested. No thank you, Agent."

"I will meet you anywhere else in the world, except Russia."

"Neutral ground?"

"Yes, neutral ground."

"Paris. I like Paris."

"I do, too."

"Good, one week from today, same time. In front of the Louvre. Since you have my phone number, I will assume you have my email address."

Kruger looked at JR, who nodded. "Yes, I do."

"I will remember not to underestimate you, Agent Kruger."

"And I will not underestimate you, Mr. Orlov."

"That would be wise. Send me details of what you want to discuss so I can be prepared."

"See you next week, Mr. Orlov."

The call ended.

JR smiled. "Have you ever been to Paris?"

"Once, on an investigation. Why?"

"Great city, but don't meet him by yourself. You'll need back-up."

"That's what Gibbs and Knoll are for."

***

"Have you ever been to Paris, Steph?"

Stephanie Kruger was standing at the kitchen counter preparing a salad for dinner. She was displaying a wide smile.

"No, I haven't. So when did you decide we'd be going to Paris?"

"This morning, when I scheduled a meeting."

The smile faded. "A meeting?"

He nodded. "If it lasts more than an hour, I'll be shocked."

The smile returned. "All the way to Paris for an hour meeting? That seems a little wasteful."

"Not if it results in finding out where the missing college students are."

She stopped and turned to stare at him. "Who are you meeting?"

"A Russian banker named Dmitri Orlov, who just happens to have ties to the Russian mafia here in the states."

"How would he know?"

"Good question. I hope to find out."

"Sean, we aren't going if you're going to be in any danger."

"I'll have back up. Jimmie Gibbs and Sandy Knoll."

She noticeably relaxed and returned to preparing dinner. "Good."

"Sandy's bringing his wife."

She jerked her head up and stared at her husband. "Sandy's married?"

"Yup, twenty three years. They have two boys, both in the military."

"How come you never told me about it?"

"Because I didn't know it until this afternoon."

"He never talks about her."

"I know, I asked him why."

"What'd he say?"

"He indicated it was an agreement between him and his

wife. I understand, I don't discuss my family at work."

She folded her arms over her chest. "And why not? Are you ashamed of us?"

He smiled, walked over, and embraced her. "You never know who might be listening." Changing the subject, he asked, "Is your passport still valid?"

"Yes, when we got married, I had my name changed on it."

"Good. We'll plan for a week's stay."

"What about the kids?"

"Brian and Michelle already agreed to watch them."

"Guess I'm going to Paris."

"Yes, you are."

CHAPTER 46

Paris, France

Kruger stood on the west side of the Pyramide du Louvre, Jimmie Gibbs on his left and Sandy Knoll to his right. All wore jeans and, to ward off the cold Paris afternoon temperatures, leather jackets. They faced the Place du Carrousel as a black Mercedes S560 pulled to the curb.

"This must be him." Knoll said.

Kruger nodded, but remained quiet.

A heavy-set man in a black knee-length overcoat exited the curbside rear door, stood, and buttoned his suitcoat underneath. A man, roughly the size of Knoll, joined him, having exited the car on the opposite side. A tall, slender man exited from the front passenger door and also surveyed his surroundings.

Gibbs leaned in and spoke quietly to Kruger, "Big guy is Boris Volkov, ex-Spetsnaz and current director of security for Orlov. Skinny guy is Yuri Popov, last known to be associated with OMON."

Without taking his attention away from the approaching Russian, Kruger asked, "What's that?"

"Special Forces of the Russian Federal police, equivalent to our SWAT and Rapid Response Units."

Nodding, Kruger turned to Knoll. "When was the last time you saw Orlov?"

"June 2000. I was on the team making sure our new Embassy was secure. Orlov attended one of the receptions. Smart guy, well connected with the Politburo. Don't believe too much of what he says."

"Wasn't planning on it."

They watched as the Mercedes pulled away from the curb, and the three men walked toward them. Kruger maintained a neutral expression as did Gibbs and Knoll.

When the newcomers were within ten feet, Orlov smiled, "Agent Sean Kruger, it is pleasure to finally meet you."

Kruger nodded. "Nice to meet you, Mr. Orlov."

The Russian chuckled. "Call me Dmitri."

Nodding again, Kruger kept his hands in his jacket pockets. Neither man offered to shake the other's hand.

Orlov turned his attention to Knoll, "Benedict Knoll, it's been, what? Twenty years?"

"Eighteen, actually."

"Time flies."

"Indeed, it does."

Turning to Gibbs, the Russian smiled. "James Gibbs. I understand your swimming records still stand within the ranks of the U.S. Navy Seals."

"Don't know. Haven't checked lately."

"Ahhh… Trust me, they do."

He turned to the slender man standing next to him and spoke in Russian. As the man was speaking, Gibbs leaned over and translated for Kruger.

"He's telling Popov about my swimming records," he whispered. "Apparently Popov is a swimmer, too. He seems impressed."

Kruger nodded, not taking his eyes off Orlov.

The Russian turned his attention back to Kruger. "Excuse my manners." He motioned to the larger man. "This is Boris Volkov, he is our bank's Director of Security. My colleague on the left is Yuri Popov, Mr. Volkov's assistant."

Nodding at each man as they were introduced, Kruger tilted his head slightly. "I believe you were concerned about your visa being revoked, Mr. Orlov."

"Ahhh, yes, the American propensity to get right to the point. I agree, no need for chit-chat. Let us walk, Agent Kruger. It is a beautiful crisp fall day in this lovely city. Is this your first time here?"

"No, I was here about ten years ago on an investigation."

"I have an office here. I prefer Paris to Moscow. Moscow is too cold."

Kruger remained quiet as they started walking west, falling into step next to each other, Gibbs and Knoll slightly behind Kruger's left, Volkov and Popov in a similar position to the right of Orlov.

As they crossed the Place du Carrousel, Kruger started the conversation. "It is a lovely city. Unfortunately I didn't get to enjoy much of it last time I was here."

"You should bring your wife sometime. It is such a romantic city. Best restaurants in the world and, in my opinion, the best wine."

"So I've been told." Kruger chose not to tell the Russian that Stephanie was here and they were planning a week's vacation after the meeting.

As they crossed through Tuileries Garden, Orlov switched from pointing out historical spots and finally got to the point.

"I wanted to ask you why you have an arrest warrant on me. I need to travel to the States several times a year on business and this will create great difficulties for me."

"I understand. The Department of Justice is the one who issued the warrant, not me."

"Yes, but it was your investigation of Robert Burns Jr. that resulted in it being issued."

"True."

"So why do you think I was involved?"

"Were you?"

The man walking to his right laughed. "Of course not, Agent Kruger. I am a businessman, not a criminal."

"Do you know someone by the name of Yaakov Romanovich?"

"It is a common name, but I don't believe so. Why?"

"He tried to kill me in Washington, D.C. He missed. However, he knows you. He indicated you two were, ah…" Kruger glanced at Orlov, "acquainted."

Orlov did not respond as he watched a young couple walking toward them.

After they passed, the Russian shook his head. "I can assure you, we are not, as you say, acquainted."

Kruger smiled slightly. "I see. Yaakov was shot before he shot me. He survived, but, then you knew that. Anyway, when he recovered enough to understand the penalties for attempting to kill an FBI agent, he developed a severe case of diarrhea of the mouth."

Orlov shot a quick glance at Volkov, who nodded slightly. Turning his attention back to Kruger, he asked, "What did this Romanovich individual say that has your Department of Justice so upset?"

Smiling slightly as they continued their walk on the Champs-Elysees heading toward the Arc de Triomphe off in the distance, Kruger answered the question.

"He told us you offered a twenty-five thousand dollar bounty to anyone who could stop my investigation of the Burns family."

"Nonsense."

Kruger shrugged. "Just telling you why there is an arrest warrant out on you. You asked."

"That I did. How do I get it lifted?"

"Rescind the offer and tell me why Robert Burns Sr. and Junior, and Joel Moody were so important to Russia."

"It is hard to rescind an offer I did not make, Agent. But, I will make inquiries."

"Thank you. What about Moody and the father and son?"

The Russian could be heard chuckling. "That is more complicated."

"How so?"

"You must remember I am not involved with these matters."

"Of course you aren't, but being a well-connected businessman you have probably heard things."

"Agent Kruger, Robert Burns Sr. was not always rich. In fact, there was a time he could not get a loan from any of your American banks."

"And you graciously loaned him money."

"I did not, but the bank I was associated with at the time did. I was the individual who negotiated the loan for him."

"So you've had a long relationship with Burns."

"Correct."

"Is that why he decided to run for the Senate?"

Orlov shrugged. "He did not tell me the reason he ran."

"It wasn't to help ease bank regulations to help with the profits of your banks?"

"Of course not, Agent." Orlov turned to Kruger with a menacing stare. "That would be illegal in your country."

"Yes, it would." Kruger returned the stare with the same expression. Neither man averted their eyes from each other for several moments.

Orlov smiled. "Enough about Robert Burns. How do I get this ridiculous arrest warrant rescinded?"

"Tell me what happened to the girls."

"What girls?"

"Don't insult my intelligence, Mr. Orlov. We know Burns paid Russian nationalists to get rid of Junior's victims. Where are they?"

Silence was Kruger's answer. He glanced at Orlov as they walked. The man was staring at the windows of the shops they walked past. Kruger remained quiet, waiting for a response.

Finally, Orlov said. "It is a sad part of my country's past."

"Past?"

"Yes. My government has made much progress over the last decade to prevent this activity. However, due to the profits associated with human trafficking, certain criminal elements continue to be active. The women you refer too were involved before this crack-down occurred."

"Where are they?"

Orlov took a deep breath. "I do not know. I can speculate if you want."

"Please."

"A few died of their injuries at the hands of the son. Most did not."

Kruger frowned. "Were they killed by the men who were paid to clean up?"

Orlov shook his head. "No, they were drugged and sold as sex slaves in the Middle East. Many rich Arabs, while expounding religious edicts, have yearnings for young western women and are willing to pay huge sums of money for them."

Closing his eyes, Kruger was silent for a long time as they walked. Finally he asked. "What happened when the men who bought them grew tired of them?"

"I do not know. But they were never allowed to go home."

"So they're dead."

"I would assume so."

"That's why their bodies have never been found. They weren't even on the continent."

Orlov nodded.

"Why was Burns Jr. killed and his head shipped to the father via a FedEx box?"

"Did you see the movie *The Godfather*, Agent Kruger?"

"It was a message?"

"I would say a powerful message. Certain individuals were not happy with the loss of money and time they spent getting the son elected to the Senate."

"I thought the elder Burns put up the money."

"Yes, yes, that is what he wants everyone to think. He did not."

Kruger's suspicions were finally confirmed, but he had one more question.

"How many other politicians are compromised like Burns?"

Smiling, Orlov didn't answer at first. "How would I know that information, Agent Kruger?"

"Silly question. Sorry I asked."

Orlov nodded his head. "Now that I have answered your questions, I have a question of my own."

"I'll try to answer it."

"Why are you so concerned about these women, Agent Kruger?"

Taking a deep breath, Kruger closed his eyes for a brief moment. Once his emotions were under control, he replied, "I don't like rich guys thinking the law doesn't apply to them." His stare was fixed on Orlov.

Returning the glare, Orlov nodded. "I see. I appreciate the honesty. Now, what about the warrant for my arrest should I return to New York City?"

Their walked ended as they approached the circle drive around the Arc de Triomphe.

"I don't suppose you have any connections with your government's Foreign Service division, do you?"

Orlov shrugged. "Possibly."

"If they could find out where the bodies of these women are located, that would go a long way in getting the arrest warrant cancelled."

"An interesting thought, Agent. I will make some calls."

"One other request."

"The price of my freedom grows."

"Yes. The price of freedom is expensive."

"What is your request?"

"A name."

"I can give you a lot of names. Whose name?"

"The name of the individual who organizes the sale of the women."

Orlov was silent as he stared at Kruger. Finally after almost a minute, he nodded. "The one you seek is actually a Syrian who now lives in Oman. He knows many rich Arabs and has been in business over twenty years. However, he is no longer involved with these types of transactions."

"Oh, what is he organizing now?"

The smile Orlov gave Kruger told him a lot. The Russian wanted something done about this individual.

He gave Kruger the name. "It seems he has cast his lot in with a group of extremists in Yemen. He is now using his knowledge of several rich Arabs to extort money. That money is being diverted to ISIS in Yemen."

"I take it the Saudi House is not happy."

"No, and neither is a friend of mine. It seems some of these extremists have organized attacks on our brave troops in Syria."

"This gentleman seems to have pissed off a lot serious individuals. Why don't they do anything about him?"

Orlov gave Kruger the smile again. "Politically impractical for either party. We were hoping for some assistance."

"I'm not in a position to offer any, I'm afraid."

"No, but your friend Benedict Knoll is." Orlov nodded in Sandy's direction.

"He's with the FBI."

"Yes, I forgot. My mistake."

"So, what are you proposing, Dmitri?"

"I give you the location of the graves and the location of this individual. Then the Department of Justice drops all charges against me."

"I'll talk to the Attorney General and see what I can do on my end."

The Russian smiled at Kruger. "Then we have a deal?"

Kruger nodded and extracted his hand from the leather jacket pocket.

Orlov shook it and returned the nod.

The black Mercedes pulled to the curb and stopped. Volkov stepped ahead of the older man and opened the rear passenger door. Just before stepping into the back seat, he turned to Kruger. "I am glad we had this meeting, Agent Kruger. Some of the information may have been painful to hear, but, as we both know, the world can be a cruel place sometimes."

With this statement, Orlov and his companions entered the car and drove away, within seconds disappearing into the chaotic traffic surrounding the Arc de Triomphe.

Knoll spoke first. "Do you believe him?"

"Some of it. The Russians want something done about this Syrian. If we can arrange something to happen to him, they will give us what we want."

Gibbs pressed his cell phone to his ear but before the call went through, he looked at Kruger, "Now what?"

"We wait to see if he comes through with the location of the bodies. Then I have to tell a few families the truth."

CHAPTER 47

Hannibal, MO
Three Weeks Later

Kruger rang the doorbell on Paul Kelly's home. Sara Kelly answered before he could remove his finger. She stared at him and opened the door.

"Is this about Linda?" she asked.

"Yes, Sara, it is. May I come in?"

"Yes, sorry, please come in."

"I thought you were going to sell this place?"

"Not till we know for sure about Linda. Have you heard anything?"

He nodded. "Can we sit somewhere? This could take a few minutes."

She blinked rapidly, stared at him, and then nodded. "Would you like some coffee?"

"No, thank you."

"I believe I will. Excuse me."

She offered him a chair at a small kitchen table. Watching as she poured her coffee, he noticed her hand shaking slightly. When she was sitting across from him, he took a breath and smiled gently.

"The news I bring is not pleasant, Sara. Is there anyone

you would like to call?"

The blinking returned. She then studied her coffee cup. "No, I'll be fine."

"You sure?"

"Yes. What about Linda."

"I can confirm she is dead."

Sara Kelly glared at Kruger, closed her eyes and bowed her head. "I was afraid you would tell me that. What about her body?"

"That's the difficult part. There's a team of FBI forensic experts on their way to Oman."

She looked up and frowned. "Oman?"

He nodded slowly.

"Why Oman?"

"Through the help of the Russian government, the Oman government has revealed a mass grave of western women who were kidnapped and held as slaves by one of the Sultan's brothers. When it was discovered, the brother was quietly executed, and the entire affair swept under the rug in 2010."

"How long had this brother been doing it?"

"Early 1990s"

"Is Linda in that grave?"

"We believe she is."

Sara stood suddenly. "But we won't know for sure until the DNA is checked. Is that what you're telling me, Agent?"

"Yes, ma'am.

"So she might not be there?"

"There is always a chance. But it's a small chance."

She sat again. "How was this information discovered?"

"We caught the individual who abducted her and her friends."

"Are her friends there too?"

"We believe so. One of my associates is collecting DNA samples from their families today as well."

"Who took them, Agent Kruger?"

"Robert Burns Jr. We're not sure what happened after they left the diner that night, but he turned them over to—

uh—individuals who drugged them and smuggled them out of the country."

"Why?"

Kruger took a deep breath. "This is the hard part, Sara. They were sex slaves."

All she could do was stare at him without comment. A tear slid down her cheek as she turned her attention to the window behind the table.

He remained quiet as she struggled with her emotions.

Silence was Kruger's response. He sat and let her collect her thoughts.

Finally she asked. "How many women are in the grave, Agent Kruger?"

"We were told about forty."

"Those poor families. Do you know who they are?"

"No. We have suspicions of about ten, but some may never be identified."

"Are they all Americans?"

"No, the majority are from Western Europe, and a few from South America. Interpol is involved as well. They may be able to help identify some of the victims."

Tears flowed down her cheeks again.

"Sara, you're Linda's cousin. I need a DNA sample."

She nodded unconsciously. "Would hair samples from her father be of use?"

"Yes, better, actually."

"There's still a brush of his in the bathroom. You can have it."

Kruger nodded.

Silence descended upon the kitchen again. Both individuals lost in their own thoughts.

Finally, Sara said, "I was just thinking about how frightened she must have been."

"Sara, if it's any consolation, we think the women were drugged constantly and may not have known what was happening."

"But, what if she wasn't. She would have been so scared

and angry."

"Yes, she would have been."

Sara closed her eyes as more tears leaked from them. She took a deep breath and then started to shake.

"Can I call someone, Sara?"

She shook her head rapidly. "No, I'll be alright in a minute."

He waited.

"Will we get her body back?"

"Yes, as soon as the DNA analysis is confirmed. The State Department will be in contact concerning the date. They will work with you on the arrangements."

"Thank you."

She was quiet for a few more moments. "I want to thank you for not forgetting about Linda, Agent Kruger."

"I promised your uncle."

"I'm sure he knows you fulfilled your promise."

All he could do was nod.

***

Beverly Moody sat across from Kruger and Ryan Clark in her attorney's office. She was dressed comfortably, not in the orange prison jumpsuit she wore the last time they met. Her attorney, Mary Atwater, was a matronly figure in her late fifties, wearing a nondescript pantsuit. Her gray hair was professionally styled around a round face. She sat next to her client across from Ryan Clark.

Kruger smiled. "We've notified your attorney the FBI is dropping charges related to the false passport, Beverly."

"Thank you."

"We appreciate your help in the case against your husband."

"We weren't really married. I'm going back to my real name, Gayle Patterson."

"Good."

"What about the other charges, Agent Kruger?"

"Those are Washington State charges, Gayle. I don't have a say so there. But I'm told they will work with you if you tell them what you know about the human trafficking in Seattle."

She nodded. "Mary's working with them. I appreciate your help."

"Not a problem." He paused for a brief moment. "I would like to ask one question."

"Okay?"

"You knew Joel better than anyone. Why did he kill himself?"

She took a deep breath. "I've been thinking about that a lot, Agent Kruger. The only reason I can come up with is that he knew if he went to prison, he'd be dead in a week."

Kruger nodded.

She continued. "Joel also had demons, Agent. He had them under control when he was with me. I believe he truly, truly loved me. I may have been the only person he ever felt that way about. But, when he went to work for the elder Burns, those demons came back. He never hurt me, but there were times…"

Kruger waited, but she did not finish the sentence. Finally he broke the silence. "We have evidence Joel murdered ten women in the eighties and nineties. Where you aware of that?"

She nodded. "Those were the demons he kept inside."

"When did he stop?"

"After we met."

"Did he tell you about them?"

"Yes."

"When?"

"The second time he caught me with drugs. We drank a lot that night. He used booze to self-medicate and ease his conscious. He was falling down drunk when he told me. Then the next morning, he didn't even remember the conversation. I never brought it up again, nor did he."

"Gayle, Joel had ten million dollars in an account in the Cayman Islands."

"Yes, I knew about it."

"Did you know Joel set it up so that if anything happened to him, it was the property of Gayle Patterson?"

Gayle Patterson stared at Kruger, her mouth open and her eyes wide. It was at this moment he chose not to tell her that JR Diminski was the individual who set up the transfer of ownership. A secret he would keep between him and JR.

Mary Atwater smiled and patted Gayle's arm.

Kruger continued, "Once you file the proper IRS paperwork, what remains will be yours. I would ask your attorney to suggest a trust fund manager to pay your legal fees and set up a fund to earn interest."

"I don't know what to say."

Smiling, he and Clark stood. Before they walked out of the conference room, Kruger turned.

"Gayle, this is an opportunity to start over. Take it."

CHAPTER 48

Washington, DC

Kyle Sandifer's hand shook as he returned the phone to its cradle on his desk. He closed his eyes and took a deep breath. Placing the palms of his hands flat on the desk in front of him, he struggled to maintain his composure. Joseph Rothenburg sat in a black leather wingback chair in front of his desk. He leaned over, placed his elbows on his knees, and buried his face in his hands.

"Damn," was all Sandifer could say.

Rothenburg straightened to ask, "Any chance we could renegotiate the deal?"

"No. Their interest in our firm vanished along with the billings Robert Burns Jr.'s defense would have produced."

"They were interested before we got the Burns case. Why drop out now?"

"It was an excuse, not the reason. With the FBI looking into the affairs of the elder Burns during his tenure as a senator, they feel lobbying firms will also be under scrutiny as well. So, for now, they are walking away from the deal."

"Lobbying is only half of our revenue."

"They know that, but their goal was to increase that revenue stream once they bought us."

There was silence from Rothenburg as he looked over Sandifer's shoulder at a distant point only he could see.

Both men were lost in their own thoughts for several minutes. Finally, Sandifer broke the silence.

"Whoever Burns contacted was not happy with him."

"Obviously."

"I need to talk to Ms. Sanders."

"How could that possibly help?'

"She may have learned something during her interviews with him. It won't hurt to ask."

"Very well, I'll get her."

***

"Disappointing turn of events, wasn't it, Ms. Sanders."

"Yes, sir."

Jolene Sanders sat ramrod straight on the edge of the wingback chair in front of Sandifer's desk. Her attitude was defiant with the anticipation of being fired for letting her client escape and losing the millions of dollars they would have billed for his defense.

"I assure you, the firm does not blame you for what happened."

She nodded, and Sandifer noticed her shoulders relax slightly.

"During your interviews with your client, did he mention anything about who might have helped him escape?"

Her eyes stared at the top of his desk as she sat back in the chair, she was silent for several moments. "I'm trying to remember. Looking back on the interviews, it was hard to determine when he was lying and when he was telling the truth."

Sandifer nodded.

"I believe it was the last time I spoke to him, he mentioned something about getting in touch with friends of his father."

"Obviously not good friends."

"No, apparently not."

"Anything else you can remember about your interviews?"

She slowly shook her head. "No, he was more interested in proclaiming his innocence."

"Very well. If you think of anything else, let me know."

***

The morning passed while Sandifer attended to matters of the firm. At forty-two minutes after eleven, his cell phone rang. Looking at the caller ID, he noticed an international number. After a slight moment of hesitation, he accepted the call.

"Kyle Sandifer."

"Mr. Sandifer, my name is Dmitri Orlov. We met last year at a banking conference. You were the keynote speaker and gave a brilliant presentation on international banking laws."

Sandifer's mind raced as he tried to associate the name with a face. "Yes, Mr. Orlov, I remember you. I'm glad you enjoyed the presentation. How may I help you today?"

"It is more about how I can help you."

Frowning, Sandifer did not respond for several moments. "I see. I'm not sure what I need help with. Would you care to enlighten me?"

"This morning you received some rather unpleasant news about a business venture you were planning."

"Life can be full of disappointments."

"Yes, it can be. However, this particular disappointment may offer you and Mr. Rothenburg a different opportunity."

Sitting up straighter in his chair, Sandifer's brow wrinkled and his eyes narrowed. "I should probably ask how you came about this information, but I doubt you would tell me."

"You are correct. However, a group of investors and I would like to enter into negotiations to acquire your firm. Our terms would be similar, if not more lucrative, than your previous offer."

"I see. When would you like to start these negotiations?"

"This afternoon. My representative will be available to make our presentation at a convenient time of your choosing."

"Two p.m."

"Excellent, I believe you will be pleased with our proposal."

***

The office was quiet as the sun set over Washington, D.C. Kyle Sandifer and Joseph Rothenburg sat across from each other on matching leather sofas in Rothenburg's office. Each held a crystal lowball glass of Glenfiddich Scotch.

"What do you think, Kyle?'

"It was better than the private equity offer. I liked it."

"As did I."

"Will you stay to run the firm for a year?"

"I'm thinking about it. What about you?"

"No. The wife already has a place picked out on the South Carolina coast."

Sandifer nodded. "It won't be the same around here without you."

Smiling, Rothenburg was silent for a few moments. "A year will go fast, Kyle."

"Yes, I know."

"I was a little disappointed they will be closing down our criminal defense division."

"Yes, that is disappointing, but understandable in this town."

Rothenburg only nodded.

Silence fell between the two men as they sipped their scotch. Finally Rothenburg tilted his head. "Do you believe they told us the truth about why they want to buy the firm?"

"I have absolutely no idea. After a year, I won't care."

***

Dmitri Orlov smiled as he answered his cell phone. "What was their reaction?"

Peter Yanovich, Orlov's representative in Washington, D.C., chuckled as he answered, "If they could have signed the contract today, they would have."

"Good. How curious were they?"

"I got the feeling they were desperate after their original contract fell apart this morning."

"Yes, interesting how that happened."

Another chuckle. "Dmitri, do not give me additional details. I do not wish to know."

"When is your next meeting?"

"They asked for a few days to discuss it between themselves."

"Tomorrow?"

"Probably."

"Good. Keep me informed."

"Without question. What else do you need?"

"I need background on an FBI agent named Sean Kruger."

"How deep?"

"As deep as you can go."

"May I ask why?"

"He has become an irritant. I need to make sure he does not interfere with our business in the future."

"When do you need it?"

"Let's get the Sandifer and Rothenburg deal closed, then we can concentrate on the FBI agent."

"Excellent, I will follow up with Sandifer in the morning."

"Good."

CHAPTER 49

Springfield, MO

JR brought the bottle of a locally brewed lager to his lips and took a gulp as his friend, Sean Kruger, closed the lid of the now clean gas grill. He could hear the sound of a distant lawn mower, a barking dog, and a cool spring breeze rustle leaves in the background as he stood on Kruger back deck.

"Are you declaring the case closed?"

Kruger nodded. "Yes."

"You don't seem pleased."

Glancing up at JR, Kruger gave him a grim smile. "I am. The bodies of the college students have been returned to their families and they have closure. It's just…"

There was a long silence as Kruger stared at the stainless steel lid of the grill.

"Just what?"

"There are so many unanswered questions about this case."

JR took another sip of beer. "Some questions don't have answers."

"Not in my world, JR." Kruger chuckled. "I don't have that luxury."

"Maybe I can answer one of them."

Kruger shot JR a frown. "Since when?"

"Late today. The right time to tell you hadn't presented itself."

"Go on."

"When Orlov told you Burns wasn't always rich, you didn't seem to question the statement."

"I had no reason to, I figured his wealth came when he inherited his father's properties."

JR shook his head.

"Care to share this newsflash with me?" Kruger's voice betrayed his impatience.

The corner of JR's lip displayed a small smile. "I've been doing a little digging into Burns' finances. At one time, all of those wineries had multiple liens against them. The father was technically bankrupt when he passed away. Senior didn't inherit wealth, he inherited debt."

"Huh."

"The liens disappeared within a year."

Blinking several times, Kruger asked. "You think the money came from the Russians?"

"I couldn't confirm it, but with what Orlov told you, that would be my guess."

Kruger was quiet as he stared out over the growing twilight in his backyard. "So Burns needed cash to get the wineries out of debt and start buying the tech companies he wanted. And the only place he could get it was from the Russians."

"Yup."

"There's the connection, JR. It started with Senior."

"Seems that way."

Silence fell over the two friends. A variety of birds could be heard chirping in the growing darkness of evening.

"You're more familiar with the serial killer mental state than I. Why did Moody stop his killing while he was keeping tabs on Junior?" JR asked.

"Junior wasn't really a serial killer in the classical definition. He was more of a violent sexual predator. Moody, on the other hand was. There could be numerous reasons why he stopped. My suspicions are his needs were met by dealing with Junior's victims. But, without being able to interview him, the truth will never be known."

JR nodded as he stood beside Kruger and watched darkness settle over the numerous mature trees behind the residence.

"I appreciated your help on this case, JR. As always you made my job easier."

"Glad to help. What's next for you?"

"I'm staying with the agency. Stef has made it perfectly clear it's my only option. I tend to agree with her."

"And?"

"My interview with Orlov in Paris raised more questions than it answered. Paul wants me to start looking into his activities both abroad and here in the states. He wants me to do it quietly and behind the scenes, so I won't be using agency assets."

"Makes sense."

"What to help?"

A smile came to JR Diminski's lips.

EPILOGUE

Al Dhafra Air Force Base, United Arab Emirates

Retired Special Forces Major Benedict Sandy Knoll stood behind two MQ-9 Reaper operators as they concentrated on the monitors in front of them. The man in the left seat piloted the unmanned plane, and the other officer manned the drone's sensors. Knoll crossed his arms over his massive chest and stared at the images beamed back by the aircraft's forward camera. His attire was Desert BDUs, minus insignias, and his favorite desert tan tactical boots. A man of similar size and dress stood next to him.

Phillip Farnsworth was an old friend and colleague of Knoll's. Both served together during several tours of Afghanistan and Iraq. Both were highly trained retired Special Forces operatives. Farnworth had a dark complexion with black hair and a thick bushy mustache. He blended into the local populace with ease. Like Knoll, he was retired from Special Forces, but currently worked under a CIA umbrella.

He pointed to the pilot's monitor on the left.

"The Reaper will be on station for another four hours before we replace it."

Knoll nodded, but remained silent.

The Reaper he referred to was a remote piloted aircraft

flying a lazy figure-eight pattern ten miles southwest of the town of Salah, Oman. The unmanned craft flying at 25,000 feet was, for all practical purposes, invisible to any observer on the ground. Attached to the weapon pods underneath the small airplane were two AGM 114 Hellfire laser guided missiles. Far below the center of the lazy-eight flight pattern of the small airplane was a walled compound near the foothills of the coastal high country.

Turning to look at Farnsworth, Knoll said, "Jimmie's with the Seal team inserted on a beach three miles from the compound."

The black haired man nodded.

"Let's hope something happens."

Farnsworth took his attention away from the pilot's monitor and looked at Knoll. "My orders were to give you operational control, but it didn't say I couldn't be curious. Who is this guy you're after?"

"Let's call him The Banker."

"Okay. And?"

"He provides al-Qaeda in Yemen financial support."

Farnsworth smiled. "Bullshit."

Knoll chuckled and looked at his old friend. "He does, really. But that's not why we're after him."

"Good, I hate it when you lie to me, Knoll. Tell me."

Taking a deep breath, the retired Special Forces Major pursed his lips. "He helped an Omani prince obtain western sex slaves. Of which we've positively identified nine Americans."

"I don't like the sound of this."

Shaking his head, Knoll kept his attention on the pilots monitor. "It gets worse. They were found in a mass grave along with forty-seven other women from various countries."

"Ah, geez. Who was the prince?"

"Faheem al-Salem. The Sultan found out about it, and one night the guy disappeared from the face of the earth. Of course no one bothered to tell anybody about the mass grave, they just let the dessert hide their dirty little secret."

"I take it someone found out?"

"Yeah, my boss at the FBI."

Farnsworth nodded and decided he had asked enough questions.

Silence fell between the two men as they watched monitors.

Five minutes later Knoll heard a squelch in his earbud. "Something is happening."

***

Jimmie Gibbs was back in his element, a mission with his beloved brethren Navy Seals. After landing their F470 Combat Rubber Raiding Craft on a deserted beach south of Raysut, Oman, their mission was to observe and inform. The walled compound they observed was isolated from other populated areas in this remote part of Oman.

Three men comprised the team, Gibbs as the representative of the FBI and two Navy Seals, Josh Arrington and Ben Chavez. All three were dressed identically, blending into the desert background. Gibbs and Chavez studied the compound with their Steiner 7x50rc M50rc Commander military binoculars, while Arrington kept watch on their surroundings. Their position was on a small rise west of the compound, which allowed a good view over the eight foot surrounding wall.

It was approaching noon, and the semi-arid landscape was starting to heat up. Jimmie didn't notice; he was concentrating on two Toyota Land Cruisers parked in front of the main residence of the compound. Several large men with automatic rifles stood watch over the vehicles. Five men emerged through the front door and stood by the front SUV. Focusing his binoculars on a tall figure in the middle, he spotted the target of their mission. Yasser Hussein.

"There he is in the middle. Ben, do you concur?"

"Yeah, that's him."

"Once we know which truck he's in, we'll paint it when it

leaves the compound."

"Got it."

The two fell back into silent concentration. As soon as Hussein got into the back seat of the lead Toyota, Gibbs tapped the transmit button on his handheld radio as Chavez prepared the laser target designator. He heard in his wireless ear piece a response from the pilot of the unmanned drone Gibbs knew was five miles above them.

As the two SUVs exited the compound, Chavez aimed the laser on the lead vehicle. Gibbs heard the disembodied voice of the drone's sensor operator in his ear.

"Target acquired. Stand by."

***

The sensor operator turned to Farrington.

"Target is painted, sir. On your word."

Farrington nodded and looked at Knoll. "Your call."

"Do it."

"At your discretion, Lieutenant."

"Yes, sir." The sensor operator turned back to his monitor and prepared to launch both Hellfire missiles.

***

Gibbs watched as the two-vehicle caravan turned onto the main highway and sped west. From their vantage point, they would have the trucks in sight for several more miles, so he expected the show to begin immediately.

As the three men watched the trucks speed away, they heard the distinct sound of incoming Hellfire missiles. Several seconds later, the two SUVs disappeared in a cloud of fire, dust, and metal debris. The sound from the explosions reached their location six seconds later. Gibb trained his binoculars back on the compound and saw the guards' reaction to the explosion. No one seemed in a hurry to investigate. They were more interested in looting the compound and getting the heck out of there.

Chavez was already packing his laser in his backpack. He looked up at Gibbs and asked, "Do we need DNA?"

Shaking his head, Gibbs studied the smoldering remains of the two SUVs off in the distance with his binoculars.

"Wouldn't have any samples to compare it to. We both confirmed the target visually; they'll have to be satisfied with that."

He smiled and removed his eyes from the binoculars.

"Besides, there's nothing larger than a soccer ball left in that mess."

About the Author

J.C. Fields is an award winning writer living in Battlefield, MO. He enjoys creating short stories and novels in the mystery/thriller genre, with an occasional foray into science fiction. He is a member of the Springfield Writers' Guild, and Missouri Writer's Guild. He has written and published numerous short stories and three full length novels: *The Fugitive's Trail*, published in 2015, *The Assassin's Trail* released summer of 2016, and his third novel, *The Impostor's Trail*, in July 2017.

All three novels are available on Amazon.com, Barnesandnoble.com, booksamillion.com and other online retailers. Audio versions also available. Visit his website at www.jcfieldsbooks.com. Follow him on Facebook at www.facebook.com/jcfieldsbooks/

Made in the USA
Columbia, SC
02 March 2023

13039686R00193